GOD SAYS NO

GOD SAYS NO

by

JAMES HANNAHAM

McSWEENEY'S
Grove Press

First published in 2009 by McSweeney's Books, San Francisco

Printed in the United States of America

ISBN-13: 978-0-8021-4496-6

Grove Press
an imprint of Grove/Atlantic, Inc.
841 Broadway
New York, NY 10003

Distributed by Publishers Group West

www.groveatlantic.com

10 11 12 13 14   10 9 8 7 6 5 4 3 2 1

for Daniel

GOD SAYS NO

"*Supposing you'd asked God to do some-thing,*" *said Philip, "and really believed it was going to happen... and you had faith, and it didn't happen, what would it mean?"... "It would just mean that you hadn't got faith," answered Uncle William... {Y}et he didn't see how he could believe more than he did.*

—W. Somerset Maugham,
Of Human Bondage

Hast thou not poured me out as milk, and curdled me like cheese?

—Job 10:10

I.
PLOTLESS PLOT
A play based on an illusion

ONE

Russ broke my Jesus, and I was mad. I don't know where all my anger came from—my roommate must have smashed up my good manners, too. Leaping up from the bunk bed, I shoved him across the room. He stumbled away, bumped his thigh on a chair, and limped around, rubbing it. I lay back down on the lower bunk and pretended to sleep, but my blood kept boiling. A moment passed and then—surprise!—Russ dove on top of me, his muscley frame on my beanbag chair of a body, landing vicious punches on my kidneys. I hollered and pushed, but he was much stronger than me, and he held tight. He tore my shirt and spat in my face. When I got my arms free from under his thighs and boxed his ears, he took to howling something fierce and tried to poke my eyeballs out with his thumbs. I lifted my arm to cover my face and elbowed him hard in the cheek, somewhat by accident. By that time, the RA had heard the commotion from down the hall and rushed into our dorm room to pull us apart. Later, Russ got a shiner on account of my elbow.

Russ broke my Jesus in October of 1988, during midterms freshman year at Central Florida Christian College in Kissimmee. I'd come home that evening to find he'd shoved all my belongings into one corner and divided the room with a long strip of red tape. Behind a pile of my dirty clothes, I saw the shattered remains of the little statue I prayed to every night. It didn't make sense. My Jesus couldn't have fallen and broken into that many pieces. Russ had to have chucked it at the wall.

Russ didn't like me, or people like me. In September I'd overheard him on the phone asking somebody, "What'd I do wrong that they put me in with a fat coon?" As if I wasn't there, as if I wasn't that fat coon. Since late August, we'd made it a point to stay apart. Taping the floor was the first time he'd acknowledged my existence in a whole month. Insults aside, the message I got from him destroying my Jesus was *Russ hates me more than he loves Christ.* A hate that deep spooked me.

After the fight, I gathered up the plaster shards in an old shirt and rested them on my desk. My skin still tingled with an adrenaline rush, and I had a fresh memory of Russ's warm, strong thighs pinning me against the bed and the wall. I felt alive, the way you do after saying something you've kept to yourself for a real long time. My crotch woke up. Feeling confused and looking down at that smashed-up Jesus, holding His broken head and His hollow body in my hand, just like when Joseph took Him down from the cross, the white dust falling through my fingers—it sure was the start of *something.* The broken Jesus wasn't the real beginning of the story, though, just the point when I admitted I had a story at all. Because right then it struck me that I might never be a normal Christian man—definitely not a radio preacher, like I dreamed of—and I started to panic something terrible inside.

I was fixing to put Him back together, but I didn't have any glue, so I had to calm myself down and head out to the nearest convenience store, a piece down the road. As I lowered Jesus onto the desk, the shards made tinkly sounds like wind chimes. I sped out of the dorm feeling more upset than I should have, but I couldn't control myself, or think why not, except that everybody got stressed out during midterms. Tears welled up in my eyes and I started sniffling—I felt dopey on top of the sadness. I kept telling myself, "Stop your blubbering, Gary. What are the stationery-store people going to think?" Nobody special had given me that Jesus. I had bought it myself on after-Christmas discount at Keegan's, the gardening center where I worked in high school. Had I been worshipping a graven image instead of the real savior?

I spent a while in the store, pacing the aisles and trying to decide which glue to get. Then an Asian girl I'd seen working in the dining hall came in to buy cola and snacks. She was short and heavy, with long wavy black hair and glasses. We had always been cordial over the serving trays, and she must have noticed that I looked mighty troubled, so I ended up telling her about the fight, and my busted-up Jesus. She listened sympathetically, recommended a certain brand of superglue, paid for her things, and left. That was Annie, the girl I'd marry in less than a year. Funny how one person in a relationship always has a different set of memories from the other. Annie doesn't remember that night, but her kindness fell on me like loaves of bread from the sky, and I suddenly became calm, the type of peacefulness I'd felt as a boy when my fears kept me awake and my mother let me sleep in my parents' bed.

Back in the dorm, I spent the next three hours fitting Jesus back together like a 3-D jigsaw puzzle. But I couldn't find this one chip right at the rib cage. I got on my knees and looked under the furniture and everything, but it had disappeared.

I really dislike confrontation because of how my daddy used to beat up on my family, so I wrote Russ a Post-it note asking him to either replace the statuette or reimburse me. I left the note on his pillow and went to sleep, though it took a long time to drift off. Russ came in from biology class the next morning at ten, shook me awake, and explained that the statue had been on the shelf, and when he dusted up there, it fell down and broke.

"If you'd known what you were doing, Gary, you wouldn't have put it so close to the edge," he hissed. I couldn't believe he blamed me. I nearly started another fight.

School policy made getting new roommates tough. Instead, they encouraged healing differences and fostering brotherhood through the teachings of Christ, along with regular counseling. If we chose the second option, the elders said they wouldn't call our parents. Neither of us wanted that, so we tried to make amends.

Once the elders made me and Russ like each other, I forced myself to notice the good about him. It came a lot easier than I reckoned it would. But he didn't have abstract qualities like intelligence or honesty. I'd think, I sure like his Alabama accent, it sounds nice when he keeps his voice low. I watched his lips move—full, red, and soft like a girl's—and how that bright, pale, athletic body of his practically glowed in the dark. Russ is a good guy, I'd think. A real good guy. At first I didn't believe myself. But I thought it a whole lot, and something shifted in my head. Truth be told, I started watching him when he undressed at night. One night I said, "Russ, man, I wish I had a body like yours."

"What? White?" he asked, tugging up his pants by his belt loops.

"No," I stuttered, sort of peeved. "You know that isn't what I meant."

"Skinny?" He fake-smiled with his full teeth, tunneled into a polo shirt, and left. Growling to myself, I turned to the wall and pretended to read a magazine.

Eventually, to make things look good, Russ let me sit with him in the cafeteria, and we found that we had some things in common. We both liked cocker spaniels and collies (though I hated German shepherds). We both liked fire-and-brimstone preachers. Our fathers had the same birthday, September 17. By and by, he replaced my plaster Jesus with a heavier porcelain one that had golden hair and a blue robe. But someway, I never could get used to that one. I only felt better if I put them next to each other. I thought maybe a prayer to both of them would be twice as likely to reach. But whenever I prayed, I'd face the original to the right so I wouldn't have to stare into that hollow chest.

Back home in Charleston on Thanksgiving break, I went to St. John's A.M.E. Zion Church on Sunday to hear Rev. Isaiah Lovejoy, my favorite preacher ever. St. John's A.M.E. wasn't one of those fall-down places like out in the Sea Islands, but if people felt the spirit, they'd raise their arms and shout "Glory to God!" "Hallelujah!" and "Yes, Lord!" I had always admired Rev. Lovejoy's speechifying. He'd stand straight as a lamppost, but he'd use his hands real expressively, playing the crowd like an organ. His sermons against crime and adultery were the best, but he didn't do so well at preaching brotherhood.

I studied him carefully, because I also wanted to help people experience the reality of God. That Sunday, Rev. Lovejoy talked about Jonah and devotion. The spirit got into him so much that he tore the underarm of his jacket and his glasses got all fogged up. He took them off and kept going. First everybody in the pulpit leapt to their feet, then the whole congregation. We applauded and shouted almost like folks in those other churches. At one point, Rev. Lovejoy described Hell in so much detail that Mrs. Addison, a dignified lady with yellow feathers in her yellow hat, burst into tears and ran right out of the church. A bunch of people, including me, followed her with their eyes, guessing why she thought she was going to Hell.

I was awed by Rev. Lovejoy, and a little jealous. I wanted the power to make people know in their hearts that God and Jesus and Heaven and Hell were true, but I had stage fright. I thought if I preached on the radio, I wouldn't have that problem, so I decided to major in Communications.

Back when I was eight years old, my folks and I used to listen to radio station WGWT, "God's Word Today." WGWT played Mahalia Jackson records and preachers with rough voices. Reverends from all over the country would prove through biblical logic that Satan controlled the world. The only way to stop him was to let Jesus into your heart. I had done that, of course. One day Mama sat me down on a bench outside the post office where she worked. She asked me if I wanted to be saved, so I said Yes, Ma'am, I sure do. Then she told me to put my head down and ask Jesus to come into my heart, and I did that, too. When I heard Jesus tell me that he wouldn't ever desert me, my skin tingled and I got teary-eyed. I said Thank you, Jesus. Mama read from the beginning of Matthew 18—"Whosoever therefore shall humble himself as this little child, the same is greatest in the kingdom of heaven." Then she wet my forehead with kisses.

After I accepted Jesus, I begged my mother to get my father to take us to a revival meeting up in Bishopville to see Rev. Ebenezer Poyas, who was my favorite before I discovered Rev. Lovejoy. Daddy thought that only Baptists, whom he called "fool niggers," went to revivals, but it turned out he liked Rev. Poyas. Poyas—you pronounce it "pious"—was a Methodist who thought the Bible should be the law, that sinners should get the old-time punishments like stoning, that you should burn offerings for the Lord and the whole enchilada. He sang the words "Praise God!" and took a gulp of air between every phrase during his sermons. But his big thing was faith healing.

The meeting was all black folks like us, dark women and girls in pink and white and lace-trim dresses looking like chocolate bunnies, with fellows old and young in serious grays and red ties, here and there a cummerbund. Not as colorful as at home, where the ladies would come dressed in all lime green, and even my father, who never wore anything but black to the law firm where he was a runner, sometimes wore a cobalt blue suit on the hottest, humidest days.

Rev. Poyas wore a suit the color of a chalkboard. His heavy forehead beaded with sweat, and he promenaded through the crowd, swinging the microphone up the aisle. I closed my eight-year-old eyes, hoping that he would put that hand on my head and I'd feel God's healing electricity zap me. I couldn't see him through all the tall people around me, but when I heard Reverend Poyas's voice coming closer, I froze.

He searched the crowd for a woman who turned out to be standing next to us. I opened my eyes. The lady wept as she told Rev. Poyas all about her brain cancer, and then she took off her straw hat to reveal a baldie bean. I had only seen that hairstyle on a boy, so I nearly laughed. Everybody else stayed serious. The Reverend laid his hand on the lady's shaved head, and her eyes rolled back so only the whites showed. Her knees gave out. I took a breath; it wasn't funny anymore. She dropped the hat in the aisle and went into convulsions, stumbling and saying "yip-yip" like a little dog. I braced my hands, hoping she would fall on me and some of Christ's healing power would rub off. But instead she fell into the aisle.

Everybody lunged over to keep her from hitting the ground, but we missed. She hit the grass and rolled around, and Rev. Poyas had everybody singing Hallelujah! and Praise Jesus! The organist played dramatic chords and whooshed his finger up the keys.

Soon the woman got up on her knees and told Rev. Poyas that the pain had gone and there was no more brain cancer in her head. Everybody under the tent applauded. I asked Mama how the woman knew the Lord had cured her brain cancer. She frowned down at me and said, "'Cause Jesus took away the pain, that's how. Such foolishness."

At that time, her explanation satisfied me. Like a lot of folks, when somebody in the know confirms what I already want to believe, I swallow it whole. Because if the Lord could heal something serious like brain cancer, he'd have no trouble granting my little wishes. The organist's magnificent chords rang out, loud and astounding as salvation itself. Some people in the front leapt up and down, and their whole bodies shook. Mama wailed and nodded, her eyes full of tears. Daddy nudged me and smirked as if to say Fool niggers. Did he mean Mama, too?

I kept my eyes glued to the brain-cancer woman. Kneeling in the muddy grass of the tent floor with her arms raised, greenish brown stains all over her blouse, she wept and kept thanking Jesus. She held on to the crabgrass like she was trying to keep her joy from catching the wind and taking her right off the planet Earth. I just knew from watching her glossy eyes, staring toward the sky like she could really *see* Jesus, that the disease had left her body. I wanted to know what she saw, to feel what salvation felt like. As she cried out to the Lord, I looked where she was looking, but I only saw the crook of the tent, where a lost starling clung to the ropes, flapping his wings.

Ten years later, in college, watching Reverend Lovejoy's Hell sermon during my Thanksgiving break, I still wasn't sure what the brain-cancer woman had felt. Even after scaring Mrs. Addison, Reverend Lovejoy hadn't healed anybody. He kept describing Hell like he'd just come back from there. "The canyons are gigantic smoldering coals!" he shouted. "Hallelujah! When the blue flame touches skin, the seared flesh will bubble! Hallelujah! Floating down a river of lava, you'll hear millions—*millions!*—of sinners, shrieking for mercy in vain! Hallelujah!" The congregation gasped. My eyes flowed over with tears of repentance.

Our neighbor Debbie Ross walked us home after St. John's. She had the gift of gab. She got my mother into a discussion about nothing, so I could think my own troublesome thoughts as we walked over the broken sidewalks back to Romney Street. I couldn't stop praying for forgiveness and worrying about seared flesh bubbling. I imagined the skin on my forearm melting like pizza topping. I've got to tell Russ about Rev. Lovejoy, I said to myself. He'd love Rev. Lovejoy. Russ loves a tough sermon like Rev. Lovejoy's. I love that guy.

By the time we got near my house, Debbie had kept Mama back a couple of doors, still talking. I came to the front gate and touched it, but for some reason I couldn't move to open it. I stared up at the I-26 overpass with my mind finally blank and listened to cars whooshing up there, their wheels drumming against the concrete. I saw the sky, boy-blue and full of feathery clouds. I love Russ. I'm in love with Russ, I thought, laughing to myself and shaking my head. I knew that wasn't possible. Russ hated me more than he loved Jesus, and plus he was a boy! A laugh rumbled up from my stomach, but then I got that seasick feeling you get when something's so weird and bad and wrong that it's got to be true. For a minute the air filled with a sweet scent—a weird one for November, hibiscus maybe—and I felt hundreds of tiny needles poke my skin in a wave that went from my heart to my feet and back. My nervous laugh burst out and frightened a bird from a nearby bush. Mama showed up behind me without Debbie and asked what was funny. I grabbed the fence tighter and said Me, because I can't get this here latch undone.

TWO

There was only one way to wrangle with my crush on Russ. Officially, I couldn't hate him, but I couldn't get near him either. So I made a schedule that sidestepped him. I'd leave the dorm at 6:30 a.m., before he got back from his morning run, and come home at 10 p.m. curfew. We got into the same biology class second semester, and probably would have been lab partners, but I switched out, even though the sight of him pulled me like the moon does the tides. If he minded, he never let on, and that broke my heart more.

My closest friend freshman year was a woman named Joy. All the time I would have loved to spend with Russ I spent with her. She had curly blond hair and a wide smile, and she made herself available to anybody in need. I felt she could help me sort out my feelings. At Central I finally had a social life—I could never keep friends as a kid because I was "too friendly," as one schoolmate told me—and I didn't want to screw up.

On a kayaking trip into the Everglades, Joy and I shared a boat. She was a large person too, so we had an extra-large boat—it didn't tip up out of the water at all. She rowed, and I sat behind her to keep the boat steady. We spent a couple of hours off on our own, rowing through the tall grasses, stopping to watch cranes take flight, looking out for gators and cottonmouths the whole time. The heat tired us out, and the natural setting put me in a peaceful frame of mind. I said to myself that I would tell her that day. She couldn't turn around in the boat, so I wouldn't have to look her in the eye.

"Joy?" I finally said. "I have been experiencing some... un-Godly desires." I was so nervous I just about fell out of the boat. It wobbled, and I tried to stabilize it by standing up, but that only made matters worse. I sat down and the water lapped up the side.

"Desire is not un-Godly, Gary," Joy reassured me once we got set right again. "God intended for men to find women attractive."

"But this is different—"

"Believe me, most boys have trouble controlling their lustful urges. That's completely normal and natural, Gary."

"This— But these are not—not for girls. The desires." I'd said as much as I could, but I didn't feel better. My hands shook. I'd come over pretty queasy and dizzy.

"Oh," she said, puzzled. She plunked an oar into the water beside us and pulled it forward. The boat made a sharp right turn. "Then what are they for?"

The splash of the oars in the lake sounded as loud as a dam overspilling to me. Then Joy let out a little gasp, almost as soft as a regular breath, and let her oar drop before the next stroke. Russ appeared in my imagination—no pants on, as usual. No way could I say that this had anything to do with him.

"Have you acted on it?" she asked, turning around.

I downplayed my powerful cravings. "Well, it's not a lot," I shrugged. Also, I wasn't sure what counted as acting on it. Truth was, Eugene McCaffrey, a kid I tutored in junior high, had kept daring me to play with him, and I did it once, but maybe not just because I wanted to—because of the dare, too. I'd stand by his bedroom door, upstairs from his parents' burger-and-fish joint, Gizzy's. The heavy smell of fried food would drift up from the shop. I was always fixing to run and never quite getting around to it. Euge would unzip his jeans and lower them down his chunky thighs to his sneakers. Then he'd peel off his drawers and sit down, his belly and his legs turning his crotch into a cave with a dirty blond brush sticking out of it. He'd spread his legs and massage his male part, bright white compared to the tan and red skin everywhere else. He'd touch himself for a while and then spit into his hand. I'd whisper that he should stop, that his daddy would come upstairs, and he'd only laugh.

"Touch it," he'd say, or "Put your mouth on it."

"I don't want to get my clothes dirty," I'd tell him. "My daddy doesn't like me coming home all dirty." Daddy often beat me and my brother, Joe, for the least thing wrong, like an unmade bed or a dish with a gravy stain. He didn't just hit us with a switch—sometimes he did it with a dustpan, a broomstick, or his bony black fist.

Euge would laugh out loud, his mouth wide open. "You're funny, Gary," he'd say. "You ain't like none of the other colored boys I know."

I didn't dare ask what the other colored boys were like. I didn't like that there were other colored boys, and I didn't like him thinking I was different from them.

The fourth time, he didn't laugh. He'd just taken his pants down and his thing poked out from his round body like the wick on a short candle. Euge glared at me. "You can't come over no more. I'm telling your daddy that you ain't a real tutor." He said snotty things like that all the time, but he meant it for once. Shaking, I shut the lights so Jesus wouldn't see, and groped around in the dark for that wick. My nervous fingers found his big stomach, tickled their way down, and grabbed on tight. I milked his thing like a cow udder for a couple of minutes, until he groaned like somebody putting down a sack of lime. Once he got done, I kept my dirty hand still. I wished I could have unscrewed it and left it there. Euge found his shirt and wiped my fingers, and I ran out of the darkness into the bathroom and scrubbed both hands real hard with Lava soap.

Thinking about that scared the stuffing out of me freshman year. So I didn't.

"Don't you have any feelings for women?" Joy asked. I could hear a little disgust under her question, same as when kids at school would ask, "Y'all don't got a TV at home?"

"Yes!" I blurted out. "Sort of. But something might be a little wrong."

She tossed her hair and picked up the oars again. "Have you prayed?"

My nervous laugh burst out. "Have I ever."

"Nothing?"

"Nope. Not yet. I did, and then Jesus stopped talking to me."

"Jesus would never stop talking to you, Gary."

I laughed, kind of bitterly. Joy took a deep breath and let it out. A breeze skidded across the water right then, like her sigh had done it. "You know, I had kind of hoped that we…"

A strange kind of happy sadness welled up in my chest. What a relief to tell somebody about my problem. And what a surprise for her to say that she liked me like that. Joy, a pretty white woman, who could have easily had a white man. But it was just awful that my confession had to disappoint my friend. I thought of saying that this didn't rule her out, but that didn't seem like a good idea.

"Will you help me?" I asked.

"I've heard about people who have overcome this."

Joy thought that an exorcism might work. In the library, she looked up a special prayer to bind the demon and cast it out. We met in the chapel in mid-afternoon when nobody was there. Joy had copied the prayer down in her notebook. I read it first. It was addressed to a demon of homosexuality, but I asked her not to say "homosexuality" in case somebody heard. She began, and right before the end, she touched her palm to my forehead. "I cast you out!" she cried, ferociously but quietly. "Leave this man, demon of—!" Her mouth snapped shut and she hummed the seven evil syllables.

"Did you feel anything?" she asked, wiping my sweat on her long polka-dot dress.

"Yeah," I said. But I had trouble saying what, aside from hot and worried.

To test whether the exorcism had worked, I went back to my dorm immediately. I wanted to see Russ, because if it took, he and I could be pals for real.

It was a muggy night, and he never liked the AC, so Russ was sitting at his desk wearing boxer shorts. A glass of water and a pitcher sat next to his books, sweating. He coughed up a flat hello. His tight chest had a shadow under it, a dark bird flying above his navel. With my eyes, I couldn't help tracing the silky trail of hair in the middle of his stomach down to his waistband. Far as I know, there's no name for the emotion that's both intense sexual attraction and a whole lot of shame. But the first time I tried to ride a bike, I did it without anybody helping me for about fifty yards. I said "Hot dog, I can ride a bike!" Then I crashed into a car and fell and split my lip so bad I needed four stitches. Looking at Russ right then felt like reliving that whole experience.

Eight days later Joy and I tried exorcism again, in a more hidden room where she could say "homosexuality," but I still didn't change. I asked if she would marry me anyhow.

"I need to get married," I insisted. "That's the only thing that'll stop it." She said no.

"You need a real minister to solve your problem, Gary," she said one morning in the chapel. Joy sounded tired of me now. "I'm only a freshman." Behind her, next to a stained-glass window, I stared at a sculpture of Christ suffering on the cross. His eyes rolled up into His head, eternally going through the unbearable moment when He thought God had forsaken Him. The pain pierced my heart because the statue was very accurate—the crucifixion nails even went through Jesus' wrists. If the Romans had nailed through His palms, I'd read, the nails would've sliced through the tendons and He'd have fallen off.

Later I heard from other people that Joy was tired of what she called my "lack of initiative." When I saw her, I could tell she didn't want to hang around, but we knew we'd have to see each other on camping trips, so we had to be polite.

By winter break I got sadder and more frustrated. Joy started avoiding me. I steered clear of my other friends and skipped lots of classes. Whole afternoons I spent hunched over in the TV room, watching inspirational shows that did me no good—they just reminded me of how far I had to go before I could be holy. I had the same problem with my weight. When I figured how much I'd have to do to get slim, I felt like somebody standing at the bottom of Mount Everest with a trowel and a shoestring. My grades plummeted.

Almost every night on the phone Mama asked if I'd met any nice young ladies. The pressure went so high that I told her about Sareena, a Phys Ed major I'd only spoken with once. She had big bones, dark skin, and a quiet way about her—exactly the type of girl my mother thought I ought to marry. I let Mama think that we'd held hands in church and played putt-putt golf on a date. "She's a bougie gal from Atlanta," I said. Sophisticated folks impressed Mama. "Her father owns a Christian record label, Clarion Records." I made up that company, and lots of other facts, and pretty soon Sareena and I had a history so complicated I had to write it down to keep it straight. Then that February my folks invited her down for a weekend. I had to find out where she stayed and eventually caught her at home. She was a senior. As I told her about our history and my parents, she raised one eyebrow and folded her arms.

"You could have just asked me out," she said. She was quiet but frank. "I'd have said no, but you'd have saved yourself a whole lot of effort." Supposedly she had a boyfriend back home in Alabama, but it sounded like they might break up soon.

"Will you please come meet my folks?" I begged. "And there's something else. I'd like to show them pictures. So if you don't mind, can we make some pictures of us on dates?"

"What's in it for me?" Sareena wanted to know.

Once I agreed to pay her, Sareena turned out to be a great sport. She memorized our history and came up with her own ideas as well. We took pictures on the beach, at putt-putt golf, and by the fountain in the Osceola Square Mall. Mama still has one of those pictures on her fridge. At supper Sareena charmed my folks with her manners, and acted like an honest-to-God girlfriend. So when they went to bed, and we sat out on the veranda drinking sweet tea and listening to the locusts and the highway, I got my courage up, figuring our fake thing could turn true pretty handily and maybe even change me.

"So," I said, smirking so I could backtrack if I needed to, "do you want to make it official?" Sareena burst out laughing, and I was hurt. "Why's that a funny idea?"

"Because you're a fruitcake, Gary." She raised that eyebrow again, and it chilled me like the Evil Eye. "You need the Lord's guidance. I've looked at you looking at what you look at." She scratched a mosquito bite until a raw red dot opened on her biceps.

"A nice girl don't make an accusation like that on a man in his own home," I growled. "Especially just from looking at looking."

The next weekend, around Valentine's Day, I told Mama we broke up because she'd cheated on me. We only spoke again once (I slipped payments into her campus mailbox), but the aftermath of our fake relationship made me more uneasy, and curiously lovesick.

During this time of trouble, Annie, who I called Superglue Girl in my mind, started talking to me more on the serving line. I knew that she thought I got more helpings because I wanted to flirt, but I was only dumping food on top of my problems. I did like her, though. She wore a hairnet, a sea-green smock, and glasses, but underneath you could see diamonds in her eyes. Her easygoing manner and the way her pudgy face glowed reminded me of the good parts about Euge. She had a special way of clinking the spoon against the plate when she served the mashed potatoes—three clinks, the second two closer together. Then she'd smile.

Before Joy, I had never considered that a woman might find me attractive. Mama had let me go on Christian group dates in high school, but that was different. After Joy, it became sort of a fun game for me to figure out if a girl liked me.

So when I saw Annie in the library one day, out of her dining-hall uniform, I complimented her flowery dress. Then I ran into her walking across campus late one morning and we decided to have lunch together. She wanted to major in Business, and I had started in Communications. We talked about how well the program at Central combined the principles of business and communications with Biblical laws. The conversation didn't make much sense—it was the kind of dumb chitchat you make when you're desperate to keep somebody near you. At the end of it, I asked for her phone number—in case she wanted to go to study hall together. It didn't make me too nervous to ask; I knew she'd say yes. A month after my breakup with Sareena, Annie agreed to come on my next camping trip, to Lake Kissimmee. I began to feel like something of a ladies' man.

By the time we went to the lake, Annie and I had developed a special bond. During the drive out there, we sat in the backseat, real close, and said silly private things to one another that Joy and her new boyfriend Steve couldn't hear. The next morning we left Joy and Steve sleeping in their separate tents at the camp and went on an early hike.

Annie came from a place called Samoa, in the South Pacific. I had never heard of it, but I supposed it couldn't be too different from Hawaii. I knew a little about Hawaii because one of the preachers on WGWT broadcast from there. It surprised me to hear that Samoa was part of the United States. Right when I opened my mouth to compare it to Hawaii, she told me she didn't like for people to compare it to Hawaii. Samoans had a bunch of interesting folktales about brothers who turned into mountains and volcanoes with spirits in them. They sounded kind of satanic to me, but nobody took it serious anymore, Annie said, and most Samoans were good Christians.

Joy and I got a moment together on the second night of camping, when Annie and Steve decided to go fishing. The day was winding down. A hot breeze hung on from the sweltering afternoon. Hot as a goat's butt in a pepper patch, as Euge used to say. In a clearing, Joy and I gathered sticks to make a fire. We tried to find oak because that and hickory made the best-smelling smoke, and it would seep into the food.

We stooped down like slaves. Joy wasn't used to bending over and gathering things, so I teased her about how her people couldn't handle hard labor. A plane left a long, beautiful streak of smoke across the sky, and our conversation got quiet. Crickets chittered and frogs croaked. Twigs broke under our feet.

"Have you told Annie yet? About yourself?" Joy asked.

"No," I admitted. I was enjoying myself so much with Annie. The way I figured it, saying something might destroy the whole relationship—the way it was doing with Joy, really. "I suppose I will when the time comes."

"As I become more intimate with Annie," Joy warned me, "this knowledge puts me in an awkward position. The longer you wait, the more I feel it is my obligation to let her know." Joy had never spoken to me so stiffly, like a second-grade teacher. She talked real proper for a Texan because she came from money. But she'd never seemed quite as nasty to me as right then. In that moment, I felt *good* about our friendship falling apart.

Angry blood rushed into my face. "But Joy, it isn't really your business."

"If I didn't know, I feel I could agree with you, Gary. But by helping conceal your problem, I'm helping you deceive Annie. It isn't Christ-like."

"But Joy—" I said. Annie and Steve's rowboat came into view. We wouldn't be able to keep the conversation going. In a rush, I agreed to tell Annie as soon as the trip ended.

But I didn't. After Lake Kissimmee, Annie and I spent so much time together that I never had to officially ask her out. Everybody assumed that we were dating, though we looked a comical, mismatched pair. We dressed in thrift-store clothes. She wore nerdy-looking glasses and I sported a pair of generic sneakers with a hole in the toe. She stood 4'11" and I was 6'1".

We were both overweight, but Annie carried her extra pounds like my mother. Her cheeks glowed like full birthday balloons. If I kept her smiling, the same way I did with Mama, I could make her life perfect.

Once or twice I thought about telling Annie, and I wondered if I was giving in to Joy, who thought that keeping a secret was the same as lying. It didn't feel that way to me. I had to share my trouble with Annie in my own time, not because Joy wanted me to hurry up. My attraction to Annie would make me normal soon—I could feel it. Why bring up the past?

On our first trip to Disney World, I pulled Annie right to the teacups. She loved spending a day there almost as much as I did, so it hadn't taken long for us to end up there on a date. On the ride, Annie made up for her short size with strength and stubbornness. She spun our teacup faster than I'd ever done by myself. When we got off, we stumbled in a zigzag and held each other up and laughed. We bought burgers and Cokes and sat in the picnic area. In the middle of the snack, she said, "I wish my whole life could be like this. Just fun. Only pleasure."

I breathed in, tasting the warm air, full up with the smell of sugar and grease. Delicious. I tingled all over and smiled. "Me, too," I said. She stared into my eyes and blinked and giggled and looked away. I gently stepped on her toe with the ball of my shoe.

"Can I call you Pookie-Pie?" she asked, still giggling.

"You can call me anything you want, except late for dinner."

I swear I had real feelings for her. But what are real feelings when it comes to love? If the love doesn't work out, feelings that drove you stone crazy one year could feel like a feather in your ear by the next. Feelings feel real enough when you've got them, but sometimes they don't mean much more in the scheme of things than what the weather was on this same date last year. When you think about it, it gets tough to put your emotions into boxes called Real and Not Real, or even Sexual and Not Sexual. The way a friend of mine puts it, the problem with attractions might be that they're *all* sexual.

Annie and I finished our meals, tossed out our trash, and headed for Tomorrowland. When we stood under the monorail, she slipped her fingers between mine.

We went back to Disney World all the time. I didn't need an excuse. Annie loved Big Thunder Mountain Railroad and the Indy Speedway, but she also wanted to be near families. She had left her mother, three brothers, and two sisters back in Samoa. Her grandfather on her mother's side was also still alive. She wrote a letter to all of them at least once a week. Sometimes she wrote personal messages to other relatives in the margins.

One time she went up to a Samoan family outside Spaceship Earth. It turned out that they had known her father. The mother spoke of Annie's dad as somebody who had been very kind to their family. I would have liked him, I knew. He was a tuna fisherman, a devout Christian, and a generous leader in his community. When Annie was seven, his boat capsized in a storm and he drowned.

The Samoan family insisted that we spend the day with them. While we strolled through the park, they explained the Samoan perspective on life. It sounded a lot like Christianity in the South—you had to do everything your parents said, even after you grew up and got married. Annie whispered that that was why so many Samoans committed suicide.

When we had all gotten tired of walking, we found a table by a snack bar. The mother, Mrs. Tatupu, brought out a couple of Tupperware containers filled with a delicious beef dish called *supasui*. She handed out forks from a cardboard box and sat down next to Annie.

"Anone, how is it you've come to the mainland?" she asked. I hadn't heard my new girlfriend—I loved to look at her and think the word *girl-friend*—tell the whole story myself yet, so I leaned over to listen.

"I came to study," she told the older woman. "The Bible." She smiled. "And I thought Florida wouldn't be too big a change in climate."

"But everyone said—" Mrs. Tatupu began. Her expression became curious. She glanced at me, trying to answer a question she had about me without asking it. "Oh," she sighed, though her face still appeared confused.

"No," Annie said to Mrs. Tatupu, touching my knee. "It's not what you think."

Once we got done with the dish, though, the family said a few words in Samoan to Annie and left us, rushing ahead to the Living Seas exhibit instead of exploring France. I tried to convince them to continue on with us, but Annie stepped hard on my foot.

We said good-bye and entered the neat gardens of the France pavilion.

Annie didn't say very much during our walk, and when we got to the bridge between France and the United Kingdom, she stopped and gripped the stones at the edge. A strong wind threw her hair up, so she knotted it tightly and folded her arms, staring across the reflecting pool at the geodesic dome.

"I did something foolish," she said, "because I wanted to leave Samoa." Annie had placed a personal ad in several Florida newspapers, after a friend told her how to do it. She thought she could find a rich man to pay her airfare. In the ad, she called herself exotic and leggy. A few men responded, and she started writing back and forth to one of them, a guy named Kent. Without her asking, he sent her a plane ticket. Knowing that her mother would never allow her to go under any circumstances, she ran off to Pago Pago without telling anybody, not even her best friend, and got on a plane to Tampa.

For three weeks she lived with Kent, a survivalist type with a bushy beard and a beat-up truck. He did inventory for a software company, but he spent his spare time researching how to live in the wilderness. Neither of them thought the other was a good match, but Annie didn't have any money or anyplace else to go. Soon Kent decided that she owed him sex, and he tied her to a chair in his basement for four days, only letting her go to the bathroom once a day, when he got home from work. During the time she sat in the chair, she promised Christ that if He got her out of that situation she would serve Him for the rest of her life. On the fifth day she untangled the restraints and crawled through a basement window. She ran away on the public bus and found a church that helped her. Going to Central Florida Christian College was part of fulfilling her promise to God.

As she told me all this, the corners of her eyes filled with tears. "My family disowned me when they found out I had deceived them. I guess I hoped Mrs. Tatupu didn't know. But she didn't have to bring it up. Why couldn't she have let me pretend, for one day?"

"But what about all the letters you send home?" I asked.

"They never write back."

Well knock me down and steal my teeth, I thought. They abandoned her. I stooped down and wrapped my arms around her. She wept, and a jolt of electricity went through me, because I realized for the first time that Annie was as cut off from her community and the rest of the world as

I was. My toes tingled and went numb, a punch landed in my rib cage, and for a few seconds I couldn't breathe. I had no way to explain this fantastic sensation, so I came to the obvious conclusion. I meant it more than I had ever meant anything.

"I love you," I said.

In church they said that premarital fornication was a sin, but I didn't realize that fornication meant sex. Everything I learned about men and women came from kids on the street, or the echoes of right and wrong that you pick up in polite conversation. I had figured out that you kissed a little, you squeezed the breasts, the penis went into the vagina, and the man thrust it in and out a whole bunch. It sounds loco now, but I never quite put it together that that added up to sex, and a child might come along as a result. Sex just sounded like a funny thing everybody wanted to do but couldn't, or did too much and suffered. Above everything, you had to keep it a secret.

Annie and I got closer than a boy and a girl were supposed to at Central, and we created our own private rules. She had the key to the kitchen and we would raid the refrigerator at night sometimes. Since we were boyfriend and girlfriend, I figured that the man had to want sex from the girl, but since all the secretive business scared me and I didn't know if I wanted it or not, or whether the Lord would get angry, I pretended to want it, and that made it a joke I could take back if need be.

On our kitchen nights, Annie would tell me what time she'd be in there and I'd come find her. We couldn't turn on the lights because that would attract attention and get us in trouble. I didn't want my supply of free pralines and mud cake cut off, no sir.

One time I got to the kitchen late because I'd run into Russ on campus. Actually I saw him across the quad and went out of my way to bump into him. I missed and loved and hated him and simmered with jealousy because he had made the Dean's List. He had grown his hair out slightly, and a recent shower had slicked it and separated it into ringlets. He was extremely handsome and fresh-smelling. Chilly breezes kept tickling the green, making his nipples stand out under his dress shirt—I couldn't stop looking at that. Thankfully, Russ never looked at my looking, but he seemed genuinely concerned about me for once, and I wanted to soak that up.

My erection pounded hotly along my thigh as I arrived in the kitchen. I tiptoed across the cold room, thinking maybe Annie had left. But she'd waited for me in the dark under a long metal table. She barked, leapt out from under the table, and grabbed my leg. I let out a big gasp like a lady. Annie kept pretending to be a dog and we wrestled playfully and shoved each other around. I joked with her about wanting to make love. Then I kissed her and the joke disappeared. We ground our faces together and went all the way. We scrunched against a bunch of big sacks of cornmeal flour while we did it and flour got all over our clothes and in our hair. Annie whispered that I should pull out, but too late.

"Gary," she breathed, lying on top of me, chin to chin. "That wasn't cool."

We heard footsteps outside and froze. The shadow of a head passed the square doors on the far side of the room but didn't stop.

"I'm sorry," I panted. "I'll ask God's forgiveness."

A worried expression branched out across her face and curled her eyebrows. She answered quietly, through her teeth. "That might not be enough."

THREE

A few weeks after we met Mrs. Tatupu, we stood up in church, as we always did at the end of the service. A younger minister, Michael Woodson, a man of color with a shaved head, red lips, and a complexion like tea with milk, was filling in for Reverend Franklin, who had a family emergency. He encouraged us to call him Mike. Unlike his elder's hard speeches and deep, booming voice, this young fellow preached a real personal, friendly sermon about reconciling with your family, using the story of Joseph's father as his basis. Not my thing at all, but I gave him a shot.

Minister Mike described his grandfather's stubbornness about making peace with his son, who had suffered under the demon of alcoholism for many years. I thought of my own daddy's problem with the bottle. Minister Mike's father had developed bone cancer and died before his father could humble himself. You'd think the grandfather wouldn't care, but he was devastated. Mike stressed the point that there was only time to patch things up while your relatives were alive. The congregation broke into applause, which I had never heard in that church before.

As the sermon came to a close, Mike called on us to open our hearts to Jesus, and encouraged anybody who felt the spirit to go on up to the altar. I looked at my shoes. I'd never had a true baptism of the spirit, like everybody approaching the stage.

When I turned thirteen, after what Euge and I did, I prayed every night for a year for Jesus to change me into a likeable person. "Yes, my son," He'd say, in a deep voice like a preacher on WGWT. "It will happen any day now, Gary." But nothing changed. Was He too busy? Did it just take a long time? Why would Jesus promise and then not do it?

"What does Jesus say when He talks to you?" I asked my brother Joe. Joe was big like me and good in science. He kept a chemistry set under a corner of our bed, potatoes on sticks in plastic cups on our windowsills, and a hurt bird in an animal hospital in the yard.

Without looking up from his forbidden X-Men comic book, Joe said, "Jesus don't talk to me. He don't talk to nobody. That's some hokum they say at church."

Confusion and fear came over me. Joe stared at me like a puzzle he didn't feel like solving. "You think God's talking to you? In your head? Boy, you're stone crazy." He iced his rejection with a sneer.

"No I'm not. If that's not Jesus, then whose voice is answering my prayers?"

"Gary. Damn. I must say, I've never known anybody who could fool themselves as good as you. That's your own voice. You're pretending that it's Jesus."

"No. He really talks to me."

"Prove it."

"I don't say 'thou' and 'thee' when I talk. Jesus talks the old talk to me."

"Boy, if Jesus is answering *your* prayers, you must be asking for the wrong shit."

Joe rolled over and ignored me. I tried to tame my doubts, but they crept in anyway, and when I prayed after that, I couldn't hear the voice anymore. Every night I tried to hear His voice again, and nothing happened. I followed Christianity, but in my heart, I believed God had hung up on me.

A hymn played quietly on the organ. Minister Mike's voice became soft and serious as he invited us up for a baptism of the spirit. Annie slid her glasses off and set them on the pew behind us. Then she raised one arm to the sky and whispered "Jesus, Jesus." At first I thought something was wrong. But soon I knew that Jesus had filled her heart. I stepped back so that she could walk down the carpet, toward the front of the room. Still repeating the Lord's name, she sauntered up to the minister, until I could no longer see her in the crowd of believers at the pulpit. What about me, Lord? I said inside. Reach into my heart!

My shirt collar and tie felt tight. The salvation period had almost ended. Fewer people moved to the front, where raised hands swayed back and forth like royal palms in a tropical breeze. The hymn grew louder. Sweat soaked my shirt, so I tucked it further into my slacks and loosened my tie.

Two weeks before, the many classes I skipped had caught up to me. Notes from professors had been arriving in my dorm mailbox, warning that I would soon reach the magic number of absences that guaranteed a failure, but I had slipped them under paper towels in my garbage pail to ease the forgetting. On Saturday, though, I'd gotten one from the dean's office that said I had to take the next year off. I tried to burn it, but I set off the smoke alarm. I blew out the note and tried to silence the high-pitched beeping by fanning the alarm with my hands, but I couldn't reach. By that time people had started to bang on the door, so I let in a neighbor and he took care of it.

In the middle of my panic, I'd put the note down on Russ's desk. Later that afternoon, sitting at his desk, he held it up behind his back, displaying the charred edge. I'd been daydreaming about his successful future as I watched him study.

"I'll miss you," he said, without turning around.

I said my worst fear. "No you won't."

He spun around in the swivel chair and flung the note at me like a ninja star. "You're right," he said. The note zipped behind our bunk. I left it there.

There wasn't a reason to stick around. I answered a newspaper ad and found a job doing telephone interviews at a market research company called Daytona Reports, and moved into the Heritage Estates Condominium Apartments. I decided to tell my folks I had enrolled in summer classes. With all my school friends shrinking away, I needed church pretty desperately if I wanted a social life. But everybody else had gotten saved.

The way our classmates talked about it, getting saved came naturally, like a sneeze. Jesus would illuminate your soul and touch your heart until it blew like a volcano into ecstasy and new life. Color and peace would flood your world. Annie's friend Sam had fallen off his bicycle on the way back from church. "Jesus hit me with an energy beam!" he exclaimed. His girlfriend, Lydia, said salvation was like trying to think of a name you couldn't remember. It would come faster if you didn't force it. Maybe getting saved and liking women happened the same way. Maybe if I let go and let God in, He'd mend everything.

I raised one timid arm into the air, then both. "Thank you, Jesus," I said. "Thank you, Jesus. Thank you, Jesus." I stepped into the aisle and took baby steps to the altar, gaining confidence with each one.

Nobody's energy beam hit me. In fact, I feared that the Lord would strike me dead for pretending to experience the power of His love. I had so much nervous guilt inside me that my hands shook. Of course, that made it look like the Lord *was* healing my soul. I glanced around the crowd of people, all in rapture, eyes closed, heads thrown back, hopping in place, sweating, pumping their hands to heaven: old folks, children, middle-aged women, everybody. I envied the honesty of their belief. None of them seemed as unlucky as me. The faith of a child is so precious, I thought. How can anybody ever get it back?

By the time I spotted Annie in the crowd, I suppose I did seem to have changed. She gasped with delight when I showed up at her side. She pushed her hair out of her eyes, clapped her hands together, and wept, overcome with gratitude to the Lord. She wrapped her arms around my waist. The entire congregation raised their voices to sing a beautiful hymn of reconciliation between fathers and sons, inspired by the parable of the prodigal son in the gospel of St. Luke:

O where is my boy tonight?
O where is my boy tonight?
My heart o'erflows, for I love him, he knows;
O where is my boy tonight?

Once he was pure as morning dew,
As he knelt at his mother's knee;
No face was as bright, no heart more true,
And none was so sweet as he.

Go for my wandering boy tonight;
Go search for him where you will;
But bring him to me with all his blight,
And tell him I love him still.

The room vibrated with the sounds of our voices. Music swelled from the organ, whose many golden pipes shone across the front walls of the church. Minister Mike brought his own son, Chester, up out of the choir and hugged him, and they both cried. Chester's meaty thigh was right at my eye-height, straining against the fabric of his suit, and I followed it up his body. I immediately fell into his sexy, maximum-size features: a bowed upper lip that almost breathed me in, a pair of large, reddish brown ears, ripe for nibbling. The energy of a racehorse seemed to flow through his brawny limbs, even as his father held him and he wept. He was one of the most attractive men I had ever beheld. Unconsciously, I wet my lips.

I wanted the power of the voices of Minister Mike's congregation to lift me out of the pain I felt. I tried to ride those voices to salvation. But even though strong emotions overtook me, I knew they were coming from my sour memories and guilt, not a joyous rebirth in Christ. I wept, and though it looked like salvation, I knew I was weeping because I could feel Jesus falling *out* of my life.

My father once tried to teach me to change my drawers every day by rubbing my face in a pair of dirty ones. When I got a B+ in fifth-grade math, he socked me in the mouth after our meeting with the teacher, and his wedding band chipped one of my teeth. I spat out the chip too close to a storm drain and couldn't save it. We couldn't afford to get it fixed, so I had to live with the broken tooth. For many years I kept my upper lip down so nobody would see, especially not Daddy, and I had to smile and hide the smile at the same time. To keep me and Joe from standing up for ourselves, he'd make fun of us if we protested. He'd call us rabbits or girls. "You should've seen your face," he'd guffaw.

As the first-born son, Joe had it worse because all my parents' expectations got dumped on him. He couldn't take it, and he acted out a lot. The be-all end-all was when he went and got a Gullah girl pregnant. When Daddy found out, he threatened to slice Joe's neck open with a pair of gardening shears. He didn't just say it, though—he had Joe's neck jammed between the blades, his elbows cocked, about to behead his son easy as you would a dandelion. Joe reached for a monkey wrench and slammed Daddy in the face with it a bunch of times, breaking his jaw in five places.

After that, Joe couldn't come back home, no way. He moved to New York and eventually got work as a recording studio engineer. I'll never forget watching his white shirt fluttering in the dark as he rushed off down Romney Street. I thought I'd never see him again. Daddy curled into a heap at Mama's feet, spitting droplets of blood and tooth fragments on the dirt front yard. For my parents, I made a show of caring for Daddy and hating Joe, but in my heart of hearts I reckoned Daddy had it coming. I secretly kept in touch with Joe through friends, but Mama and Daddy stopped even mentioning him. They talked like they only had one child and nobody but me would carry on the family name.

Thinking about all what Daddy and Joe had done, I turned to the stained-glass window, but I saw in the far corner the depiction of David aiming his slingshot at Goliath that I usually avoided looking at. Some Sundays I imagined myself stroking the clean-cut victor's back, other times the hairy brute would attack me. That was a double whammy, that particular window.

Finally, fixing my eyes on the cross, I tried to understand the intense suffering of our Lord and Savior. Through His mournful eyes, I tried to feel what He felt. But He didn't touch me inside. Silently, I begged His forgiveness for my phony revelation, hoping that He would take pity on me and bowl me over with His incredible power, or even change me gradually— I would have settled for anything. My salvation might have been bogus, but my plea for Him to make it real was completely sincere. That should have counted for something.

FOUR

With no job, a forced leave of absence from school, and no way to go home without shaming my family and getting a thrashing, I reckoned my life had bottomed out. But it hadn't. I lost Annie, too. The last weeks of April she had finals; I'd see her twice a week instead of every day. When we did meet up, she'd greet me with a limp wave from two feet back—no more bear hugs. I would leave messages on her machine and smooth Post-it notes against her door, but she took her sweet time responding. I decided to wait and see how long it would take her to reply, but after three days of hugging and biting my stuffed animals at night and banging my head against the drywall by my bed hard enough to dent it, I caved. At 3 a.m. on May Day I put a comforter in the passenger's seat of my car, drove to her apartment, and spread my bedding across her threshold. I lay down on it and slept uneasily. She couldn't step over me—she'd need to move my fat body to leave.

Even still, the next morning Annie put a chair in the doorjamb and was fixing to jump over me, but a cross-breeze whooshed through the door and stirred me. I came to as she landed on my other side. She leaned over me, trying to push the chair back into the apartment and reach back in to pull the door shut, but I took hold of her ankle.

"It's over, Gary," she said. "Let go."

"Why, Annie? What did I do?" I lost my self-control. Tears spilled into my nose. I wrapped my forearm around her shin.

She loooked a little bit ill. The skin on her face didn't fit well, and the rest of her body had a downright unhealthy gray tint. I figured she was ashamed that we'd done it and angry with me about being a bad lover. I was ashamed, too, about the sin, but also a little proud in a manly way that made the shame bearable. But if she left me, I'd have to go through life alone—that I couldn't handle.

"You didn't do anything, Gary." Annie met my wet gaze, then her face contorted and she rocked forward. For a second I thought that I'd disgusted her somehow, but in a heartbeat she turned to grip the iron rail of the balcony. I had to let go of her ankle and rise to follow her. She bent her neck over the railing and sent the contents of her stomach splattering to the blacktop on the ground floor.

"Are you okay? Annie? Are you sick?"

"No, I'm okay. I'm fine." She coughed and spat until her throat went back to normal.

I padded over the comforter into the apartment, ran a cool glass of tap water for her, and delivered it as she stepped into the living room.

"Sit down?" I suggested, and she did. "Have you been to see the doctor?"

She made a noise in between a breath and a laugh and drank the water in one go. Even after the water had fallen into her stomach and cooled her down, I kept staring at her as if I was waiting to hear about her doctor visit. She didn't say anything for a long time, and a tiny parade of very different thoughts marched across her face. The corners of her lips turned up, then one corner more than the other, then they both fell. Her eyelids flared. She sighed. Something dark came over her. She bit down on the rim of the glass. Annie's expression finally rested in a plain, unemotional position. I thought she was trying to look a little dumb so I wouldn't expect an answer.

I hadn't peed all night, and the pressure in my bladder had built up pretty strongly. "I'm going to the facilities," I announced, pushing myself away from the dividing wall between the kitchen and living room, feeling lucky just to have entered her apartment.

As I washed my hands after doing my business, my eye fell on a scrap of white paper sitting on top of the toilet brush. It seemed like it had fluttered down only to miss the garbage pail. It had small writing on it, like the directions you get with foot creams and wart medicine. I dried my hands on Annie's face towel and reached down to toss the scrap of paper into the bucket, but then I got the notion that it might hold the key to Annie's sickness and read the fine print. The paper said, "Dip the test into your urine." It said, "A plus sign in the round results window means you're pregnant."

Instantly I remembered Joe's neck between the garden shears. Daddy's sweaty face and open, howling mouth. Joe's bugged-out, fearful eyes, Daddy's cocked elbows. Mama screeching at Daddy to let Joe go, trying to tear him off by the collar. I thought of the monkey wrench banging against my father's face, the splintered bones in his chin. Of the many months Daddy spent with his jawbones wired shut, drinking liquid meals. Of all the curses he wrote down about Joe on scraps of paper. How they were so mean that I burned them in the backyard while I prayed to Jesus to forgive Daddy. But mostly my mind fixed itself on what his girlfriend Desiree had done, and how she couldn't have children as a result.

I returned to the living room a zombie, still holding the pregnancy test directions. I sat myself down across from Annie, who had laid down on her couch to recover. Jewels of sweat collected on her forehead, so I found a paper towel and knelt beside the sofa to mop them up, leaving bits of fluff around her eyebrow. I put the directions on the coffee table. Her eyes traveled to the paper and then to my eyes.

"You're not sick," I said.

Annie groaned. "It's not yours," she said. I didn't believe her but I accepted her version of the truth. A bunch of questions came to mind— Why hadn't she told me? Whose else could it be? Was she planning to get rid of our baby?—but I kept my big mouth shut and let her lead the conversation. She turned her head sideways, locked eyes with me, and looked away several times. When she looked, I tried to let her know, without saying anything, that I was opening my whole life to her and putting it square in her palm.

"That doesn't bother you." It was an observation, not a question.

"You weren't going to have an— Were you going to— Without—?"

She groaned again. "Okay. We'd better get married. Let's get married."

I was already kneeling, so I proposed and she accepted. We set a date and everything. It had to be before she started showing. I hugged her and there was a pause. "I do love you," she said, like a cop letting me off with a warning. "And I lied. It is yours." I well nigh grinned my face off.

A tense couple of months passed as we planned the ceremony, while I worried that Annie might change her mind, and tried to find a full-time job. Neither happened.

Four days before we were supposed to leave for my aunt Vietta's house in Savannah, where Annie and I would get married, I interviewed at yet another company. The interviewer, a bald man with a red face and a loose neck, looked at my résumé and told me that I didn't want to work there. I said that I thought I did, but he said I wanted a different job, in the mailroom, or as an admin. He didn't ask how I felt about his opinions, and if he had, I wouldn't have been dumb enough to contradict the man. So I asked about other jobs, but the bald fellow said there weren't any that fit my experience. He slid his papers together and shoved them into his briefcase.

Since the formal part of the interview seemed to be over, I asked, in a friendly way, if he knew about any jobs that *did* fit my experience, maybe at other places. He said no and left the room. I folded my résumé all neat and stuck it back into my jacket pocket as I walked out to my car. I sat in the driver's seat with the door open and my legs outside and looked at the office. Because the blue glass building reflected the sky, it didn't seem to be there. Maybe the whole experience wasn't real and my life was truly Hell. I felt that I could not support my future wife and child, and the fight against my desire for males dragged on.

With my heart heavier than ever, I slid into my car and headed down I-4. I wished that Florida had more bridges, cliffs, and high buildings. I could drive or jump to my death from one of them. Suicide was a sin, I knew, but I was guilty of worse ones. I looked at the many tall signs along the highway advertising hotels and fast-food restaurants, wondering if I could climb one, leap off, and bring my suffering to an end.

It was typical of me that reading all those restaurant names made my suicidal thoughts fade into regular hunger. Pretty soon I pulled over at a Waffle House. In my mind, I already had an image of a thick brown waffle, dripping with syrup, and a scoop of butter on top that looked like ice cream. I passed the sign between where I parked and the actual restaurant. This was one of those super-tall poles you can see for miles back, seven or eight feet around and painted with black enamel. I walked over and hugged it, the surface rough and cool against my neck and chin. I looked straight up and saw how incredibly high it went, like an express lane up to Heaven. I was sorry I couldn't climb it. Anyhow, it felt good to hug something, even something tall, black, and heartless.

Only one other customer was in there, sitting at the counter. She chatted with the staff like a regular. Business had died down after lunch but hadn't yet picked up for supper. I sat down in a booth by the door. The waitress came over and called me Sweetheart and Honey, which I liked hearing even if she didn't mean it. The friendly service improved my mood a little, and so did the fact that I could see the highway from my seat. It reminded me of my backyard growing up, right next to I-26. All those cars rushing past, going somewhere, while I stayed still, barefoot in the crabgrass.

Waffle batter sizzled and spilled out from the sides of the hot iron as they filled my order. I ate too fast and got the hiccups.

A man in a jumpsuit walked in and sat down in the next booth, facing me. He was white, but kind of dark and hairy. His eyebrows connected in the center and his face was thin. The guy kept his mouth still but he looked around a lot. The fact that we were facing one another in the nearly empty restaurant connected our lonelinesses in a way that embarrassed me. Sometimes our eyes met. It made it so we had to nod and say a silent hi.

My hiccups made the whole thing even stranger. Every time a little frog sound hopped out of my throat, the man in the jumpsuit stared at me. I tried to get rid of the hiccups by drinking water and holding my breath—no dice. I even thought about scaring myself, but how do you do that? The tics stopped for a while, but as soon as I thought they'd gone, another one would jump up out of me. The silence got extra silent. I hiccupped. The waitress laughed and brought me another glass of water.

As I drank, I glanced at the man. It's kind of hard to take a big gulp and look someplace else, so I think I spilled a little on my shirt. When I put the cup down, the man raised his lower lip and cocked his head like he wanted me to follow him somewhere. He raised his eyebrows, put his coffee cup to his lips, and slurped like he really meant to make a slurp sound. I looked out at the highway, but my eyes kept drifting back toward him. Every time I took a look over there, he'd look right on back. Then he made that same funny gesture. When we'd done a few go-rounds of this, I had a hard time pretending nothing was happening.

I leaned forward over my empty plates. "Excuse me, sir?" I asked.

He pulled back, put the coffee cup down, and peered at me like somebody trying to solve a math problem written on my forehead. He made that same gesture again, swallowed his coffee, got up, and walked stiffly into the restroom.

It came to me that maybe the fellow didn't speak English and he had a hiccup remedy he wanted to show me. So I followed him without thinking too much about it. In order to do what I wanted, I always needed to tell myself a cover story. That way my desire could stay mysterious to my own self, like some kind of weird music coming from the far side of a hill. When I got over there, I'd be surprised to find out that the music was coming from inside my head all along.

At first I didn't see the jumpsuit man when I got in there. Just my own big body in the long mirror over the sinks. The area by the urinals was empty. The doors of the stalls gaped like open mouths.

"Sir?" My voice rang out against the bathroom tiles. I went a step farther. Suddenly I noticed the man's reflection in the mirror. He was standing in the last stall, not moving a muscle. I heard him breathing. "Sir?"

On tippy-toes, I went back there. But before I could say one word more, he took me by the arm and tugged me into the stall. He grabbed the back of my neck and stuck his tongue in my mouth. He pushed me backward so the stall door closed and then let out a long moan, like somebody in a TV commercial enjoying a rich dessert. Outside in the dining area, he had seemed trapped inside himself. Now he came alive. He was an animal clamped to my face, kissing me.

But I had the opposite reaction. I was kissing an animal! I panicked and shoved him away. He lost his balance and fell backward, catching himself against the toilet paper dispenser and the tile on the wall. I tried to turn and run but he held my wrist.

"Hey," he said quietly. In English and with a Southern accent, to my surprise. There was a gentle part to his voice, and it sounded like he had something else to say, so I stood there a moment.

"What are you doing?" I asked. He let go of my wrist and stood there for a minute, breathing, staring at me like I was the next one down the food chain. The longer he took to answer my question, the stupider my question got. Blood rose to my face. The fellow zipped the jumpsuit down real slow, studying my face like a snake charmer. At first I worried that somebody would follow us in and get a look at what was going on, but everybody outside was a female. I stared right back. Just how far down did he intend to unzip that garment? Zipper noise echoed through the room.

Now, I suppose I shouldn't have been surprised that he had no drawers on. But at the time, I didn't know that people could just *decide* not to wear drawers. The man straddled the commode and the jumpsuit flopped down like shed skin. Once he got to the end of the zipper, he opened up both halves of the suit. His man part swung free and swayed from side to side right in front of me. Then it kind of twitched and stuck straight up like a tree branch. Underneath, his sac hung there like a pair of pantyhose with a couple of eggs in them. He put his hand around the base and pumped it a couple of times.

I wanted to run, but I had to stay put. Reaching behind me and fumbling with the stall door, I figured I couldn't open it without stepping so far forward I'd have to touch the guy's pecker. My need to do sexual things and my agony at the thought of doing them slammed together in my head like two semis on a one-lane highway. A long, sour blast of guilt, disgust, and unspeakable lust wailed in my head. All I could think was Annie, I'm sorry, I'm sorry, Annie. I'm sorry for this disgusting thing I think I'm maybe gonna probably do.

"You can't turn this down," the guy whispered, with perverted pride sparkling in his eyes. "Look at you. You ain't never seen a hog like this 'un. C'mon now." After a tense moment and a silent plea for forgiveness, I reached out and touched him with the back of my hand. The skin felt real hot to the touch, and much silkier than I expected. My knuckles slid up and down. Then I curled my palm around the shaft. To my surprise, my fingertips didn't touch my thumb. I flicked at the edge of the helmet. "That's it," he said. "Yeah."

In my head, I was already bargaining with myself that this one sex act would purge all the years of pent-up evil thoughts. My senses caught fire, and I squatted down between the door and the toilet. My mouth opened wide, partly out of astonishment—this fellow had a real monster down there. I didn't do all that much, but pretty soon he got done.

Spinning paper off the roll, the man said his name was Dickie and apologized that he couldn't shake my hand. He said he had a special machine at home that you could put on yourself and your friends, like a sucking machine. He didn't know it, but during puberty I had once used our old vacuum to pleasure myself and pulled a groin muscle. So when he suggested we go to his place and use the machine, I got offended, because he'd come pretty close to discovering the evil I had done in total private.

"That's disgusting," I said flatly. Inside, I was going berserk with shame. I backed out of the stall and washed my hands and face with lots of pink soap. Since we were still alone in the bathroom, Dickie kept on harassing me, asking if I didn't want to change my mind. "Don't you want to get off?" he prodded.

Just when I'd had enough, he came right up next to me and whispered in my ear. "I love me some chocolate chubbies," he said, giggling. "It ain't enough around these parts for me."

The use of cutesy words upset me, and Dickie's lust made me sick and ashamed. I hated my body, and I couldn't imagine why anyone would want to be naked with it. The saggy, baggy folds of skin depressed me. If I never looked at myself, I could imagine that I had a normal body, like other men, and go about my day. When I saw my hugeness in a mirror, the slabs of fat hanging on my womanly chest and waist destroyed that fantasy.

Without looking back, I skedaddled right out of that bathroom with my hands still soapy, dropped a few bills on the table, and left the restaurant. It didn't occur to me until much later that my hiccups had gone.

"Thank you!" the waitress called. "Y'all come back now!"

Outside, a heavy Florida thunderstorm was already in progress, and I had to duck into it to cross the parking lot. The rain was so heavy it blinded me, running down my face and into my eyes. I almost couldn't find my car. The raindrops stung my shoulders, and then a bunch of little mothball-type things started crashing down on my head and bouncing everywhere. Hail. It made a frightening racket on the hoods of all the cars, like a huge drum corps, like my punishment coming down direct from Heaven.

I drove slowly, with the windshield wipers on high. I could hardly see through the gray-green water coming down like a curtain on my Chevy Malibu. Since I had to drive so slowly, I worried that Dickie had decided to follow me. No telling how far he'd go to get a chubby.

When I got home, I pulled the chain across the door. I kept trying to decide how to confess to Annie, trying to second-guess the future. Would she cry? Would I? Would she leave me? Would I even have the guts to tell her? Wouldn't that ruin her life? I took off my wet things, sat on the bed, and stared through the sliding glass window. After a time, the rain trickled away and children came out to splash in puddles all over the parking lot. Laughing and chasing each other, they could have been the same kids who'd shunned me at school, staying forever young while I grew older.

I put my Jesuses side by side and knelt by the nightstand. Clasping my hands, I put my forehead right up against them. "Lord, I can't live this way," I said. "You've got to change me right this instant. I have to be normal by Saturday."

As I waited for His response, I tried to see a message from Him in everything that happened for the next hour. The clouds broke, and solid beams of light poked through them. Was that it, Lord? The phone rang. That was strange because I had no service. Was the Lord contacting me by phone? Slowly I reached out and picked it up. A man's voice on the line asked for Connie. Was he an angel? "I'm sorry, there's no Connie here," I said. "Good-bye." I really was sorry; I hated disappointing anybody, even strangers.

I got myself up off the floor. Now I thought I had proof that the Lord would never work a miracle in my life. He had nothing to say except a hailstorm. The storm hadn't even been a personal message to me, because it had fallen on the entire area. God wasn't singling me out. The thought made me almost happy—I finally had my answer. Nope, the Lord wasn't listening, watching, videotaping, or anything.

Annie's reputation would be okay. People would know that I'd meant to marry her. I stood and went to the medicine cabinet, where I found a plastic bottle of pills that Mama gave me when I had trouble sleeping freshman year, and shook two into my palm. I tried to swallow the yellow and blue capsules without water, but I choked. I got up, filled a glass, and sat back down on the bed. I gulped two of them down, then another two. Then four. I got up to twelve and ran out of water. Once I refilled the water glass,

I downed one more. Was that enough? I stuck my finger into the bottle and poked around, but it was empty.

Sitting on the bed again, I watched the kids outside, waiting for the pills to take effect. Their sounds of happiness would be the last thing I ever heard. I opened the window to let their joyful noises bounce around the stucco walls and brighten my lonely room. Taking the pad and pen from beside the phone, I thought about what to write as a suicide note. Nothing came to me except what I had said to the wrong-number man. "I'm sorry. Good-bye." I wrote that and put down the pen.

I lay face up on the bed, my hands at my sides, getting comfortable for my final rest. I thought back to corpses I had seen in coffins at funerals and tried to put on an expression like theirs, sort of serious and sad, but also peaceful and satisfied, like life hadn't been a total bust after all. I closed my eyes and waited. I took a few long, deep breaths and let them out very slowly, wondering if maybe I'd exhale my soul with the last one.

A slew of memories went through my head as I tried to settle on a final one. Kids slapping my back after the one home run I ever made in a kickball game. Ocean mist tickling my face on a boat trip. Licking sweet potato pie batter off my Mama's finger as a little boy. Drinking sun tea out of a jar as big as you please after me and Joe picked tobacco for one of Daddy's friends, tar all over our hands. Annie and me riding Space Mountain, screaming, lifting up our hands, falling into the darkness.

I sat up with a sudden jolt. I had no thought except a violent feeling that I didn't want to die. I'd go to Hell, definitely. Annie would be a single mom, and my baby wouldn't have a daddy. My own daddy would curse my name and Mama would probably die of grief. I didn't want to have to face Mama in the afterlife—she'd come down to Hades to get me, crying and giving me a tongue-lashing for all I'd done. Let alone Daddy, who would surely beat my behind back to life. It was harder than it seemed to leave behind everything and everybody I knew. Even though life had made me miserable, even though I felt like it would kill me *not* to leave it. I know now that this happens to a whole lot of attempted suicides. We think that death will take away our problems, but nobody's life is all problems, and the Grim Reaper doesn't let you keep the good parts. Once it hits us that we can't come back—never, ever—we don't want out anymore.

I ran to the bathroom and leaned over the commode, pushing down on my tongue with my index finger. When that didn't work, I stuck the handle of my toothbrush down my throat. But I couldn't gag. Trying to cough up the pills, I must have sounded like a cat spitting up a hairball.

Desperate and sweaty, I left my apartment to search for a phone. My neighbors weren't home. The kids outside had no supervision and wouldn't let me into their apartments. So I hopped into the car and drove around like a crazy person until I spotted one outside the Publix supermarket in the next town. By that time I was panting like a dog, convinced that I was going to fall asleep and crash the car. I parked about twenty yards away from the entrance and walked over, careful not to trot because that might make the drug spread through my bloodstream faster.

At the bank of phones, I dialed the emergency number and found myself talking to an operator immediately, like she'd been waiting on the line already.

"I took some pills," I blurted out.

A few clicks sounded on the line, then it went silent for a second until a male voice crackled through.

"Poison Control."

At the sound of the man's voice, it dawned on me that although thirty minutes or so had passed since I first swallowed the sleeping pills, I didn't feel drowsy at all. My arms and legs and eyelids didn't have any heaviness in them. Come to think of it, those pills hadn't worked so well when I took them freshman year, either.

I watched shoppers taking buggies and turned around toward the slow parade of cars to test for any shift in my alertness. I didn't feel different. My balance was stable; I wasn't dizzy. I thought of the paper label on the bottle of pills, yellow and buckled from years of resting on my mother's dressing table. I reckoned the active ingredients had lost a whole lot of strength.

The Poison Control man asked for my location. He wanted me to stay on the line, talking. I was right about to hang up, too, but I couldn't, because, well, the guy sounded like he might be sort of handsome. He had a silky Alabama drawl, kind of like Russ.

"Taking thirteen sleeping pills, I should feel something after a half hour, shouldn't I?"

"Yes, sir. Most people would be out cold by now."

"They must have been duds."

"Just stay on the line, sir. We're sending a truck out."

"Yeah, they must have been duds." I got the shivers when I thought about what the cost of the ambulance and the hospitalization would add up to. I had no health insurance. What if this was just a false alarm? I couldn't even afford the ambulance part, what with buying all the clothes and food and rings for the wedding.

I didn't notice any change during the call. I had to work the 6:30 to 10:30 shift at Daytona Reports that night. I could still get to work on time. "I think I'm okay," I said to the guy. "Tell the ambulance not to come. I'll call you back if I start to feel like something's really wrong."

"Sir—"

I shoved the receiver back into the cradle—fast, like it might bite me otherwise.

There turned out to be a small ice cream stand right at the supermarket entrance. When I moseyed over there, I found that they sold a smorgasbord of rich flavors: mint chocolate peanut butter, vanilla nut cookie dough, coffee marshmallow Heath bar. It took a few minutes to decide which one to get, but eventually I bought myself a large pistachio fudge in a waffle cone with multicolored sprinkles.

Just as I pulled money out of my wallet, I saw an ambulance turn in to the yellow striped zone at the front of the lot. An EMT worker hopped out. He walked toward the entrance and searched the horizon for me. Even though I hadn't told him what I looked like, I turned away. I dropped my change out of nervousness and went inside.

Walking around, I thought I'd see how I felt and maybe go to my shift. I didn't want to die anymore, but I couldn't quite figure how to start over again, either. Could I keep my secrets from Annie without the guilt overwhelming me? The pistachio fudge made life okay, but only for right then. In the chilly aisles of the supermarket, I remained well aware of my sobriety. As I moved through the merchandise, daydreaming of meals, I eventually relaxed.

Entering the dreamy state of the other shoppers, I pushed the last nub of cone into my mouth and licked a blotch of green cream off my thumb. I wiped my hands and grabbed a basket from underneath a checkout belt in the front of the store. I tried to remember what I had written down on the grocery list at home. Canned corn, I thought. Cheerios.

My thoughts kept flashing back to the shameful part of the day, so I shopped more aggressively to keep everything that had happened with the bathroom man from flooding into my mind. The most thrilling memory hadn't stopped looping in my brain—when I felt the spasms of Dickie's climax right before that colossal boner erupted everywhere. That moment kept repeating, so I said "Cheerios" out loud to stay focused.

Publix had a sale on the thirty-six-ounce size of Cheerios, and only a few boxes remained. They sat on the bottom shelf, where the Cheerios always are. I had to lean over to see them—they were hiding in the back. It turned out that a few had toppled over on the very rear of the display shelf, their packaging ripped and crushed. I decided to look closer at the damaged boxes to see if they might be worth my while, so I put my basket down, squatted, and reached for a box. I couldn't get at either of the two left. I had to kneel. In due course I wound up with my head and shoulders on the shelf and the rest of me lying across the aisle. The linoleum floor was freshly waxed, so I didn't worry about my knees getting dirty. I stuck my head and shoulders in above the empty metal pegboard.

Finally I grabbed hold of a Cheerios box. Its nutrition panel had been sliced off and the plastic bag inside had a rip in it, probably from the box-cutter. Little Os had scattered across the shelf like mini life preservers after a mini shipwreck. I stared at the back of the box, disappointed that it was no longer okay to buy, wondering if somebody had damaged it on purpose to steal the baseball cards inside.

The scramble puzzle on the back of the box had me stumped, and the sound down there made me think of being inside a metal room. I sang a note to hear how different my voice would sound, but the note was sour and rang in my ears. Still, something made me stay down there, in the weird private place between the shelves. Something slowed me down. My head felt heavy. I put my face against the cool green shelf, and wouldn't you know, I slept for the next nineteen hours.

FIVE

On waking up many hours later at Florida Hospital, an IV taped to my arm, a tube up my nose, I saw Annie camped out by my bed. The doctor had told her I had blood poisoning; I suppose he didn't want to assume I'd tried to commit suicide. In the gap left by that half-truth, I saw a way to make things easier, so when she asked, after massaging my feet and moisturizing my face for a while, I muttered that I'd been bitten by a snake. On the TV, CNN showed a whole mess of angry Chinese people and tanks.

"We'll have to postpone, won't we?" she sighed. The wedding was going to happen in three days. Struggling in my bedclothes, I said no as forcefully as I could, assuring her that I'd recover quickly.

"Everybody's already made plans," I wheezed. Whatever excuse we gave for postponing we'd have repeat to all my relatives, who had organized the event. And it went without saying that if we waited any longer, the truth would come out about the baby. I didn't want to raise the slightest suspicion that anything had gone wrong with me or Annie. Keeping one big secret felt impossible, but keeping three huge, interlocking secrets was unavoidable—almost easy.

"You're sure?"

I muttered something jumbled. They kept me another two days at the hospital; I went home the night before the wedding. I felt okay, physically.

On Sunday, June 11, 1989, at my Aunt Vietta's farm outside Savannah, Georgia, Annie and I were joined in holy matrimony. I wore a peach tuxedo to match Annie's satin gown. The day was fresh, warm, and windy. Large, slow clouds with flat bottoms flew near to the ground like blimps in a white sky stained with a bit of blue. Vietta had arranged plastic forks in all different colors in a fan shape on a table and put tiger lilies in the punch bowl. Hand in hand, Annie and I climbed the small steps Vietta had decorated with bright fabric and gardenias, to listen to the minister speak of the perfect union of one man and one woman. My mother sat in the front row, sobbing.

"Do you, Gary Gray, take this woman, Anone Palolo, to be your lawfully wedded wife?" the minister asked me. He'd pronounced Annie's name wrong, and I nearly told him, but Annie nodded at me not to say anything. I swallowed spit and said "Yes!"

The minister squinted at me. "I mean, I do." My head grew light and I thought I might pass out, so I took a deep breath. The minister said I could kiss the bride, so I bent down, which helped with the lightheadedness, lifted the veil, lowered my lips toward Annie's, and we kissed. I was downright ashamed at where my lips had been only a few days before, and so shaky that I wobbled slightly. Our teeth banged together and I almost bit her, but if anybody noticed, they didn't mention it. When I stood up, I was married, and almost normal. I had just turned nineteen.

My nearby relatives and friends of mine and Annie's made up most of the guests. My brother Joe even came. I hugged him and squeezed his shoulders and slapped him on the back. For me it was like he had come back from the dead.

But Joe and my parents stayed on opposite sides of the wedding. They denied him like two Peters. I overheard my mother tell somebody that I was her only child, even with Joe across the yard. The person just nodded his head. What Joe had done wasn't moral or honorable, that's true. My father never went back to work. But that wasn't all Joe's fault, because Daddy had also developed a disease that made his skin and toes get hard and his mouth dry up. He needed my mother to help him move around the lawn and up and down stairs. When the photographer took pictures it upset me to pose with my arms around my mother and father while Joe watched from afar.

Later, in a private moment by the buffet table, my mother leaned toward me, staring at Annie as she fixed my eighty-six-year-old great uncle Linton's boutonnière. "So one her parents black and the other Chinese?" she asked, a pin between her teeth. Annie's skin had grown tan from our trips to the beach. Timidly, I shook my head.

"What *is* she?"

"She's from Samoa."

"Sam-*who*-a?"

"Samoa. It's in the South Pacific."

"And she not mixed at all? I swear that girl is mixed. You mean to tell me that with that flat nose—?"

"No, Mama, there's no black."

"Samoa," my mother repeated, the way she might have if I'd brought home a girl from another galaxy. "That's a new one."

Great Uncle Linton showed his teeth and said, "Have Samoa."

Aunt Vietta had set a group of round tables along one edge of the property for the reception. On another set of long tables, she'd put an eye-popping spread of crab cakes, pots of greens and gumbo, candied sweet potatoes, and chicken fried chicken on trays that looked just like real crystal. Two huge bowls of bright yellow wedding punch rested on a complicated arrangement of palm leaves and irises.

The wedding had been a gospel wedding, so polite dancing was allowed at the reception, and the party went on quite a long while—until about 10 p.m. Mama and Aunt Vietta had chosen the music, so we all had a wonderful time clapping and waving our hands to old-time gospel tunes like the Reverend James Cleveland's "Get Right Church" and "Something's Got a Hold On Me," and Mahalia Jackson's "Didn't It Rain."

That last song's about the Great Flood, so when Hurricane Hugo destroyed a whole lot of Charleston four months later, I remembered that moment. The winds came toward the barrier islands at 135 miles per hour. Lots of houses in my old neighborhood were torn apart. They couldn't save anything at the Wards' house. Moochie McKee's roof got blown down the street intact and blocked the road for a month. Dogs drowned in the flooding. A whole restaurant on Folly Beach, a few blocks away from Gizzy's, the place Euge's family ran, got washed into the ocean.

Mama said that Daddy refused to let anybody evacuate him. He said he would rather go down with the ship, but she pushed him out of the house, both of them screaming in the wind and rain. They got on the evacuation bus and stayed in a school near Columbia for a couple of nights. Then they moved in with Vietta for a while, coming back to clean the house and repair some of the damage. Annie and I helped them on weekends when we could. We never did get it all fixed. The roof still leaks in some places.

When the music was turned off and most of the guests had left, Vietta started the cleanup phase. She approached me as she crossed the lawn, collecting used plastic cups. She had a glow in her eye as bright as the string of colored lights zigzagging across the field. The breeze kept lifting strands of her amber wig into the air. "Don't you and Annie want to get on home?" she said, pursing her lips. "I can hold down the fort." She repeated Great Uncle Linton's joke—he'd repeated it about two hundred times, to my embarrassment, but nowhere near Annie. My new wife froze when she heard it. I scooped her shoulders and led her off to our crazily decorated car. "Did she say what I think she said?" Annie asked.

I pretended I hadn't heard the question. The car sat under a live oak that blocked out the streetlight. In the dark, Annie moved my hand to her bosom, chuckled, and said, "Well, now that we're married, you can."

Annie went into the bathroom at our motel to slip out of her bridal gown, brush her teeth, and put her hair up. By the time she got out, I had fallen asleep in front of the television, still in my peach tux. She poked me but I didn't stir, so she let me sleep.

The next morning I half-figured that Annie would bring up the fact that we hadn't done anything sexual since that night in the kitchen. But we had to leave pretty early, so she was already getting set by the time I stuck my feet into my slippers. I reckoned she thought of it as the man's job to initiate sex, and she'd had that bad experience with Kent and everything.

With the no-sex thing hanging in the air between us all day, we drove to Disney World in the Malibu and stayed at the All-Star Sports Resort. The hotel didn't cost much, and I guess it was sort of cheesy, with a collage

of team pennants and famous athletes decorating the wallpaper and match-
ing sheets. But we had already talked about how the low price would let us
spend more money in the park. The hospital bill hadn't come due, so that
fooled me into thinking that I still had some money.

At the park Annie and I went a little berserk, even for us. In the morning we made our way from Main Street backward to Tomorrowland, where
we stopped and had rare and juicy deluxe hamburgers for lunch. We got
crispy wave-cut fries with the burgers and sipped bucket-size grape Cokes
through fat straws to wash it all down.

Then we headed across the hive of automobiles to Epcot, hand in hand.
I am married, I thought to myself periodically. I am a married man. I'm
just a normal, married man. I'm gonna be a daddy. I love my wife. We are
good people. On top of our own kids, we're going to adopt orphans from
foreign countries and disabled children nobody wants. *People* magazine will
photograph us for having such a big, loving family.

We finished the day at the Ohana restaurant in the Polynesian Resort
area. By the time we got back to our room at the All-Star, I had no energy
left. My feet had swollen up and throbbed from all the walking. I had a
blister on the side of my foot where my new sneakers—we'd gotten match-
ing pairs as a wedding present—had rubbed against it. I took off my sock
and poked at the tender bubble. Annie flopped down on the bed and let
out a long sigh. She mussed up her hair and raised her head from a lying
position, then peeped at me through the wavy strands.

"How are you feeling?" she asked. "You're not tired, are you?"

"I sort of am," I told her, not looking up from my injury.

Annie pushed the hair from in front of her face with both index fingers,
like a curtain opening on a stage. She pursed her red lips; she must have
freshened her lipstick when we got home. I found a paper clip and walked
over to the desk, then lifted a pack of matches out of the ashtray. I unbent the
first turn of the paper clip and set it down. Annie didn't take her eyes off me.
I returned to the armchair, which had basketball players on the fabric, and
massaged my instep, searching for the right place to puncture the blister.

"I'm bored," she announced.

"Wouldn't you love a peanut butter fudge sundae right now?" I asked.
"With M&M's and crushed walnuts on top?"

"Sort of, I guess."

I felt that I *had* to make love to Annie that night, even though she was three and a half months pregnant. She wanted me to, and I didn't like disappointing her. I had known all along this moment would have to come, of course, but I hadn't planned for it. I'd only thought that I probably could do it again. At this point, even after the failed exorcism, I still wouldn't put a name on what I was, because putting the name would only make things sure and I couldn't come back from that. I meant to fight it.

I got up from my chair and spoke with all the masculine gumption I could bring up. "Let's go eat now." Reluctantly, she followed me out. We had chicken fingers and a couple of large Cokes with no ice, and shared a banana fudge sundae with piles of nuts and whipped cream on top, Nilla wafers stuck in around the sides like a fence, and M&M's whose colors rubbed off on the white fluff. All drenched in butterscotch sauce.

We got back to our suite around 11:30—bedtime. On top of the exhaustion, my feet hurt pretty bad, since all the walking had chafed my blister. My stomach bulged and churned with half-digested slop to the point where I was fixing to spit up.

I brushed my teeth, washed my face, and slid into my pajamas without leaving the locked bathroom. Annie and I prayed together, asking the Lord to look down and bless our marriage. Silently I added my usual wish to be changed.

I got under the covers. With the lights out and a heavenly glow from the neon display outside coming through the drawn curtains, Annie climbed into bed beside me and asked for a goodnight kiss. I rolled over and puckered up. As we kissed, she kept her lips pressed against mine, then opened her mouth and tried to wedge her tongue between my lips.

"What're you doing?" I struggled to say against her tongue.

"It's our honeymoon, Gary!"

I didn't respond. Instead I listened to her breathing, hoping we could let this drop and go to sleep. No way could I have a marriage where sex had to be important.

"Gary," she said carefully, "I would like to express my devotion to you in Christ through the act of love."

"Is that what you told Kent?" I asked, not realizing how bad it sounded.

"If it bothered you that I wasn't pure, you should never have married me," Annie said. "You knew that going in. You even made it worse! But it wasn't my fault—any of this—and it isn't fair for you to blame me!" Tears came up in her voice, but she held them in.

Saying stuff like that, I started to feel like somebody who wasn't me, who backhanded his wife and called her a whore to keep her from getting to know his inner thoughts. I hoped it was over and we could go to sleep. I felt like a guard dog in a scrap yard, pacing around and snapping at anybody who got ideas about nosing in on my territory. So I didn't apologize until the next morning. Instead, I tugged some of the covers back from my new wife and went to sleep, a little uncomfortably, almost like a normal man.

Until a little while after Cheryl was born, in late October, Annie kept her one-bedroom in Longwood, on the second floor of a complex called Tudor Valley. She thought it looked like Smurfland. Every time we went to her home, she would sing the Smurf song and pretend to be Smurfette. The place was kind of small but it had two bedrooms and it was closer to my work. I loved sleeping there with my wife. It felt very comforting to join a community of millions of married people who did the same thing night after night.

Though I enjoyed my time there, I couldn't perform my marital duties. Her pregnancy lowered her sex drive, but sometimes Annie hinted that we could still make love. I would ignore her, leaping to describe how difficult my workday had been or spending a long time complaining about a petty dispute I'd had with a coworker. I made a mental list of Bible quotes that laid out strict rules about sex, just in case.

If Annie pressed up against me in a way I found too sexy as we sat on the couch with a family movie or a romantic comedy, I would embrace her tenderly, snuggle, and kiss her, usually with my mouth closed. I'd remind her that having relations might not go well for a pregnant woman. When her hand traveled up my leg, too close to the softness in my lap, I'd bring up Romans 8:7—"The carnal mind is enmity against God"—and her hand would fly back to her side. I didn't get aroused, as much as I tried to fool myself into thinking I felt something I didn't. Only a tiny tingle of delight shimmered in my pelvis when her warm body pressed against me, like hugging my mama. Even that small feeling, though, sometimes meant more to me than the animalistic frenzy people called normal sexuality.

Annie never complained about the lack of sex, but I saw her frustration rising like a flood tide. She knew that the Bible required her to submit to her husband, but she wasn't afraid to express herself, either. "What happened to 'Go forth and multiply'?" I heard her sigh to herself once, as she changed into her nightgown. She had just left me on the couch as the second volume of *Dances with Wolves* played out on the VCR.

One Saturday at the supermarket, a family of five passed by us. The three children pushed the buggy by themselves as the adults shopped up ahead. A boy of about six pulled the buggy. His younger brother sat in it, opening a box of crispy snacks, and an infant girl dangled her legs from the toddler seat, sucking on a pacifier. Annie and I saw her happy, wise expression at the same time. We kootchy-kooed her fat cheeks and talked baby talk to her until the mother took control of the cart. She had messy white hair and a big head like an owl. She looked us up and down, so we moved to a different aisle.

"Do you really want this kid?" Annie asked, rubbing her stretched-out belly. Coincidentally, we had moved into the diaper section.

"Of course I do," I told her, though I sped up our buggy a little to avoid the images of babies on all the products around us. I pictured them flying off the packages like cherubs and dancing in the air around our heads. "The kingdom of God belongs to children."

"So you want more than one?"

"I sure do."

We got to the end of the aisle and Annie checked the traffic on either side. Without turning back to me, she said, "Well, I only know one way to make a baby!" An unusual undertone of anger pinched her voice. I waited to say anything.

"Look, there's a sale on peas," I remarked as we passed a pyramid of cans.

Annie's outburst at the supermarket made it clear that a time was coming when I would have to see whether I could perform with a woman. But it wouldn't be fair for me to use her as the guinea pig, especially if I couldn't hack it and we had to get unhitched. Unfortunately, I had painted myself into a tight corner on this one.

* * *

On October 22, 1989, the Lord blessed Annie and me with a healthy child. We named her Cheryl, after a friend of Annie's, but we kept her conception date a secret and told everybody she was a preemie, betting they wouldn't square that with her fit little body. Cheryl was plump like us and exotic, with curly dark hair, almond eyes, and a wide smile. It shouldn't have surprised me, but she really looked like a perfect blend of me and her mother. Watching Cheryl, I enjoyed seeing how a new person could have a full personality. Cheryl never slept more than three hours at a time and always woke up howling something fierce. I worried that she might grow up to be a rock-and-roll singer. She liked peach baby food, but Mama couldn't even get creamed spinach in her mouth; she clamped right up. She had a sweet tooth, just like her daddy.

For the first few weeks, I took care of Annie. Gradually, as she gained strength, raising Cheryl became mostly her job. When I changed diapers, they always came loose, and if Cheryl cried and I rocked her or bounced her on my leg, she screamed more—like a banshee. I was half-afraid she hated me already. The pressure to keep Cheryl safe scared the bejeezus out of me, and all the drooling, the poop, and the pee turned my stomach, as cute as we tried to make it sound. The messed-up sleep schedule soon made me a completely exhausted wreck.

Whenever I lay my baby's trembling, vein-covered head in my palm, I worried that I'd accidentally let go or twist her limbs into a painful position. I guess that came from my father always calling me incompetent. On a beach trip once, Annie passed her to me as we stood on a jetty, and as I tried to balance her body with my arms, I fumbled in a real dangerous way and almost dropped her. Annie gasped. If I hadn't grabbed Cheryl by the ankle and under the thigh at the last second, she'd have knocked her head against a rock and been brain damaged or dead with her brains everywhere. It would have been my fault.

After that episode, Annie demanded that I give Cheryl to her, both right then and in a kind of permanent way. An awful tide of bad-father guilt rose up to my neck and made me shiver. My inside voices laughed, saying, This is already a mess, and now you're gonna mess up the mess, too.

* * *

In my downtime at work, I fretted about my troubles. I didn't see any way out. I regretted that I hadn't let anything develop between Joy and me. How had I missed her signals? Could she have saved me? I would ask myself these questions over and over, tugging a paper cone from the dispenser by the water cooler and filling it with cold liquid.

The Daytona Reports office, where I still had a part-time job, stood on the second floor of a strip mall just at the edge of the part of town considered nice. A hairdresser, a tattoo parlor, and a live-music bar were its closest neighbors downstairs. Sometimes, during the night shift, we had to contend with loud sounds and unruly behavior. A colorful segment of the population, a lot like the folks from my neighborhood, gathered there in the dim alley that led to our upstairs office. If I thought about it at all, I pictured myself in the Christ-like situation of working among those who most needed salvation. One of these days I could lend a hand to a wayward soul.

Every so often at work, they'd cut a survey short for some reason—especially market research polls. On a late shift one Friday night, the higher-ups told the boss that the night's deep-freezer questionnaire had been pulled. Ahead of us we had either an hour of twiddling our thumbs or an early departure. To our surprise, the boss let us go.

Careful not to act too eager, I sharpened my pencils and put them back in their yellow plastic box. I poked my time card into the slot and it made a pleasant clunk sound. Then I swung the door open into the sweet humidity of a real Florida night. Something about going from the chilly air-conditioned world of the office into the outside stirred me. When I stepped into the humid breeze and cricket noise, I had a vision of another glass door, one inside me. One that opened into real air and freedom. An hour of my own time—time I wouldn't have to account for when I got home.

Before I stepped into the alley, I hadn't thought of spending that time anywhere other than at Annie's. I dug down in my pocket for my keyring, deciding to surprise her with a treat—doughnut holes, maybe, or a bucket of pistachio ice cream—to make up for what I couldn't figure out how to provide.

When I got to the bottom of the steps, I heard muffled rock-and-roll drums coming from inside the bar. To my left, leaning against the wall, I saw a lady in a pink Tweety Bird T-shirt and spandex leggings counting a small roll of bills. On the ground, closer to the stairwell, sat a scratched-up car seat with a child in it. The kid was adorable, and he had on a faded blue jumpsuit. My attention went directly to the baby, who was sucking on a pacifier the color of beer. I waved at him and his eyes opened wide. The kid seemed more awake than the woman, who focused on her counting and said, "For-ty-sev-en!" in a happy voice when she got done. She folded the bills tightly, wrapped them with a rubber band, and zipped them into her fanny pack.

Continuing to wave and smile and say "Hi! Hi! Hello!" to the infant, I moved on to other baby talk. I had plenty of practice now, and this child had a magnetism about him—alert, shiny eyes and velvety skin. For an instant I couldn't help imagining him as the fine-looking man he would someday become, but I tried not to let that fantasy run away with itself. I squatted and dangled my car keys above the boy's hand, hardly realizing that his mama's eyes had traveled from my shoes to my head and back again.

"Oh, hello, sir," she said. She had a nice, sugary voice. I looked up, a little embarrassed at how much attention I'd paid to her child and not her. Mortified, I thought she could tell I had attractions for men because I liked playing with her male child. I shouldn't have worried.

This lady had dyed her hair blond as straw and stretched it back into a ponytail. It stood out against her cardboard-brown forehead. She stretched her neck and said, "I hope you don't mind my asking, but are you going in the direction of Pinecrest Avenue? I'm supposed to be staying with my sister. She doesn't drive and her husband's out of town and she's over there waiting, but my ride didn't show up." She indicated the car seat. "And it's just too heavy carrying this one around." Her casual laughter put me at ease.

"Sure, you can ride with me," I said, though I hadn't heard of Pinecrest Avenue. The boy batted my keys and bounced slightly. "What's his name?"

"Dyson. I'm Penny." We shook hands and I introduced myself. "Ordinarily," she continued, "I wouldn't ask a stranger, but I can trust you. I could read a face real well."

"Yep, I'm pretty harmless," I said, with a nervous chuckle. I stood and stretched. She picked up the handles of the car seat and lifted it to knee-height. I noticed that her arm was muscular for a woman's and thought that might be on account of carrying Dyson around. I helped her secure the car seat in my car and we pulled out of the parking lot.

"Turn left," she told me. We rode in silence for a moment, going in the opposite direction from Annie's place at Tudor Valley. I opened my mouth to ask Penny for directions to Pinecrest Avenue, but she spoke first.

"So what do you like?" she asked.

"Food," I answered. "Man, I love food. Hamburgers. Strawberry ice cream. Egg foo young. And Disney World. And cartoons, and family movies. I just got married and I have a beautiful daughter. How about you? I mean, what do *you* like," I said, "not are you married, too." She cackled loudly, and a worldly, piercing expression that reminded me of Sareena crossed her face.

"Are you for real?"

"Sure," I said, slightly taken aback. "I'm very for real."

"You're not a police officer, are you?"

"No…"

"Say it. Say, 'I am not an officer of the law.'"

I said it.

"So what do you like?" Her tone got sort of impatient.

"I told you," I said, trying to match her edge with some of my own. "But you never answered my question about what *you* like."

"It don't matter what I like. C'mon. Tell me what you like. Like, what do you *like*." She pressed down on her words like she was trying to mash extra meaning out of them. She lit a cigarette and rolled down the window part of the way. "Mind if I smoke?" I did mind, but it was too late to say so.

"I told you what I like."

She blew a cloud through the crack in the window. "So you want to go get some ice creams, honey?" She burst out laughing, and I laughed with her, though I didn't know what was so funny.

"Sure. You know, there's a Dairy Queen just up the road here." She doubled over, laughing so hard that she couldn't make noise anymore.

"Wow, you're really a fun person," I told her, although I was starting to wonder. "How far is… was it Pinecrest Avenue?"

She was still laughing. "Sugar, there ain't no damn Pinecrest nothing." Smoke drifted out of her open mouth. She tapped her ash out the window and suddenly got dead serious in a way that seemed almost mean. Her jaw tensed. She took a quick glance at her wristwatch and slapped the dashboard as she spoke. "So what do you want to do, Mister Gary? *To me.*"

She cupped her breasts and stuck her hand between her thighs, grunting and gesturing in a very impolite way.

"Oh," I said, with a start. Did she carry the child around to fool the police about her profession? Was it even her child? I felt swindled. Still, I decided that if she found my innocence funny, I would play it up. She probably didn't get much of a chance to laugh in her line of work. And introducing her baby to that kind of life! I was worried, especially for Dyson, and nervous that somebody might see us together. My eyes burned from tobacco smoke, and I needed to air the car out. So I swerved into the Dairy Queen lot and pulled into a parking space lit by the fluorescent glow from inside.

"What's your favorite flavor?"

"Honey, I'm sorry, I'm lactose intolerant."

"They probably have frozen yogurt, or Tofutti."

"Look. You're very nice, but I'm trying to work here. Unless you paying for my time, I can't be all up in no soda shops on cute little dates and whatnot. This ain't 1953."

"I can pay. And it isn't a date. I'm married."

"Gee, I've never heard that line before," she said, laughing again. There was something cruel in her voice now, like the thought of my being nice to her and treating her like a human being made her sick.

I returned with a container of large fries for her, a Pecan Mudslide for myself, a sample-size sundae for Dyson, and a small, undecorated Just Because cake to share with Annie later. What an interesting opportunity, I told myself, thinking about Christ's ministry to women like Penny, and deciding to tell her the good news about being saved. That made me less nervous about anybody seeing us together. We sat in the car and ate our treats together. Penny spooned sundae into Dyson's mouth. Mostly it went on his shirt. She used a handful of napkins to wipe his chin.

At first Penny wouldn't believe that I didn't want what men normally wanted from her. But as we sat, I showed her respect. I asked her about her life and she stopped fidgeting. Penny told me that she had come down from New York for the weekend to visit and her sister had thrown her and Dyson out of her house because she figured out what Penny'd been doing for a living. She needed to get enough money to either change her Amtrak ticket back or pay for a hotel for the next two nights.

She said that Dyson's daddy was a prominent city councilman in the town she came from, and that I could look him up if I went there. I wasn't sure whether to believe all of her stories, because she talked so big. But I gave her some extra money to help pay for the ticket and told her that Christ could offer eternal life and salvation. She sucked her teeth and wouldn't look me in the eye when I said things about Jesus. Maybe she had come from a religious background and the Lord had shown her to me as an example of what happens when you go against His word. Maybe He had put me in her path so that she could hear about Christ's mercy.

When we finished our food and threw our garbage out, I asked her where I could take her. She told me she wanted to go back to the rock club because she still needed money. I didn't have much cash left.

"You've got to leave this life behind," I urged.

She demanded that I take her back, so I started the ignition. The car vibrated and sputtered under us. She glanced my way, triumphant and nasty. The scary feeling came over me that she could read my thoughts. Or worse, that she could see other things, like the thoughts *under* my thoughts—stuff I couldn't even guess at.

Since the moment I'd figured out the situation, I'd thought that this might be an opportunity to find out once and for all whether I could fix my urges myself and put them toward a female. Maybe God wanted me to do this instead of having Him correct the problem overnight. I couldn't imagine that He'd want me to use one kind of sinfulness as a weapon against another. But how else would I find out the truth, spare my wife the pain of blaming herself for my difficulty, and keep anybody in my life from knowing about the terrible feelings that were rotting me out from the inside? Now it's easy to go back and piece together what I might have thought as I stared blankly back at Penny. In my eyes she must have seen the look of every married john, the dull face that says Help me avoid the blame.

"You just pull around back," she said.

When I walked through the archway at Tudor Valley, $116 poorer, dragging my feet with disgrace, the Just Because cake I bought for Annie had softened into a goopy mush, dripping out of the box into the plastic bag and leaving a trail of milky droplets behind me. At that point, even showing it to her would make her ask why it had been sitting out for so long. I would have had no explanation. I tied the plastic handles together twice and forced the bag down into the swinging door at the top of one of the public garbage cans near the statue of a knight with a lance in the courtyard. Penny's voice played on a loop in my head as I dawdled there, watching the shadows of headlights play across the horse's bronze backside. *It's okay*, she'd said. *It happens to a lot of guys.*

You learn more from failure than success, as my daddy always used to say unless he failed. The experience with Penny hadn't gone well, but it did give me a little bit more confidence. I reckoned it like this: sure, I blew it with Penny, but if I could give it a go with a prostitute, what kept me from trying it with my own wife? Plenty of ungodly men cheated on their wives with hookers. But what kind of scalawag *only* cheated with hookers? The longer I chewed on that bone, the madder I got with myself.

The only two pieces of proof I had that I didn't like women were the fact that I'd never had any sexual feelings for them, and my lack of experience. Big things, sure, but here came experience, ready or not. One night, as I sat on the edge of the bed taking my shoes off, Annie stepped toward me and put her knees between my thighs. I pulled her further in toward me. Once she realized what I had decided to do, she giggled, but I could hear a little bit of irritation behind the laughter. Weighing Annie's breasts in my palms, grabbing hold of her waist, and poking my tongue into her mouth, it comforted me to know that God approved of what we were doing. His okay alone raised my level of excitement higher than it could have with Penny, and my years of unsatisfied urges had made it so that touch carried a charge all by itself. Contact alone aroused me about 55 percent. Once we'd gotten undressed, my male part stood out enough to be convincing.

Probing around in the folds of her thighs, my fingers kept expecting to find a hole somewhere, but they got more and more lost. I'd had a whole lot of beginner's luck that first time. Sex turned into a project, and I got so frustrated with the job of it that I lost track of myself. I gave up trying to find the hole with my fingers and probed around with my penis instead, sort of aggressively. After the kissing, I got Annie onto the bed, tugged down her panties, and climbed on top.

"Ow! Gary! You're crushing me!" Annie cried out. Embarrassed and apologetic, I leapt backward off her and twisted my ankle. That hurt so much that I rapidly began to lose my hard-won 55 percent. Now, if a woman sees you lose your erection, I figured, that signals to her that either you don't like her or you don't like women at all, so I panicked. For a split second I wondered if I was allowed to masturbate, but time was disappearing, so I didn't worry. I got back to about 45 percent and raised myself up on the bed again. In a minute or three I had succeeded in penetrating my wife with my floppy johnson, pinching it tight at the base to make it seem harder. But by then I had lost another 5 percent. My male ego hung in the balance there, so as a last-ditch effort, I thought about Russ and jammed myself into her over and over, using the repetition to erase reality. In twenty seconds I went up to 95 percent, but by the twenty-fifth, it was all over.

"That was great," I said, confident I had beaten back the demon of homosexuality a little bit.

Annie smiled weakly and pulled the covers over her head.

One slightly chilly night the next January, we'd pulled the covers up to our necks, and I woke up to feel the comforter taking in air and blowing it out like a bellows. A warm, moist pressure weighed down my crotch. I'd just fallen out of a wonderful dream about hand-crabbing on Lake Kissimmee. Thinking I had wet myself, I reached toward my groin area to find that the pressure was my wife's body on top of mine. She had pulled me through my boxer shorts during one of the natural cycles of arousal that happen to a sleeping man, and was riding my body up and down. It felt kind of like falling asleep at the wheel. I nearly jumped up and pushed her off, but I then I got the notion that her scheme might work, so I went with it.

Annie grunted as she threw herself down on me, gently at first. Our round paunches connected like continents slamming back together after ages apart. *Bump. Bump. Bump.* About one per second. For a little while, I played possum to avoid breaking the spell. But then her success made me sort of proud, like I had made it happen, too. My breath caught in my throat, thinking for a moment that my prayers had been answered at last.

I groaned to let Annie know that I was awake, and stepped up the pace. *Bump bump bump.* I reckoned that if she got pregnant again, she'd want to know that I knew I could be the father. Within minutes, though, my manhood started to droop. Desperate to keep hard, I thought about a muscular fire dancer I'd once seen at Disney World's Ohana restaurant, and went wild with the pace. *Bumpbumpbumpbumpbump!* It helped that Annie didn't wear feminine perfumes, makeup, or much jewelry. I reached up and dug my fingers into her shoulder muscles so they'd seem bulkier. All women have mustaches, and fortunately for me, Annie didn't bleach hers. In the dim room I could see light reflecting off the tiny hairs under her nose, so I focused on them. I bucked so hard I almost tossed Annie off the bed, but I finished what she'd started.

Once Annie had broken the ice, she discovered that she liked making love. I doubt it had anything to do with me—I wasn't much of a lover. I sweated a lot and usually didn't get so manly. I didn't know the first thing about bringing her to orgasm. She never admitted to wanting sex out of lust, probably because of the Bible passsages I always quoted.

Once when I tried to sidestep her advances, she caused me to jam my index finger against the kitchen counter. That kept me in a splint for a good while—a good excuse to avoid the sex act. But the afternoon we came home from the hospital, she wanted to use the time for intimacy, even with my hand wrapped up in aluminum and gauze. I brought up Christian chastity stuff again. But now when I did that, Annie knew how to fight back. She quoted the verse from Corinthians where Paul says that couples should only be celibate if they both agree to it. She took my injured hand and yanked me into the bedroom.

"I'm beat," I sighed.

Annie wasn't discouraged—no sir! "I will be your strength! Build your rock upon me!"

We went on into the bedroom and she stood in front of me with her arms at her sides, just like the young man I pretended to see in her place. When she demanded lovemaking, she'd follow up by waiting for me to take charge. It felt kind of unfair. Every time I stood there dumbstruck, like a cow chewing cud. I always forgot what had gone well the time before. I had to make everything up again. I'd take a step forward and hug her. She'd moan and loosen her spine, and I'd squeeze one of her breasts.

"Ow!" she'd say. "Not so hard!"

I'd move my hands to her waist and touch her more gently there.

I'd lean down and kiss her, first on the side of the mouth, where tiny hairs stuck me. In my mind they'd become a beard. That would excite me, so I'd press my lips to hers and work them open and shut. I'd keep my tongue far back, because when we were kids Joe showed me a nature magazine picture of two slugs mating, tangled together and hanging from a tree by a thread of slime. The thought of tongues wrapping around each other always brought that image back into my mind. Annie would open her mouth wider, so I'd move mine away and kiss her cheek for a while. She'd raise a finger to her ear and tap it to say I should kiss her there, but I didn't like the idea of earwax one bit more than slugs, so I'd make like I hadn't seen her do it. In a few more minutes I'd let go and take a step back.

"That's enough of the kissing part, right?" I'd ask, sitting down on the edge of the mattress. When I sat, we'd meet eye to eye.

Annie would step forward, tucking her plump legs between mine. With the palm of her hand, she'd stroke the flat surface my hair had been buzzed into. She'd play with the collar of my golf shirt, raising and lowering it in a flirty way. I'd unbutton her blouse and take off my shirt and pants. She'd shimmy out of her skirt and panty hose, then turn to give me access to her bra hook. I'd tug at it too hard and it would get frustrating. I must have pinched her up front doing that. Finally she'd tell me, gently but firmly, how to take it off. Then she'd climb on top of me and I'd have to lie back on the bed.

We'd roll around, kissing and touching, and I'd think about Mama. How her cholesterol levels were rising, or how she was trying to change her diet. I'd worry that she was going to die of a heart attack. I'd wonder if we should try to get Cheryl into a good nursery school, even though we couldn't afford one. Then I'd remember that I should concentrate on what I was doing. A boy would appear in Annie's place, and I'd become more excited.

But usually Annie started talking to me and calling me Pookie-Pie. Her feminine voice wouldn't allow me to get involved in the fantasy as much as I needed to. Eventually she'd push her panties down to her knees, hook her toe into the elastic band, and slide them off and onto the floor. That meant I should probably to do the same, so I'd get off the bed and take my boxers down.

Every time I turned around, her face would fall. I hadn't been able to perform sexually very often, or for very long, and Annie got frustrated by that. She wouldn't mention it too much, but I'd see confusion and hurt bubble up in her eyes. One time it took on a special intensity, pinching the corners of her face in a way that made her look older, so I climbed onto the bed and pulled her toward me. She held back a little. Outside, somebody started a lawnmower.

"It's okay if you can't," she began, making me think about the awful time I'd had with Penny, who kept trying and trying for twenty minutes with me in her mouth and didn't get anywhere. "But I would like—I have been talking to Minister Mike about this, and he says that the Lord—that God wants married couples to experience intimacy and pleasure in the bedroom, not just to make children."

"Well, I disagree with Minister Mike."

Annie went silent, stewing for a while. She swung her legs under the covers and brought the sheet up over her nakedness. I followed suit. The buzz of the mower came closer and then moved away. "Is there somebody else?" she asked, almost in a whisper, once the noise died down.

"Of course not."

"Do I— Are you not attracted to me anymore?"

"No."

"No as in no you're not?"

"No, no as in that isn't it. I've just been working so hard. I'm not used to it. I come home exhausted every night, you know. And now this—" I raised my splinted hand into the air.

"Minister Mike said you might be somebody who has a secret turn-on that he is too shy to share with his partner. Is that true? Do you have a secret turn-on, Pookie-Pie? You can tell me."

"You're talking about turn-ons with Minister Mike? This is hard enough as it is. Don't make it harder."

"I wish I *could* make it harder," she joked.

"Don't act like a street whore!" I blurted.

Before I knew what had happened, Annie brought both of her fists down on my chest, nearly knocking the wind out of me. I gasped both for breath and in shock. She growled and grabbed hold of my splint. "I swear I'll break it if you ever say something like that to me again. Dishonor our blessed union with that kind of filthy talk one more time and I will kick you out in a minute, Daddy or no. I have dealt with tougher men than you." Waving my splint in the air as if that would ease the pain, I thought of telling her that I'd meant to say Don't *talk* like a street whore. But then she might have asked how I knew what street whores talked like.

"I must be the only newlywed wife in Florida who has to argue her husband into bed."

I let her anger fall off for a few moments. "Maybe there's something wrong that you feel you need sex so much," I whispered.

"Huh? Maybe it's a huge part of marriage and a fun way of expressing love and trust. I thought sex was only ungodly before marriage. I feel tricked!" She put a pillow in her lap and pulled on the corners like a pet's ears.

"Just because something feels good doesn't make it right, even when you're married."

"There's nothing kinky about the missionary position," she harumphed, turning on her side and embracing her new lover, the pillow. "Missionaries did it!"

One of the other survey-takers left his job at Daytona Reports and started working in the marketing department of a company called Bradley's Biscuits. He recommended me for a position as a junior account executive. Bradley's Biscuits had started out selling dough in pop-open cylinders, but they made more money selling Dietz's Special Potato Chips. They were popular with auto mechanics and landscapers. I loved working for a company where eating potato chips counted as part of the job.

On the evening I came back to Tudor Valley with my first big pay-check, I was so happy that I showed it to Annie. I smoothed it down on the kitchen countertop for her to admire.

"That's a whole lot of numbers there, isn't it?"

I wore a suit and tie every day—the same one until my first paycheck arrived. Later, I bought a brass money clip and a nice watch with a little crown on the face. With dental insurance, I finally fixed the tooth my father had chipped back in sixth grade. Bonding it made me smile more, and healed some of the bad emotions I still held against him. Cheryl got a beanbag doll of Ariel from *The Little Mermaid*.

Annie, Cheryl, and I left the old condo and moved into a larger apartment in a complex called the Ponce de León. It had wavy terra-cotta tiles on the roof, a fountain in the courtyard, and blue porcelain numbers stuck in the blinding white concrete walls outside the front doors. It was a place where you thought you would see a flamenco dancer married to a bullfighter in the next apartment. The Ponce had a washer-dryer, and a refrigerator with an ice-maker. Suddenly I could consider myself a real American man. I felt like I had gotten away with something. The marquee above my life advertised a movie called *Totally Normal*. If only I could stay silent. Because the thoughts in my skull were a different story. My same-sex desires hadn't gone anywhere. They had backed up inside me like water in a bent garden hose. The harder I choked them off, the harder they'd spurt out whenever I let my guard down.

Unlike at Daytona Reports, a whole lot of the guys on my floor at the new job were handsome, well-groomed, and clean. On my fourth day, as I stood by the elevator about to leave, the doors opened on Hank, a friendly, sandy-haired fellow who always seemed like he'd just come from swimming. His hair gleamed brighter from chlorine in some spots, and it looked wet. I'd only met him once before, but since then I had found out everything I could about him without asking. I guess I had a thing for blonds.

Hank beamed as he held the door open. "Gary!" he exclaimed, like somebody talking to a long-lost friend. Holy smokes, I thought, Hank remembered my name! Nobody else was in the elevator, and we would probably get to ride to the parking lot alone.

"Oh, I left something at my desk," I said. "You go on ahead, Hank."

"You're on the Cheeze-A-Roonies account, right? You should come by and talk to me. I've been reading up about oil-based lipid substitutes." Bradley's Biscuits was fixing to expand into Bradley Foods, and they'd started making nonfat versions of all their snacks.

"Sure thing," I said. "Have a good night."

"Happy trails," he said, giving me a military salute as the elevator doors shut. Once the doors closed, I hid my face in my hands. You have to beat this thing, I told myself. You can't let it interfere with your work. Let Jesus guide you.

At a big meeting the following week, I put my binder down in a seat close to the head of the table, to the left of a no-nonsense woman named

Harriet. I would have to cross her line of sight if I wanted to moon over any of the guys who always sat in a group at the far end, including Hank.

Before the meeting, we milled around the refreshments. A chocolate-chip muffin caught my eye. It sat on a tray next to Hank, who stood past-ing cream cheese onto a bagel. He had on a wide gold wedding ring, so tight it made the rest of his finger plump up like a hot dog. Since I didn't want to get too near the warm space that surrounded his body, I edged around him and picked the muffin up. Oh boy, it was hot. I peeled it out of the frilly paper and broke it in half. The muffin steamed slightly and the chips inside were gooey when I bit down.

Just then Hank's crisp North Carolina twang tickled my ears. "Hey Gary. You said you were gonna come by last week. Were you just swamped? Why don't you swing by after the meeting and we'll talk Olestra. It's pretty exciting what's going on. Sounds like a great opportunity."

With my mouth full, I made a noise that didn't mean yes or no.

"Great!" he said.

I poured myself a cup of coffee to wash down the thick wad of muffin. By the time I served myself and took a sip, Hank had sat down and the meeting had started. I spent a lot of time fretting about what was going to happen later. When I stood next to him, I could always smell his flowery shampoo.

Hank pulled me aside after the meeting and demanded that I come by his desk right then. His way of doing it was real good-natured. I wanted to be near him, so I didn't say no. I stood just outside his personal area, and used the cubicle wall to brace my shaky legs. The odor of Hank's hair was kind of herbal, but syrupy. It shot up into my nostrils and made me woozy.

"Why don't you sit down?" he said, pulling a plastic chair toward him. I said I had a presentation to get done in two days, so I couldn't stay too long. He shrugged, printed out a few articles, and handed them to me as he raved about the miracle fat substitute. When he handed me the print-outs, his silky hand accidentally touched mine. Well, my ghost just about jumped out of my body. For a split second I wanted to feel all that hot skin against my own nakedness. I pictured us at work after hours, grinding our flesh together on the carpet-guard under his desk.

Stomping the thought out almost as quickly as I'd had it, I hugged the photocopies to my chest. I was grateful that he didn't have his own office, and that the temperature always stayed pretty chilly at work. Careful to show no emotion, I thanked him and hurried back to my desk. I rolled the chair up to where my belly touched the edge and thought hard about dead dogs to keep my erection down.

Hank's presence distracted me enough that I had to take the stairs all the time. I told people I wanted the exercise, but we were only on the second floor. It got to the point where I needed to spend less time in the office. I kept an eye out for opportunities to leave town and avoid him.

The first couple of business trips I took were short ones, to nearby cities like Tampa and Jacksonville. As part of a team putting together a proposal, I spent most of my time with my close associates. Some of those guys I liked, but not a one of them sent me over the edge like Hank. We usually stayed in the hotel room, ordered room service, and pored over bullet points and PowerPoint files. We only went out to meetings, not to socialize. That's probably why our proposals were mostly big hits. I can do this, I thought sometimes. I'll be fine.

My third trip was a weekend conference, a small convention of pork rind brands that my boss, Mr. Price, wanted me to check out. He sent me by myself. The plane ticket came to my desk and I noticed that I'd been scheduled for a Sunday return. I thought it was a mistake, so I knocked softly on Mr. Price's door, even though he always kept it partway open.

"Mr. Price, I think Rhonda made a mistake. The convention is only Wednesday night, Thursday, and Friday."

Mr. Price, a vice president of marketing, was still pretty young for somebody so accomplished. His black hair had only a few needles of white in it. He was a Yankee. He dressed casually and he treated his employees like friends. Instead of following the rules, he wanted everybody at the company to think outside the box. He was the first person I ever heard use that expression. For a long time I thought he'd made it up, because so many of our products came in boxes.

"Spend the weekend," said Mr. Price. "Explore a little. Chicago's a great town. You'll like it."

"What would I do in Chicago?" I asked.

His voice boomed so much that everybody outside his office could hear him. "Have you no curiosity? Go to the top of the Sears Tower! You can see all the way to Canada from there. There's a cross-section of a human body in half-inch sections on display at the science museum. Wouldn't you like to see that? Go to the ballpark, the lake, go look at the hammerhead sharks in the aquarium. Visit the goddamned Robie House. But I'm not changing your plane ticket and that's final." He smiled like a game-show host handing me the keys to my new car. I didn't even ask him not to swear.

Annie's face fell when I told her my plans had changed. I repeated something Mr. Price had said about wanting his execs to experience the world and have class. She didn't completely understand, maybe because she had seen more of the world than I probably ever would. "Maybe I can join you there," she said. For a moment she got excited by the idea and grinned. "But I have to work." Annie had just started a job at a travel agency. "That's okay. Take lots of pictures!"

The next morning she made a special breakfast of boiled rice and eggs all stirred up in a pot. It warmed my insides as I stepped into the street with my bag. Annie shuffled out to the curb in her housecoat and slippers to see me off, pushing her thick black hair out from behind her glasses and throwing a brave little smile up at me. She deserves a much better man than me, I thought, one who doesn't keep big secrets and can satisfy her in bed. Sometimes I wondered if she was such a good person that she'd figured it all out and still decided to stand by her man.

The cab driver unlatched the trunk and it bounced open like the car was happy to see me. Once I got in the back, he asked where I was going, and I said Chicago. Laughing out loud, he said he couldn't drive that far, but it would be a good fare.

SIX

After it became a habit, I gave it other names—"getting a favor," "guy stuff." Not sex. Not sin. Not infidelity. That is, if I admitted anything to myself. By any darned name, though, I knew Annie would be devastated if she found out, and I would've had one heck of a time explaining what it *really* was. So in order to keep a sense of morality, I made up a whole mess of rules about it in my head. One of them was to limit my guy activities to business trips.

My responsibilities at work kept increasing, unfortunately, and I went out of town more often. It always felt good to get away from the demands of having a child and a wife for a little while, even though I missed them both. But temptation lurked in every airport bathroom stall and public park, and since nobody suspected anything, I got bolder. The more I did it, the less guilty I felt. Each encounter with a different fellow added to a pattern and they all became the same man, instead of sticking in my mind as individual earth-shattering events. By and by, the tune in my head changed from "I've Got to Stop This" to "It's Not Like I'm Having an Affair."

The possibilities of Chicago stunned me. From the plane that evening I could see its whole shape down there, the long avenues scratching pink scars across the shoulder of Illinois, the giant curve of Lake Superior cutting them off in the northeast. The taillights of cars stopped and started across the city like blood cells pumping through a gigantic heart. I had a hard time believing that so many people could live in one place. How did they make a city so huge without using up the world's supply of brick and metal?

On Friday morning, after munching on pork rinds all day Thursday, I woke up with some powerful gas. I called Annie and she told me to drink a large coffee and a glass of water. Thanks to her, my gas mostly went away, so I managed to go to some of the panels. By 3:30, my stomach began growling again. I swapped business cards with a few people I thought Mr. Price should know, but I decided to skip the rest of the networking session. I went back to my hotel room and had another glass of water, then lay down and flipped through all the cable TV channels. My stomach growled and whined like a sad dog. My boredom mixed with horniness—a dangerous combination.

Using my tiredness as an excuse, I paused on the sinful channels. German bodybuilder and former action star Klaus Rassmussen had a half-hour show about the Ab Crunch Machine. Mr. Rassmussen never wore a shirt, and his oily torso glowed in the reddish spotlights. A white neon line ran around the border of his perfect silhouette. I couldn't take my eyes away.

As soon as I'd given in to the urge to look, though, the program ended. My stomach had mostly calmed down. It dawned on me that I had a whole bunch of free time ahead of me. I could run through the wild, crazy avenues of Chicago, where nobody knew me and nobody was watching. Nobody from back home would ever find out if I did something ungodly, as long as I kept it to myself.

Of course, God was watching. But God never spoke about what He saw. Certainly not to me. How long had I pleaded with Him to help me, to fix me, to show me a sign, only to be ignored? If you thought on it, God let everything on Earth happen. God plunked Himself down at a big desk and okayed *everything* with a fat rubber stamp. Should it be a sunny day? Why, yes! Today, let's wipe out the coast with a hurricane. Great idea! Should there be roller coasters? Yeah, let's build a whole mess of 'em! How about a train wreck, Lord? Fine with me! Do we need a snack food called Cheeze-A-Roonies on Planet Earth? Heck yeah, bring on the Cheeze-A-Roonies! What say you create an evil dude named Adolf Hitler? Yessiree!

Seemed He didn't even *have* a rubber stamp for No. He let good and bad stuff happen all the time and didn't care if folks did what they pleased if they could handle the consequences and keep the secrets.

But maybe there wouldn't be any consequences.

For a moment, after Klaus Rassmussen's show ended, the tide of my lust went out. I changed my mind about going out and getting a favor. But then a food-processor infomercial came on, and the young, attractive man and woman on the show demonstrated the salad spinner. The fellow, whose name was Paul Cantor, appealed to me with his dimples and honey brown eyes. When he broke a dripping wet head of lettuce in half with his thumbs, it was the sexiest thing I'd ever seen. Water went everywhere, dotting his thick, manly hands and hairy forearms with fat droplets. Carefree, he dabbed his arms with a dishtowel and cranked the mechanism. Lettuce leaves flew around willy-nilly inside the cage. Overcome with desire, I knelt on the plush carpet and kissed his lips through the screen.

When that show got done, I turned the television off and imagined Klaus Rassmussen's stomach. His abs poked out like an upside-down muffin pan. I let myself think about them and got semi-hard. Automatically, I crawled over to the side of the bed and found the phone directory on the bottom of the nightstand under the Gideons' Bible. I spread the book and flipped my way through the tissuey pages.

The yellow pages didn't list anything gay. The entries went from "Gauges" right to "Gears." I couldn't force a new category to appear in the space between them, so I looked up "Homosexual" and even "Lesbian." Nothing. It was like same-sex desires, after torturing me for so long, had been erased from the world as soon as I decided to seek them out.

Usually this kind of situation would've made me give up, but this time, determination growled in my gut. I stood up, put on my winter clothes, turned the lights off, and strolled right out of that hotel. Of course, I didn't have the gall to ask the concierge where was gay to go. But I decided I had to do something. Even though I didn't know where I was fixing to go, I couldn't stop myself from gamboling out into the freezing afternoon like a primitive hunter with a mean hunger and a spear full of poison.

The notion that acting on my secret lust wouldn't bring any consequences was a bet against the reality of Hell. But no matter how much I believed I would burn, I couldn't shake my desire. Like a demon with his claws in my shoulder, desire tore at my flesh, howling, trying to make me defy the Lord's word and throw away eternal peace for earthly delight. I couldn't get the Lord to respond to my prayers and make it stop no matter how hard I tried. If this problem had turned into a choice between my flesh *probably* being burned but not consumed in the hereafter and my body and mind *definitely* being consumed but not burned in this life, it had begun to feel like I should take my chances. Was this Satan's influence corrupting me, or the voice of my true self? Was my secret sexuality my true self? More true than my wife and family? I didn't have an answer—I was a walking question mark. I only knew what I wanted—and not even specifically.

Outside in the Loop, I followed men I saw walking alone, or in pairs, searching for signs in their walks and actions. It was December, though, and everybody's winter clothing made it hard to tell anything about folks from the way they moved. The men I singled out waddled into steakhouses and sports bars. One of them stepped into a station wagon full of groceries, and another met his girlfriend with a passionate kiss in the crystal lobby of a department store decorated with poinsettias and holly. I stayed outside, watching the lovers, my hot breath steaming in front of my face.

The Yuletide display before me was a wondrous landscape of toy trains, elves, miniature houses, and tinsel-covered trees. Putting down my sadness, I welcomed the pure joy of Christmas into my heart. Laughing boys and girls had gathered there with mothers and nannies, squealing, pointing, and running to follow the path of the train around the foyer. The store had even rigged up a flying sled with a Santa Claus that waved, while his reindeer carried him through the sky inside the diorama. Flakes of Styrofoam fell over the miniature countryside, and a xylophone version of "O Come All Ye Faithful" played on the speakers. I marveled at the delightful scene until my nose got numb. Then I decided to go on into the store.

I'm not sure when I admitted the real reason I decided to go in. Maybe a couple of attractive men passed by the display on their way in, and their reflections revved my drives into fifth gear. Maybe something in the display triggered me—even a cute elf or a reindeer with rounded haunches could've ignited my passions at that point. But even though I spent an hour searching through the forest of housewares (I convinced myself that Annie wanted a blender for Christmas) and itchy overcoats (I had just bought a parka), I had walked in to find the men's restroom.

Every place I went, I noted the signs that led to the john and moved to a closer department. Finally, I spotted it. The bathroom was located down a short corridor in the very back of men's outerwear, lit with a strange orange light—I pictured the gates of Hell. While I pretended to comparison-shop for coats, I could see in the corner of my eye anybody entering or leaving the bathroom. As I watched, my entire body became electric. Eventually I decided that I had to use the bathroom for real reasons. "I have to use the facilities," I said aloud, to nobody. Maybe to God.

Huge snowflakes hung from the ceiling, glittering ornaments and mannequins wearing Santa hats lined the main walkways, but all thoughts of God and Jesus left my mind. I felt like I had injected freedom directly into my veins. I feared doing what I wanted so much that I tried to pretend I wasn't there. Then something strange happened—the fear bubbled over until it joined up with the sexual thrill, and I fell in love with the idea of being a sinner. I felt that I never wanted to stop engaging in guy stuff. Which I suppose made me a for-real homosexual sinner, instead of just a straight fellow with some problems, although I still couldn't put the words to the feelings.

Full of swirling needs, I made a beeline for the restroom like I was Mrs. Addison running out of church. Staring at the shiny floor to keep my face from view, I made a game of keeping my feet inside its checkerboard pattern. When I got to the door marked MEN, I noticed that somebody had added a crude drawing of the male organ to the familiar stick figure's crotch. I swung the door open and it creaked with an almost human cry.

Despite how closely I had tried to watch the comings and goings of men walking toward the back of the store, I had calculated wrong. The restroom was empty, and as an added insult, it stank like human waste and lemony cleaning fluid. That nobody was in there relieved and disappointed me at the same time. I had imagined—hoped, feared, desired—that I would barge in on some immoral activity in progress.

I chose the farthest stall and drew the small bar across to lock it. Though I had been indoors for a while, my skin felt chilly and numb. Regardless, I took off my coat and hung it on the hook. I tugged down my corduroys, and then the long johns I had bought not long after settling in at the hotel. Then I took down my drawers to find that it really was colder in the bathroom than in the rest of the store. Maybe management had turned down the heat in there to save money. My exposed skin became tight, and goosebumps spread out all over my big behind and thighs. When I lowered myself onto the seat, it was ice cold, and I flinched. You'd think a department store with such a pretty Christmas display would have spent more on heating the bathroom.

I knew that men did things in public bathrooms, from having read the graffiti there, and from my experience with Dickie. Once I got used to the seat, I realized that I would have to wait awhile. A peephole had been drilled, or ripped open someway, between my stall and the next one. Somehow I recognized that this place had puzzling new rules and customs to learn. I had no idea what ought to happen next. Was I supposed to watch something happen in there? Did you pass the money through that hole? I checked my wallet. What would seven dollars get me?

I put my eye up to the hole, but I couldn't see much of the tiny room next door. The things I imagined happening would probably have taken place nearer to the toilet seat. My body spasmed from the cold, so I made fists and blew into them to warm my hands up. Nobody came into the restroom for a long time, and my crazed lust started to wane. Maybe I'd done enough for one day.

Then the door squeaked open, and my spine tensed like it was connected to the hinge. I leaned away from the hole and heard dress shoes scratching against the tile. Somebody sat down in the far stall and did his business. It made me uncomfortable to hear that—it reminded me of the abnormality of homosexuality, how queers had to find partners in the same places where people relieved themselves. A third man walked in.

Between the echoing plops and squirts and the freezing cold in there, I decided I'd had enough. I reached down to pull up my drawers. But then the third person swung open the door of the middle stall. I could see his shoes under the wall, a pair of brown loafers with tassels attached at the tongue. He wore gray socks.

After a moment, his dress pants fell and a belt clinked against the floor. I heard the man sit down. The far toilet flushed and the first man left as the sound of rushing water roared through the room, then faded. For a while I listened to the dripping faucet, waiting for the man to make the normal sort of sounds, but he didn't. The amount of time started to speak for itself. I figure he must have known I was there, too, and that I wasn't doing anything either. Just waiting. I reckoned I ought to use the hole to communicate with the man, to whisper through it or something, but I wasn't sure.

The hole was positioned far enough forward in the stall that you couldn't see the person next to you unless you got up and deliberately looked through it. I tried to lean forward as casually as possible and see what I could in the corner of my eye accidentally on purpose, but it was pretty tough to get a view.

All that shifting around in the stall must have tipped the man off about my intentions. I heard the belt jangle, then his shoes disappeared and his knees came back in their place. A wide green eye looked through the hole at a sharp angle. It moved quickly from side to side, painting me with shame, then it disappeared. Even after the eye left, I wanted to cover myself. I thought of the evil eye and how it could kill you.

Somebody sighed from over the wall, and then a voice said, "Fucking fat nigger troll." I was stunned. At first I didn't realize the words had been directed at me. I just knew they weren't nice words to say; all those curses and hurtful expressions jammed into one horrible phrase. I have to stop this fellow from being so rude, I thought. I forgot where I was for a second and knelt down at the hole to scold him. "How dare you!" I whispered. "You shouldn't call people nasty names. You ought to be ashamed—"

As an answer, the guy shoved his man part through the hole, right into my personal space. I didn't get the opportunity to complete the sentence. From the other side of the wall, I heard him demand something from me that I had already begun to do, in spite of my wounded pride, with a whole lot of gusto. I relaxed the back of my throat so that his entire self could fit in my mouth. I licked fast up and down to tickle him, and I tugged his nuts through the hole, too, and weighed them gently on my tongue. I wanted this rude fool to have the best experience he'd ever had from a Fucking fat nigger troll. How would he feel about chubby black men after *that*? I reckoned he wouldn't be able to use such hurtful language about us anymore. I reckoned he'd most likely go out trying to *find* some FFNTs, like Dickie, who I guessed wasn't such a bad guy after all.

If that man's thing had been a Tootsie Pop, I would've gotten to the center in no time flat. It didn't take long before it took to twitching and spurting. I aimed it against the wall, but some still got on my shirt. So much tension had built up in my own body that I didn't have to touch myself much before I finished, too. The man pulled himself in and zipped up his pants. I tried to get a look at his face through the hole, but I only saw his hand. Like me, he wore a wedding ring.

Bradley Foods soon made a big push to go national. My hours went later, and Mr. Price sent me on more trips. Annie wasn't happy about that, but when I tried to bring up my status as a new dad with my boss, I found that I couldn't say anything. Part of me knew that by working harder I was doing more to fulfill the duties of a dad. That meant bringing home more bacon, or, as Annie said, "bringing home the bacon-flavored snacks."

With all our expenses, we sank further into debt. Being a responsible man meant I had to get us back on our feet. Unfortunately, this meant more man-on-man encounters.

Eventually it stopped making a difference, because I broke my rule about waiting until business trips. Whenever I could leave work before nine, I would go to parking lots and rest areas by I-4 or I-95, or parts of the Old Town area of Kissimmee. Men like me would sit idly in our cars, not really reading the paper, or making like we were having a beer. We'd sneak little glances at one another. Success in the game always depended on how well you could pretend not to want anything at all. It reminded me of fishing.

In time, if one of us looked good enough to the other, we would step out of our cars and into a nearby wooded area. We had to keep from doing anything definitely gay until we actually touched each other. We never knew who might be a cop. A man getting out of his car and going into the woods could say he needed to pee. A fellow loitering on a park bench could just be brokenhearted with no place to go.

On rainy days, I would visit the bathroom of a local department store. It was a popular spot for the sort of person I had become. After a while I started to see the same men there on a regular basis. I got to know their faces, and some of them I gave nicknames. Once, in the hallway of a company where I had a business meeting, I passed one of the men I had done things with in the woods, a man I called the Librarian in my head because of his crew cut and 1950s glasses. Our eyes met for a split second, and the Librarian's eyelids flared. Mine must have, too. We turned away carefully.

One Friday at the end of a very tough week, Mr. Price let me leave work at about 5:30. I had spoken to Annie earlier to let her know that I would be working until nine. I always told her that I would be home later than I thought so that when I showed up early she would be happy and not suspicious.

The bathroom in the nearby department store's basement was perfect for my needs. It was near the men's department, and before you got to the stalls and the urinals there was a large room covered in old tile. That room must have had a purpose in the days when the building was built, but there didn't seem to be a reason for it anymore. The old door creaked something awful when you walked in, and that noise would tell anybody in the stalls that somebody had walked in long before the newcomer could cross the first room and see what was going on. The urinals didn't have metal blinders between them. That made it possible to see your neighbor and reach over if he let you know it was okay. The stalls were also old-fashioned, with doors that went all the way to the floor. Seemed like the more modern the design of a men's bathroom, the more it tried to prevent the perversions of the male sex.

In my many trips there, I had figured out a special trick. I knew that if you opened the door real quick like a bunny, it wouldn't creak. If you swung it open and then tiptoed across that big room, you could sometimes catch somebody in the act of doing something. Since I wasn't attractive to most guys, I sometimes had to console myself by just watching the activities or sneaking in a little poke or a feel-up instead of jumping right in like some of them. Usually if you walked in on a couple of guys and one of them recognized you as a member of our little fraternity, they wouldn't pay you any mind. They'd just go back to doing what they were doing.

On that day, I used my door-opening trick more effectively than ever. If somebody was in there, he wouldn't have heard me coming in at all. I walked real slow, so that the sound of my footsteps wouldn't bounce off the walls. I even held my breath.

One man stood at the bank of urinals. He was short and hairy and bald. He pretended to do his business, but he turned his eyes to me as soon as I walked in. He sized me up and then turned back to the charade. I knew something about me had disappointed him, but I didn't know if it was my black skin, my weight, or something else. I could never tell for sure. Maybe I wasn't a heavy enough fucking fat nigger troll for him.

As I went on into the main bathroom, I saw two fellows against the far wall. One of them was kneeling with his back to me. The other had his back against the wall, facing me. He was slim, with thick glasses and a neat beard. We made eye contact, recognizing each other as regular bathroom hounds. I had been attracted to him once, but he had snubbed me. He nodded slightly, with a gentle frown, embarrassed maybe, but still having himself a good old time. I noticed that the kneeling man was black. That might mean I still had a chance with the standing man. Maybe I had caught him on a day when he felt more open to somebody like me. My spirits lightened.

One of the stalls was open, so I positioned myself just inside. I unzipped my trousers and pulled myself through the layers of clothing. I could see just enough of the other men, and if somebody suddenly entered the bathroom without using my door trick, I would hear the creaking and lock myself in the stall before anyone knew what I had been doing.

The man at the urinal turned. He saw what I was doing and joined in from the bank of urinals. Then he moved closer, occasionally looking back toward the door. He stopped in front of the sinks for a better view. He looked into the mirror, where the angle probably made for a perfect eyeful.

Because of the tense atmosphere, the men were trying not to make any noise. The sounds they did make were intense and erotic because they had to whisper, even though they probably wanted to let loose. The body of the man leaning against the wall tensed up. He clenched his teeth and looked toward the ceiling. His body went through a series of spasms. "Oh God," he said through his teeth. "Mmm. Oh, sweet Jesus." I didn't like to hear the Lord's name used this way, but I couldn't deny that ecstasy was taking place in his body.

When the young man stood up, he turned toward me, and I recognized Minister Mike's son, Chester, the gorgeous boy who had hugged his father the day Annie was born again. I hadn't identified him immediately, because he had let his hair grow out. We were face to face. I couldn't hide what I was doing, and he couldn't hide what he had just done.

I covered my private parts and looked down, as if that would hide my identity. My first urge was to try to save him from this kind of behavior. I couldn't tell if he recognized me from church, but he gave me a look like he was about to vomit and hurried out of the bathroom. I couldn't help watching his powerful shoulder blades as he left.

The possible meanings of this chance encounter raced through my mind. I kept still for a while, letting a hundred fantasies come to a boil in my head.

"Hey, hey," the bearded man whispered. "You. Blackie. I could go again, man." He grimaced. I reckoned it was better to be called Blackie than Fatty. My opportunity with him had come, but at such a time! All of a sudden the idea of sex with the man made me so sick that I almost didn't want it anymore. I stood there stunned, waiting for the sound of the door closing behind Chester, thinking that if I didn't hear it, he'd turned back, maybe. But the door creaked shut, so I turned to the bearded fellow and kneeled.

Even though my one-year eval went well, Mr. Price came to me two months later to say that my performance hadn't been satisfactory for a promotion. By that time I was doing the same work as somebody with a higher job description. I struggled to understand this turn of events. If my performance had been unsatisfactory, why hadn't he given me a poor evaluation or fired me instead of trusting me with more responsibilities? He had always treated me real well. He didn't seem like somebody who would discriminate against me.

Later, through other colleagues, I learned that the C.E.O. had told Mr. Price who to promote. Circumstances forced him to tell me that my performance was unsatisfactory, because he couldn't admit that he had no power. Knowing this, I should have felt better. Brian, one of the people placed above me, was a former forklift operator who had gone to another company and come back. He had hit home runs for the company softball team, and he was white. I couldn't help thinking that Bradley Foods hadn't treated me fairly.

I spent most of Brian's first day helping him. He didn't understand such simple things as the proper way to prepare a fax cover page. Once I had introduced him around the floor, I brought him over to my own desk. I had him sit down so I could teach him the voicemail system. Brian had just learned how to transfer a call when a buzz began to stir in the nearby cubicles. Geoff Bradley, the C.E.O., was on his way. He rarely came down to the level of the account managers.

"Where is he?" I heard a voice say. "Where's the softball star?"

As the training session continued, I lost patience with Brian. He didn't understand anything. Normally it takes a lot for me to get upset, but I had to stop and recite the names of the disciples to myself at least twice to keep from raising my voice. Brian didn't know the job, but he acted toward me like he already knew everything. He had a Yankee accent, along with the haughty attitude that Northerners sometimes have toward people from the South. But I wasn't above him in rank, so I had to maintain a cordial attitude.

I left work feeling grumpy. The day was like my mood—chilly for Florida, and mostly cloudy. It had been that way all week. Because of my bad mood, I knew that I would probably stop off somewhere to be with men. It would make me happier, if only by releasing my frustrations for a few minutes.

I was driving down the highway in the opposite direction from home when I noticed something under my windshield wiper. The Chinese/Japanese restaurant and the optician in the strip mall next door would often leave flyers on our cars, so it didn't surprise me to find something there. But this looked like a piece of notebook paper. Not thinking, I accidentally engaged the wiper. It slid up the glass choppily, and nearly released the piece of paper. When I noticed that the paper had handwriting on it, I quickly shut off the wipers. Was it a personal note?

I pulled off to the side of the road into the gravel there. The page dangled off the edge of the windshield and flapped in the breeze made by a passing semi. I swung the door open, got out, and pulled the note from under the wiper. I smoothed the paper out on the hood of the car, which was pleasantly warm, and read it. In block letters, somebody had written FAGGET.

The feeling that came over me as I read the note does not have a name. My chest hurt when I inhaled. My throat got so tight that it could've been twisted into a knot. Weakness spread through my legs like scum across stagnant water and raced up into my head.

My thoughts crisscrossed over each another. I couldn't think who could have written the note. At first I tried to force myself to believe that the writer didn't have any proof of my desires. I knew the word *faggot* didn't always mean a man with my problem. But I couldn't help thinking that some evil person had decided to torment me about the exact thing that was already ripping my life and soul in two. Though I could hardly see through my moistening eyes, I read the note again. The word grew and grew until, at twenty feet high, it fell over on me.

This note had to be destroyed. I knew I had to get rid of it before I went home. I tried to memorize things about the handwriting, so that if I saw it again I would know the culprit. The block lettering didn't look unusual, except for the capital *A*. I vowed to keep my eyes out for anyone who made *A*'s shaped like triangles.

I got back into the car and put the paper between me and the steering wheel. I ripped out the part with writing on it and crumpled up the rest. Carefully, I pulled tiny pieces away from the note and placed them on the seat next to me. I tore the tiniest pieces I could, with the smallest part of my fingernails. If I could have separated every atom of that sheet of paper from every other atom, I would have done it. I sat there for so long that a man with a goatee pulled his pickup truck off the highway and stuck his head out the window to ask if I needed help. At least I think that's what he wanted.

"I'm fine, sir, thank you!" I yelled back. He waited a moment and then drove off.

In a few more minutes I had created a pile of shredded paper that a hamster could have called home. When I got done, I jumbled all the pieces together. The paper hadn't mentioned me by name, but if anybody saw me throwing it out, I didn't want there to even be a possibility that they could put it back together and get the idea that I was a homosexual. It didn't matter to me whether they believed it or not. I wanted to make sure that the thought itself could never cross anyone's mind *at all*, because I wasn't a homosexual, I just had same-sex attractions, and I did guy stuff sometimes, but I could sort of perform with my wife sometimes now, so that was that. To make absolutely sure, I separated the pieces of paper into four piles. I stopped at four different city garbage cans along the side of the road. Checking to make sure nobody saw me, I threw a cottony lump into each of the four trash bins. Only then did I start to relax.

The note had been planted near my workplace, so I worried that somebody at work wanted to expose me and ruin my career. Hank, my coworker crush, never wrote with block letters, so that relieved me. A few of my other colleagues sometimes talked trash about fags, but

I always agreed with whatever they said, and sometimes added my own comments. Eventually I decided that Chester must have lashed out at me for discovering his own activities. I didn't think it through—my panic-stricken brain jumped right to the conclusion and stayed there. Why had he responded so hatefully? I wondered. To keep people from figuring him out?

Annie greeted me at the door with a white plastic device in her hand. "I bought a deionizer," she announced. She had a habit of adding to my worries by going on shopping sprees for Cheryl. My anger from work was at its peak, and she made it worse by preventing me from getting inside.

"A what?"

"It was only $260." Finally I made it around her, into the kitchen, and poured myself a glass of ice water. I tried to hide my fury.

"Do we really need that stupid thing?" I held my hand out and Annie placed it in my palm. To me it didn't have $260 of weight.

"Stupid? Are you so cheap that you'd let your daughter get sick to save money? Don't you love her more than that? Or did you drop her on purpose? Oh, I shouldn't have said that." Annie covered her mouth.

Suddenly the rage inside me came to the surface, and I broke the tumbler in my good hand—the one without the splint—against the kitchen counter. Glass, ice, and blood went everywhere. I opened a big gash in my palm.

Annie gasped. Grabbing my wrist and saying my name many times, she plucked out the big pieces and washed the wound, but I still needed a doctor.

In the hospital, Annie sat in the room while the doctor stitched my hand. As he pulled the thread through my flesh, she gently mentioned that I had slipped away from God's word. She said she had noticed that I seemed like a zombie in church, like I was just going through the motions of loving Him. She encouraged me to turn to Christ again.

"He will not desert you," she said. The doctor left the room for a moment to attend to another patient. The room hummed. The silence between me and Annie hurt almost as much as the cuts in my palm.

"Look at me, Annie," I said, raising my hand. "He deserted me long ago. This isn't stigmata. This here is my own foolishness."

"But you're saved, Gary."

"No, I'm not. I tried so hard. But Christ won't come into my heart the way He's in yours."

"But I was there with you."

I chuckled hopelessly. "Oh, I walked up to the pulpit, all right. But in my heart, I felt nothing, Annie. I've tried hard all my life. I've done everything! Should I have prayed harder? Louder? Why, of everybody we know, am I the only one Christ won't touch?" I came very close to telling Annie about my homosexual desires then, but instead I decided to leave that last statement alone, an unfinished bridge she would have to complete and cross by herself.

"This is called a crisis of faith, dear. But you'll get through it and you'll be stronger than ever in Christ. You need to talk to Minister Mike. I'll call him for you myself. Would you like that?"

I didn't say yes or no—I couldn't imagine talking to him. How could I tell him what had happened? Annie took my silence for agreement. The doctor came back in, so the conversation had to end. Keeping my mangled hand raised for the doctor to continue his work, I crumbled into the crook of my elbow. I would have sobbed, but my sadness was too vast, too nameless for tears.

Annie arranged the meeting with Minister Mike. They scheduled it two weeks in advance, and as the date approached, I got real jittery. I tried to watch my car from the window of the building at all times, but my designated parking space was on the opposite side of the lot. I'd need to be in Hank's cubicle to get the best possible view. I was in agony, obsessing over whether the note had been a random event or had been from somebody who wanted to blackmail me and ruin my life.

The next time I saw Chester at church, he turned his eyes away, even when we neared each other head-on. That was all I needed to prove my hunch. One time I said his name, because I had a conversation in my head that I wanted to have with him even though I was scared to, but he acted like nobody had said anything. Finally, one Sunday, Annie went to use the john right after services, and when I went outside to get the car, I discovered Chester standing on the church steps. He had his face turned up to the sun, drinking it in. He turned his eyes to me for a second and then turned away fast. Nobody else stood near us.

"Chester," I asked in a hush. "Why did you do a thing like that?"

To my surprise, he chuckled, with a hint of a superior atittude. He stuck his hands in his pockets. "Same reason you did. Let's not talk about it. Especially not here." There was a long pause, and he took a step down and away from me.

"Wait. What do you think I mean?"

"You know. *That*."

"Oh," I said, scared out of my wits. "I meant the—the other thing." I couldn't tell him what he'd done, because he'd just deny it. See, I had to get it out of him that he knew what I meant in order to prove he'd done it.

"Other thing?"

"With the car. On my car."

He turned his neck but not his body and screwed up his face. "I don't know what you're talking about. But Daddy's almost done in there," he said flatly.

At that point, I started to feel a little crazy. Like most new dads, I hadn't been sleeping through the night much, and that made things worse. I thought maybe the note thing hadn't happened, or I'd dreamed it. Maybe somebody put it on my car by mistake, or it said something other than what I thought. In my head, doubt and certainty took each other by the forearms and twirled around, laughing, until they got dizzy and fell down.

In the darkest moments of those next few days, when I thought most of confessing to Annie and bringing on a divorce—always for her sake, since nobody deserves a relationship with somebody who doesn't want them sexually—I always changed my mind, thinking how bad I wanted Cheryl to have a father—a good father, nothing like mine.

When the day came for my meeting with Minister Mike, I insisted that Annie let me go by myself. She stared at me with doubt. Watching her with Cheryl, I thought of Mary nursing the baby Jesus and felt damned.

At the sight of Chester's sports car in the church parking lot, I drove past the building and kept driving. I drove and drove. Driving pacified me. I flew up I-95 to a truck stop outside Daytona Beach. If I'd taken a right turn, I could have gone to the ocean. I pictured driving the car into the surf and drowning myself.

Minister Mike's kind, sympathetic face appeared in my head. At that moment he must have been sitting at his desk, waiting, checking his watch. I invented an excuse to tell him later. Wild with lust, I parked my car and found the men's room.

Cheryl turned two and a half the week that Mr. Price sent me to three snack-food conventions in a row. The Philadelphia Pork Rinds and Cracklings Expo was the first. Hank had a wedding in Asheville to attend, and Brian's hotel room was on a higher floor, so I had plenty of time alone. Walking around town that night, I stumbled on the city's gay area. It didn't dawn on me that I'd found it until I saw two men walking a poodle. I put my good hand out for the dog to sniff, and he touched his wet nose to my knuckle and licked it hungrily with his big old slippery tongue. The eagerness of the dog's licking embarrassed me, so I pulled my hand away and looked at the owners to apologize. They were two men with mustaches, and they were holding hands. I excused myself and hurried away.

I skulked around that part of Philadelphia timidly, peeking into card shops with rainbows pasted to the windows to see what the men looked like. They wore faded jeans, leather jackets, heavy boots, long hair, and goatees. There was something satanic, I thought, about their style choices. Some of them really tried to look like the Devil.

Eventually I found myself in front of a coffee shop, pretending to read the menu while I watched men—gay men—biting into croissants, sipping hot drinks, and chatting. I moved to leave the storefront and realized I had been standing by the glass door of a gay community center. In the hallway, a staircase led up to the office above the coffee shop.

I peeked up the staircase. It was almost 9 p.m. on a Thursday night, but they had their lights on. Before long, a person who could have been a man or a woman walked down the stairs and left, almost touching me. The door was unlocked.

For the next hour I circled the building. Even after all the guy stuff, I still believed that homosexuals were evil people who risked eternal hellfire by defying God's law, as stated in Leviticus. Homosexuality was punishable by death. Take a step toward it and Christ, the Bible, and your family would condemn you. If one of the sex viruses didn't kill you, loneliness would. But a community center didn't seem as threatening as a bar. The phrase made me think of chat groups and bake sales, things I already found familiar and safe.

I'll go in at 9, I said. But 9 turned into 9:05, 9:10, 9:15. At 9:55 I took a bunch of full-lunged breaths from across the street. All that stood between me and revealing the truth about myself was a light green door with a square window in it. I started across the street, but the horn blast from a truck blew me back. I squatted for a moment between two cars and caught my breath. Strangely, the adrenaline rush gave me the extra courage I needed to walk up that flight of steps. I checked up and down the street for oncoming traffic, crossed, and pulled the door open with exaggerated confidence.

I bounded up the steps and found myself in a lobby. A man—definitely a man—rushed around closing folding chairs, double-locking doors, and chucking paper cups into the trash. I wanted to talk, to unburden a life of suffering on him, but he didn't seem interested. The man had a blond bob and a silk shirt with Eiffel Towers and French breads tumbling all over it that flowed over a pair of tight orange jeans. Taking tiny steps, he wiped crumbs off different folding tables. We were the only two people in the room. I wondered if something would have to happen between us sexually before he'd help me.

The man kicked a rubber doorstop to close an empty conference room. "Can I help you?" he asked. His voice was feminine and impatient. He pushed his hair back into place and stood with the other hand on his hip. Gay, I thought. Gay gay gay. I couldn't stop thinking Gay. He's gay. He knows about me! If I ever told anyone, I knew, I wanted people to be able to look at me and think other thoughts than that I was gay. The words *He's gay* kept repeating in my head.

"I..." He's gay, he's gay, he's gay. He knows. He knows.

"Listen, I don't know if you're gay or whatever, LGBT, Lesbigay—BLT for God's sake—maybe you're looking for a drop-in—heck, I don't know if you're about to firebomb the place—alls I know is I have to get out of here *toot suite*." The man swung his head around in order to fix his bangs again. He dragged his vowels out when he spoke. He's gay, I thought. Gay gay gay gay.

"I'm already fifteen minutes late for my physical therapy," he sighed. I noticed he had a slight limp. "Drop-ins happen every second Thursday of the month in Room 216... Okay, thanks!" He held the door open. I didn't even have time to grab a flyer. I bumbled out into the street, not knowing where else to go. I walked and walked and eventually found myself on a park bench, sitting by a little statue of a goat. Fog came up the river and muffled the city.

On the next night, June 11—my wedding anniversary—Hank showed up. His cousin had postponed the wedding, he told us, because she came to her senses. But a reservations glitch had left him without a hotel room. The tall ships were in town, so our hotel had no vacancies and neither did any others. I didn't speak up about it, but Brian remembered that I didn't have a roommate on account of my snoring and volunteered me to let Hank spend the night in my room. However, my room didn't have double occupancy. I pretended not to think anything either way about that. But when he piled his stuff in, the exhilarating smell of his hair quickly filled the tiny room. At such close range, I knew I would give myself away. I wished I *could* give myself away. I couldn't keep my eyes off his arms. They were as solid and strong as steel-belted radial tires.

"I'm putting the game on," he announced, just after sliding his bags up to the edge of the bed. He settled down into the recliner. At the desk, I found a copy of the morning paper and skimmed the sports section so I could have a conversation with him. Talking to him meant I could look at him. Out of the office, Hank's hair fell casually over his forehead. His honest round eyes peeked out from behind his disobedient bangs. Even though he liked cheap beer and could talk your ear off about race car drivers and turkey shoots, he was soft-spoken and easygoing. He'd read books by philosophers and knew the names of artists and the parts of plants. It made me like him more to find out that he wore boxer shorts with pictures of trucks on them and the words FILL 'ER UP written around the waistband. "Don't laugh," he said with a bashful smile. "My wife got them for me." I made a dumb comment about wives to stomp out any suspicion. Man, I could have looked at Hank until I died.

The game was baseball. As we chatted, I made sure that I looked at the TV screen sometimes instead of staring at the sprouts of hair growing out of Hank's boyish chest. I wanted to stroke them, to move my hand across the gentle curves there, then down his side, to grasp his love handles. And then.

Annie called. I apologized to her again for the untimeliness of my trip and wished her a happy anniversary. To soothe my guilt, I guess, she said it couldn't be helped. We talked about celebrating the following Monday. She asked me how my meeting with Minister Mike had gone. "Good," I said, hoping she wouldn't ask for details. "I feel sorta better." Cheryl got on the phone and yelled that she loved me before she went to bed.

The orchids I sent had arrived, Annie told me. Annie said Cheryl couldn't stop pressing their velvety petals between her fingers. I got up and moved to the chair near the window, staring at the downy fuzz on the nape of Hank's neck as he shook his head, watching the Phillies trounce the Braves. I bet the fuzz felt like the orchid petals. Annie talked for a long time, longer than the Phillies played the Braves. But I wasn't paying very much attention. Once or twice the line went silent and she asked if I was there.

"I'm listening," I told her, but by that time Hank was slipping into the bed we would share that night. He rolled over on his side, facing away from me, and turned out the light beside him.

Eventually, the time came to hang up.

"I love you, Pookie-Pie," Annie said.

"I love you, too," I said. But as I told Annie I loved her, I directed the words at Hank. It shocked me how honestly those words came when I thought of him instead of her. I had never said "I love you" to my wife so passionately.

I admitted to myself then that I didn't love Annie. I liked her a great deal. More than that, I *needed* her. I relied on her judgment for everything. I depended on her to find my house keys, move my underwear off the kitchen table, and talk me through my worries. Her opinion meant more to me than Mama's. I enjoyed all the amusement parks and lovey stuff we did together. She had a terrific sense of humor and had given me a wonderful child. I loved the meaningful things that kept our marriage standing. But I loved stupid things about Hank. Like the shape of his eyebrows, his blocky handwriting, the roll of dough above his hips. I even caught myself loving the way he stirred coffee: three stirs in one direction and then one in reverse. "That's scientific," he explained when he saw me staring. "It gets the molecules moving." My love for him had passion in it. Compared to this crazy love, my marriage felt like a workplace.

A few delicious minutes later, I slid under the covers with him. There wasn't enough room to keep my fatness from touching his broad back, smooth except for a few moles. The heat of it felt like somebody dumping butterscotch sauce all over my body. The burning, sweet truth could have drowned me: I loved Hank—a man I didn't even know so well—more than my wife. I thought about lifting my arm and wrapping it around him, and freely breathing in the smell of his shampoo. But I might as well have started building a nuclear bomb—I would've gotten it done faster. I spent the night in a cold sweat.

In the morning, I couldn't breathe. I struggled awake and found that the comforter and sheets had wrapped themselves around my head. I clawed my way free and saw Hank watching me from a chair by the bed, his fists propping up his chin. Dark circles puffed under his eyes. "Did you have, like, a really terrible nightmare?" he asked.

"No," I said, puzzled. "I don't dream. Why?"

"Damn, Gar, they said you only *snored*. You kept me up half the night, crying in your sleep. It sounded like somebody torturing a house cat, man! How does your wife stand it?"

"Gee," I mused. "I had no idea. She's never mentioned it. I'm sorry, Hank."

"No, *I'm* sorry. I could've suffocated you when I put those bedcovers over your head."

Hank drank an extra cup of coffee and went to the day's first seminar, "Point of Purchase in the Age of Cable Television," but I stayed. I thought for a long time as I watched Philadelphia's streets, bustling with so much more purpose than my life. How thoughtless. Hank had almost suffocated me and didn't care. He had as much love for me as a street dog. He might as well have stabbed me.

Finally I came up with a solution. The hope I saw in the end of my troubles filled me with happiness. I whistled to myself as I prepared for the day. I sailed through all the presentations on new varieties and flavors of cracklings and pork rinds. Lime and chili, cheddar cheese, low fat—how'd they do *that*?

When I got back to my hotel room, I flipped through the Philadelphia yellow pages. I took the El to Kensington and bought a .38 from a rude

Polish guy in a dusty shop. He tried to persuade me to buy a set of cleaning patches and rods to go with it, but I told him "No, thanks. I don't need any of that." I was so excited I forgot to get scared. When I returned to the hotel, I still had time before supper, so I prayed.

"Lord," I said, "either change me in forty-eight hours, or give me a sign that you have plans for my life. If you don't, I'm going to shoot myself in the head at twelve noon on June 13 at the Radisson Hotel in Atlanta."

Having done that, I showered and changed into my nice clothes. I sprayed cologne behind my ears, slapped my cheeks, and smiled at myself in the mirror. Hank had already gone to supper. He'd left me a note, which I read and then kissed. I folded the paper and slipped it into my breast pocket, right over my heart. About to leave the room, I turned back and fished the .38 out of my bag. It was dark and rough; its heaviness made my palm sag. Unlike all the threatening questions circling above my life, the pistol had the weight of an answer. "Salvation," I whispered, tracing the barrel with my finger. I slipped it back into its case and hid it under all my dirty clothes.

Galloping down the stairs to the ballroom, I thought about the long train ride I would take the next day. Philadelphia Pork Rinds and Cracklings wouldn't even be over before Snaxpo started. I'd asked Rhonda to give me a night on my own in Atlanta. So I could do some man activities if I wanted.

Even in the dim light of the ballroom, I found Hank immediately. I was a compass and he was due south. He greeted me with quiet enthusiasm, and I dreamed he was a lover welcoming me back to bed. Now that I knew what to do, this new twist—love, I guess—didn't even matter. I was almost amused that it came when it did—too late.

I didn't move my knee when it touched Hank's lightly. A VP of sales at Nabisco with the weird name of Delico Organ had already started the after-supper coffee chat. But Hank—perfect, considerate Hank, trying to make up for the suffocation and failing—had saved my meal under a plate next to his. Knowing it might be my last supper, I ate slowly, concentrating on every flavor as it took a long trip over my tongue. Stuffed filet of sole. Garlic mashed potatoes. Julienned green beans almondine. And for dessert, strawberry shortcake topped with a sweet cloud of whipped cream.

II.
TRANSFORMATION OF CHARACTER

*A method of playing more than one person,
or morphing from a tree to a person, a bird to a tree, etc.*

SEVEN

On Amtrak's Crescent service to Atlanta late the next afternoon, a woman from Decatur told me how pretty she thought Orlando was. The woman and her daughter were on their way home. She had never visited Kissimmee, but she thought she would like it, too, from what I told her about the golf courses and theme parks there. She had been to Disney World, so we talked about that some. They had also gone to Sea World several years back and the daughter had petted an Orca whale.

Still thinking about my plan, I only half-listened to the woman. The woman's daughter sat with her cheek smushed against the window, humming a sad melody as industrial lots and suburban condos blurred past. The mom said the daughter would graduate from the theater program at Temple University next year. A paperback copy of a book called *Plays and Masques*, by somebody called Ben Jonson, lay split open on her thigh. That caught my eye because I'd known a kid named Ben Johnston in school. In the girl's face, I saw the kind of sadness that would end for me the next day. I smiled. When depressed people commit suicide, everybody says that they rally right beforehand. I was rallying.

The girl's mother said, "For my husband, I bought a sweatshirt with a picture of a flamingo—" Then came a loud noise like a thunderclap, the sound of hard steel scraping, and an explosion. We were thrown to the front of the car, and a pole slammed into the woman's chin. I tried to stabilize my fall with my hand and slammed against the automatic door. The mechanism jerked, unable to open. The train car pitched backward and rolled over. Snack packets, cardboard trays, and plastic cups rained on us. For a moment or two I lost consciousness. The next thing I knew, I was lying on the grass, my fingers scratching Georgia clay. It all happened in about ten seconds.

Flexing my joints, I checked for broken bones and picked safety glass from my hair. My skull throbbed. I didn't know how I'd made it out. I figured the doors had sprung open. Nobody big as me could have fit through the exit windows in the bar car. Later, I'd find that I had multiple cuts and a sprained wrist. But praise the Lord, I was still alive.

Prickly darts of fire shot out from the windows of at least seven cars up the way. They lay burning on top of each other like logs in a fireplace. A tornado of toxic smoke climbed up out of the wreckage. Our train had smashed head-on into another one—loaded with acrylic acid and ethylene oxide, the news would say. It could have been worse. Kids were playing in a schoolyard up the tracks. Bitter chemical fumes burned in my nose and throat. Covering my mouth with the sleeve of my sweatshirt, I searched for other survivors.

Aside from from the accident, it was a beautiful day. Clear, sunny, and cool, with still air and infinite visibility. Birds sang and cabbage moths darted through the bushes, like a picture from a children's book.

As I stood and came to my wits, a powerful presence made itself known to me. Jesus appeared. I couldn't tell from where. He had on the robes that you always see Him in, a close-cropped beard, and an otherworldly glow surrounding Him. But His hair was pretty dark—black even. In the flesh, He looked more Arab than in the picture books, plus He was a lot shorter than you'd expect. So I didn't recognize Him at first; I thought He might be an angel, maybe a disciple. When He lifted up His hand in the classic Jesus gesture, I thought, Darned if this fellow doesn't have the best posture of anybody I've ever met. Then I noticed his crucifixion scars—they were on His *wrists*, not His palms. That's how I knew it was Him, and I freaked out. I hollered so loud that I scratched my throat. I fell to my knees and wept, at first because I thought I had died.

"Hush, my child," He said. "Never would I desert thee."

When I heard that, I cried tears of joy, because I understood that my prayers had come true. Again and again I shouted "Jesus! Jesus!" until I lost my breath. Finally I recouped enough to ask, "Jesus?" but I couldn't form a whole question after that, because, well, where would I start? The Lord nodded slowly—of course He knew what I needed, and He'd already said His piece. Gradually, the halo around Christ's body vanished and He faded away, becoming part of the smoke that still drifted around the wreckage. Now I knew how and why I had survived. The Lord had plans for me. I took to sobbing again.

But when my tears stopped, I didn't understand what the Lord meant to communicate. I'd come over so starstruck that I'd missed His message. What did He want me to do? I searched myself for a minute or so. Then it came to me, like the lightning bolt that knocked Saint Paul off his horse.

I checked the underbrush for a trail. Down a nearby hill, two clumps of kudzu had been pushed apart to make a passageway. The vegetation rose high enough so that nobody would see me. Somebody had dug a hole underneath a nearby fence to bypass the razor wire. It even looked large enough for me to squeeze under. I jangled in my pockets for my wallet, removed the cash for safekeeping, and edged closer to the burning part of the train. I tossed my wallet into the wreckage. They would find it, burned just enough to prove my death. I thought about the picture on my driver's license catching fire. I pictured Gary Gray's face buckling and melting into hot blobs, the way a movie burns when the sprockets jam.

I thanked Jesus. Oh, how I thanked Jesus! I started to move away from the disaster, toward a fenced-in parking lot full of cement mixers. Then I heard a cry. When I looked down, I saw a woman's hand in the dirt a few yards back. Without thinking, I stepped over and grabbed hold of her wrist. It was the Decatur lady's daughter. It felt like her arm had popped out of the socket, so I scooped her up and dragged her out from under a piece of the wreckage. A bright red stream flowed from a wound on her other arm. I yanked off her sock and bandaged the cut. Moments later, it was sopping wet.

"Don't worry," I said to the girl. "Help is on the way." People from the shopping district on the nearby road had rushed over, but farther down, on the other side of the train, where the worst damage had occurred. I could hear the commotion. This side had only a small group of trees and a series of factories, and nobody had arrived to help yet. The girl and I waited in the long shadow of a toppled car.

Since I was such a heavy person, I couldn't imagine climbing to the top of the train car and waving my arms. "That's a very pretty blouse you have on," I said, trying to keep the girl calm. She reminded me a little of my college friend Joy.

Once I helped her, I would make a break for it. But then Cheryl's face appeared in my mind, giggling at an affectionate purple dinosaur we had seen on TV. Immediately the gentle laughter I imagined sharing with her got to me, and she became the gatekeeper of my soul. Was her spirit inside this injured girl, begging her daddy to reconsider the plan? Or was the Devil putting her image in my mind to distract me?

Thinking I heard somebody coming on our side, I took a few backward paces to look. I stepped on something brick-shaped and lost my balance. It was the girl's paperback. At the same time, I saw a group of samaritans marching down the little hill, probably toward the area of thicker smoke. Dressed in plaid shirts and baseball caps and carrying axes, their hasty but careful movements let me know they were part of a rescue operation. I reached down for the book and it sprang open. Balancing it in one hand, I put it in front of my face to keep my identity secret and dashed toward the group as quickly as I could. Peeking around the pages, I steadied my direction. As I ran, I hollered at the samaritans to follow me—a girl needed help.

The group leaped into action at the sight of the girl. Her eyes had rolled back into her head. Fortunately, everybody was too busy to ask me any questions. I held the book in place. After a few quick glances under it, I felt sure the girl would survive. A kind, red-faced woman from the group spoke to her loudly and sincerely. Two of the good old boys spread a sheet out at the girl's side and lifted her onto it. They didn't seem to know where to take her at first. The remaining pair steadied the operation and searched the area for more wounded. They shared a comment comparing the scene to Vietnam.

I took small steps toward a parking lot beyond the fence, thinking the rescuers might notice me before I could excuse myself. Even though

Jesus had shown me the way, I felt ashamed and scared to do His will. I considered throwing the book down and forgetting about the whole thing. But I had lived for a very long time as I appeared that evening, hiding my true face under a pile of false actions. I couldn't bear it any longer. Leaving behind my dishonest life was the only option. And Jesus had given me my only chance.

Much later, some pessimistic type said that I must've seen the Lord because of head trauma from the train wreck. But to me that proves it more. Because maybe belief does come out of your own mind, but how does that make God not real? Folks see evidence of God's work everywhere they look—they live on the evidence. Heck, they *are* the evidence. Disbelief's like saying that the phonograph isn't real because it came out of Edison's mind. Could be that vision of Christ was like a safety valve God put into the head when He invented the head.

Sirens howled, coming closer. The girl woke up and moaned loudly. My heart warmed to see her conscious again, but I pretended not to hear. I set off on a course away from the railroad tracks, away from the sirens. As I scuffled down the dirt path toward the parking lot, I thought I heard one of the men ask the other who I might have been.

My sweatshirt got stuck on the fence as I went under it. I tugged at the cloth with everything I had. Then, after a yank that practically tore my soul in two, I pulled it free and scrambled across the lot, out of breath. I'd ripped a big hole in the sleeve and scraped my forearm, but I made it.

I jogged across that parking lot, past rows of cement mixers covered in white dust. When I passed each one, I felt like something just as heavy was leaving my distressed mind and floating away. I exhausted myself running. The front exit of the lot was open to the main road, so I sped through it, following a grassy path. Hustling along next to the road, I got nervous that somebody had followed me.

Though my heart throbbed in my chest, and enough sweat ran down my forehead to sting my eyes, I picked up the pace. Trucks and delivery vans zipped past me in both directions. A shudder of relief made my head tingle. Not only had I made a clean break with my painful past, I had saved my wife and daughter from me. I really did think that my secrets were poisonous to my family, like a bum appendix about to burst. At first that kept me from feeling a lot of doubt about doing as the Lord had ordained.

I reminded myself of how Jonah sacrificed himself to the sea to save his companions on the ship. But where was my whale?

Soon I had to slow down on account of feeling lightheaded. I walked for about forty minutes until I came to a strip mall.

The accident had happened in a town called Duluth, about twenty miles northeast of Atlanta. By the time my walk ended, I had reached the next town, Norcross, a Mexican part of Georgia, believe it or not. Many of the signs on stores were in Mexican. I got the sense that I hadn't just escaped my life, I had left the country, too.

A mile or so down the road, I spotted a restaurant called La Valentina. For a few minutes I stood outside the restaurant in the parking lot and caught my breath, nervously turning to make sure that nobody had seen me. Gradually, I stopped panting and stood up straight. I brushed the dirt off my clothes.

The restaurant had a festive atmosphere, even without many customers. I smelled garlic in there, and tortillas warming up. Despite my hunger, I made a beeline for the restroom. I plucked the mess out of my hair, rolled up my torn sleeve, washed out the cuts on my arm and face with soap, and dabbed them with a paper towel to stop the bleeding. I walked out looking more or less presentable. It didn't seem like a restaurant that cared much about your presentation anyhow.

In the dining area they'd draped striped poncho-type blankets over the chairs. Tissue papers with complicated designs cut out of them hung in a string across the back wall. The top half of the wall was made of mirrors, and they'd taped up a bunch of heart-shaped decorations around the counter. Only one customer sat at a small table, a man the color of a peeled potato wearing a grease-stained jacket, smoking and guzzling a beer. Mexican trumpets played softly on the radio.

Jesus had created this situation so that I could start my life over without hurting my wife and daughter. Annie and Cheryl would never know that as a husband and father, I was a complete fraud. They would grieve at first, I knew, but now they could carry on with dignity. Our neighbors would think of them with sympathy and caring, not rumors and scorn. They'd never have to lay my pictures facedown on the home entertainment center.

I began to think of everything that happened to me as another communication from God. The hearts on the menu meant that He loved me.

Trumpets sounded when angels had something to say. These signs made me smile and stop and rest, shaking my head with awe and gratitude. God really could do anything, the way I'd believed as a child.

Full of excitement, I sat down and thought about what to do next. What would be my first meal as a new man? What different choices would I make to show Him how I had changed? How could I express my thanks to the Lord through the things I did in the new life He had given me? It made me shake my head to think that I'd really met Jesus and had really been born again. I felt sure now that the Lord would change me into a normal person so I could go back to Annie and Cheryl. I didn't think I would be away for too long; just long enough to get over my problem. It's tough to go back and piece together my logic. My mind was jumbled; my body in shock.

The man in the jacket paid me no mind. He got up and turned on the television. The accident had already made the news. From the report, I found out that lots of people had been injured, but so far nobody had been killed, even in the big explosion that happened after everybody got out. Not even the engineers. That made it clear that the accident had served one purpose alone. It was a message for me.

The waitress had teased hair and penciled-in eyebrows. She came by with a plastic pitcher of ice water, shaking her head and clucking her teeth as she poured. She handed me a menu and a set of silverware wrapped in a napkin.

"You're not from around here, are you?"

I paused. "No." I picked up the girl's book, which I'd rested on the table beside the sugar dispenser, and hid it on the chair next to me.

Several other customers walked in at once. It seemed like they worked nearby and had all decided to come together. The waitress greeted them like she knew them, and forgot about sticking around to hear where I came from.

Like a shepherdess, the waitress kept an eye on her customers. My tumbler hadn't even reached the halfway mark when she came up behind me and gave me a refill. Maybe she'll ask about my past, I thought. Since I couldn't tell anybody my background, I would have to make up a new one. Staring at the ice melting in my glass, I thought about what name to give myself and became lost in my thoughts, hoping and praying that Annie and the rest of my family wouldn't take my disappearance too hard.

Suddenly the theme song of the news broadcast caught my attention. The first thing I noticed when I looked up was the handsome newscaster. The newscaster's name—Robert August—appeared right below a square jaw, eyes as honest as Hank's, and a short, smart haircut. I took August as my new first name. I had always liked names that were also months, and all the rest were girls' names. Scanning the room for a last name, I flipped through *Plays and Masques*, but I didn't understand too much behind all the flowery language. I considered calling myself Ben Jonson, but that was almost as boring as Gary Gray. I had always wanted a name with more zing, one that made people's eyebrows go up when they heard it.

My eyes went back to the menu. I turned it over a bunch of times, searching its greasy front for a word that would make a good last name. By and by, it dawned on me that the name of the restaurant itself would make a pretty good last name if I made it sound not Spanish. It had very positive associations—of love, gifts, and chocolate candies. Yes, I would be August Valentine. I repeated it to myself softly, like I was introducing myself to a stranger. *August Valentine. Pleased to meet you.* It had an important ring to it, like maybe the name of some well-known company should come afterward. August Valentine, Merrill Lynch. August Valentine, IBM. August Valentine, CBS News.

The waitress must have seen me lay my menu down to watch the news broadcast, because she swung over with her pen and pad ready. With a strange kind of pride, I ordered things Gary Gray didn't like. August Valentine had the huevos rancheros with pickled jalapeños and spicy green sauce, rice and beans, and a coffee. When the waitress brought it, I reached for the sugar dispenser and held it above the cup. Then I changed my mind. Gary Gray had a sweet tooth. August Valentine didn't. I put the dispenser down and pushed it far away on the table, next to the pink packets of sugar substitute.

August had a taste for salty, not sweet. He enjoyed bitter, weird flavors, like olives, dry white wine, and hot peppers. August Valentine's flavors were grown-up—sophisticated tastes somebody like Mr. Price would admire.

The waitress loitered near my table, leaning her hand against the back of an empty booth, watching the television. She said more about the disaster and what a shame it was. I nodded, popping the last pepper into my mouth, then excused myself from the conversation to call a cab. With a friendly nod to the waitress, I paid my bill and waited outside.

"August Valentine," I said, like I was answering an office phone. I looked up toward the evening sky. Suddenly the air tasted like fresh strawberries, and then it didn't anymore. Right when all the streetlamps came on, a white cab pulled into the parking lot and stopped in front of me. I planted myself in the back, away from the driver. He had dark skin and a full head of white hair like my father's. Imagining how he would look in a cobalt blue suit like Daddy's, I pressed myself into the backseat as hard as I could.

"Downtown Atlanta," I told him. I had very little idea how far away that was. I had only a few hundred dollars on me. He raised an eyebrow and cranked the wheel toward the main road.

"My name's Luther," he said, turning to face the road. Like the Reverend Dr. Martin Luther King, whose headquarters are in Atlanta, I thought. Another sign from the Lord. The trip would be expensive, but I didn't want to hitchhike or to try to figure out the public transportation system of a strange town at night. He told me a few more things about his personal life before he asked for my destination.

"The Radisson?" I didn't know the name of anything else in downtown Atlanta.

Through the cab window, America went by. One of the things I'd learned while traveling so much for my job was that I was always at home in America. I liked having a base in Florida—Disney World was my capital city, not Washington, D.C.—but seeing so many familiar stores in new places always put me at ease. I counted three Elco gas stations, a Hot Tomato restaurant, two branches of Harry Moses Fried Chicken, and a Crenson's Homemade Ice Cream Bakery. My whole identity had changed, but not the outside world. I sank back into the seat, thinking my new name and pretending to read the Ben Jonson plays so that Luther wouldn't ask more questions, but that didn't work.

"So why do you need to take a cab from all the way out in Norcross to Atlanta?" he asked. "It's kinda far, ain't it?" His questions made me wonder if he suspected that I had walked away from the train derailment. Since when did a cab driver have the right to ask you a reason for taking the cab? I thought he should be happy he had such a big fare.

"My car broke down," I said, trying to sound bored.

"Did you hear about the big train wreck?"

"No, I didn't. What happened?"

We arrived in Atlanta. Many of the avenues had the name Peachtree, and they fell on top of each other like pickup sticks, so I could get lost easily. I never had any idea what direction we were facing, but being lost in a maze soothed me. I could hide here. We turned a corner and pulled into the Radisson's driveway. I paid Luther thirty dollars and got out. Welcome to Atlanta, August Valentine, I thought.

Carefully, I walked into the lobby, a huge, open atrium with balconies full of hanging plants. A skylight glowed at the top, even though it was night. This was the hanging garden of Babylon, with only the faint light of the Lord to save the decadent city. Next to me a fountain burbled, and I threw in a penny. (Guess what I wished for!) I spent a few minutes in a dark corner of the lounge, making sure that Luther had really gone, and then I left the hotel, keeping my head down. I walked out and quickly got lost.

The downtown area hadn't been revitalized yet, like it would be in the next few years. Most storefronts were boarded up, and bright green puddles of antifreeze dotted the gutters, ugly and beautiful at the same time. Paper napkins from fast-food restaurants skidded down the streets, hurrying faster than the people on the sidewalk. A whole lot of vendors sat around in booths with plastic curtains, selling cheap watches, perfume, bootleg videotapes, and handbags with designer labels. Women bigger than Mama watched me from the MARTA buses. Their eyelids drooped and their straightened hair flew in all directions. Some of them wore bold floral dresses or African patterns, but they all looked overworked and unhappy.

After some wandering, I found myself in the Auburn neighborhood. This area contained many housing projects and soul-food restaurants. A huge deserted hotel called the Savoy set the tone for the place. Though its windows had been boarded up, you could tell it had once been glamorous. Auburn looked like a perfect place to start over.

With my choice of low-budget hotels, I settled on the Patriot Inn. The plastic banner across the window said $22.50 a night. A group of people stood out front, maybe waiting for somebody. The lobby was a tiny room with a fluorescent light and one ripped-up chair in it. A woman from outside walked in behind me and greeted me like she knew me, but she just wanted to sell me something. "You're a prostitute, aren't you?" I blurted out, thinking about my Dairy Queen date with Penny. She stopped in her tracks and said, "You want some kinda prize, Poindexter?" In the doorway, an older man argued with a muscular boy in ripped jeans who kept shouting, "I said fif-*ty*, not fif-*teen*!"

The woman at the front desk had on a nameplate that said MARILYN. Marilyn had something wrong with her face bones, and I noticed it with a little jump. I hoped she didn't notice me noticing.

"Name?" she asked. I could tell from her scratchy voice that she smoked a lot.

"August Valentine," I announced. I said it slowly, with a space in between, enjoying the sound of it. She wrote it down, and I leaned in to watch her write. Seeing my new name in writing gave it more of an official reality, so I puffed my chest up a little.

"Can I see some ID?"

"My wallet was stolen."

Marilyn lowered her chin and gave me a sad, disbelieving glance. "Don't you got nothing on you? What's your social?"

"Uh, I never memorized it, ma'am." That was true. "I used to have a card, but it—"

"—was in the wallet. Of course." Marilyn sighed long and loud, like my lack of ID was a personal problem for her, but also one she dealt with from other people every day. She squinted through the safety glass. "Aw, you don't look like a troublemaker," she groaned, a little dismissively.

"I'm not," I told her in a cheerful tone, like I could prove I wasn't a criminal just by acting happy. She pressed the dash key on the computer in the ID spaces. "I'm a really nice person."

"How many nights?"

"Not sure."

"All right, open ended. Just show me the ID when you get it replaced, okay, Sugar?" I nodded. Marilyn gave me room 206. A brown carpet stain peeked out from under the dresser, and a palmetto bug scampered down the bathtub drain when I turned on the light. I soaked my aching wrist in hot water in the sink for a while, then I went to the five-and-dime and bought a toothbrush, a map, an Ace bandage, a set of hair clippers, and a three-pack of drawers.

Once I'd settled in, I kneeled on the carpet by the bed and prayed. I thanked Christ for his mercy, for not ever deserting me, and I apologized for the many times I'd assumed God had condemned me or didn't care. I shaved my head and mustache. I couldn't help giggling in the bathroom mirror at how funny I looked without hair. After everything that day I felt tired, so I lay down on the bed and watched television. Soon I fell asleep.

I woke up a little later with an erection. The orange neon glow from outside lit up the wall in front of me. The TV was still on, an episode of an adventure show I had heard other kids talking about as a child but had never seen before. I watched for a while to change my state of mind, but the lead actor was too attractive, so I changed the station. But handsome men showed up on other channels, too.

As usual, being in a hotel room in a strange city and feeling the way I felt made me eager to seek out the company of men who shared my problem. But I started to worry. Jesus wanted me to purge my desires by getting them out of my system. He wanted to show me the evils of the gay lifestyle so I could go back to my family a changed man. The Ghost of Christmas Past had done something like that to Scrooge; I felt my time in Atlanta would have the same effect on me. Just to make sure, I prayed for guidance.

Jesus didn't reappear, though, and no message came to me. Puzzled, I stood and watched the street scene through the window. Maybe something out there would give me a sign. I closed my eyes, put my palms together, and begged the Lord to show me what He meant for me to do.

I counted to ten and opened my eyes. Just then a bus pulled up to the stoplight downstairs. The whole side of the bus was covered in a colorful advertisement for a bank that wanted to lure new customers with its low fees. In red letters, the side of the bus said FREE CHECKING*. In smaller letters, much lower and to the left, it said, *FOR ONE YEAR. Next to the words, the image of a handsome businessman with the same beard and caring brown eyes as Jesus beamed out at me.

It was all right there. For the next year, I could purge the unwanted feelings for men from my system in a way that protected my family, because I would have a different name. Then could I see my way back to Christ, and I would be cured. The more I thought about it, the more sense it made. I had even heard of religious groups doing something exactly like that:Amish kids went into the outside world to experience a year of sin. Most of them went back with greater faith.

The room had become stuffy, so I opened the window. The bus pulled off and I breathed in exhaust. The heavy smell reminded me of my childhood home. Lots of people were walking around outside, talking loud in the warm evening. I could hear conversations happening right underneath my window. Everybody in town seemed happy to be alive in the outdoors that night. An electric sense of possibility rode through the streets on the breeze, so I shoved the hotel key into my pocket, closed the window, and went downstairs to join the excitement.

EIGHT

In the jumble of Atlanta's streets, I turned every which way. I checked everywhere for signs of male hangouts, poking my head into alleys, parking garages, and twenty-four-hour copy centers. Don't ask me why on that last one. Soon I became frustrated and fell back on an old trick. I followed random men, especially the ones traveling alone.

Just a few blocks from the Patriot Inn, one of the men I was trailing passed the neon sign for a dirty bookstore. He didn't go in, but I stopped. I couldn't walk into the place immediately, so I stood a few stores away, pondering my next move. Snaxpo had already started. Most other parts of town seemed full up with people carrying tote bags. Would I run into somebody from my past? I thought I should keep as low a profile as possible. Maybe leave town. But I only had a few hundred dollars from my wallet, and no income.

I crossed the street and loitered at the bus stop, pretending to wait for a bus. In a while one came, and stopped in front of me with a hiss. Nobody got off. It had stopped just to pick me up. The driver opened the door, and I waved him away with a sheepish grin. He gave me a suspicious look. The bus wobbled away.

Ashamed, I decided to go back to my room. But when I stepped into that small, glowing space, I found the Ben Jonson book on the dresser. Immediately I stuck the girl's paperback under my arm and marched back out, like an invisible hand would lock me in forever if I stayed too long. I hurried back to the bookstore.

Standing across the street, I watched the signs in its windows. Oriental-Male-Lesbian, they said. I had fully entered the world of perversions, but at least I didn't have to worry that it would reflect badly on my family, Mr. Price, or Bradley Foods. I'd only spend a year in homosexuality anyway, until the Lord wiped away those feelings.

With the book over my face, I stepped into the store, searching with the corner of my eye for the all-male pornography. As usual, I found it downstairs in a separate area. Near the cash register, I saw what I needed—a directory of gay businesses. On the cover, a white man was pulling himself out of a pool, his ropy arms and hairy chest all wet. He smiled at me, promising a new world of pleasure. The guide listed gay places all over the globe. Since I didn't want to go up to the cashier, I flipped through the directory. On a tiny map of downtown Atlanta inside, I located the cross-streets for the Patriot Inn and memorized the address of the nearest gay bar, which turned out not to be so close.

After some cab trouble, I entered a nightclub called Nutz. It was in a warehouse-type district that seemed deserted, secret, and evil, like a place where demons came alive at night. Inside, violet lights turned everybody's skin greenish and made the lint on my shirt glow. The walls twinkled, too, like a spaceship. As scared as I was, I might as well have been on Mars, and everybody in there an alien.

Concerned that I might run into somebody from the convention, or worse yet, from back home, I used my trusty book trick when I walked into Nutz. August Valentine, I knew, would have entered the bar showing his face. I tried to stop myself from slipping back into Gary Gray–dom, straightening my spine and squaring my shoulders. Near the edge of the dance floor, I found an area where a spotlight carved out some of the wall. Thinking like August, I planted myself in a spot where the light hit half my face. From time to time, I lifted up the lower end of the book and checked out the scene. I thought nobody would bother me. I reckoned I looked like a mysterious intellectual, reading.

I'd gotten there before eleven, so the place wasn't crowded. I counted seven people: three older men, a tall, skinny loner scuffing his feet by the carpet at the edge of the dance floor, and a couple of Asian men disco dancing to the *thump-thump-thump* of the music. They held hands and spun each other around.

Another fellow sat at the bar, facing out and swirling ice in a tumbler. He locked his eyes in my direction. I looked away, scared that he liked me. There wasn't anything between us worth staring at, though, and I had my back against the wall. The fellow didn't take his eyes off me even once. Nervously I shifted my weight from foot to foot. Talk to me, I thought, and I'll... I didn't know what I'd do. August Valentine would be charming and talk to the man. He'd win the man's heart without trying, and break it the next morning, I bet.

Several more men trickled in over the next half hour. The staring man had another drink. Slowly the disco ball turned, shooting out beams of light, like when God creates a new planet. I changed locations, and all of a sudden the man from the bar appeared next to me, trying to see around my book.

"She it is, in darkness shines!" he shouted. I peeked around the book. The man had big, wet red eyes and his hair was blond on top but dark at the roots. He giggled and waited for a response. Though I didn't move, he went on. He struck a funny pose like an actor doing a play from Old English times. "'Tis she that still herself refines! By her own light, to every eye, more seen, more known when Vice stands by." Belching quietly, he touched his fingers to his chest when he said "Vice." Then he waited for me to react. The disco beat shook the bar's thin walls.

"Are you calling me a she?" I bristled from behind the pages. Homosexual men called each other "she." That was one of the womanly things they did that disgusted me. August Valentine wouldn't tolerate feminine behavior in other men, even if he did things with other guys.

The man guffawed. "Silly Billy. You're not reading that book at all, are you?"

I froze. I hadn't thought much about what book it was. Casting my eyes down, I turned it quickly to re-read the cover without showing my face for too long. It surprised me to think that this Ben Jonson fellow was famous. I had never heard of him before. I flipped the book back.

The man tapped the picture on the cover of the book, right on Ben's nose. "I played the fourth pygmy in a staged reading of one of the masques a couple of years ago. I'm with this sort of dance company thing. Are you an actor?"

"No."

"Glad to hear it." The man's face was red. Maybe he was blushing. A rush of sympathy came to my heart. He was a shy person, sort of. It must have been difficult for him to approach me. "So why are you reading that book? It's sort of obscure. Are you a drama student?"

"I build sets. I've built sets." In junior high school, I meant, for one show. Seemed that every time I said something about August, I learned something new about him and myself at the same time.

"Oh! A set designer!" He exclaimed, brightening and tucking his electric blue lycra shirt into his jeans. "Delighted to meet another man of the theater. Are you fond of Jonson? I'm a big Jonson fan. Or a fan of big johnsons, or something like that." Cackling, he threw his head back. I had no idea what he meant by any of it, but it sounded funny. As usual, I was flattered that somebody had decided to talk to me, once the terror wore off, so I took a longer glance around the book. The man lit a cigarette and folded one arm across his chest, then crossed his legs and took a drag. The move made him lose his balance slightly.

"That'll teach me not to buy my shoes at Kmart!" He burst into laughter at his own joke. "I am so ridiculous!"

He told me he was the son of a U.S. Army general from Arlington, Virginia. He had lived in many places all over the USA before settling in Hotlanta, as he called it. In order to support his career as a dance/theater artist, he worked at a gift shop called Over the Rainbow in Little Five Points. He had moved out of his parents' house when he was seventeen and his father figured out about him. Sometimes he wrote or spoke to his mother, but he didn't have a lot of contact with his family.

Naturally the story moved me. I saw the sad part of my immediate future in his lack of family contact. As he spoke, I gradually lowered the book, letting it fall to my side. Sweetness and vulnerability showed in his big red eyes—the irises might be blue, I could sort of see that in the dim light. I like him, I thought, after listening to him talk about his life for a while. What had happened to him reminded me of what had happened to Annie after she ran away from home. It struck a chord with me now that

I had begun my gay year, making me think I could preserve a little bit of my old life. The man also made me laugh the same way Annie did. A warm connection between the two of them formed in my mind. Maybe gay people could be okay if they were as funny as this man. I wondered what his name was but I didn't know how to ask. My defenses melted; I turned my whole body to face him. I considered myself right lucky to have met a potential mate on my first official night out in the world of gays. I stopped short of thanking Jesus, though.

"My name is August," I finally said, at a break in his talking. I grasped his hand with an extra-firm August Valentine grip. "August Valentine. You can call me Augie." For the first time, my new identity rushed through me like real blood. A couple of days later, I would find a head shop near the Patriot where a guy made a photocopy of a birth certificate with my new name on it. "Use this bad boy to get an international student ID, and you're good as gold," he said. "Probably you could get a passport with the ID. Just keep building on the old ID. Good luck, stranger. Don't do nothing I wouldn't do!"

"August," the gay man repeated. "That's a nice name. And a hot month. I'm Miquel. You probably can't tell, but it's actually spelled with a *q*. My Anglo dad wanted Michael and my Mexican mom wanted Miguel, so they compromised. But it just looks to everybody like I can't spell."

"You're funny," I told him. He couldn't think of a clever response and turned his attention for a second. Then our eyes met.

The glow of our sexual feelings flickered between us for a moment. Then came an uncomfortable silence. Almost like he only wanted to break the pause, Miquel blurted out that he thought I was like a teddy bear and hugged me. He couldn't get his arms all the way around my body, but he squeezed as best he could. After a minute, he stepped back and admired me, which made me uncomfortable.

"What are you drinking, Augie?" he asked.

"I'm having a..." I couldn't think of the names of drinks fast enough, so I had to confess. "I don't drink. Much."

"The hell you're doing in a bar then? Oh, I get it." He smirked. "You're here to pick up cheap dates like yours truly."

"No," I protested, "I— I—" I almost told him that I'd come there to read my book, but he wouldn't have believed that.

"Join me in a tequila shot," he begged, turning the corners of his mouth down. Struck by the deep need filling up his face, I couldn't say no. I had never had anything like tequila before. It burned my throat and I coughed so hard that Miquel slapped me on the back and asked if I was all right. Eventually I straightened up and asked for a glass of water.

At 11 p.m., men in tight clothing poured in and jammed the dance floor. They took their shirts off and tucked them into their belt loops. Soon the bar became so crowded that we couldn't move around freely. As they passed, the shirtless men scratched my arms with their shaved chests. The sensation was erotic but painful, like sexy sandpaper, if that really existed. As the space filled with hunks, their beefy bodies pushed us closer together. Soon Miquel's stomach pressed against mine. I yawned—I wasn't used to staying up late.

"Bored with me already, eh?" he said. "Shall we just skip to the morning-after part?"

"What?"

"Do you live alone?" he asked. I hesitated. He had just finished a gin and tonic. He stabbed the lime with a stirrer, drank the water, and crunched on the ice as it melted. "Well, I do. My boyfriend moved out a month ago."

"Really?" I asked. "Tell me about him."

"There's nothing to tell. He was a son of a bitch, and when he hit me I gave him his walking papers. With some help from law enforcement, of course."

A six-foot-five, muscle-bound blond man wearing a leather armband bumped into somebody behind me, who spilled his drink on my lower back and pushed me into Miquel's arms.

Miquel wrapped himself around me to see about cleaning up the spill. What luck—I didn't have to take the blame for doing what I already wanted to do. Fortunately the drink had been colorless. A few pages of *Plays and Masques* got wet, but nothing was stained. Miquel turned me around forcefully and grabbed a handful of cocktail napkins from the dispenser on the bar. He sopped them against my back. By then the crowd had swallowed the man who spilled the drink.

Miquel, still mopping vigorously with the napkins, untucked my shirt and pushed the wad down into my pants. Nobody could see what he was doing around my waistline. They probably didn't care. Miquel's other hand plunged in and he massaged me. I pulled away and turned around.

"Hey!" I complained, grabbing his wrists.

"I'm just being friendly."

"That's real friendly!" I thought of leaving him there and going home, but August wouldn't have done that.

"Don't try to tell me that big behind is untouched, Polly Prude. Look me in the eye, say it with a straight face," he mocked. "Okay, a gay face will do."

I dropped his hands and edged toward the door. "I should go," I said. I guess I liked him, and I didn't want what happened between us to be like my bathroom guys.

Miquel made a face like he'd lost the lottery. "Augie! You're kidding! Don't leave. I know I was out of line. I'm just a little tipsy. And I like you. There, I said it. How could I not like you? You laugh at all my jokes." The redness around his eyes had become inflamed. In fact, his whole face had grown bright red with embarrassment and panic. It seemed like he was about to burst into tears. His arm twisted itself around mine and he pulled himself close. "When can I see you again?"

"Sometime," I told him. "I'm pooped, so I'm going to go anyhow. But not because of you."

"Oh, Augie, don't go! We were having such a good time! I'm sorry. Sometimes my hands just... Well, I used to play the piano, so sometimes they just get carried away. Roman hands, Russian fingers..." His fingers tripped up an imaginary keyboard. "What's better than roses on a piano?"

"I don't know, what?"

"Tulips on an organ!" Miquel threw his head back and hooted at the joke. I didn't get it at first. When I did, I laughed, but not enough, and when he saw that, he shifted gears. His wide forehead wrinkled and his posture collapsed like one of those plastic dolls that topple when you press a button on the bottom of their little pedestals. The music got quieter, bubbling electronically for a while, like *it* was listening to *us*. I said good-bye and started to push my way toward the door.

"If you're so hell-bent on going, can I walk you out?"

"I guess so."

We pushed our way through the flesh. Walking around for the first time in a while made me aware that I was drunk as a monkey.

Outside the club, a long line of white men had gathered, corralled by a velvet rope, their hair slick with gel. Only a few of them looked at each other or spoke. A bulky man with tattoos kept everybody from going in. Miquel and I stood for a moment at the exit, where four taxis idled. When I smelled myself, I realized how much I stank like smoke. The drivers stuck their heads out of the cabs, hoping we would be their next fare.

"So are you going to give me your number?" Miquel asked.

"I'd love to," I said. "But I don't really have one."

Miquel arched his back and sneered. "Oh, I get it. Tamiqua is waiting at home with the rolling pin, and baby Jamal is crying his head off 'cause he wants his daddy? Or maybe it's Mom—you live at home, in the closet. 'Never done this kind of thing before,' huh? No, wait—I know. You've got two lovers named Miquel with a *q* already, and they're both waiting for you in the Posturepedic waterbed. Nothing you say will surprise me, honey. Go ahead, try." He stood with his hands on his hips, like somebody waiting for a slap across the face. I made a move toward the first cab in line. "Okay," he barked. "Have a nice life, Jumbo!" His jaw quivered.

I halted. The alcohol had blurred my sight. "Why don't you give me *your* number?"

"Oh Christ. You mean why don't I throw it into the Chattahoochee River."

"You know, you shouldn't take the Lord's name in vain." I tried to smile. "Just give me your number. I promise I'll call."

Miquel laughed bitterly and rolled his eyes. "That's right up there with 'We can just sleep together, we don't have to *do* anything.' Seriously, *caballero*, do you think I just fell out of the incubator—on my *head*?"

I searched myself. "Do you have a pen?" I asked him.

"No," he replied, without checking his pockets.

"Hey, I got a pen," the closest of the cab drivers yelled. I turned to realize that all of the cabbies had been listening in. Blood rushed to my face. I searched their eyes, but they didn't look shocked by our conversation. None of them even seemed amused. The nearest driver leaned out of the window and held his pen toward us. I took it and handed it to Miquel, who picked up one of the nightclub flyers scattered all over the sidewalk.

Using his thigh as a surface, he scratched out a phone number. He paused to shake ink to the tip of the pen. When he finished writing, he flicked the card at my nose.

"Happy trails, amigo."

"I'll call you."

"And I heard that Christ guy is coming back from the dead, too."

A surge of pity for Miquel crested in me, one that made me know I would have to see him again. I had to prove to him that love existed— especially Christ's love.

My balance was unsteady. I folded the flyer into quarters and stuck it into my front pocket. "I'm going to call you, Miquel," I said in my most serious tone.

"Y'know, it's like, the more you say it, the less I believe it. Isn't that cuuurious?"

"Good-bye."

"Good-bye already." Miquel chucked the pen at my feet, turned on his heel, and stepped over to the doorman. I picked up the pen, which had rolled into the gutter between the first taxi and the sidewalk, and got into the backseat of the cab. "Thank you for the pen," I told the driver.

"No prob. Where you headed, son?" With some difficulty, he pulled the gearshift into drive and slowly started pulling away from the curb. I gave him the Patriot's address. "Tough luck tonight, eh? The homos can be worse bitches than the women sometimes, huh?" he snorted. Only half-listening, I grunted in agreement. I had turned to watch Miquel, hoping that he would see me. I wanted him to acknowledge that something real and tender had happened between us earlier in the night.

I heard the doorman bellowing, "All exits are final! Don't make me say it again!"

"But I left something in there, Mr. Doorman, sir."

"What did you leave in there?"

"My fucking dignity, that's what!"

Craning my head out of the back window of the cab, I couldn't catch Miquel's eye as he stumbled off down the sidewalk.

NINE

That weekend I shuffled through the streets of Atlanta with no destination, searching thrift shops for dirt-cheap clothes that August Valentine
would like—subdued colors, ethnic patterns—and beating myself up the
whole darn time over what I'd done. Sunday morning I promised myself
I'd end it with a phone call to Annie. But in my travels, I made the mistake of picking up the *Journal-Constitution* and reading an article about the
derailment. I was scared to read about it, but it would've made me angry
if they'd ignored it. The paper had put the article in a small box on page
12, probably because the only death was a man named Gary Gray, whose
body they said had burned up in the fire. I hadn't expected to read that
they'd notified the next of kin. My heart kicked my rib cage like a billy
goat. A steel door might as well have slammed shut between me and the
past. I found the nearest place to sit down, a brown brick wall under a
tree in a plaza full of homeless folks and people cutting through, and my
body shook. I sat there for a good while, worrying that I'd done something
monstrous and deceitful. Then I got to thinking that a deceitful monster
ought to stay away anyhow.

Watching folks pass, I asked myself questions I never had before. Who
were these people? What had their lives been like? How much time did

they have left? How many of these men and women were like me—people who weren't who they said they were?

On TV I had seen many stories about people who moved to new places and changed their identities. Most of them had done it to avoid criminal charges. I had the advantage of not being a criminal, at least. Annie and Cheryl and Mama and Daddy would understand that my death was part of the Lord's plan.

At the fried-chicken restuarant across the plaza, I bought a two-piece, extra crispy. August would have gone to a café, but Gary had to watch his spending. When I finished eating, I wiped my greasy fingers with a napkin. I wadded the garbage up in the box, set it aside, and found a pay phone at the other side of the brown plaza.

I reached into my back pocket and found the dance club flyer with Miquel's phone number on it. I took myself a long look at that number. By the second or third time, I had it memorized. It was an easy number, with a pattern of sixes and fours. I admired the rounded, readable handwriting. A fat loop sat behind the q, a circle flew above the i.

By this time it was about three in the afternoon. I thought that would have given Miquel enough time to get a good night's sleep and a late breakfast. By now he would be reading the paper, watching television, or perhaps even waiting for my call.

Four times, I dialed every digit except the last. A thin woman in a blue hat came over and stood in line to use the phone. Finally, mustering all of August Valentine's courage, I dialed the last digit.

"Please deposit fifty cents for the next five minutes," said a mechanical voice. I popped two quarters into the slot. The phone rang. It continued to ring. I counted the rings. When they got up to fifteen I started to wonder if Miquel owned an answering machine. After twenty-five more, I gave up and put the phone down. The woman in the blue hat put her fist to her hip and eyed me, and I walked away down the plaza.

After dialing Miquel's number a few hours apart at various pay phones during the rest of the day, it dawned on me that he might have given me the wrong number on purpose. I kept on calling anyway.

Calling so much almost made me lose my fear of dialing the number. At eight I told myself I would try one last time. Then twice. Then three times. On that last time, at ring number twelve, a voice answered. I nearly leapt away from the phone booth, I was so surprised. He answered! My tongue failed me. I felt like I'd bent over and ripped my pants.

"Hello? Hello! I can hear you breathing! For God's sake, what do you *want*? If you're gonna send a fax, send a freaking fax already!"

"Miquel?" I breathed.

"Who the hell is this? How do you know my name?"

"It's August. You gave me your number the other night."

He adopted the tone of a detective who thinks you're lying to him. "Oh yeah? Where did I meet you?"

"At Nutz the other night?"

"Really? Well, I haven't been to Nutz since—since—"

"Friday night! It's Augie, remember?"

"Augie? ...of course! You're the tall short fat thin guy with the dark light hair and the brown blue hazel green eyes!"

"Still funny," I laughed.

"Listen, I'm in the middle of something. Is there anything I can do for you?"

"I'd like to see you again."

"Again. That would be interesting."

"So, 'Yes'?"

Miquel hemmed and hawed on the line for a couple of moments. "I suppose it isn't like I'm pouring boiling oil on all the suitors trying to break down my castle door with their battering rams... Come to think of it, I could use a battering ram." He muttered. Static fizzed on the line. "Can you hold on a moment?"

The bang of the phone being put down on a hard surface filled my ear. Then I heard Miquel's voice in the background, too far away to understand, but near enough to make it clear that an argument was taking place. His tone had changed.

Two or three more minutes passed. A door slammed. Fortunately, I had enough coins to feed the phone. I listened to what sounded like someone walking around on creaky floorboards. Every so often I heard Miquel mutter something angry. All of a sudden he gasped, I think, and I heard his footsteps getting louder.

"You're still there?" he asked, as if only a strange person would have waited.

"Uh-huh."

"Sorry about that."

"Who was that?"

"No one. No one at all. A void where a real man ought to be. So are you free tonight?"

I couldn't believe my good fortune. I had been sure that he wouldn't want to continue talking to me. But now—I wanted to think that I had done something to cause this change of heart, but I couldn't imagine what could have impressed him so much, other than my waiting so patiently. Maybe that was another August quality, staying power.

"I think I can fit you in." As far as I knew, I had nowhere to be for the rest of my life.

"Oh, I remember," Miquel blurted out. "You're Ben Jonson! You're the fat black guy with the Ben Jonson book!"

"Don't worry, I'll leave it home tonight."

We agreed to meet at a restaurant near Piedmont Park, in the neighborhood where Miquel lived. In order to save money, I walked there. It was far, but not too far. The early evening held a bit of a chill for Atlanta in June. Light sweater weather. The overcast sky was a blue so light you could pretend it was sunny, except there were no shadows on the ground. I got to the restaurant before Miquel, so I read the menu for a while.

Twenty minutes later, he arrived. I realized that I found him handsome, especially his eyes—always so active. He was shorter than me by about a head, but taller than Annie. He hadn't shaved. A light brown beard sprouted in different spots on his face. The hairs made his pale cheeks look like sand dunes with reeds coming up here and there. His mouth was a little red crab apple, and his forehead had a musical staff of wavy lines across it. You could tell he had been unhappy a lot. But along with the grief, anyone could see his true sweet nature and honesty. When he approached to say hello and hug me, he stared up with an openness that made my body tingle.

He apologized for being late, and we sat down to eat. In the booth, he squeezed in next to me instead of across. I didn't know what to make of that. But once we got settled, he took my hand real naturally and pressed our sides and legs together. He rested his ear on my arm and shared the menu with me. "Try the chicken strips, Augie," he said.

I was uncomfortable with showing gayness in public. I asked him to sit up straight. So that he wouldn't get upset, I asked him if he could hold my hand under the table so the waiter and the other customers wouldn't see.

"Everyone here is gay," he informed me. I peered at them for a spell. I knew about gay bars, but the idea of a gay restaurant sounded ridiculous to me. There wasn't any such thing as gay food. Nope, I wasn't convinced. Most of them looked normal.

"These folks don't look gay," I said. "I don't want them getting ideas about me."

Miquel put both elbows on the table and examined his own menu. "You're with me. They'll just assume. It's called guilt by association." I took my hand away from his to unfold my napkin onto my lap.

When we finished eating, Miquel invited me to his apartment. I refused. "We don't have to *do* anything," he pleaded. "We can just hold each other." It wasn't him I didn't trust, though. I knew that if I went to his room, I'd touch him no matter how much I wanted to control myself.

"Let's please not," I said. I thought about how August Valentine would ravish him in the evening, again in the morning, and move on to the next man. Maybe I'd do that with the next fellow. Instead we made plans to see each other the next day.

As we started to date, I found that Miquel was a sensitive person. Sometimes he thought people were talking about him when they weren't. On one date I said that I didn't like people who told lies. When I had talked in negative terms about liars for a while, he shouted, "Why are you saying this? I've never lied to you!" Afterward it took a long time to convince him that I hadn't been trying to send him a message by bad-mouthing liars.

Of course, though I hadn't told the whole truth about myself, I wouldn't have considered myself a liar at the time. As far as my background, I avoided answering most of Miquel's questions too specifically. If it came up, I said very little. When Christ had guided me to leave, the past had to disappear for a while. When Miquel asked where I grew up, I said, "Down South. Sorta near Florida."

Why did a fellow always have to dodge and feel bad so he could love another fellow? My vague responses seemed to satisfy Miquel, but I wished I could have opened up. Like a whole lot of things in life, my friend Ralph J. says, love is half illusion and half real. But for the whole thing to work, you've got to make like it's all real or it washes away, quick as a sugarcube in a hot shower.

After our fifth date, Miquel dropped me three blocks from the Patriot Inn, as I always asked him to do at the end of our nights. I walked back to the hotel, took my shoes off, and lay back watching television. Klaus Rassmussen's torso glistened on the screen, lighting up the dark room. I stuck my hand into my pants and stroked myself. About fifteen minutes had passed when I heard a feeble knock on the door. I sat up instantly, afraid that somebody had found me out. Was it the maid? Or Marilyn? I owed money on the hotel bill and she had kindly let me stay for a while, but now I had to avoid her.

Without making a sound, I went over and peeked through the keyhole. It was Miquel. He had followed me. I growled like a grizzly—he'd invaded my privacy. For a moment or two I thought about keeping the door shut and letting him think he had come to the wrong place. But crime in the area had hit a record recently, and I didn't want anything to happen to him. I slid the chain off the door and opened it part of the way.

"Augie, what is this place?" Miquel asked, like I had moved to the moon.

"A hotel."

"Hotel? More like a shooting gallery! And that woman downstairs!" he shrieked. "I have nothing against freaks—some of my best friends, blah blah blah—but putting them in service professions is creepy. *¡Que horrór!*"

"Marilyn is a nice lady. Why did you have to follow me?"

"I couldn't help myself, Augie. You're so mysterious. I just had to know. And once I found out, I knew I wouldn't be able to keep my trap shut about it, so I came to let you know that I know." He tried to step in but I kept the door rigid.

"You shouldn't have spied on me. I asked you not to."

"I know. I'm sorry. Can I come in?" He stepped forward more aggressively.

"I can't be with a spy." I held the doorknob tighter.

"Of course not," he sighed. He didn't take his eyes away from mine, and they started to glisten. We stood in silence. Miquel's foot moved back behind the threshold. "But you shouldn't have to live like this," he said.

"I'm okay here. Everybody's friendly. It's nice."

"Nice," he repeated. His eyes were rounder than I remembered. His skin flushed and his lips glowed. Miquel looked right sexy to me when he was upset. I kissed him. But in private, it's well nigh impossible to kiss somebody you like once and leave it at that. So I kissed him again, and then I had a hard time not kissing him more.

When I did stop, Miquel looked up at me. He leaned over and I let him into the room to kiss me and I kissed him deeper, tasting the garlic bread that had come with his fettuccine Alfredo. He drove his tongue into my mouth like a corkscrew. We wound up on the bed, and pretty soon we were naked together for the first time.

Miquel really enjoyed my big body, romping all over it like a kid on a muddy hill. His hands went everywhere, squeezing and twisting my flesh, holding my belly in his hands and stroking it, kissing and biting my soft chest. I was real surprised that anybody could like the way I looked. He even kissed my kneecaps and licked the soles of my feet. Then he put his face between my legs. He worked his thumb up into a place that I'd rather not say. His tongue went other places that I didn't know you could go legally. Come to think of it, not much of what we did was legal in Georgia at the time.

For a good while I lay there. I had never had sex lying down with a man. I thought it would be strange, and that I wouldn't like it. It was, but I did. By and by, the hill started to move. For the first time in my life, the freedom door opened up inside me, and I found a fire blazing behind it. I matched all of Miquel's licks and caresses with two of my own. He gripped me by the root, and I took his root in my hands and squeezed it with a kind of pulsating motion that I invented on the spot. We ground our faces together so hard that the next day the inside of my upper lip was raw. At the time, I remember comparing what I felt to the first time I ever had a real *hot* hot sauce, one I couldn't handle. It was like the top of my skull flew off. I panted like a husky dog in August and worked my jaw open and shut. My eyes watered, and all the tender parts of my face burned. Miquel stared into my eyes real seriously, without any of his usual joking manner, and I stared back, and I swore I could see the whole universe in his pupils. When I reached my climax, I accidentally got Miquel in the eye. He said it stung, but he laughed, and I laughed, and we fell into each other's arms, and somehow everything outside that room felt like nothing at all.

Afterward, Miquel dozed off. I watched the lights and shadows play on the ceiling of my hotel room as cars went by down in the street. I felt lucky. I thought, I hope it stays like this. But then Annie came to mind. I don't even wish to recall the bizarre idea I had about keeping them both in my life. In the breeze from the open window, Miquel's two-tone hair fluttered, and his wet lips parted to snore. I had become August, and I would bring the lessons I'd learned from him back with me into hetero-sexuality one day.

Miquel's apartment sat on the top floor of a cream-colored house with green trimming. The floors and doorjambs had gone all lopsided with age. But it had a porch almost the size of a veranda. He'd filled the living room with movie posters, books of modern plays, knickknacks from the fifties, and an incredible collection of painted seashells. On the wall in the kitchen he had hung a big scallop shell that had been turned into a clock. He had salt and pepper shakers shaped like dice and hula dancers and a pair of monkeys wearing fezzes and a teapot shaped like a dragon. You poured the tea and it came out of the mouth.

By the window in the living room there was a chair lined with orange fur. I liked to sit in it and stroke its arms while having a beer from the wet bar. On Miquel's nightstand there was an ashtray in the shape of a girl in a bathtub and a ceramic lamp with a leopard-print shade that Miquel said came from 1955. The comforter on his bed had a whimsical cow pattern.

What a thrilling place! Annie and I had never paid much attention to furnishings. We didn't realize that we could change our home into a place of delight and happiness. We only went to Disney World.

I got a special thrill from opening Miquel's windows; the honeysuckle vine in the downstairs neighbor's garden made the air taste sweet. He teased me about how much I liked the orange chair and refused to visit me at the Patriot. The place disgusted him and he also didn't want to relive the memory of barging in on me. Instead, without bringing it up, he let it make sense for me to want to move in with him. The passion did the work.

I would say, "Are you coming over?" and he would say, "I'm exhausted," so I'd volunteer to go to his place, because going over meant guaranteed boot-knocking. I'd rather have stayed with him than alone. So with very few possessions, and dead broke despite getting August an office temp job, I joked, "I could just throw everything into a box and get on the MARTA." An interested look crossed his face, but he didn't encourage or discourage me.

Two months into our relationship, I put my things in a cardboard box and a thrift-store suit bag, left the Patriot Inn, and moved to his place.

In spite of God's plan, I'd fallen for him. I thought I'd only stay until the sand ran out of the same-sex hourglass, that I'd break up with him then. (Or rightly, August Valentine, who could handle emotional situations, would.) But maybe Miquel would get tired of me before that had to happen. From what I'd heard, male-male relationships didn't last long. Anyhow, I didn't think much on how it might complicate things.

I borrowed some money from him to help pay off my hotel bill and had nothing in my bank account for a while. When I said "Good-bye, Marilyn," to the desk clerk on my way to Miquel's place, she didn't look up from her paperwork. Because of her face problem, she always talked out of the left side of her mouth. "Oh, you'll be back," she croaked. "No one leaves here for long." Marilyn raised her head, looked me in the eye, and cackled.

Miquel and I had a dinner date that evening, and I showed up early, before he got home from work. He had given me his keys after a few dates, in case I wanted to use his apartment when he wasn't around. I put my cardboard box of belongings on the kitchen table where he'd see it and sat in the fur chair watching television, waiting for him.

When Miquel got home, he went to the fridge for a glass of water and saw the box. He came in and wrapped his arms around me from behind. He kissed me on the ear and rested the cold sweating glass on my chest. I flinched but I didn't mind. "Oh, Pookie," he cooed. My body stiffened. Annie's pet name flooded me with regret. I forced a smile.

For a while, our life together was like that moment when the waiter sets a creamy dessert in front of you, long before you have to pay. When he wasn't working on a show, Miquel would fix fancy suppers for us, grilled chicken and salmon. He would dust them with chili and squeeze a wedge of lime over the plate to add flavor. Every salad had at least one plant I had never heard of, arugula or pine nuts or daikon. I got a lesson in botany every time I sat down to eat. August memorized all the names.

On warm weekends we would drive to Tybee Island and spend hours strolling down the flat silver beach. Miquel flew kites as a hobby, so he would bring a box kite or his rainbow bird and we'd stay out until the sun faded behind the marshlands.

Savannah was too close to Charleston for comfort, though. My aunt Vietta lived there. Tybee was mostly white folks; I didn't worry about running into her there. I'd switched my wardrobe to the kind of thing that lots of gay men wore in those days: acid-wash jeans, a black polo shirt, a black belt, and Doc Martens shoes. A leather jacket didn't suit me, though. If it got cool out, I wore a denim one with a tan corduroy lining. Even with my disguise on, I'd sometimes think I spotted somebody from my past, usually a kid from high school or college. I would have to turn away without letting Miquel see.

Sometimes, in my horniest moments, I thought maybe I shouldn't go back after the year of free checking. Then I'd quickly remind myself that Christ Himself had personally made this strange bargain possible so that I could eventually live the normal life He wanted for me. My dog-eared Bible said that fornicators, adulterers, effeminates, abusers of themselves with mankind, thieves, coveters, drunkards, revilers, and extortioners would not inherit the kingdom of God. But I trusted that the Lord wiped the slate clean once you repented and gave up the behavior—what you'd done in the past wouldn't count.

When I saw my family again, I'd tell them the honest truth—that I had wrestled with my demons for a year and conquered them. Even so, I longed to get back in touch with my mother to tell her that I was alive and that I hadn't deserted her. I didn't like to think about how upset she must have been about my death. I had a quiet celebration of Cheryl's birthday for myself, sticking three candles in a cupcake at a Denny's in Decatur and blowing them out.

After living with Miquel for six months, though, I started thinking the Lord's plan was working. The wild nights of September had cooled down a lot by early February, and my attraction to him had fallen off. We hadn't had relations since month three, and now, when I watched him take his clothes off for bed, I could only think of how funny his thing looked soft, like a cigarette butt sticking out of a pinch of tobacco, and how strange it was that my lust had ever paid it any mind. Sometimes I found myself attracted to other men, though, and I couldn't make head or tail of it.

Of course I also felt bad about not finding Miquel sexy anymore. To make up for it, I agreed to help build sets for Loco Motion, the dance/theater troupe he worked with, thinking it would mean we could spend more time together and that might fix things. Gary didn't have any interest in the arts, but August felt that dance/theater troupes were more necessary than football teams. At first I didn't understand what to do, but building sets for dancers isn't astrophysics. The dancers need to use most of the room, so you keep it real simple.

The piece we worked on seemed decadent to Gary, full of randomness and godless themes. I suspected that Satan enjoyed seeing the disorder that groups like Loco Motion called dancing. Laurice, the director, had a lot of avant-garde ideas about dance. But to me, the dancers appeared to be in pain or gesturing for help. I couldn't figure out the point of it. People threw their arms and legs around like in the crazy-house. Cheryl could have choreographed it. But Laurice had studied at famous places for dance in Europe that made people raise their eyebrows and say "Oh." So had most of the dancers, including Miquel, who went to North Carolina School of the Arts. A dancer named Dakota Wong had been at Temple University, and another named Jane Rosedale had gone to Sarah Lawrence College, which was almost as fancy as where Laurice had gone. August had attended the University of Wyoming, I decided. That was far enough away from everything that nobody would know or check up on it. It turned out I never needed to tell anybody, though. August Valentine adored modern dance, and when he heard everybody call Laurice "the next Merce Cunningham" he picked up on that phrase and repeated it a hundred times before he'd ever seen a picture of the guy.

As Gary, I felt that Christ would have rather seen stories like the ones in the Bible: easy to follow and with a moral at the end. He would have paired the men with the women and had them move together gracefully. And I knew for sure the Lord didn't want dancers to perform for such small audiences. On one night, only four people came to see *Kafka Dances*, and one of them left. Hiding your light under a bushel was a sin.

Miquel always got home exhausted. If I had to go to a rehearsal, I'd come home exhausted with him. Usually I would have to go to one of my new office temp jobs the next day, too, so we would just kiss goodnight and conk out.

The weekend after *Kafka Dances* closed, we were sitting up in bed Sunday morning. A woodpecker outside knocked against a tree in the backyard. I got up and stared at it to make it stop, and I thought maybe it understood, because it stopped. But then it started again, so I tried to block it out.

Back in bed, Miquel demanded to hear my opinion of the show, which he had done several times before. I made a Frankenstein monster out of a few phrases I'd heard. "Laurice is the next Merce Callahan," I said. "Her work is incredibly of the postmodern. In fact, it's almost pedestrian." I squinted; August could sometimes be extra serious.

"Cunningham," he sighed. "You think it's silly, don't you?"

"It doesn't matter what I think, Frosty," I said, petting his arm. I called him that because of his hair. How had he heard the truth under my B.S.? He turned away and pulled himself out of bed. From my perch I could hear him knocking around in the storage closet. Soon I heard him in the living room, vacuuming the shag rug. He vacuumed to drown out everything unpleasant in life, especially things between us.

I wondered if Miquel was jealous—not love jealous, but work jealous. This kooky fellow named Rex Messina, who ran a theater company called Concerned Relatives, had asked me to be assistant director on his next show. In this world, manpower was short, so people changed jobs all the time. You built the set on one show and performed in the next. You didn't hold auditions; you asked your friends or people you met at parties for help. My first impulse was to say heck no, but then I figured August would jump at the opportunity. So I said yes, even though rehearsals happened from 6 to 10:30 most weeknights and then for five hours a day on weekends. Rex was independently wealthy, so he paid his actors and crew, and I needed the extra income. Loco Motion had squat. They didn't even have the nonprofit status that lets you apply for money from foundations and the government. During *Kafka Dances*, Laurice hosted a benefit party at a restaurant downtown with long breadsticks and calla lilies in glass vases, but none of the important people she invited showed up, and the company only broke even.

Miquel started using the time between shows to go on weekend-long antiquing or kite-flying trips without me. He liked furniture, I knew, but suddenly it became an obsession. He discovered faraway warehouses that dealt in sixties furniture like the hair chair I liked so much. A few times, I went with him to help move things. But lifting all that furniture left me with an aching back. "You don't have to come with me," he said. "Don't do it out of obligation." By the time we got home, he'd shout that my attempts to please him were "belittling."

Despite my efforts, I couldn't convince Miquel that I liked the dance/ theater world. He thought August was a phony who had gotten involved because of him. My new wardrobe made him doubt my sincerity. The starchy shirts, high-waters, and Hush Puppies from the Salvation Army that I used to clunk around in had amused him. Now I wore those only to my temp jobs. Those clothes made me seem naive, and I suppose naive people are easier to understand and love.

"You just don't seem like yourself in those clothes," he'd say.

I had a hard time believing that the clothes I wore could make somebody love me or not. "Are you serious, Frosty?"

Miquel didn't like having to bring up all the emotions in our relationship, because he thought I should learn to do it, too. But his silence got too angry for me to fill. I couldn't explain all the trouble I'd gone through to be with him—I still had to keep my whole life before I met him a secret. To me, a same-sex relationship had to be twice as strong as a straight marriage, because the whole world was against it happening—sometimes even other homosexuals.

Of course, not having sexual relations played a big part in our troubles. Even when we did go to bed, I wouldn't do the thing gay men are famous for. It scared me to be either person. Getting it would hurt and giving it would be dirty. I wanted everything else a whole bunch before it happened, and during, but afterward it got me pretty sick. The smells of another person and the liquids coming out of them made me queasy and a little afraid. Probably it was all the sex diseases they talked about in the media.

Words from the Bible still rang in my head a lot, too. I could hear the preachers on WGWT and see a certain Reverend Rodney Pinckney in my memory. He was one of Mama's favorites; we'd gone to see him when he came near to town. Rev. Rodney growled, shouted, and sweated, preaching against men with men, quoting Leviticus like they all did. "Both of them have committed a abomination!" he'd yell. "Praise God! They shall be put to death! Praise God!" With a little white handkerchief, Rev. Pinckney would wipe the sweat off his brow and then slip the cloth back into his pocket. "Death!" he would shout one more time, hopping on the balls of his feet as the congregation cheered.

These memories burst out powerfully, but I still had trouble thinking God would kill people for falling in love. In my new church, the Stop Suffering Center down the street from the Patriot Inn, a woman preacher kept repeating, "Dios es amor!" (I went to a Spanish church for a while to avoid running into people from my past. I didn't tell Miquel, even though I needed him to translate, because it would have seemed suspicious and he wouldn't have gone anyhow.) The woman said *Dios es amor* so many times I had to nudge the lady next to me and ask what it meant. She said "God is love," and nodded, in agreement with herself. I nodded, too, but I got to wondering. Now, if that was true, why would He make you fall in love and then strike you dead for obeying Him? Clearly, the Lord didn't mind the *love* part of homosexuality. It was the *sex* part that got Him mad. If two men could love each other without giving in to animalistic urges, I bet they could still be good Christians. I took that as the main message for my year of free checking.

One morning during an intimate moment, right after I'd started working with Concerned Relatives, Miquel and I got into a fight about the famous thing. Desperate to avoid the issue, I commented on his anatomy in an immature way that I regret to this day. At first, Miquel didn't react. But the next night he decided to sleep on the couch.

I didn't connect the two events at first. "What are you doing putting all the sheets on the couch, Frosty?" I asked. I expected that if I started a fight we would make up before it could get too angry.

"I can't sleep in there. All that noise from the space heater. *Coño!*"

The winter had been a little chilly, but it didn't get below freezing too often in Atlanta, so we had only used the heater once.

"We can just turn it off."

"I don't want you to be uncomfortable."

"I won't be. I like it a little chilly. You're the one who likes it warm in there in the first place." He said nothing. After a few more nights of back-and-forth, I got the hint. But by then it was too late to bring up the real reasons for him moving out of the bedroom. Underneath what we said to each other, secret knowledge dripped like dirty water in a sewer.

The new arrangement made me sad and happy at the same time. I still loved Miquel, and now I had won. My intimacy problem was solved, and we could still live together until the time came to say good-bye. The transition would make our separation less painful. According to the schedule in my head, it would only be another three months.

August had held his ground pretty well, with only a few slip-ups. That Christmas, Miquel had given me a white terry-cloth bathrobe to match his own. After a burst of happiness and thanks, I thought of Annie and Cheryl, as I often did in my happiest moments. It was my first Christmas without Annie since we'd met. I pictured my wife and child sitting on our dark green corduroy couch, Annie's shoulders hunched over in front of our miniature plastic Christmas tree and crèche.

"You're probably wondering why Mommy's crying," I imagined Annie saying to Cheryl. My daughter lay next to her in a pink jumpsuit, sucking and chewing on a pacifier. "Christmas was such a special family time for me that whenever it comes around, I can't help thinking of your daddy, honey. I miss him so much. I know God has a plan, but why did the Lord take him away from us?" Annie wept. I cried for real, wishing I could tell her about meeting Jesus, and all the stories from my new life.

A surge of doubt and regret hit me as I stroked the terry cloth of the bathrobe and pressed it to my cheek, and though I tried to force it out of my face, Miquel didn't miss it. He tried to get me to tell him what was the matter. I shrugged off the seriousness of my mood swing, but he didn't like that. Anger crinkled up his face. Smoking and sipping a glass of chardonnay even though it was 10 a.m., he started to tell me about a few of the problems he had with our relationship.

Miquel said it frustrated him that I wouldn't share certain parts of my past and my emotions with him. The word *withholding* kept coming out of his mouth. That led him to talking about the new sex problems he had with me. First, I didn't want to have as much sex as he did. Then, I didn't want to touch him anymore.

This time, instead of the famous thing, he complained that I wasn't comfortable kissing him. "You don't open your mouth, and you won't use your tongue." I braced myself for him to open the discussion into talking about the famous thing. Even a person as thick as me could tell that he was working his way up to it.

But he didn't. Since Miquel hadn't told me he had any sexual problems with me other than the famous thing, I'd assumed that everything else was fine. At first, things had been fantastic, but somehow, getting to know him better made me more uptight. Now I couldn't deny his accusations. I had never thought of myself as good in bed. But I didn't think I was as bad as he made me sound. After this dressing-down, I knew I'd been mistaken.

Miquel talked about our problems for a while without stopping. I didn't respond. Instead, as I watched his lips move without hearing anything, I thought about how nobody teaches you to make love. You're expected to find somebody who has the same thoughts about lovemaking as you do, but if you want to be moral you have to fall in love and marry them before carnal knowledge. So why doesn't anybody say anything about their likes and dislikes before they get into bed? They just make up the whole thing as they go along, like the herky-jerky improv dancing in Loco Motion's rehearsals. There must be an awful lot of misunderstandings about that, I said to myself. For a second I thought about my parents in bed. Then I waved the thought away like a pesky fly.

Miquel paused, pursed, his lips and asked, "August, who are Annie and Gary?" He held up a wedding ring he had discovered at the bottom of my side of the sock drawer. We had engraved our names on the inside.

The shock of hearing those names from his mouth was so great that I didn't react at all outwardly, but my windpipe was fixing to twist itself into a knot. I sat in the fur chair and stroked away the sudden rush of adrenaline. "Oh," I said casually. "That came from a pawn shop. It's real gold. Probably worth a lot." I waited for him to react, but he didn't. I hoped he didn't notice my shaking leg, so I wiggled it deliberately. "Why were you going through my stuff?"

"We live together. You're a slob. Your stuff is all over my stuff. I can't help it."

"Why can't we just accept each other as we are, Frosty? Without name-calling, like 'slob.' Don't you trust me?"

Eventually he softened. "Oh, Augie Bear. I'm sorry," he said, stumbling over the rug on his way toward me. "I didn't mean to upset you, I just want us to communicate better." He sat in my lap and we kissed a while.

The cuddling hadn't led to sex in a while, but this time it did. We wanted to prove that we forgave each other, and we did it by throwing our bodies at one another, eagerly, violently, like these bull elephant seals I saw on a nature show once. It always made sex good when you had a motivation. We needed to do something, anything, to keep from talking.

TEN

"Concerned Relatives makes silent plays that deal with universal struggles," Rex, the director, told us on the first day. "Not mime." Even though he'd hired me as an assistant director, I had to do what he called "the training," so sometimes I'd wind up doing a theater exercise or two. In one of the routines, Isla Moroff, a short Russian girl with gray circles around her eyes, played a peasant woman, and two of the guys—tall, big-headed boys from deep-country Georgia named Miles and David—played her sons going off to war. In another, I acted as the Everyman, who goes through all the events of a normal human life in a few scenes. Many of the things I had done for real, like growing up, falling in love, going to work, getting married, and becoming a father. While I did it, though, I couldn't shake the feeling that somebody else should have played that part. For somebody black outside and damaged inside to do all those things felt wrong and not normal, even to me.

Other folks had trouble with the rehearsals, too, but none of it ever fazed Rex. In the middle of one of our marathon rehearsals, Dakota Wong, a Chinese American lady who had quit Loco Motion with me to work with Concerned Relatives, became frustrated with how much time the process took and quit in the middle of a rehearsal, tearing her plaster mask apart and storming out dramatically. Rex sat there for a moment without moving.

"This is good," he announced, once her footsteps had faded down the staircase and we heard the door slam downstairs.

Erica, who hung on every one of Rex's statements, laughed and said, "Rex, you're amazing. You could find the positive side of a fatal plane crash."

In a calm voice, he replied, "Increased safety measures."

Now, Rex had seen this documentary movie that he liked called *Titicut Follies* that you could only see at the Georgia State library. The movie showed a day in the life of a bad mental institution. I mean *real* bad. The inmates there were always naked and abused or wearing hats and singing show tunes. He showed us the movie and said that he wanted to use it as inspiration for a new piece. The theme would be madness in the individual and in society. I wasn't too keen on the idea, seeing as I didn't think the Lord wanted us to dwell on negative things like that, but I didn't think I'd have to perform, so it didn't make me any nevermind.

Rex called it *The Titicut Project*. Rehearsals extended far into the night, past 11 p.m. Miquel didn't think this was fair, but I couldn't confront Rex about shortening rehearsals. To satisfy Miquel, I tried to get home faster instead, but it didn't work all the time.

One evening, two weeks before what all the performers hoped would finally be opening night, three more company members quit. Everybody paced around, fretting and twisting up their hair, except Rex, who fixed his eye on me.

"August," Rex said, "you've done the training with us, and it's too late to start someone new, so you'll have to be in this show. I'm just going to redistribute the roles, as we did when Dakota left. Everything will be terrific. The show will be a huge hit."

Panic stabbed me. *In it?* I was the assistant director, I couldn't perform. I wanted to tell everybody that I couldn't do it because I was too fat to be a dancer, or I was a devout Christian. But that would have made them either laugh or try to convince me that I was wrong. They would talk down to me with pity and I would look like an idiot.

"I've never been onstage," I said, laughing nervously between every phrase. "I can't fill in for three people." I thought I saw Erica smirk about my size when I said that. Sometimes I needed to behave more like August Valentine and I just couldn't. Fear yanked on my nerves, like somebody pulling the emergency cord on a speeding train.

Rex stood up, his chair making a scraping sound on the floor. He wrapped one leg around the other and bent his torso to stretch his hamstring. Although he wasn't facing me when he bent over, he continued the conversation. The rest of us—Erica, Spitz, Isla, Helene, and I were the only ones left—watched him intently.

"I really can't budge on this, August. If we're going to open in two weeks, there simply isn't time to train anyone else. We'll modify the choreography to accommodate your body type, but you're going to have to do it. You can't let me down." Jumping into August's skin, I bit the bullet.

Over the next two weeks leading up to the show, my stage fright didn't worry me nearly as much as my fear of trying to be a dancer, since I disliked my body so much. All the movements in the show were awfully complicated and specific. I had to learn exactly when to nod or stick out my elbows. I had to listen to the music and move my body along with changes we heard. I didn't have the technical experience to learn the movements the way everybody else did. I felt like Hyacinth, the hippo from *Fantasia* who dances in a tutu.

Luckily for me, Rex was also interested in artists who used chance as a way to make their dances. He'd included some improvised parts in the show to demonstrate that. One of them was the dervish section. It happened at the climax of the piece, two thirds of the way into the two-hour show. When the dervish section started, Isla would toss her curly hair over her head as a signal. After the signal, the tight rules of the rest of the choreography would disappear for a while. The performers could follow our creative energies and take the spirit of the performance in whatever direction we chose.

The dervish section didn't even have a set time period. In order to end it and go on to the next choreographed section, there had to be agreement among the dancers. To let everybody else know that you wanted to end the improvisation section, you would go upstage, to the back of the space. You would move your mouth angrily and point your finger with your arm stretched out. This was a movement made by a mentally damaged inmate in the film who gave long speeches about God that nobody could understand. Erica had to stand on her head and sing praise to the Lord at the same time. When everybody was mouthing and pointing upstage, the choreographed part of the dance would continue.

"In theory," Rex explained, "this performance-within-the-performance could go on forever—maybe for the rest of your lives—unless you all agree to end it." He laughed. "This is when the show becomes about the madness of society. The way in which real freedom in a society made of individuals becomes an asymptote, a 'moving toward' that never arrives at a pure expression of itself, whatever 'self' means." To emphasize these difficult qualities, Rex said we should change our minds frequently about stopping the dervish section.

Just before the opening, Rex added an hour and sometimes two to the regular rehearsal times, and stopped giving us Fridays off. I prayed that Marco, the guy who owned the big warehouse where the show would run, would get a paying customer for the space so that we could have more time, but that didn't happen.

Finally, on May 10, opening night came. I didn't want to appear onstage. Secretly I hoped nobody would come, even though I had put a lot of cards out on tables in coffee shops and record stores and at Over the Rainbow. As nervous as I was about the audience, I feared Rex and his judgment even more. He was always kind, but some of the things he said could be devastating because they were true, and the truth always hurt more if someone said it in public. After one run, my only note from him was "Slower." But more often he would sit in the stands during the run-throughs and notice with a sharp eye every small thing that I did wrong. But he never brought up that I might fail, and nobody had ever treated me so well.

The first night, Miquel came with Jane from Loco Motion. I asked them to sit in far chairs so that I wouldn't get nervous. I needed to feel like nobody was watching me, or I would freeze up. Although I knew it wouldn't make other people happy, I was thrilled that the house wasn't full in the huge Atlanta Lumber space.

As a concept for the set, Rex spread out the seats in the warehouse. Each chair had a few feet of space around it. Rex said he wanted to "force a physical confrontation between the so-called sane individual and his mentally ill counterpart." People who came to see *The Titicut Project* were immersed in the environment of the mental institution. Rex said it would "emphasize the isolation and stigma experienced by the insane." Putting viewers in with the performers would also make them question their own sanity. I wondered if dancing could really do all that. In the end, I had to trust all the people who had studied in famous places.

We wore bodysuits that made us look naked, and white masks. I had a bodysuit close to the color of my skin but not quite dark enough. Isla, in her funny accent, said it made me look like my skin had been ripped off.

We moved around the raw space in ways that were sometimes graceful but mostly not. Some movements threatened the audience, but none of them hurt anybody. Even in the sunny light of the upstairs rehearsal space, I worried that *The Titicut Project* would scare folks. From the depressing nature of the movie, I should have known. But when we moved it into the musty warehouse and played all the creepy music, I felt in my heart that *The Titicut Project* really did tempt Satan. That might explain what happened that night.

See, I had a lot of nervous tension before the curtain went up. When I get real crazy nervous I belch a whole lot, so I tried to do it quietly, away from others. I also used some breathing techniques for reducing stage fright that Alexandra Spitileri, the dancer we called "Spitz," had taught me. During the first few minutes of the show, I nearly passed out from nervousness. But as I watched other people dance to help me remember the steps, I had less time to concentrate on the fact that people were watching me and that Rex was judging me. So I got through the difficult part. The strict choreography kept me waiting eagerly for the dervish section, when I could see what it felt like to really let loose.

By the time we hit the three-quarter mark, I had become more comfortable doing the movements. The mask worked like Rex had said it would: it gave me a feeling that I could do anything I wanted, with no consequences and without anyone watching. Unlike most of the rehearsals, we didn't stop and start the dance—we had to go through the entire thing, like the first few moments of a roller-coaster ride after the highest drop. I couldn't keep my eyes off Isla, who had a solo during which she used her graceful neck to approximate a patient who had a twitch that made him nod and shake his head. At the end of that section, she tossed her head forward and the dervish section started.

A storm of excitement broke in my head. Crazy drumming from Burma started on a tape. Suddenly, adrenaline washed through my body as I spun around the space. I got dizzy, and for a moment I forgot my clumsy, bulky body. Aping stuff I had seen in the film, I stomped on a part of the floor that made a drum sound with my bare feet. I did many jumping jacks. I pretended that somebody was bringing me downstairs to feed me through a tube in my nose. I lay down on the floor and flopped like a fish. I imagined that somebody had cut my face while shaving me. Another movement from the film I did was to bend my arms and wave them in front of me like somebody doing the dog paddle.

Soon Erica and Helene stood upstage, making silent speeches and pointing. The freedom door had opened inside me—but what a time for it to happen! I couldn't stop myself from expressing the emotions that had been in my system for such a long time. I pushed away the seat behind me with my foot. Then I kicked all the empty chairs off to the side one by one, until I had formed a pile. Then I picked one up and beat it against the concrete, thinking of my father's abuse, the nasty note, Annie and Cheryl's innocence, my own shame and guilt, and somehow, worst of all, Hank! How I longed even now to run my fingers over the down at the nape of his neck! Lord, I could have screamed, *What is so wrong with that?*

I didn't notice for a long time that Isla, Alexandra, Helene, and Erica had all moved upstage. But their agreement that I should stop only made me more upset. I knew that in silent pantomime theater we weren't supposed to speak or make noises. But in that moment I forgot myself. In the film, a man goes into his cell, squats facing the wall, and screams. Just like him, I bent my knees and let out an unearthly yell like somebody possessed by the devil. Maybe this moment should go on for the rest of our lives, I said to myself.

But then in my vision, a skylight opened up in the warehouse just above me, and a light came down on me and touched me everywhere. It rolled over me like an electrical storm compressed to the size of one person, devastating every small town up and down the coast of my body. Like sheets of rain and hail pummeling me, purging all the bad emotions.

Finally exhausted after fifteen minutes, I fell down. I wasn't sure what had happened. In church, I'd have known what that light was. But in a theater, it had to be something else. But what? Did one of the kliegs go out? Or did it have to be anything? Exhausted, I clambered up and took my place among the other dancers upstage. I shook as I moved my mouth and pointed with two fingers. The performance continued. At the end, the audience applauded politely and filed out. I thought we deserved more praise.

"Gosh," Miquel said afterward, in the booth of a twenty-four-hour fifties diner with stars on the chairs. A stack of pancakes puffed in front of him. "You were really *on* tonight, Augie." I told him about my vision of light and he nodded, but didn't comment.

Most people hadn't said anything about the performance. In fact, most people who showed up hadn't even stayed long enough to see the dervish section. Rex had said congratulations to us backstage and given us all roses and cards, but he seemed none too happy about the way the show had gone.

Miquel peeled the wax paper off a pat of butter, scraped it off the cardboard with his knife, and slid it between the cakes. "Honest, I've never seen anything like that before."

"Did you really like it?" I asked him, smiling. Then I remembered our earlier fight about how I couldn't criticize dance pieces and thought maybe I shouldn't have asked. I changed the question around. "Do you think I could be a dancer?"

Miquel's eyes slid from my face to his napkin. He grabbed his glass like a kid and took a sip of water. "It was really intense, the whole thing," he kept on. "I'll bet that's why so many people left. They couldn't stand it. The intensity. I'm going to have to rent the movie it's based on. Jane had to go, by the way. She told her boyfriend she'd meet him at 9:30 before she knew how long the show was going to go. She said to say mazel tov and tell you how much she enjoyed it and how bad she felt about having to leave."

Miquel had brought me a bouquet of carnations for opening night. They had been grown in food coloring, and the flowers had turned blue and green and purple. The bouquet rested on the far part of the table until the waiter brought my Belgian waffle with ice cream. I moved the flowers to an empty seat. From doing the show, my hands still had a nervous kind of lightness in them, and I breathed easily. I was acting a little drunk, even though I hadn't had any alcohol.

Gazing at the carnations, I said, "I wish you had brought me those on a regular night," as I poured syrup in a zigzag motion, filling the waffle's squares.

Miquel cut a wedge of his pancake stack. He paused when I talked. Still holding the knife and fork up, he shot a pained glance at me, then sighed and put down the utensils. "Augie," he said. After a few moments he picked up the knife and fork again, poked a chunk of sausage to go with the pancake, and stuck the food into his mouth. A song played on the radio that said "Turn, turn, turn," with words I recognized from Ecclesiastes.

I knew he was about to bring up a relationship topic but I had to wait until he finished chewing. "I suppose there's a lot we need to talk about," he finally said as the song finished.

"Don't break up with me, Frosty," I blurted out.

"Jesus, you're paranoid! What gave you the impression I was winding up to do that?"

"You shouldn't take the Lord's name in vain."

"Oh, for Christ's sake! When I go to Hell I'll be really surprised if it's for taking the Lord's fucking name in vain. *Mierdakotexteta*!" That word was his father's way of trying to curse in Spanish.

"Miquel, I get so scared for you when you talk like that." Soon after we moved in together, he had demanded that I stop trying to save him after I bought him a religious self-help book for his birthday. "Catho-lick!" he said, waving the book in his hand. "Got it? I was raised Catholic, and I'm never going back *there*, let alone evangelical Christianity. I'm plenty crazy as it is."

I held back from proselytizing now, but I couldn't stop completely. I wanted the best for his eternal soul, plus I felt like Heaven wouldn't really be Heaven without him. "I don't want you to go to Hell."

He touched my cheek jokingly. "You're not fooling anyone with all that piety. Without Mr. Jesus, you'd be as big a whore as me. You're gonna be my cellmate, Angelcake. It'll be *Kiss of the Spider Woman 2*!"

"You're drunk," I said, leaning forward and whispering it to him like gossip.

"Good call. And Mars is the goddamned Red Planet, FYI." He removed a new pack of cigarettes from his back pocket and banged them on the Formica, then ripped the red thread off with his teeth. Once he got one lit, he took an extra-long drag, leaned back, and exhaled like somebody expelling his ghost into the air above him. I watched for a while, a little disgusted, and then coughed. It was a real cough, but it sounded fake. I could tell from his expression that Miquel thought I was pretending, but I couldn't help that.

"You s—" he began.

"I what?" He said nothing, but lowered his chin so that his pupils went halfway under his eyelids. That razor-sharp stare spooked me.

Miquel flagged down the waiter, a thin boy about eighteen years old. He had a strong jaw and eyebrows like charcoal marks under wavy gold hair. Neither of us could keep our eyes off him.

His smile was an ear of white corn. "What can I do for y'all?"

Slowly, one corner of Miquel's mouth curled into a smirk. He turned to the boy, and if he'd done with his hands what he did with his eyes, he'd be in jail now. "What can you do for me? Geez, I don't know where to start," he purred.

I kicked him under the table and missed, jamming my toe against the chair. The waiter heard the noise, but only chuckled nervously and scratched his arm.

"Do you guys need a couple of minutes?"

"With you? Maybe a couple of hours." This time my foot connected with Miquel's shin and he yelped like a coyote in a snare.

"I'll— I'll just come back, okay?"

I took the opportunity to grab the waiter's forearm. It was tan and covered with silky yellow hairs. I had been watching the vein in his biceps appear and disappear as he flexed his arm to lift his pad and pen. "Oh no," I said. "He's ready. Tell him what you want!" I twisted my face at Miquel and clenched my jaw. I held the warm arm until the boy deliberately stepped out of my reach.

Grumbling so low that the waiter had to ask him to repeat himself, Miquel ordered a Bud Dry. It arrived quickly, and he sucked at the bottle like a newborn chugging at Mama's tit.

"So what should we do?" he asked into the empty bottle, making him sound like a lonely guy in a basement.

"Do about what?"

The waiter passed by and Miquel raised his hand to get his attention.

"Another," he said, pointing to the empty beer bottle.

"You've had enough," I told him. There was still a swallow left in the bottle. I slid it toward me. Slyly, Miquel eyed the waiter's rear end. "Why is it that homosexuals can't think about anything but sex?" I wondered aloud. I still thought of this time as a good transitional phase. When my year ended in a few months, I'd only want his companionship, and I'd enjoy straight, normal sex forever more. It made sense for the Lord to do things this way.

Miquel tapped an ash into his water glass. "Are you kidding? Can you imagine how ugly the world would be if homosexuals didn't think about fashion and architecture *more* than they think about sex?" He swung his shoulders crudely, shifted in his seat, and pulled hard on his cigarette. Miquel knew I didn't like it when he acted womanly, so he played it up. He pursed his lips and stroked the back of his neck as he rested the cigarette on the edge of his saucer. The waiter placed the beer in front of him and he followed the boy's behind with his eyes again, this time in an obvious way, to mock me.

"See?" I gestured at the guy's butt, like it somehow proved my point. "Why does sex have to be so important?" I growled. "Can't we just cuddle?"

"Darling," Miquel said, "I can cuddle with a cocker spaniel. With a human being, I want some ack-*tion*." Miquel started to sing and make feminine dancing motions with his hands. "*I want to live! Ack-tion, I got so much to give. I want to give it, I want to get some too!*" Then he made some cat-like noises, still singing. I wanted to slide under the table and die.

"Shut up, Miquel," I snapped, with August's gumption pulsing up my neck. People turned around. He pretended I hadn't said anything. He continued to sing, even raising his voice a little. "Please, cut it out."

He sang directly to my face. "*I love the nightlife, I've got to boogie, on the disco round, oh yeah!*" Dancing with his shoulders, he leaned across the table and stuck his lips out to provoke me. Furious, I stared at the knife on my plate and wondered what would happen if I stabbed him right then. Probably nothing, since it was a butter knife. In any case, I felt that Jesus didn't want an attempted murder charge for me.

Eventually Miquel got to a point in the song where he had forgotten the lyrics. He finally shut his trap and finished his pancakes. I watched him chew, thinking I'd never liked how he opened his mouth partway when he ate.

"You think we can be boyfriends without ever having sex, don't you?" he suddenly exclaimed, his mouth still full.

"What's wrong with that?"

The waiter returned. "How's everything?"

"Terrific!" Miquel responded, suddenly chirpy.

"Another Bud Dry?"

"Don't you have anything stronger?"

The waiter laughed nervously and rocked on his heels. "Beer and wine is it, I'm afraid."

Miquel rolled his eyes. "Okay, I guess." The service bell rang and the waiter sprang off toward the kitchen.

"Wouldn't it bother you when I brought other guys home?"

"Other guys?"

Miquel played with his hair, thinking of a response. I wanted to hug him, but I could see that he might have wanted to hit me in the face. "Wait a second. You want to be celibate *and* monogamous?" He snorted.

"Yes, Miquel. I want to be celibate *with you*." That way of putting it came to me right then. It sounded so original and holy. August, for all his worldly ways, never forgot what Christ had done to make him possible. He and I remained devoutly Christian. In Atlanta, nobody found that too strange.

Miquel's face muscles tensed. "That's almost funny," he said. He looked away for a while, like we were stranded in a rowboat and he thought he'd spotted land. Violently, he smashed his cigarette out in his syrup and immediately lit another. He stuck one in my face and I held up my hand to decline. "Jesus Christ deluxe with onions."

He knew that comment would get my goat. A rubber band in my head popped. I slammed my open palm down on the tabletop and the silverware jingled. "Stop it! Stop it!" I shouted. "You know I can't stand it when you blaspheme against the Lord!"

Miquel turned away when I yelled. When he turned back, his eyes were red and sore. His lower lids were filling with tears. It was the wounded look I found so irresistible. He rested his chin in his palm, covered his face, and wept. Then he turned all the way around. His back shook, but he didn't make any noise. That made me very uncomfortable. I touched his spine to comfort him and he wriggled away. I pushed a napkin into the cage under his elbow, but he shoved it back through with his opposite hand. I watched the waiter more passively now, and the other customers, too. Some them were still looking at us out of the corners of their eyes, in case we flared up again.

It took a few minutes, but Miquel raised his head, found the napkin on his own, and wiped his eyes. He breathed in deeply and let it out slowly. Soon I could no longer stand the lull in the conversation.

"Hey," I said in a soothing voice. "Think of it this way. You've already made it most of a year without having sex. This will just be a continuation." I announced this while Miquel cried himself out, as a compliment to his stick-to-it-iveness, a way of thanking him. "Why is it all of a sudden such a huge issue?"

The waiter dropped a wet bottle of beer between us in passing. Miquel raised it to his lips and soon all the liquid vanished into him. He straightened his spine, put his elbow on the table, cupped his hand, and rested his cheek in it. "No," he sighed. "I didn't make it almost a whole year without having sex, Augie." His lips formed a pathetic smile.

My first thought was that he had figured out a way to trick me, the way Annie had done with my nightly erections. I opened my mouth to say something like that. Then the truth sank in with an ugly chill.

It didn't matter to me that I would be straight soon. In fact, I completely forgot that aspect of my future in that moment. Besides, if Miquel had done this six months earlier, he might have transmitted some awful disease from whoever this was. What good would straightness be then? It might mean I could never have another child, or I'd die.

But then I panicked, imagining Miquel kicking me out of his magical house into the street, like Adam out of paradise, or like my daddy banishing Joe from our lives forever. I would never stroke the furry chair again. My name hadn't been added to his lease. I had no legal right to be there. I couldn't afford much else on a temp's wages. Shivers passed through me when I thought of what Marilyn had said about the Patriot Inn. *No one leaves here for long.*

The question almost refused to leave my mouth. "Did this happen— Is there a time— When...?"

"Last week, when you were in tech." The technical rehearsals had lasted from 9 a.m. until midnight for four days. "I was lonely."

Slightly relieved, I took a big breath for the next question. "Is it— Are you in... Is he another man?" I sipped my ice water, hoping I could survive whatever fate he dealt me.

Miquel spat a "Ha!" across the table. "The last experience I had with a woman was when I left the womb."

In sketchy terms, he described an encounter a lot like my bathroom stuff. With Annie, I had put my times with men into a box that said Not Cheating. But I thought differently now that I was in her position. As angry as I was at Miquel, it came to me that letting him see me get upset would mean admitting to myself that I'd done something wrong when I skipped out on my family. Miquel might also decide to leave me. Annie's presence grew so strong in my imagination that I could almost see her sitting in the empty chair, clutching the bouquet of carnations. Hoping that she would have mercy on me if she ever found out, I went against my boiling rage and tried to forgive Miquel. This is what Christ would have done, I thought, if His boyfriend— Of course I couldn't finish that twisted, blasphemous thought.

"It's okay," I said.

"It's okay," he mocked. "You're full of shit, Nelson Mandela. Next you're going to give me another sermon about turning your cheeks, or the Prodigal Son's loaves of bread or something. It's not okay and you know it."

"What do you want me to say, Frosty?"

"Get angry! Get jealous! Show me that I matter to you, dumbass!" Then he muttered, almost to himself, "Why do you think I did it in the first place?"

Way to turn it around on me, I thought. I couldn't do any of those things on command. Cleaning my fingernails with my other fingernails, I waited for an answer to come into my mind. The sounds of pop music, the dishes clattering in the kitchen, and the hum of conversation grew louder in my head. The noise drowned out the sensitive reaction I wished I could have.

"Calling people names isn't polite," I managed. "I should be the one calling *you* names." The waiter skidded past with two plates resting on his sleek forearm. Leaning into his path I asked, "Can we get the check, please?"

Miquel folded his arms and glared at me. The busboy cleared our dishes away carefully, like somebody defusing a bomb. Somehow the restaurant had emptied out without my noticing. Miquel lit another cigarette and blew smoke rings. His open mouth looked as rude as a blow-up doll's. The expression on his face rejected me, and the more I thought about the day when we'd break up, the more tears came to me, like a locomotive whooshing up the tracks. Miquel's mouth opened and he reached across the table to touch me. I let him stroke my arm.

"Oh my God," he said. "I'm sorry."

Once I raised my head and blew my nose, I figured we ought to turn the conversation back to more pleasant matters. "Did you really like the show?" I asked.

His words slid out of his mouth as carelessly as the smoke. "I hate Rex Messina's work," he said. "He's so pretentious. He thinks he's the Dalai Lama of Mime or something. As if mime needed a Dalai Lama. What mime really needs is to be put out of its misery. The only good thing about that show was the lighting design."

These words crushed me more than his confession. I wanted to ask, Not even me? But by the time I understood how much more that comment had struck home, we had paid the bill, so I got up and went to the parking lot instead. The night was sticky-warm, so humid I felt I could almost drown in the air. We got halfway home before I remembered the carnations. Miquel never mentioned them, and I never reminded him.

On the last night of *The Titicut Project*, the cast went out with the audience to celebrate. The run hadn't ended so well. The last audience had fewer people in it than the cast, one of the saddest things that can happen in the theater. The only folks there were a couple who worked with Helene and a trio of young guys who piled out when we still had ten minutes left. Helene's friends wanted to congratulate her by taking some of us out to dinner, so they stayed and watched us break down the set and lights.

Rex gave us notes, and Spitz took to grumbling that the notes didn't matter, since the run had ended. Everybody else knew Rex would disagree with that, because for him, notes had as much to do with life as the show. If he could have followed us home and given us notes about what we did there, I bet he would have.

Afterward, the cast went to one of those Japanese restaurants where you sit on the floor. Raw fish didn't strike my fancy. Instead, I ate a big plate of shrimp tempura. At supper Rex fairly talked his jaws off about the value of doing shows without an audience. He sat at the head of the table and his nose vibrated as he spoke.

"Small audiences don't bother *me*, guys. On the contrary," he said. "For centuries, writers have made their work for one person at a time to receive in silence. There's a timeless beauty to that phenomenon of silence and a one-to-one audience—even when it happens in a theater." Ever since Miquel insulted him, I believed him less, and that night his conversation just sounded like an excuse for nobody showing up. It even took him a good while to get Erica on his side; she carefully sipped green tea and pouted instead of agreeing. I felt real bad for all of us.

Miquel had the car that night, so Isla gave me a ride home. I threw up the tempura on her dashboard. Once I'd helped her clean up the mess and gone upstairs, it was 11:30 on a Sunday night. I quietly slid the key into the lock to keep from waking Miquel up. I dumped my tote bag by the shoe area, as usual, pushed off my Doc Martens, and yawned. The empty couch soaked up pink light from the streetlamp outside. Usually Miquel left the sofa draped with linens, but not that night.

Probably he hadn't come home yet; some nights he went out to drink. But when I tried the door to the bedroom, it was locked. This was unusual, since the door to the bedroom didn't have a lock. I jiggled the knob gently at first, then pushed hard on the frame, but it wouldn't give. Miquel had probably moved the dresser to block the door as a way to take back his bedroom. That made me angry. He could have asked for the room back and I would have said yes. How could I say no? I just lived there; it was his apartment.

I was fixing to pound on the door and wake him up, but in the silence, I heard a steady knocking. I had heard that sound before, whenever I sat up and leaned back too far watching TV in bed. But this noise came regular as a clock. Between the knocks I heard an animal-type growl, not a noise I had ever heard Miquel make. The growl turned into a voice I had never heard either. It told somebody to do a bunch of things—nasty sex things. It called out names and cursed and told the other person that he enjoyed everything like a dirty whore. It could have been the voice of Satan. And the person hearing it had to be Miquel.

Well, I flipped. I knew Miquel didn't agree with the celibacy idea, but I thought I had let him know that I didn't want an open relationship. He hadn't said he would or wouldn't, but having sex and moving the dresser left no doubt. Did he even care where I slept? I pushed myself against the door, but even my bulk couldn't budge that hefty dresser. By that time they'd built up momentum, and I don't think Miquel or the satanic man heard the sound. Maybe they ignored it.

Standing and listening for a bit, it dawned on me that I didn't want to meet that growling man. He sounded pretty mean. I was angry, but he sounded like a man with a knife or a gun. By and by he would finish his little adventure with Miquel and they would come out of that room. I didn't want to see his face, or any proof of their carnal passion. Maybe this really was the Devil. Thank the Lord, I thought, I'm going to turn straight one day and leave all this behind.

I spread linens out on the couch. They smelled dryer-fresh, so I put them up to my nose like in a commercial, then tucked the fitted sheet around the pillows and pulled the flat sheet up to my waist in the night air. If I slept, the growling man would be gone when I woke up to get ready for work, and I could avoid a fight. I lay down and closed my eyes.

Of course I couldn't sleep. I lay on my back with my arms folded, fuming, then opened my eyes and watched the ceiling fan spin. I made myself dizzy trying to follow just one of the blades with my eyes. The only way to avoid them once they got done, I knew, was to leave the apartment. Since I was having trouble sleeping already, it made sense for me to get up, get dressed, and take a walk through Piedmont Park. So that's what I did.

The night was clear and balmy, with a half moon, a few stars, and a breeze. God had polished everything in the sky. The heavens had a silvery sparkle that hung on all the edges of the leaves and the blades of grass, too. I stuck my hands into my pockets. I sure wished we had a dog. Walking him in the wee hours would have kept me from looking so suspicious. Holding a leash would've given me something to do with my hands. Everybody knows about idle hands.

Now, by this time, I knew what kind of men hung around in public parks at weird times of the night without dogs. Though I couldn't see any of those men on the street once I got up to the park entrance, I couldn't stop myself from expecting, maybe hoping, to see them. A young lady in a sports bra whizzed by on her bicycle. Across the street, a couple were having a disagreement in a hatchback. I saw a homeless man sleeping on a bench with his head under a crumpled newspaper. Satan whispered in my ear how exciting it would be to find a man and have a sexual encounter. But that would make me no better than the sodomites I'd left upstairs. If everything went according to schedule, I'd start to want physical closeness with a woman pretty soon. Maybe this bad luck with men had the purpose of weaning me off them.

Soon after I entered the park, another set of footsteps mixed with the sound of my own. When they got loud enough, I turned around and saw a muscle-bound white man leading a dachshund on a leash. The dachshund scurried ahead of the man. His red T-shirt fit tight around his barrel chest, and his trousers were made of a shiny black material, probably leather. My blood started to race, so I turned away quickly before he got too close. But I couldn't stop myself from taking another look.

Even though the situation frightened me, something about this guy seemed friendly and familiar. He raised his chin and said hello under his breath. I did the same, trying to imitate him exactly. His bent nose made his face more interesting. I slowed down.

"Great night, ain't it?" he said. I turned and he stopped, so I had to stop, too. We had paused in an area where a huge magnolia tree blocked out the glare from the lamps on either side, as well as the moonlight. The man might have stopped there deliberately. The shadows of leaves made us look unfinished, like the night had bitten chunks out of our bodies.

"I suppose so," I said. "Almost like room temperature." My nervous laugh hopped out of my throat. The dog stood on his back legs and steadied himself on my shin, peering at me and wagging his tail.

"That's Percy," the man said. "Short for Percival."

"Oh," I replied, bending to stroke the dog's neck.

"He's always looking for something to hump. Just like his daddy," he laughed. I recognized the man's accent as one from South Carolina. He could have been Euge McCaffrey grown up. In fact, I longed for any connection to my past so much that I thought I might be trying to turn the guy into him with my mind. But I couldn't see him so well, and he hadn't recognized me. Wouldn't Euge have remembered? A powerful surge of homesickness swelled in my heart. I longed for my old bad life as I hadn't since the Lord had shown me the way. That gave me the courage to ask the one question you simply don't ask until all the business gets done.

"What's your name?"

"Lance."

He wouldn't admit to being Euge. I had no idea where I stood, so my spirits quickly sank. "You from South Carolina?"

"No. Why?"

"No reason. You just sound like you're from there is all."

"Near there." He backed away casually and tied the dog's leash to a nearby bench. "You wanna take a walk? Like a nature walk?" Without waiting for an answer, he left the path and went up a small hill to another tree that stood farther back, in a darker, more secluded area. When I hesitated, he checked behind him to make sure I was following. My legs moved up the path almost by themselves.

His back narrowed into his waist and flared at the hips. If Euge had slimmed down, fixed his teeth, and dyed his hair, I thought, this could be him. I recalled that Euge had three blemishes by each corner of his mouth. This guy had four. Or had Euge had four? Why had he told me his name was Lance? Why was he denying me? Some gay friends of Miquel's used special fake names when they picked up guys. Could this so-called Lance have been like me, living under another name? My eagerness to find out the truth became unbearable. But in order to know for sure, I would have to risk opening the door to my old life.

When I joined him again, he had found a cozy spot on the far side of the tree. He leaned against the trunk, seductively. The natural canopy of broad, flat leaves made it so dark that I almost couldn't see him, but the dim light gave his body a faint aura. Following the light with my eyes, I realized that he had unbuttoned his jeans and pushed them to his thighs. He called out to me.

"Hey, you. Dude." Since I couldn't decide on which name to tell him, I didn't fill in the name part. "Over here." I got closer. I pushed aside my guilty conscience and opened my mouth for a kiss. But instead of pressing his face against mine, he took hold of my shoulders and pushed down on them real hard. One by one my knees bent and made contact with the mud. A little defiantly, I kneeled too far from where he stood. I made it so that he would have to step forward to get me if he wanted me to suck him off.

"Isn't your name Eugene?"

"Nah."

"McCaffrey? From Charleston? Gizzy's your mama? Had lymphoma? Maybe she passed?"

He let out a breath that was a laugh and whispered like somebody else might hear. "Who I am don't matter in particular, do it? If you need Eugene McCartney to get off, that's cool, I'm Eugene McCartney. Just hurry up and polish my knob, dude. Percy's got issues. Too much longer and he'll start howling to beat the band. Now get sucking."

While my knees got waterlogged, I remembered the early tutoring sessions when I had been paralyzed in this same position. Scooting forward, I started doing the exact thing I had been so scared of back then. Up and down, like a piston, until my jaw ached and almost got locked in the open position. Of course, I watched myself for signs of excitement, and I was proud to find very little. Soon, I was sure, normal, healthy desires would fill the cavity that homosexuality had hollowed out in me. From there, I patted myself on the back for evening the score with Miquel. Only then did I figure out that I'd left the house with that mission already.

The meeting came to an end, and I stood up. Lance didn't pay me any mind as he raised and zipped up his jeans, yanking on his belt loops to adjust himself. But he had stepped into an area of brighter light, and I got to look at him for a good long while.

"I swear, if you ain't Euge..." I breathed, almost frightening myself. "It's me. It's... Gary." I'd gone almost a year without admitting who I was to anybody. Saying that name frightened me just about as much as it would have to admit my same-sex desires in public. To get his attention, I grabbed his arms and shook him. He curled his hands around and took hold of my wrists. My sadness from before came right back. "Gimme your wallet, Gary," he said, making it sound like a friendly request.

I laughed, in part because in my mind, robbing me confirmed that it had to be Euge. But he didn't move any part of his face.

"I was your math tutor," I reminded him.

Down the hill, Percy took to yowling. He sounded almost like a human child. The sadness in me mixed with disconnection. Though I had shed my secret past, I always felt that it still belonged to me. The blank expression of this man in the dark, pretending to be a stranger, proved that my past could forget me back. Of course, I didn't think of that then, because at the time I was terrified. Lance shook my hands impatiently. "Fucking gimme your fucking wallet, dude!"

He let go of my hands so I could pull my billfold out of my pocket. I put it down in his palm. He stuck it in the back pocket of his jeans and tore off down the hill. Something made me want to stop him, to tell him that everything in my wallet was phony except the seventeen dollars inside. If he looked at my ID, he wouldn't even think that I was his old not-friend-anymore Gary Gray. But before I could catch up with him, he'd untied Percy, wedged the dog under his arm, and run off.

"Euge!" I called after him. The name, echoing in the empty park, seemed to rattle the night. I tried to chase him, but quickly became short of breath. Could it mean something that I'd lost my fake ID?

Exhausted but still in a hurry, I exited the park. I thought I should try to cancel my August Valentine credit card before Lance/Euge had the opportunity to use it. Also, I didn't want anything else to happen that night. Nothing had turned out well all day. Sometimes only a fresh morning can stop a lousy day from stinking.

On the porch at the apartment, already stunned and ashamed, I realized I didn't know if I'd stayed away long enough for the growling Satan to leave. Miquel never took a long time to finish making love. But every pair of partners has a different way of doing their business. Maybe the growler could do a sex marathon, or a tri-sexalon—in the bedroom, the bathroom, and the kitchen.

I inched the key into the lock and turned it real carefully. I made sure to open the door so slowly that nobody inside would feel a draft or notice the outside sounds coming in. On tippy-toes, I went back into the apartment and shut the door. I found the cordless phone and took it onto the porch to deal with my bank. I began to think that the theft of my ID by somebody from my past meant God was about to change me back into my old self. But I didn't feel ready, especially after the incident with the guy in the park.

When I went back into the apartment, a white light glowed from the kitchen. Mumbling came from the area where we had a card table and some chairs by the window. I heard a calm version of the growling man's voice describing an episode of *The Simpsons*. Miquel said "Yeah" and "Uh-huh," and spoons tinkled against the sides of tumblers.

As I crossed the living room, I avoided the spot with the loose board that creaked. The linens still covered the sofa. Jealous and disgusted that Miquel would let this guy use our breakfast nook for their after-sex chat, I crouched down and slid onto the sofa in a way that kept them from seeing me. I pulled the thin sheet over my head, but it didn't block out any sound. I tried the pillow but it made my face hot.

"Do you have a boyfriend?" I heard the gruff voice ask.

"Um—"

"'Cause I saw a bunch of pictures on the dresser of you and some black guy."

"Oh, August. He's... well..."

"Bet he's got a big one. You like that, huh?"

"No, he doesn't live up to the myth. I stay with him because he's fat."

"Oh? But I'm not fat. Am I fat?"

"No, you're not fat. It just means he won't leave me." I couldn't tell if Miquel meant that or if he said it to make fun of the growling man. By now I should have been able to tell when he was serious. It bothered me a whole bunch that I couldn't. The growling man laughed, and I hated him as much as I could hate anybody I didn't know.

"But you don't sleep with him, do you? I can tell."

"Are you some kind of psychic?"

"It's like a pattern with me. You're the fourth guy I've gone home with like that this month," he said, laughing. "I'm in an open relationship, too. That means you can fuck anyone you want, as long as it ain't your boyfriend."

"Actually I think they call that a hot, open-faced relationship," Miquel replied.

"So where is he?"

"I think he came in, put sheets on the couch, and went out again. More tea?"

"What? Is he coming back? Is this caffeinated?"

"Lemon Zinger generally isn't. He fears confrontation, so probably not for a while. Sugar? And I mean, so do I, but I fear it a lot less than celibacy."

"No, thanks. On the sugar *and* the celibacy." He guffawed at his own joke.

Something about the sound of the iced tea gurgling out of *our* Tupperware jug and splashing over the ice in one of *our* glasses for *him* brought me to a state of primal rage. The liquidy sound was like an insult on top of on their horrible chitchat.

"Miquel!" I shouted. "I'm *here!*"

He muttered something obscene, and I heard the sound of him clearing the card table.

"Hi, Augie," he said, his voice suddenly sweet. He must have been putting the dishes in the sink. The tap gushed.

"I'd better go," the growling man announced. He hurried through the living room to get his clothes from the bedroom. I lifted my head for a second just to see. He was naked, his white back and buttocks glowing in the streetlight even though they were covered with hair. Just like the Devil, he reminded me of a goat. It was hard to imagine Miquel's taste including men as different as him and me.

Miquel came and sat on the edge of the sofa, wiping his hands with a dishtowel. His body blocked my view as the growler rushed out of the bedroom and fled through the front door with his shirt still over his head. Miquel said good-bye without looking at the man, finished drying his hands, and folded them in his lap. He talked to me like your mama trying to make everything all right. "It was just this once," he said, grasping my calves like they were oars and he meant to row them away. "I'm sorry. I just couldn't stand it anymore."

"Frosty, you promised."

"No, I never promised."

"Promise now."

He frowned and switched to massaging my calves, pinching each hair and pulling upward gently. "I can't do that."

"I guess it doesn't matter," I sighed.

"What do you mean?"

I took a breath, thinking I should tell him about the year of free checking. But I knew that because he didn't believe hardly anything I told him, there wasn't much of my story that he wouldn't criticize. There weren't too many facts in my life then, so I had to hold everything together with a heap of faith. I had always considered faith more important than what's what, anyhow.

"I mean, I guess this is okay. We can have an open relationship."

"You're really okay with that?"

I said yes, knowing that I had pledged never to have sex with Miquel again, and thinking that the point wouldn't matter in couple of weeks. He kissed me and made a speech to thank me, about the importance of making sacrifices in relationships. First he called them important, then he called them beautiful. As an example, he described the plot of some German play where an army general lets himself get killed in order to save his lover. I nodded, half-listening, dreaming about the day in the near future when I would return to my wife and child as a real man—a heterosexual man—and see their faces light up, delighted to have me back. It would be a real miracle, a resurrection.

ELEVEN

June 12, 1993 arrived—the day I thought God would start making me straight. Miquel considered this date our anniversary, because he counted from the night we met. The anniversary I thought of as real had taken place the day before. The slow breakup of our relationship and all the lingering memories of Annie and Cheryl made it hard for me to completely honor the date Miquel thought of as ours to celebrate. I bought him an anniversary gift of a stuffed Hobbes tiger. The night before, he'd told me he'd planned a complicated surprise for me.

Miquel woke me up that morning from my new place on the couch. He had insisted on taking back his own bedroom. I agreed because I thought it would make my transformation to a straight man easier on him. As soon as I woke, he had me sit up. He blindfolded me so that not even the tiniest sliver of light could get behind the black cloth. I listened to him prepare things in the kitchen. He turned on talk radio so I would have something to listen to.

I wanted very badly to see if I had any attraction to women, and I was frustrated that I wouldn't be able to tell yet. For men, attraction has a lot to do with looking. Women's voices on the radio didn't arouse me. I imagined sexy women's bodies attached to the voices, but that didn't do anything either. Taking off the imaginary women's clothes in my head wouldn't have been the Christian thing to do.

Miquel escorted me outside and into the passenger seat of the car. Since I couldn't use my eyes, I became more aware of my other senses. I heard far-off traffic, birdcalls, and the wheels of a tricycle creaking down the sidewalk. In the air I sniffed the oniony scent of freshly mowed grass, with pollen and dog poop under it.

Miquel drove around the neighborhood in a maze-like pattern, trying to confuse me, and then we got on the highway. I had no idea which highway or what direction we were going in. Mostly I thought about how to break all the news that I had for him. First I would say that I liked women, once I made sure that the Lord had taken care of that. Then I would reveal my real name to him. Then I would let him know that I wanted to return to my old life and my real family. It seemed like a lot to confess at one time. I wondered how he would react. He liked old thriller movies where lovers turned out to have secrets, so maybe it wouldn't be so bad.

Miquel talked about celebrity gossip for most of the trip. Liza Minnelli was one of his favorite topics. She had recently had back surgery again. About an hour and a half later, the traffic became stop-and-go, and I could tell we had almost arrived somewhere. The car stopped, and the engine sputtered and shut off. Miquel walked to the other side of the car and guided me through what I reckoned was a parking lot from the strong smell of gas and warm rubber. I wanted to open my eyes to discover I was in Disney World. But I knew we hadn't driven long enough to get there.

I had a depressing hunch that Miquel was taking me to Six Flags. He knew I loved amusement parks, but he must have thought that I loved all of them equally. I hated Six Flags. Six Flags didn't have any cartoon characters of its own, or a history, or a community to go with it. It only had flags—six of them. Its roller coasters didn't have personalities or fairy tales. Sometimes they were just big, boring corkscrews. You waited for an hour and a half to ride once, forward and backward. Sometimes the ride only lasted a minute. How could Miquel know me and forget how I felt about Six Flags?

As we arrived at the gate, Miquel told me to stick my fingers in my ears. I didn't do it all the way. Then he paid my admission. I heard the gatekeepers welcoming people to Six Flags Over Georgia. When we had passed through the gate, he went behind me and slowly undid the knot in the blindfold. The black ribbon fell from my eyes and onto my chest. I masked my unhappiness and non-surprise with a shout of pleasure and wonder. "I had no idea!" I said. Pressing my palms together and raising my eyebrows, I gasped right in his face. I wondered if he could see through my overdone act. But he didn't even notice how fake it was. From his expression, I could tell he was proud of himself for getting me there without my knowing. With so much news for him at the tip of my tongue, I thought I should keep from spoiling things.

"What do you want to ride first?" he asked, clasping my shoulder. The excitement in his question made me think that he might want to rekindle everything from the beginning of our relationship. A cloud of dread floated across my day. I loved Miquel. I didn't want to let him go. It didn't have anything to do with him being a man or a woman. Sometimes I'd caught myself wishing he were a woman, so I could stay with him and be August Valentine and forget Gary Gray ever existed. These feelings started to pass through me as often and as strongly as the sense that I needed to go back to Annie and Cheryl. Most everybody leads at least two lives, I bet. Generally, folks keep the second one locked up in their head, but without that dream life, you can't have a future. Me, I mixed them together so much that I couldn't tell which version of me was truer than the other. But being with a woman came with maturity and acceptance, things I needed pretty badly back then.

I decided to ride Rolling Thunder first. Rolling Thunder dropped you down, did a loop-the-loop, and came back backward. It had an hour wait. Standing in line, I spent a long time thinking about something that had happened to me in the Magic Kingdom, where Annie and I used to greet all the Disney mascots in the judges' tent after the parade. We always wanted to be last in line, because we loved the place, and we wanted the little kids and old folks to go ahead of us. Our goal was to get a little extra time with Mickey. The person inside the costume usually doesn't use his normal voice, but I think they'd hired somebody new to play him, or a substitute. Annie and I got on either side of Mickey to pose for the picture, and before the flash went off, the big cartoon head turned a little toward me, and the fellow inside muttered something. I was caught off-guard, so I don't remember his exact words, but it sounded like "So, we meet again." I knew I must have fooled around with the man, but who the Sam Hill was in there? I still wonder. In the photo, my face has a shaken, confused look.

While we waited, Miquel told me a long, gossipy story about Darby, the manager of Over the Rainbow. Miquel told stories about Darby just to make me squirm. Darby was an older gay man who enjoyed the leather community and was always seeking out newer thrills and younger men, or "chicken." He was tough and hairy. Once a hustler pulled a .22 on him and said it was a stickup, but Darby grabbed his gun hand and squeezed it so hard he almost broke it. Then he took a shotgun from under his bed and said, "Think again, Chickenbutt. I believe I'm robbing *you*." He took the hustler's clothes and gun and wallet, tied him up, and raped him in the behind with the handle of a spatula, and made the boy go home naked during a tropical depression. I couldn't stand hearing Darby stories.

The whole time, I paid special attention to the ladies nearby. It was a warm day, and people were wearing revealing clothing. The line snaked around a metal guardrail so that you were next to people on either side. A twentyish girl in front of us had on a pink cut-off T-shirt with FORT LAUDERDALE ironed onto the front. The shirt barely contained her breasts—you could almost see the bowls of them peeking out from the bottom of it. The girl wore black tights and high heels. Her hair had been dyed blond and her eyes had dark outlines of mascara around them. She chewed gum without thinking and stood next to her boyfriend with her weight on one hip. She was good looking in a way any normal man would have agreed on.

I stared hard at her, but that didn't get me excited. Then I changed my approach. If getting saved and liking women were like sneezing, I thought, maybe the less effort I put into it, the easier it would be. I supposed that after going for a long time without any response to a woman, the process would happen slowly. Maybe she just wasn't my type. Beyond Annie, I didn't really know what my taste in women would be, if I had any.

I looked at a wide variety of women, from teenage girls to grandmothers. But it wasn't until I spotted a beefy, longhaired man with a handlebar mustache several places behind us that anything stirred my sex drive. The floor dropped out from under me. I lost patience with the Lord's mysterious ways. He'd promised to straighten me, and now, again, nothing was happening! What was I supposed to do? I wanted to cry with my whole body. The fellow wasn't even that good looking.

A few dull coasters and fattening snacks later, Miquel and I walked in on the last half of the dolphin show. The graceful dolphins wiggled their powerful tails, skidding upright across the surface of the water. When that ended, we played Skee-Ball for a while. We pooled our tickets and got a medium-size panda bear. Miquel invented a criminal past for him and gave him the name Sing-Sing. By then we were too exhausted to wait for most of the rides, so we sat and had supper. I had a look at the map as I finished my burger and noticed that the park had a theater in it, so after lunch we strolled across the park and found it, a wooden building nestled in a grove of pine and oak trees.

"This has been the happiest day of my life," Miquel said. It wasn't the sort of thing Miquel ever said, so I believed him and gave him a short hug.

"Me too," I echoed.

On the other side of the wooden building sat a comfortable amphi-theater, about half-full. Onstage, a children's theater troupe was acting out the story of a lonely whale. A mean ship captain with a peg leg chased the whale with a harpoon. Everybody cheered when the captain missed and the whale ate him up. Then the whale was happy in the big blue ocean. He swam and swam. Everyone shouted, "Yeah, whale!" After the show we waited around and Miquel and I spoke to the actors.

One of them introduced himself as Jack. He had pale skin, dark floppy hair, and Asian eyes. Without asking I tried to figure out if he was part Samoan. Jack and I talked about theater for quite a while. He turned out to be the troupe's director. I tried hard not to notice his athletic body and his filled-out tights. I asked him, almost as a joke, if Six Flags needed a mime troupe, and to my surprise he told me they were doing a search at that very moment. Jack passed me a business card and Miquel practically dragged me away.

Of course, he accused me of flirting with Jack and ruining our special anniversary day. I didn't want to spoil things further, so I apologized, but that meant to Miquel that I admitted to the flirting, so he kept saying nasty things to me. The nasty things made me want to confess everything I had to confess, but I couldn't bring myself to do it. Instead I made threatening statements about things I *could* say but wouldn't, in order to spare him. He dared me but I didn't take the bait.

When we got home, Miquel boiled rice and fried chicken for supper. He continued to dress me down for the flirting. Then I backtracked, saying that I hadn't been flirting but hadn't wanted to upset him by arguing that I hadn't been flirting. That upset him more. "That's a lie on top of a lie," he said. "That's, like, a layer cake of lies."

He was really getting my goat—no, a whole herd of my goats. I begged him not to ruin the day more than it had already been ruined. But once he started to ruin things a little, Miquel would always make an effort to ruin things completely. He broke down in tears and demanded that I move out. I told him his tears said that he didn't want me to leave. He told me that he knew better than me what his tears told him. I begged him not to break up with me. He said that moving out didn't have to mean breaking up, but I didn't believe that. At the end of the fight he tried to make love to me, but I folded my arms and my body wouldn't respond. Part of me thanked the Lord for my lack of excitement, but another part wanted to weep at how much I had lost.

The summer passed, and my sexuality didn't change at all. Gradually, it set in that the Lord wasn't going to turn me straight, maybe ever. The whole fantasy I'd kept locked in my head for the last year crumbled as soon as reality touched it. Up until the time expired, I had used every ounce of faith I had to convince myself of what the Lord's signs had shown me. An important part of that strategy was never mentioning it. My attraction to Miquel had faded, but for other men it had actually increased. I admitted to myself that I really had been very attracted to that Jack fellow.

Taken together, these revelations meant I had misinterpreted *all* the Lord's signs. I had screwed up my entire life. I felt the dreadful disappointment that comes from believing something will happen and then suddenly realizing that it won't, that you've fooled yourself. For the first time since college, I skipped church for weeks. I stopped taking the bus over to the Stop Suffering Church. Maybe a couple of the Spanish ladies missed me for a week or two, but they must have gone on with their business, like folks do.

At home, I watched TV constantly. That kept me from having to relate to Miquel. He seemed relieved. We said only pleasant things to one another, and never had deep conversations, especially not about us. It became real comfortable, even. Sometimes he made comments suggesting that I should leave, but he never laid down the law.

One of my temp jobs, at a bank downtown, took me on as an administrative assistant, so I worked steadily. In the evenings, I rehearsed with Concerned Relatives, who had started working on another piece. This one was called *Omd*, which meant "baptism in still water" in Aramaic, the language of Jesus. Rex said it would explore the empty ritual of religion. This sounded like a satanic theme to me, but I had started to go over to Satan's side a little, and August had gotten there a while ago, so I let myself enjoy it.

This time Rex demanded an even more intensive rehearsal period. We didn't get any nights off. During rehearsals I went through the motions, but my thoughts remained in the doldrums. I gave Rex Jack's card and told him about the need for a mime troupe at Six Flags. Rex took it, flipped it through his fingers, and nodded when I explained where it came from, thanking me, but when I asked later, he didn't remember and said he'd have to find it again.

At one of the lower points of my depression, in February of 1994, I started walking home so that I could visit public places and do things with men again. Piedmont Park became one of my favorite haunts, and I started visiting public bathrooms again. In those places, guys mostly did quick stuff, almost never the famous thing. That activity always required the kind of close attention you'd give to a science project. So I never had to deal with that. I thought about going to bars, but I only wanted a moment of release and then to go home to Miquel.

During this sad time, I got an unexpected phone call.

"August, I need to talk to you." It was the cigarettey voice of Dakota Wong. She called on a Saturday when Miquel was at Over the Rainbow. I was so surprised to hear from her that I agreed to meet, even though I knew Rex considered her an enemy for quitting. She said what she wanted to talk about was urgent. I thought she might want to rejoin the company and needed advice about how to approach Rex.

Dakota didn't want to meet in a place where Rex or anybody we knew might show up. So we met at a fast-food restaurant in Stone Mountain, just off I-85, with a lumberjack as its mascot. The interior of the place was all white, except for the red seats, which were attached to the chairs and swiveled like rides in an amusement park. I ordered a couple of burgers, jumbo fries, and a large Coke. When the food came I chose a seat in the window where I could watch the highway and the comings and goings of the patrons until Dakota showed up. Fast food made me feel good until I thought about where it went on my body, so I made an effort not to think about that.

Soon Dakota arrived. She brought a salad in a plastic box to our table. She put the salad aside, pulled a manila envelope out of her shoulder bag, and set the envelope down on the table in front of her. Somehow that blank surface made me real nervous.

"August, do you know a woman named Lisette Franklin?"

"No," I said. I couldn't imagine what this was about, only what I didn't want it to be about. "But I hope nothing happened to her."

"Lisette is a friend of mine from college. She joined the theater company I started after I left Concerned Relatives. We weren't so close before, but we've become very close. One night after rehearsal she told me that she was involved in that train derailment that happened a couple of years ago. Someone pulled her away from the wreckage. That man's name and picture appeared in an obituary. But when she recovered some of her memory, she remembered seeing him run away from the wreck. Lisette is very spiritual, so for a while she thought that the man's ghost had helped her, or maybe even Jesus Christ. Then she did some investigation on her own and discovered that they'd found the man's wallet, but never his body."

My nervous laugh broke out. "That's— That's incredible!"

Dakota unclasped the manila envelope and slid out a photocopy of a newspaper article. The article was a brief obituary for a man named Gary Gray. I stiffened. It listed all the basic facts about Gary Gray, like where he went to school and that he worked for Bradley Foods in the marketing department and that he was survived by his wife, daughter, mother, and father, but there was no photograph, so I was relieved a little.

Seeing all the facts of my old life laid out so coldly in the article cut me pretty deep, but the mistakes hurt worse, because I couldn't correct them in front of Dakota. I hoped I could prevent the fury from showing on my face. The article said Annie had come from Guam. Near the end, they had left out the *r* and written "Mr. Gay." It felt deliberate. I squirmed, but I smiled at Dakota so that she wouldn't see the squirming.

So much had changed since then. I hadn't really become August Valentine, but I had definitely left part of Gary Gray behind, the part that believed in my innocence, and I knew that not everybody would be happy to have me back. I thought of that satanic ghost story where the family makes a wish for their son to come back from the dead. Then the zombie version of him knocks on the door and they can't open it, because it's too sickening for somebody to come back from the dead for real, so they use their last wish to wish him dead again. Maybe they'd given away his possessions and his little brother had already moved into his bedroom.

Many times I had daydreamed about the moment when I would return to my old life. But faced with the reality, I couldn't make one person out of August Valentine and Gary Gray. I didn't want Miquel to ever meet Annie. Maybe everybody from my past life would be better off using that last wish.

"Lisette saw *Omd* because I suggested she take a look at what was going on in town. She told me she stayed until the actors came out because she wanted to see what everybody looked like with their masks off. The cast came out and she saw you. She was sure that you were this Gary Gray person who saved her. But she flipped out and ran away. She lost her mother in that accident, you know."

"Oh." I smiled and nodded, still trying to keep up the impression of somebody this had nothing to do with. I curled my toes up inside my shoes as hard as I could to keep from breaking my calm outside. This took a heck of a lot of effort.

"All this time she has been trying to reach the man who helped her, so that she could thank him for saving her life."

"That's common," I said. "I get mistaken for a lot of people."

Dakota nodded with sympathy. "That's what I thought too—at first."

Tensely and unevenly, I swallowed air and watched the highway. A big truck went past, loaded with pine logs and little orange warning flags.

"But then I saw the photos." When she said *photos*, I thought I might have to give up. I bumped my shoes together to keep from panicking and giggled at nothing. Dakota stared at my face very seriously and I excused myself, giggling again.

Dakota opened the envelope again and tugged out a group of photocopies. All of them had different pictures of the man I had been on them. She spread them across the table in front of me. One of the photos came from Bradley Foods' marketing department. Another had been blown up from a snapshot of me with Annie and Cheryl. None of it seemed quite real. But then again, neither did my life as August Valentine. It had been an ordeal to replace my credit cards and ID after the Euge man robbed me in the park. At any moment I thought I might be discovered.

"August, you're Gary Gray, aren't you?"

"You think that's me?" I said, chuckling. "You think all black people look alike, don't you?" I put my hands in my pockets and pulled them out, and then began to tear the wrapping my burgers had come in into long strips.

"August," she said sternly. She pulled out a color photograph of Gary Gray and covered up the flat-top haircut. Then she poked the picture with her index finger. "This is *you*." She pointed out that the moles on his face and mine were identical, and showed me a nick on the forehead of the man in the photograph that we had in common.

"That's not the same side," I said, a little less confidently. "His is on the left and mine's on the right, see?" Why couldn't I admit it? Maybe Dakota would help keep my secret.

I wanted to be sure nobody in the restaurant overheard our conversation, and I didn't want to say any of the reasons why I had left. None of them would make logical sense if I shared them. Other people wouldn't understand. They would only make fun.

I put my hands down on the table and pushed myself to a standing position, fixing to leave. But I changed my mind to avoid seeming rude and sat back down. My worst fear was coming true. My lives had started to overlap. I went so weak from fear I almost fainted when I sat back down.

Dakota pulled her salad over. She popped open the box and crunched into it with her fork. "Listen. I know that people don't walk away from their whole lives just because. There must be some reason you did this."

I played along, but refused to admit anything. I didn't have another chance to keep things the way they were. I trembled. "Like I killed somebody, right?"

"I would have a hard time believing that, but yes. What happened, Gary? Did you commit a crime?"

"You're like a policewoman on a TV show."

"No, I'm a real person, Gary. Stop bullshitting."

I didn't have the strength to fight Dakota's evidence any further. But I didn't want her to expose me, and I was foaming mad that she was robbing me of the power to return to my family in my own time, so I still wouldn't confess. Instead, deliberately looking toward the highway, I let out a long, angry sigh, one I'd learned from Miquel, designed to make a person feel very stupid, and said, "Please don't use that kind of language with me."

After that I clammed up for a long time so I could hold on to the feeling of not confessing and of being August Valentine until the last possible moment. But I couldn't drag the moment out forever. "Are you in touch with his family, this Gary Gray guy?"

"No, just Lisette. But she has contacted them, yes. Actually, she's here." Struck dumb, I stared at Dakota. "In the restaurant. Do you mind if I call her over?"

I took a deep breath and massaged my temple with one hand, trying to make it seem as if I was tired of the whole thing rather than scared out of my darned wits. Looking away again, I lifted a pickle chip out of a Styrofoam container and bit down on it. It didn't even crunch. Dakota nodded and waved to somebody sitting behind my back. In a second or two Lisette Franklin joined us.

Her face still had the same seriousness in it, but the sadness I had sympathized with on the day our fates crossed had gone. Lisette wore glasses and had wrapped a turquoise scarf around her head. She slid her handbag off her arm into the swivel chair next to Dakota and stared at me with wonder and satisfaction. The scene from the train wreck must have been playing in her memory at the same time as it played in mine. She sat down in the chair next to me and lifted my hand out of my lap.

"Hi!" I said. "Small world, eh?"

"Gary... I just wanted to shake your hand and say thanks. So... thanks."

"You're welcome." I remembered that I still had her book.

"You saved my life. You're a hero."

"Yeah, I suppose you're right." And you just ruined mine, I thought.

"That was a beautiful thing you did." She stared at me like I was a famous guy on a red carpet, and my embarrassment must have showed, so she clapped her hand against my shoulder to show her thanks. Had she knocked over my carefully stacked-up new life just for that? She continued to smile and shake her head. "Can I have a sip of your Coke? My throat is so dry. I was so excited I only just realized."

"Sure."

She leaned over, took the straw between her fingers, and sucked hard. Not much was left and she made a loud noise as she finished.

"My mother, she was injured pretty badly in the accident, you know. She was in the hospital for a while, and eventually passed away. She was the only fatality." Lisette managed a sad smile. I was horrified. Knowing now that somebody had really died shocked and scared me, because it made the Lord's plan unclear. If somebody else had died, the accident couldn't have been a message for me only. And I'd thought things couldn't get worse.

"I'm sorry." I was sorry, but just as sorry for myself, feeling as if a house made of my own lies, every lie a brick, had just toppled over on me and crushed out my breath.

"You were the last person she ever had a conversation with." Lisette's voice broke slightly. "Did you know that?" She picked up one of my napkins and wiped her hands.

"No, I didn't know. That's sad. What happened to you afterward?"

"A bunch of stuff. I graduated from Temple and I live in Atlanta now."

"You're still involved in theater, huh?"

"Yes."

"I'm in theater, too."

"I know. I saw the piece. You were great."

"Thanks."

"There's so much I want to say," she said.

"Thank you is enough."

A puzzled look crossed her face. Then she brightened up suddenly. "I have a husband and a beautiful baby boy named Lawrence now. He's six months old. Would you like to see a picture of him?" She lunged over the table for her bag and fished out a wallet bulging with snapshots. Lisette and her husband had a lush backyard and a cocker spaniel named Frank. The pictures showed Lawrence in the playpen with a rattle, in the yard with the husband blowing soap bubbles, and with Frank licking his face. I was happy for her, but jealous at the same time. If I didn't have same-sex desires, I could have a normal life with a wife, children, a Kentucky bluegrass lawn, and a happy dog, too. I cooed extra hard to hide my bad emotions and keep her on the subject of herself instead of me.

At the end of lunch, Lisette told me that Annie had started a restaurant and that it was doing well. Cheryl had gotten sick, but it wasn't anything serious. Mama had pneumonia, and she would definitely make it through, but Lisette warned me to contact her soon. She gave me Annie's information and my mother's. Annie wasn't mad, Lisette told me, just real upset and confused about what happened. When Lisette hugged me good-bye in the parking lot, I promised her I would get in touch with them again. I especially wanted to contact my mother, who they said had taken my death very hard. I asked about my father's health and Lisette paused and said it hadn't improved. However, nothing had changed about their addresses and phone numbers. That relieved me, because so much else had changed in their lives.

Even though I thought about getting in touch with Annie and my mother and people I had known, I couldn't muster up the courage. Rehearsals ended too late, or it wasn't the right time, or I would feel too exhausted to go through with it. I also needed to keep them from hearing anything about August Valentine and his homosexual lifestyle, especially my mother. That might make her get worse. I had done enough damage.

Every couple of days I would get a message from Lisette on my answering machine, urging me to contact my family, but I would delete it as soon as I heard her voice. Once or twice I picked up the phone when she called, and I promised her that I would call or write everybody, but I really wanted the whole problem to go away. At the time I wasn't much happier as August Valentine, but I had gotten used to it. My personality had gotten stuck between August and Gary. The new Concerned Relatives show would go up soon, and I couldn't drop out of that even if my family wanted me to come back and be Gary Gray again. Also, I couldn't face them without mentioning my struggle with homosexuality. Especially not my father, who would probably disown me. That would mean I'd have to go back to being August Valentine anyway. I didn't think it was worth the risk.

I had plenty of change happening in my own life, though. Miquel finally demanded that I move out—I think he'd started seeing someone—but there was little I could afford on a temp's salary and uneven work schedule. Fortunately, around the same time, Rex decided that some of the Concerned Relatives should move into a live-work situation. He had rented a run-down Victorian house in Cabbagetown for that purpose. We fixed it up, sort of, and rehearsed in the large living room. Erica, Isla, Helene, and I would move in when we finished renovating. Spitz lived with her boyfriend not far away, in Decatur. Rex also convinced a friend, Kenny, to take one of the rooms and handle some technical issues for the company.

Miquel's home had been so delightful to live in that I felt banished from Eden. I wished he would take me back just to live there with him, but he didn't even wait for us to finish renovating before he kicked me out. I had to find a stopgap fast. Instead of the Patriot Inn, I checked in down the street at Colony Suites until the house in Cabbagetown was ready. Colony Suites cost a couple of dollars more, but there I could avoid the feeling of failure that covered the Patriot—particularly Marilyn. Or so I thought—Marilyn moonlighted at the Colony Suites, and she greeted me by slapping her rings against the Formica countertop and shouting a hearty "Welcome back!"

One night, a couple of weeks after I moved in with the group, I went alone to a gay bar within walking distance of Miquel's house. I hung around, pretending not to hope that somebody would be interested in a sexual encounter, and pretending even harder that I didn't want the possibility of love after that. Underneath it all, I also hoped that Miquel would show up. Soon the attractive guys paired up and went home together, and last call was announced.

A stocky man with no shirt walked over to the bar in a zigzag fashion and leaned against it next to me. He was covered in hair, except on his head, and had a confused expression. He peered at me.

"You look *exactly* like this dude I used to know—Kareem," he said. "Is your name Kareem?" I told him Kareem was a nice name, but not mine.

The man ordered six shots of Jägermeister and demanded that I drink three with him.

"Doing shots alone is pathetic, and I ain't pathetic," he said in a friendly way, smacking me on the back.

I told him I didn't drink alcohol much, but he became angry so I said, "Just this once," and drank three tiny glasses of the burning licorice. I enjoyed that he was expressing an interest in me and imagined he might ask me to go home or to the park. The bar started to play the final song of the evening, which was always "Desperado" because the bar had a Western theme.

Before the song ended, the man stumbled off without saying goodbye. Miquel told me once that whenever he went home alone from a bar, he comforted himself by saying that at least he wouldn't get an STD from anybody that night, but remembering that didn't help my mood at all.

I stood around in the parking lot with a loose group of other lonely men exchanging glances with each other. I wasn't good at going to gay bars. I imagined that they could be fun with friends, but I didn't have gay friends—Concerned Relatives was me, four women, some straight guys during tech, and Rex—and I hadn't gone out much when I was dating Miquel. I couldn't get anybody to look my way, so I walked off toward Piedmont Park, where a lot of unlucky men went to improve their luck. Miquel's apartment was on the way, so I stopped and stood across the street under the shadow of trees where he couldn't see me. His windows were dark. Sometimes I waited in the area and ran into him accidentally on purpose. He never said much, or let on that he knew it wasn't a coincidence.

I arrived in the section of the park where men touched each other, and pretty soon a short, confident man came over to me. He brushed his knuckles against my forearm to show his interest. I didn't take his hand away; that meant I liked him, too. Then again, I hardly ever pushed anybody's hand away unless they were real filthy or smelled too much like alcohol.

Once we had gotten friendly, I was relieved to hear him say that he lived nearby and we should go to his place. Maybe I would get to sleep in his house and get to know his life a little bit. Sometimes going home with men could be a game to see how much I could find out about their lives. If a man let me sleep over and then made coffee or breakfast the next morning it was like winning a contest, and I could pretend that I was having a relationship with him. That always pleased me, a lot of times even more than the sex.

The short man took my hand and led me out of the park. In a situation like this one, a guy didn't normally hold your hand. My self-esteem started to rise from the depths, but it had a long way to go.

We reached the exit and walked east for a few blocks. The man had rectangular glasses, a large nose, and shiny black hair. His name was Armando but he said I should call him Manny. He had a stiff, bowlegged way of walking. After talking for a bit, he asked me what I liked. I understood by then what people meant by that question.

"I like whatever you like," I said.

"Good," he mumbled, with a naughty smile. "Because I like obedience."

Right then I noticed that there was a car driving very slowly up the street behind us. I assumed it was somebody under the influence, trying to make his way home after a long night out.

When we reached the intersection of Tenth and Monroe, we had to pause to wait for a walk signal. I turned to see the car pulling diagonally into a bus stop behind us. It was a beat-up Celica, the same color as the one I had driven when I lived in Florida.

The man held my hand tightly even though the space between our palms had grown slippery with sweat. Behind us I heard the car door slam. A second later I heard a woman's voice shout, "Gary! Gary!"

I turned to see my wife. I couldn't see too well in the shadows, but it sure was her.

"Annie—" No words came to me. I couldn't even panic. I had been dropped into the eye of a storm. The moment felt like something happening in somebody else's life. My eyes danced around her and couldn't land. No excuses were possible.

"Gary!" Annie shouted, her eyes glued to the hand-holding.

I tugged my fingers away from Manny's and wiped them on my pant leg, maybe to make it look like I was disgusted by his touch.

"You told me your name was August," Manny said.

"It's a nickname," I stammered.

Annie wept and pushed tears from her eyes with both hands. I went to her and tried to keep her calm but I couldn't. She pushed me backward. "Gary! I thought you were dead! Everyone thought you were dead! Argh,

I wish you were dead! I should kill you!"

"You know this lady," Manny observed. I moved toward Annie again, like somebody about to throw a blanket over a stovetop fire.

"Annie," I breathed in a soothing voice. "Please don't be upset with me. I have a problem. A big problem. I went away so that I could fix it."

I moved closer, and light from the streetlamp fell on me. She beat me hard with her fists. I tried to hug her to keep her from hitting, but she struggled too much. New streaks of prematurely gray hair fell down her shoulders, and her eyes had wrinkles around them and puffy bags underneath. I hoped my disappearing hadn't caused all that. When hugging didn't work, I took her wrists in my hands. She kept struggling, and I had a hard time holding her back.

"It was part of the Lord's plan for me," I explained.

"But you didn't fix the problem! Are you going to fix the problem? Your daughter prays for a daddy every night. But you don't care about that. You gave her up for the flesh! You're going to burn for this!" Annie's anger reached a new peak. She kicked at me and bit my hand. I let go of her wrists and she let me have it again, punching and slapping. I didn't want to fight back, because I deserved everything. I thought about when my father used to hit me and I tried to disappear, but I couldn't.

Manny, who had stepped aside to watch until she started hitting me, rushed around behind Annie, grabbed her arms, and yanked them down by her sides. For a person of small stature, he was strong, and he held her in position as she thrashed. The two of them were the same height. I noticed that she wore makeup now, and looked prettier and more feminine. What had caused the change? Maybe she had met and fallen in love with somebody else while she thought I was dead. It would make things easier for me if she had. Jealousy entered my mind all backward, like an ingrown toenail. I got jealous, but not the way a husband gets when he wants to keep his wife to himself. I was jealous of the guy she had fallen for, because he was probably a real man.

"Ma'am," Manny breathed into her ear. "I understand that you're upset. But either you two can have a conversation about this or you can get in the car and go back where you came from. What you're doing to this man is assault. Believe me, I know. I am an officer of the law."

Annie cackled bitterly. "You're a cop?"

"I am an off-duty police officer, yes."

"What are you doing in the park, Mr. Policeman?" she spat, looking him up and down in disbelief. "Do you know what this man did? Aren't you going to arrest him? Do you know that I'm his *wife*?" She said "wife" like the sound could make him disappear.

"No, ma'am, he didn't inform me of his past histories. It sounds like he actually gave me a false name. But I did figure out that you were involved at some point by your statement that you have a daughter together."

"He and I just met tonight," I blurted out, I guess because I hoped it would make Annie feel better to know that the connection was superficial. But I had begun to admire Armando for getting involved and helping me. I sucked at the bite mark on my hand.

"Now, ma'am, if you want to talk these issues out, you and your husband ought to do so when emotions are not running as high." He pulled her toward the car. She didn't resist as much.

The drama of the scene caught up with me, and I teared up. "Annie," I said. "I always meant to come home. I just couldn't do it until..."

Annie glared at me from head to toe. I had never seen so much scorn in her expression before.

"...and I kept waiting, and it didn't happen."

She moved her head to indicate Manny. "Is this what you call waiting?"

"That was a cheap shot, ma'am," Manny said. "Now please get into the car." She struggled, but he held her with one hand and opened the driver's side of the car with the other. She got in, and he closed the door. She rolled the window down. The anger in her somehow disappeared with the final-sounding thud of the car door. Manny stood guard in case she got upset again and leapt out of the vehicle.

"Gary, we're going to get you some help, okay?" she said, calmer now.

"Okay," I said. I would have told her anything just to end the unbearable, humiliating scene. "Do you know how to find me?"

"I've been following you for the last three days. I didn't believe that you had fallen into this lifestyle until I saw you and him—" She shook her head. "I'm in touch with some people who can help." Annie started to weep again, but the tears were no longer frustrated. She twisted the key in the ignition and put the car in gear. I cataloged the events of the last three days, trying to remember what she might have seen. "We're coming to your house tomorrow morning," she said. "We're going to get you some help, okay?"

"Yes," I said.

"Can I drive you home?" she asked, with a nervous glance at Manny, who retreated to the curbside a few yards closer to the intersection, just out of earshot.

"I can walk from here. Let's take the time to calm down."

"You'll be okay?"

"I'll be okay."

Annie stroked my forearm gently and shook her head, gazing hopefully into my eyes. "Okay." She rolled up the window and drove off, wiping her eyes.

The sound of the car faded, and soon the street filled with deserted calm. Manny and I didn't speak for a couple of minutes. We watched the traffic lights change from red to green, even though no cars were waiting. Then he stepped out of the gutter and walked over to me.

"I only caught some of that," he said. "What's the story, August? Gary?" As I told him I wept openly, which I had never done in front of anybody I'd picked up. It made me feel close to him.

When I got to the end, he patted my shoulder in an older-brother way and breathed, "It's okay, buddy." A truck rumbled by, and when it had gone, the street felt especially silent. We said nothing for a long time.

"It's okay if you want to go," he said.

I felt I owed him a favor. "Do you still...?"

"The mood is definitely spoiled," he said, leading me back to the walk signal. He took off his glasses and polished them with his the hem of his T-shirt, smiling that dirty smile again. "But give me a minute." He filled his lungs with night air and stretched his wiry, muscled arms. No cars were coming, so he swaggered across the street like a bantam rooster. I followed obediently. As I crossed the double yellow line, DON'T WALK changed to WALK.

The next day started out hot and got hotter. By mid-morning, the heat under the duvet in Manny's king-size sleigh bed was so bad that my own sweating woke me up, even with the AC on. I tossed back the covers.

Manny had a lot of fluffy covers, so for a moment I had trouble finding him. When I did locate him, he was still asleep, his nose softly buzzing.

In the lemon-cake sunlight, Manny looked older. At night his hair had seemed black, and it disappointed me a little to find that it was mouse-brown with a whole bunch of silver streaks. Also, I could see crow's feet around his eyes and loose skin under his chin. But who was I to judge? I was fat. I reckoned that if he could like my fatness, I could learn to like his oldness if I got the chance. We could be like Jack Sprat and his wife. Or something. I peeled the covers off my body and looked around groggily.

The apartment was very clean and well decorated, like a showroom or a picture in a Sunday magazine. The bed matched the chairs and the couch. Everything was made of heavy, dark wood with cream-colored upholstery. For a delicious moment, I pretended that I was a rich white lady in a furniture commercial. Stretching my arms out and groaning, I struck a fanciful pose. Usually I didn't have fantasies like that, or I would scold myself if they happened, but that morning I gave myself a break. It was that pretty a day. Manny heard me groan and turned over, fully awake.

"You want some coffee? Breakfast?"

Manny made us omelets with ham and cheese, toasted a pair of croissants, and brewed some very strong Latin American coffee that he mixed with hot milk. We sat in his breakfast nook, looking out over a grove of pine trees, and I apologized for the scene in the street the night before. Without prying too much, he asked interested questions about Annie and my two lives. I found him real sympathetic to my problems and a good listener. After breakfast I told him that I needed to get myself home. Rex had scheduled a Concerned Relatives rehearsal at 1 p.m., but I didn't mention that. Manny offered to give me a ride home, and at first I said no because people had a bad impression of Cabbagetown, but by that time it was 12:20 and I wouldn't get there on time if I took public transportation, so I accepted his offer. Before we left, he wrote his number down on a piece of stationery and handed it to me.

"It doesn't have to be for a date, it could be just if you need to talk," he told me. I thanked him, folding the paper up and sticking it in my back pocket. I tried to imagine having a relationship with Manny, but it seemed impossible because of the way I had met him. I thought how strange it was that you could meet really nice people in shameful situations like public-park sex. Also, after Miquel, I didn't want to have another man-man relationship. The Lord hadn't turned me straight, but I still held out hope that I could be normal. I was like Pinocchio, a wooden marionette always begging to become a real boy.

We left the apartment and the heat nearly choked us. You could see wavy lines coming up from the pavement. Manny turned the radio to nightclub music and blasted the air conditioning in the car. We drove across town and he dropped me off without commenting on the abandoned houses, stray dogs, and vacant lots covered with graffiti all over my neighborhood. I thanked him again and told him I would call, although I didn't know how much I meant it.

Manny waved and waited until I got inside the gate before he gunned his motor and sped off. His car was an expensive BMW, so maybe he didn't want to put it at risk by remaining in that area. But there was a shiny gray sedan idling near the front gate, too—that person had no fear of crime.

As I went up the stairs, the piece of paper Manny had written his number on crinkled in my back pocket. I stuck my fingers in there and touched it. Maybe I would call him; we could be friends or lovers. I pictured us holding hands at a Disney movie and laughed at myself.

When I opened the door, I saw Annie on the couch with her hands folded in her lap. Because of the show, the living room was filled with lights, extension cords, and props and papier-mâché masks. An old couch from the Salvation Army sat at the far end for dancers to sit on between scenes. It felt like a weird dream to see her overlapping with my new life. I had forgotten to find out when she was coming, and now here I was thinking about Manny. Annie had on a polyester dress with orange and blue flowers on a white background. I remembered it as one of her favorites from when we lived together. She clutched a ragged piece of tissue, torn to smithereens. I hoped she hadn't said anything to my roommates about who she was and why she had come.

Next to Annie sat a square-headed man with a blond crew cut and gold-framed glasses, wearing a tan jacket and pants. He reminded me of one of my teachers at Central who'd also had only one long eyebrow across his forehead. Annie wore a troubled expression, but the stranger had a friendly, open face. He didn't introduce himself, though, and I needed to talk to Annie foremost.

"I'm late," I said. "I'm sorry."

"Where were you?" she asked, with a mean tone in her voice that said she already knew but wanted to hear me confess. In my mind I started to get ready with a clean answer, but the friendly man touched her arm as if to say *Hold your horses.*

"I guess we never said a time," she announced, still with some tension stuck between her teeth.

"Morning is a time. And it's gone now. Sorry."

She apologized for overreacting and trying to beat me up the night before, and I apologized back, for everything I had put her through.

"We're not even," she said. "Was there somebody else? When you ran away?"

"No."

"Did you start acting on it before you ran away?"

I had to look away to say it. "A couple of times I did some things with some guys."

Annie covered her face with her hands. Her lungs filled with air and then she let the breath out in short puffs. Then she took her hands away. "Why couldn't you share this with me so that we could work on it as a couple, as a family? Why did you have to run off like that? Why did I have to come get you?"

For a very long time, I stayed silent, wishing that everything I struggled with could just pass out of my skin and into hers. But she wouldn't let me move closer or touch her. I didn't have an answer for her questions. It felt foolish to tell her that God had said to run away, and I didn't have the words to explain that my problem was too shameful and private to share with anyone, sure as heck not my wife.

"In the back of my mind, I guess I was worried that you might have a problem with same-sex desires," she said. "But I never took those fears seriously."

I apologized again. "I thought I could handle it alone. I thought if you knew, then you'd be thinking about it every time you looked at me, and most every time we went to bed, especially. I reckoned it would get harder for me to handle the problem. I thought if I could just fix it myself without saying anything, you'd never know that it ever needed to be fixed, and everything could just be normal. I didn't want to cause trouble for you."

Annie nodded and touched the tissue to her nose. "I don't think you want to change, Gary," she continued. Hearing my real name made me feel naked. I almost corrected her, but instead I gave her a hurt look.

"But I do," I said. "I do."

Still holding the tissue, she pointed at the man. "Gary, this is Bill. He can help." I shook hands with Bill, and pulled my chair nearer to Annie, who grabbed my hand and kneaded the soft parts of my palm.

"Gary, I love you very much and I hope and pray that you love me, too, and I'm glad to know you didn't run away because of anything I did," Annie said in a rush, like she wanted to get it all out before breaking down.

I petted her hand and stared at the floor. "Of course it wasn't because of you."

Bill leaned forward and touched her shoulder. He smiled at me in a way that had nothing to do with the tone of the conversation. It resembled the smile of a man trying to pick up another man in the park. Making that judgment gave me a chill, because it meant I had started to see the world through homosexual eyes.

"Annie, can we talk about this in private?" I asked quietly.

"Bill is a friend, honey."

"Yes," Bill said, "I'm a friend." He had a friendly voice.

"Okay..." I shrugged off my puzzlement.

Rex stepped into the doorjamb by the front door. "Gary," he said pointedly, to let me know that he knew and didn't approve, "we're planning to start in about ten minutes. Do you think you'll be done by then?"

"Um, no, Rex. I'm sorry. We can go to the backyard though." The three of us stood up and squeezed down the hallway past Rex, through the kitchen and out to the backyard, where several of the other troupe members were stretching and warming up in the stifling heat. When we came out and down the wooden steps, they all perked up and went past us on the opposite side of the stairs, relieved not to have to sweat through their leotards anymore. They barely said hello, they were fanning themselves so hard. Isla gave me a look of confusion and anger; Helene smiled and batted her eyelashes and patted my shoulder sympathetically. They knew. A bucket of my emotions got dumped down a well.

Rex had followed us to the back door. "Try to keep it short, okay?" he warned. The screen door hissed as it swung, and then banged shut.

Bill marveled at the heat as I led him and Annie to a weather-beaten picnic table off to one side of the backyard by a sweet gum tree. The two of them put their legs underneath the table and I sat across from them. Finches landed on the birdbath and peeked at us. I was already sweating, and when Bill took off his jacket and laid it on the far end of the picnic table, I noticed a lot of wetness under his arms. Annie hadn't let go of my hand the whole time, like she thought I might float away or disappear again.

Annie swallowed, and her first words had saliva in them. "Honey, we talked last night about getting you some help for your problem. But I'm not sure you're ready."

"I am, though."

"Where did you sleep last night?" she asked, leaning forward a little.

At that moment, I didn't know what I wanted. The memory of Manny lingered in my mind. In fact, I could still smell his cologne on the hand that Annie wasn't hanging on to. I held that hand over my mouth and breathed in. The breakfast he'd made still warmed my full stomach. I dreamed for a minute that giving in to my gay urges would be better than struggling to rebuild my marriage and my old life.

The moral choice seemed darned obvious. My wife, the mother of my child, was offering me a true, meaningful life—one that I didn't deserve. We had a history, we shared a faith. The homosexual world, as far as I had seen, could only offer an endless string of Mannies. Though he had treated me well, every encounter I had with a man seemed to scrape away part of my soul and leave me searching for the next guy. Same-sex desire was an addiction. I didn't think opposite-sex attractions could *ever* feel as bad. I clutched both of Annie's hands. I hadn't tried everything yet. Maybe the Lord's promise would be fulfilled after all, just a little later than I'd hoped. Addictions could be overcome.

"With a friend," I said. Sweat flooded my eyebrows.

"That's it," Annie whispered, as if she'd wiped our marriage off the kitchen counter. She stood, and I tried to keep hold of her fingers but she yanked them free. "You made your choice."

I wailed "No!" and curled over into a fetal position. I had done everything in order to be a real husband and father, and to make her life happy. After something like this, I would never get to see her or my daughter again. She'd have to tell our secrets to lawyers and my family. "I'll change for you, Annie. I can do it," I promised. "Just don't give up on me." There was a long silence, and I raised my head. We took each other in, Annie searching my eyes for honesty as I prayed for mercy to arrive in hers.

Then Annie stepped forward, and so did I, and she stretched her arms as far around me as she could. I buried my face in her soft, fragrant neck. I couldn't smell Manny's smell anymore, just her rosy perfume. The hug lasted long enough for me to notice the sounds of pots and pans clattering and voices and music in the house next door to us. Annie finally sat down again. "I have a surprise for you."

She stood, still holding my hand, and gave a coy look. She tugged on my hand and led me down the alley between my house and the next one, with Bill following at a slight distance. I helped her open the gate and she brought me up to the side of the sedan I had seen outside. Her smile blossomed, and I thought of all our trips to Disney World. Still facing me, she straightened her back and knocked on the window. The house and the sky behind us were reflected in it. Bill quietly opened the front door and got into the passenger's seat. Another stranger, from the car service, had been waiting with the AC on.

The window came down smoothly to reveal the face of a beautiful girl with chubby cheeks and a pink headband pushing back her wavy brown hair. Cheryl squealed with delight when she saw me and bounced up and down in her seat. She stretched her arms out through the open window. I stepped over to the car and gave her a big hug and kiss.

"Daddy! Daddy!" she shouted.

"Yes, sweetheart, it's me, it's me!" I replied. The air inside the car was a cool, inviting temperature. Annie opened the door so I could slide in next to Cheryl. I put my daughter on my lap and hugged her some more. How could I have run away from a girl with gleaming eyes like this? I'd already missed so many important steps in her life. A tide of shame rose up in me—had I blown the chance to mean anything at all to her? Annie came around and got in on the other side.

Cheryl announced that she had just turned four and a half, which I knew. She showed me her teeth and asked me how the business trip had gone. Then she made me cross my heart and hope to die that I'd never go on another business trip again. The driver started the engine; the car moved down the street.

"I thought you weren't coming back," she said. The car doors locked.

"Don't worry, Pumpkin. I'm not going to leave you again." With a jolt, I remembered the rehearsal. "Bill, where are we going? I have to be back."

"Gary, you're really committed to beating this thing, am I right?" he said.

"Yes, but—"

"No buts. I'll bet you recognize the need to take extreme measures to solve problems sometimes. So you're willing to try anything that might help you conquer these urges of yours. Am I right?" I nodded. Bill had a commanding, fatherly authority that hypnotized me. He always asked if he was right. You couldn't say No, you're not right. Bill hadn't said much until this time, but when he started speaking a lot, I noticed that under the authority voice, he talked sort of gay-like, stretching out his vowels and saying his *s*'s like a snake. But I wasn't used to trusting my gut back then, so I didn't put it together.

The car turned onto the highway and headed south. Bill looked into the rearview mirror to meet my glance. I held Cheryl's hand and she opened her eyes wide when I turned back to her. We reached cruising speed, and Bill kept talking. "You're on your way to a place called Resurrection Ministries, Gary. It's a facility where you can get help. It's run by a group of Christian professionals who are trained to help people overcome their same-sex desires. It's near Memphis, Tennessee."

"Hey!" I shouted. "Can't I go back and get some of my stuff?"

"There'll be stuff there. You're better off without a lot of the false images you might bring with you anyway. What you need most is to be out of the environment you're living in right now, am I right? So no contact with the old world for now. You have to focus on yourself and on getting better. So no phone calls, no mail, no faxes, nothing. Annie and Cheryl can't go with you, I'm afraid, but they're going to support you every step of the way. The program's a year long, but that's what we need. For the first three months, you won't have visitors. You've gotta cut your ties." Bill's voice took on a joking tone. "But I've heard you're an old hand at that." The three of us in the back didn't laugh.

"I can't even call them and tell them to put my stuff in storage?"

"You'll be so different you won't want your old stuff," he said. "Believe you me."

In a half an hour, we reached Hartsfield airport. The driver pulled the car into the returns area. When we stopped, Bill opened the backseat on my side and Annie stood by hers. They blocked my way so that I wouldn't make a run for it. I wanted to tell them they didn't need to bother, but they had probably rehearsed all of this. Not saying that I was okay with coming meant they could do everything the way they planned it.

When Bill opened the car door, he asked me to stick out my right hand. I did so and he handcuffed it to his left with plastic handcuffs. Annie scooped Cheryl up so that she didn't notice that. I stumbled out of the car and somebody from the rental company drove it away. Cheryl held my left hand as we rode the shuttle bus to the terminal and checked in. I squatted and hugged her with the arm that wasn't handcuffed to Bill. I told her that I had to go away and she burst into tears. She made a high-pitched noise that hurt my ears and drew attention from strangers, but I took my lumps while she hit me and called me a liar and screamed. She would never believe anything I said ever again.

People stared at us like I was a child abuser. That was the worst. Over Cheryl's shoulder, I met their judging eyes with a weak smile, hoping the busybodies would just move on. I hated Bill for putting me in the position of having promised Cheryl something I had to turn right around and unpromise.

Cheryl stuck her hands in my face to push herself away and poked me in the eye. She ran to her mother and hugged her knees. Annie promised to explain things to her so that she wouldn't hold it against me. With a little difficulty, Annie embraced me to say good-bye and kissed me on the lips. Her mouth opened, but mine didn't. Some of her bright red lipstick transferred to my lips, though I didn't realize it until later. Bill and I must have looked funny going through the terminal, still handcuffed and trying to hide it, keeping our hands behind us and close together. As we cruised past the food courts on the people-mover, a couple of travelers raised their heads and had themselves a good long look.

III.

CHARACTER MARCHES

Stylized walks and attitudes

TWELVE

Outside Memphis, steel blue light disappeared behind the skyline and a clear, humid night crept in. Our shaky car rumbled through the flat main roads east of downtown, past strip malls and gas stations. In the middle of an area of shops and restaurants, a small hill poked up with a church piercing the sky at the top. Bill turned at the next street and we drove past the church, a cream-colored building the size of a small airplane hangar that had a sloping roof. The marquee said RICTUS BOLLARD CHURCH OF THE HOLY FLOCK and BEHOLD, I MAKE ALL THINGS NEW, REV. 21:5. On the other side of the church sat two buildings made of tan brick that looked like its brother and sister. "Welcome to Resurrection Minsistries," Bill said.

Many of the windows on campus glowed a warm yellow, except one on the ground floor, where a stout woman typed at a computer. The stout woman got up from her chair when Bill parked the car, and momentarily she scurried out to meet us. She wore an ankle-length denim dress and sensible shoes. She and Bill held their arms wide and embraced one another. I had to go behind the woman because I still had on the handcuffs. Their greeting ended and they turned their attention toward me.

"This is Gary?" the woman asked, pity coloring her voice. I extended my hand, and we shook. "Hi, Gary. I'm Gay." Bill chortled and grasped her shoulder playfully. My face went blank.

"You're always saying that. What she means, Gary, is that her *name* is Gay."

Gay laughed. "My parents are old-fashioned people from Oklahoma, they didn't get the memo before they christened me. It was 1955. What can I say?"

"She's an ex-lesbian."

"An ex-lesbian?" I was dumbfounded to hear people speak so lightly about something I had struggled with so seriously. These two seemed mighty comfortable joking about the worst thing in my life. Most curiously, they didn't seem too different from gay and lesbian people I had met in nightclubs and other places. Bill didn't say much about his past until later, but Gay had an easy, open manner. She was from Houston, Texas, where her folks had moved when she was five, but she didn't talk like a Texan. Her skin was very pale and her hair had a lot of shine but no curl. It flopped by the side of her face, while a pair of gold barrettes held back her bangs, looking like they belonged on somebody younger. She talked with her big chin down, like she was always laughing at herself.

"I wouldn't say ex-lesbian yet, but I am on the road to recovery. You know what they say: one day at a time. But I appreciate your vote of confidence, Bill."

"Are you going to change your name once the transformation is complete?" Bill ribbed.

"Yes. Then and only then. I'll change my name to Not Gay." She snickered real hard, and turned to me when she got done. Bill released me from the handcuffs. The light had almost completely faded, but the three of us walked around the buildings and Gay filled me in on the ministry.

"There used to be a divinity school associated with the church," she explained. "But it had financial problems and the buildings were empty for a while. In 1982, Resurrection Ministries decided to move from Seattle to here. Charlie had been looking for a place to start a live-in ministry." Who was Charlie? I wondered. "This is the men's ministry here, and the far one is the women's. There isn't a lot of overlap. In fact, I might be the last woman you see for a couple of days. So get a good look!"

Gay guessed that I was worried about what would happen at the clinic, and told me in reassuring tones that I'd be in a dorm room for a couple of days, and then I'd join a group of eleven other guys with unwanted SSAs—same-sex attractions. They had a year of fun stuff planned that would help me get rid of the bad desires.

"It feels strange now, but you'll probably look back at this as one of the happiest days of your life," she beamed. "Because it's really the first day when you'll truly begin to serve God and live for *Him*, not selfishly." Bill nodded in agreement, possibly watching many sweet memories pass through his head at once. The two of them had a special glow about them when they talked about God. I felt right at home, like I'd gone back to college.

Inside, the building even reminded me of a high school. A bunch of gray stone steps led into a glass lobby. On the right, I could see into the office through some glass walls. Like my dorm at Central, the walls were cinder blocks painted with glossy white paint. Two hallways went down either side of the lobby, lit by a series of bare bulbs screwed into wall sockets. The speckled green linoleum floor looked super clean and had a freshly mopped ammonia scent. I felt like Br'er Rabbit—they'd tossed me into a place I already knew.

"Do the therapies get rid of the homosexuality completely?" I asked. Gay looked at Bill for permission to say something, and he nodded.

"Well, we can't guarantee complete healing," she said gravely, "but I have yet to see a method with a better success rate." We followed Bill into the office. "A lot of our graduates enter a celibate lifestyle. Some of them learn to control the behavior, and a few go on to lead fulfilling heterosexual lives with husbands, or wives, and children, pets, and vacations." A colorful vision of myself living a perfect life like Lisette's opened up in my mind. I thought back to a moment when Annie and I had been lying on Daytona Beach at sunset, before we got married. Most of the people had left, and tiny waves fell over themselves one after another at the shoreline. They made a fizzy sound like a Coke can opening when they came near us. We sat in silence for a long while, trying to see the cargo ships on the horizon. The cries of gulls and the wash of the surf mixed with laser-beam noises coming from hit radio stations in cars on the strip. All of a sudden, Annie sat up and sang a Samoan song from her childhood. She warbled it sweetly, at a low volume. I'd never heard her sing before. Her voice had a gentle but strong tone that lifted it above all those other sounds.

There had been attractive men walking up and down the beach all day, oily and muscular, but I had resisted the urge to stare or imagine them sexually. I was proud of that. My lust crumbled into nothingness compared to what I felt when Annie sang, a feeling of connection to ancient, sacred things—earth, sea, sky, woman, music, and God.

"This is perfect," Annie sighed when she finished. I told her how beautiful the song was. Her words helped me to think of myself as a real man, one with responsibilities. I had given her a life of pleasure. "Thank you, Jesus," she said, "for putting this wonderful man in my life."

The practical urgency of my first night at Resurrection broke through my daydream. "First order of business, Gary," Bill said, poking me in the chest. He addressed Gay. "We've got to get this big guy registered and get him some clothes."

"Registration! Clothes! Comin' right up," Gay announced, turning on more fluorescent lights in the office. She edged around a couple of desks and touched the RETURN key on her computer. A flock of flying toasters disappeared from the screen. Down the hall, I heard men's voices. They sounded like guys playing a game, a series of sudden whoops and grunts. Hearing a sign of life in the clean, empty surroundings gave me hope.

Bill must have noticed my attitude perking up. "Say," he suggested, "while Gay sets up your files, maybe you'd like to run down the hall and meet the guys. It'll be good to have something to look forward to after Safekeeping."

"Yeah?" I said, forcing a smile. I wasn't sure what he meant.

"Is that okay, Gay?"

"Fine. Leave me here." She smiled.

Bill and I made our way down the shiny hallway on the right to a slightly open door. Four men were playing doubles ping-pong in a large rec room with a pool table at the far end. Closer to the door, a maroon sectional couch and some folding chairs hugged the walls. It looked like a place where people could shoot the breeze about important things. A low coffee table sat in the middle, with the box for the game Connect Four set in the center. One of the men, a stocky guy with a mustache wearing a yellow sweater, scampered away to the far side of the room to fetch the little ball. When the others saw Bill, they threw their paddles down on the table and rushed over to bear-hug him and pat him on the back like he'd just come back from a yearlong trip, even though they'd met him only in the last few days. "Bill!" they shouted. "How's it going, buddy?"

When the horseplay ended, Bill introduced me to the guys. I had already sized them up, afraid that I'd be prisoner in a program with lots of guys I wanted to service. Dwayne was a pale, skinny guy in his thirties who wore glasses from the 1950s and parted his hair in the middle. He stooped a little when he walked, and he breathed through his mouth. "Welcome to Resurrection, Gary!" he said, tripping over his tongue a little. "We're really glad you made it." Jake was younger, maybe twenty-six, with reddish-brown hair. He wore a dark blue golf shirt and khakis, but he had a tough-guy look in his eye, and I knew I wouldn't be able to keep up with him. He wore a Band-Aid on his neck. George had gray skin and very feminine mannerisms, thick glasses, and hips as wide as if he'd stolen them from a shapely woman. He could've been in his mid-forties. We shook hands. He had a weak, wet grip. I greeted them all, trying to match their brave smiles and go-getter attitudes. Fortunately, I didn't feel too attracted to any of them, even though I had done plenty of sexual stuff in bathrooms with way uglier men.

The fellow who'd gone after the ball returned and greeted me warmly. His name was Tom and his body looked like a smaller, white version of mine. He blow-dried his hair back neatly and his face shone with moisturizer. When he talked, Tom's double chin jiggled and his eyes sparkled. "The blessings are going to rain down on you, Gary," he promised, poking my rib cage with his index finger. "Are you ready for a miracle?"

"Are you ready for twelve miracles?" Dwayne added.

"Yeah! I sure am!" I shouted back, maybe louder than I'd meant to. The guys gave a good-natured laugh.

In the office, Gay found a clipboard with a card on it where I filled in my name and answered some questions. As my problem, I checked the box marked HOMOSEXUALITY. The ministry also dealt with drug and pornography addictions, physical and sexual abuse, incest, and child molesting. I didn't know if that meant you were the child or not, so I didn't fill it in. I didn't like thinking I had come to a place where there might be child molesters.

Gay told me that she already had my contact info on file. They'd only

contact Annie in an emergency. She led me downstairs to a damp basement area with a chicken-coop-type structure filled with shelves and racks
packed with clothing of the type you might find in thrift stores. One side
of the little area had women's clothes, long dresses in pastel yellows and
pinks, sea-green windbreakers, low-heeled feminine shoes, floral blouses
and hats, but no pants. On the other side were men's clothes, including
dress shirts and polo shirts in dark, solid colors or zigzag patterns, pants
made of polyester and khaki, and black and brown loafers.

Gay showed me to a tiny changing room with a slop sink and a mop in
it. She told me to take off my clothes down to the drawers. In there, I took
Manny's phone number out of my jeans and stuck it behind the sink before
I came out. I stood in front of her in just my drawers. Gay looked at all
the clothes I'd handed her and confiscated the ones with false images—that
meant anything sexy or popular. I got to keep my polo shirt, but she took
the jeans. The boxer briefs had to go, too, so she gave me a package with
an XXL pair of striped linen boxers in it, and a pair of khakis. Back in
the changing room, I slipped Manny's number into the back pocket of the
new pants.

To replace my Doc Martens, she gave me Hush Puppies, just like I'd
worn as a kid, but new ones, not thrift-store specials. They didn't have
much clothing in my size, but I found a couple of shirts, some pairs of
pants, and more boxers. Gay dropped my old clothes into a large bin. Then
she went through all the items I had taken out of my old jeans. "We'll save
them, but you probably won't want them later."

When she saw a picture of Russ I kept in my wallet, I held it in my
hand, away from the discard pile. "He's very handsome," she said, eyeing
me in a mock-suspicious way. Despite her joking tone, I felt violated and
untrusted. "That's Russ, my college roommate," I said lightly, as if that
meant I couldn't find him attractive. She squinted and held her hand out.
I placed the photo in her palm and took a last look at his tempting lips.

Hugging my new clothes, which smelled like the basement, I followed
Gay back upstairs to the office. She walked over to a strongbox where
they kept the keys, found the correct ring, and locked the box again. She
brought me to the third floor, down a hall where all the rooms had numbered plaques on them. I heard religious music coming out of a couple of
the rooms.

We stopped in front of a room marked 307. Gay opened the door and turned on the light—one naked bulb fixed high in the ceiling. This was my room, a narrow corridor almost, with just enough space at the far end for a large window. The window had a grate stretched across it and a dusty air conditioner stuck in the top half. On our right stood a twin mattress and box spring on wheels, with a gray wool blanket over it. Across the room sat an old wooden desk with a lamp clipped to the top, paired with a chair from an elementary school. A Bible lay open in the center of the desk, like somebody had just gotten up from reading it. Several blue Post-it flags stuck out from the pages. Right next to me and Gay stood a dresser with an electric clock, a portable cassette player, and a set of towels and washcloths, topped with a bar of soap. Immediately to our left I noticed a dark, open closet and another door that I figured might be the bathroom, but it was locked.

"Welcome home, Gary," Gay said, walking over to turn on the air conditioner. The mechanism sputtered and then hummed steadily. "We've had some trouble with this one. Let me know if anything goes wrong with it. They'll be bringing breakfast up to you at 7:30 tomorrow."

The room didn't look like such a fun place, but living at the Patriot Inn was worse, and I had done that by choice. I grew eager to go downstairs and get to know some of the other residents. I put my new clothes down on the bed and started putting them on hangers.

"Do you have any questions?" Gay asked. "Are you going to be okay?"

"I think so."

She turned to leave. I wanted to ask her to stay and talk, since she was so funny and personable, and I felt scared about this new situation. But I sensed that she had other business to attend to.

"Can I have the key?" I asked.

"Actually, Gary, the first couple of days we call Safekeeping. You need to be in isolation, focusing on God's word and on Jesus Christ for that time." She nodded and pointed at the Bible with her head. "It should just be a time of meditation and reflection on your life up until now, and what you want in the future. So you'll stay here, and someone will bring your meals. Touching yourself is strictly against the rules here, obviously. If your wife sends along some of your things, we'll have to make sure there's nothing in the package that will stimulate you, like photographs of John

Stamos, or sexy clothes, or even letters you might have received, okay? Because there's full accountability here, and if anyone finds out you have stuff like that, they'll report you. We'll revoke some privileges and you might be asked to leave the program." She swung the door back to reveal an intercom on the wall like you'd find in any apartment building. "If you need to use the bathroom immediately, or there's an emergency, just buzz downstairs and a helper will escort you down the hall."

As eager as I was not to be homosexual anymore, these restrictions made me feel as jumpy as a field mouse at a cat show. They kept the place clean and everybody acted friendly, but you couldn't leave, and that made it like you'd done something wrong, not like you wanted to get cured. As Gay held the door, I must have given her a real pathetic hangdog look.

"You're going to feel really spoiled, trust me," Gay said, smiling broadly. She locked me in the room and I turned away from the door.

When I thought about it for a moment, I realized that much of my man activity had taken place during moments of too much personal freedom. So it made sense that the program should start by taking away some of my rights and the ability to do things on my own. Before Gay could get down the hall, though, I ran to the door and banged on it. I yelled her name to get her attention. She returned and opened the door a crack.

"Is something the matter?"

"What if there's a fire?"

She sighed. "In the unlikely event of a fire… Well, first the sprinklers will go off—" she pointed to a little spigot thing on the ceiling on a pipe that went through both walls. "And then someone will come around and get you. This is a totally safe building, Gary. You have nothing to worry about. Now, I am really not allowed to talk to you until Safekeeping is over, so… goodnight."

"Thanks, Gay. Goodnight."

"Goodnight." Gay locked me in again and I heard her feet hurrying down the hall.

I sat down on the bed and tested its firmness. It sagged in the center, but I didn't think that would be a problem. I turned on the lamp, turned off the overhead lightbulb, and sat down at the desk. The chair was uncomfortable, and, of course, too small for my body. I reached forward and opened the Bible. It was a nice edition with golden edges and many color drawings inside. I opened to a picture of Shadrach, Meshach, and Abednego coming out of the furnace that didn't burn them. The picture meant that I'd get through everything fine, so I thought about reading the whole Bible from end to end, but I didn't want to wait to read about Jesus. So I skipped to the New Testament and read the first few chapters of Matthew. Whenever I read the Sermon on the Mount, I always thought about how exciting it would have been to hear Jesus saying the actual words of Jesus. Maybe afterward I could've pushed my way through the crowd and shaken His hand and gotten an autograph. I could've been one of His first followers and warned Him about Judas and told Him not to worry because one day everybody would worship Him.

Around the parables, I stopped reading and skipped through to the illustrations and the places where they'd put the blue flags. Every flagged passage was about the badness of homosexuality. Reading them became depressing, so I got up and listened to a tape of the Clymer Sisters that they'd left in the radio. I lay down on the bed and marveled as the ladies' razor-sharp voices tore through "Trust in Him," "Almighty Faith," and other hits, and mouthed along to the words. Side one finished and I got real drowsy. I stared up at the ceiling and the pattern of light that the lamp shade made against the wall, the same shape as South Carolina. Bill and Gay wanted me to think on my broken past and how Christ could fix everything, and for a while I did that. I worried a lot about whether I could stop disappointing my wife and be a man. But after a while, my thoughts wandered back to sex with Manny.

As I undressed for bed, though, I found his phone number in my pocket and crumpled it up. I had been dishonest. Then I uncrumpled it and tried to memorize it. That turned out to be harder than I expected, so I slipped it between the mattress and the box spring. I knew I was doing a bad thing. But it wasn't an actual bad thing, just an action that could lead to a bad thing, and I still believed that that didn't count.

Once I got done with Safekeeping, Gay brought me down to my new room, 210, which I would share with a struggling brother. She knocked on the door to see if he was around before giving me the key. I was so sure that my roomie would be another feminine older man with froggy eyes that when Nicky Johnson swung the door half open and leaned against the knob, my blood took a wrong turn into my legs and I nearly lost my balance. To keep myself from staggering, I took a careful step backward.

If I'd known any better, I'd have given up right then and gone home to be gay. Physically, Nicky was kind of like Russ, but he had Euge's easy ways and Hank's green eyes. It wasn't just Nicky's chestnut-brown hair, his gently crooked nose, or his skin, smooth and warm as oak tag, that distracted me from Jesus's plan. From that first moment, everything floored me: his casual posture, those puppy-dog eyelids, always half-closed, the scar that cut through his right eyebrow, the shy smile, never big enough to show real happiness, his habit of biting his chapped lips—Oh boy, I could go on. But my attraction to him was more than physical. I looked at him and I knew nothing good could come of rooming with him. I knew it like a sneeze, or like thinking of a name I couldn't remember.

"Nicky, this is Gary. You guys are bunking together. Like everybody here, Gary's dealing with same-sex attraction issues and some difficulty in his past. Nicky's dealing with the same as well as pornography, and drugs, too, aren't you?"

"Yeah, and compulsive? I'm compulsive, sex-wise, too," he said, nodding. When he talked, the ends of all his sentences were question marks.

Focusing on Jesus, I shook Nicky's hand and told him how glad I was to meet him and help him through his troubled time, and weren't we going to beat this thing through the love of Christ. He wouldn't make eye contact. Gay nodded and patted our shoulders, excusing herself to let us get acquainted before the first meeting of this year's B-group men.

I moved my things into the room. The beds were lined up across from one another, and we each got a separate dresser. At the far end of the room we had a much cheerier window than the one in 307. It looked out toward the church, across the front lawn.

Once I'd moved all my stuff in, I couldn't stop talking. It made me nervous to have such an attractive guy around. I told Nicky nearly everything about myself and then some. He listened as he got ready to go to work—we all had to find nine-to-five jobs within thirty days of getting there. I eventually found an administrative job at a desktop publishing firm.

When I ran out of things about me, I asked him about himself. Nicky told me he'd just started work at a printing office a couple of days ago, so we had a little professional talk at first. Then he said he originally came from Baton Rouge, but at sixteen, his pop kicked him out of the house when he caught him having sex with another man. He said it was even a boyfriend he loved, not a cheap encounter, but that didn't matter. His mother agreed with his father, and even his brother sided with them because they all had religion. Nicky called his dad a "fucking hypocrite."

Nicky's boyfriend was his age, so Nicky couldn't live with him. They ended up running away to Chicago. They found a place but then broke up. They stayed roommates, but then they got into crack cocaine, and things *really* started going wrong. Eventually Nicky became a drifter. I wanted to hear more, but he kept saying he had to go. As usual, I couldn't help myself and kept asking questions until he broke the conversation off and closed the door.

That night, I officially met the other men in the program. Bill gathered all twelve of us on the couch in the rec room, and after we shook hands, he settled us down to make an announcement. "What I see in front of me is a bunch of straight guys," he crowed. "That's right! From now on, you are all heterosexual men. That's the way I want you to think of yourselves, because you've taken the first, biggest step toward curing your same-sex attractions. Give yourselves a big round of applause. You made it!" We all clapped.

"Great news!" Jake said, pretending to get up and leave. "Glad that's all over with." We laughed.

"Not so fast, Mister," Bill said. "Changing your mind about who you are is only the first step. Changing your *behavior* is step two through about two million. I can't just snap my fingers and turn you all straight. I wish I could." A serious hush fell among the guys. "But we're all going to work together to help you achieve your goals: leaving sin and decadence behind, and living in accordance with the truths of Jesus Christ. Because at Resurrection, we believe that if you change what you do and what you think, you are no longer the same person. Live in Christ, and He'll show you the way out of homosexuality." Another round of applause came on its own. Then Bill talked about his own struggle, including being molested by his great aunt for five years, followed by his mother's death and a period of teenage alcoholism and violence. Right when he was about to slash an ex-friend's throat with a broken bottle during a fight outside a gay bar, a medallion of Christ's head fell out from inside his victim's collar. When he saw that, Bill broke down.

Bill telling his story opened us all up to telling our own. Nicky told us about the rest of his life. At nine, his father had forced sex on him, and that kept on until he turned sixteen and his dad threw him out. "The bastard was jealous!" Nicky shouted, with a bitter laugh. After he got to Chicago, he had a lot of sex to raise his self-esteem and then got addicted to heroin. He had a falling-out with his ex over money and moved onto the street. For a year or two he lived in a squat and slept with men for drug money. This was less than a year ago. He told me later that he thought he might have AIDS but he didn't want to take the test.

Other guys had similar life stories. School bullies had beaten up George every day on his way back from high school. His father tried teaching him to fight but that didn't work. He came out of the closet and his folks shunned him. They stopped celebrating his birthday and giving him Christmas presents, and after a while they refused to even look at him, so eventually he had to move out.

Jake's parents had split up, and his protective father died. He didn't get along with his stepfather, and eventually the guy stabbed him in the back with an ice pick. He had to have extensive back surgery and was lucky to be alive. That explained why one of his shoulders was a little higher than the other. Keith, the other black guy in the program, came from Chicago. He had gotten fired because he stayed home and masturbated to male pornography instead of showing up at work. His fiancée found out. She broke off the engagement and told his family everything. Bernard, a Catholic priest, had been recognized in a gay bar and a scandal erupted. His church paid his way to come from Champaign, Illinois. They made a deal to take him back, but only if he graduated from Resurrection.

Glenn, a shy, nervous boy from Houston, came from oil money, and his parents had said they would disinherit him if he didn't change. Randolph, who'd escorted me to the john, was a sixty-seven-year-old retired dentist from Seattle. A widower, he had gone behind his wife's back with men since before they got married. He'd even had a twenty-year relationship on the side. After he'd broken up with the fellow and his wife had died, Randy started to go to gay bars and host late-night leather sex parties in his basement. He didn't like the person he was becoming, and he didn't want his folks to find out.

Derek, a big linebacker-sized guy with very feminine ways, cried when he talked about how living in the gay community had worsened his troubles, and didn't think he could change, but everybody begged him not to give up hope. A Cuban guy, Enrique, had a history of mental illness. His family had some money, and when he told them about his SSAs, his father told him to get married and have a kid anyway. Nobody in his family would talk to him, so he couldn't tell them that he was HIV-positive. Later in the program, he got attacked in the street by some anti-gay people even though he hadn't been doing anything gay.

When I told my story, I mentioned to Enrique that marrying a woman and having a child won't fix homosexual urges. Bill agreed. "Only committing yourself to Christ can do that," he said. By the end we'd all had ourselves a good cry. It felt great to be among people who understood, who could relate to my same difficulties. We hugged one another and Bill told us he loved us and had faith that we would all succeed. Judging from our stories, we all needed that.

Now that I'd come out of Safekeeping, I gained phone privileges. Annie had called several times, so I returned the call. We sighed and couldn't think of anything to say a lot of the time. I tried to fill the dead air with stories about my day. I told her about Nicky.

"What does he look like?" she asked.

"He's just some hick with a busted-up nose," I said. "He used to be a junkie."

"Is that... attractive to you? Does it seem tough?"

"No, no, no. I don't like tough."

"But you picked up a cop."

"Darn it, Annie, it isn't like that." It had gotten stuffy in the phone booth.

"Please just stop lying to me, Gary."

"Please just start trusting me. I'm not lying." Another long silence came, one that felt as long as the hundreds of miles between Memphis and Orlando.

"This is a lot of trouble for us," she said. "I'm counting on you to work hard." She meant to remind me that she'd paid off the debt I left when I died, and that I owed her something for all that.

"I told you I would use my job money to pay the fees," I protested. "It's not fair for you to put extra pressure on me."

"Now you're going to tell me about pressure? You want to raise a daughter on your own?" This time the silence took on a chilly, aggressive nature, like a draft forcing its way through a broken window.

"Put Cheryl on the phone," I said, to change the subject. From then on, Annie always brought her to the phone during our nightly calls, but she never asked to speak to me. I had one-sided conversations with her, and then Annie came back on and we'd argue until the cows came home—more like until the cows woke up the next morning.

I also gave my mother a call. She sounded very weak and far away, even though I could tell she was excited to hear from me after all this time. "I was like to die of grief," she said. "I lost my whole family," she kept saying. You didn't lose Joe, I wanted to tell her, you disowned him. But reminding her of that wouldn't have accomplished anything. Dakota and Lisette had been softening things when they talked about my father. It turned out he had died because he refused to go to the doctor for the disease that made his skin hard—scleroderma, Mama said—and it spread to his internal organs. Mama took him once he got too weak to protest, but it was too late—Daddy's stubborn nature killed him.

With the possibility of saying all I needed to say to him gone, I felt numb. Minister Mike's sermon came back to me, about how there was only time when somebody was alive to say you loved them, or that they'd hurt you. I wondered if the minister had ever found out about Chester, and what he'd done. I became angry with Daddy for everything he'd done to me, and even more with myself for never speaking up. I got afraid that if I couldn't confront my father, I'd never cure my gayness. Like he'd died on purpose, to fix me in time.

"Are you coming to see me?" Mama wanted to know.

"I'm not sure. I'm in this place, Mama."

"What do you mean you're not sure? Why can't you get down here? You in jail?"

"No, Mama, it's not jail, but I can't leave right now."

"Oh, I know, it's like a rehab. Are you on the drugs, Gary? There's nothing so bad you can't tell your mama."

Since she had come up with her own explanation, I decided not to complicate her life any more. "Yes, this place does help people who have had substance abuse problems," I managed to say. There *was* something too bad to tell my mama. The shadow of my father's ornery nature lived on in her, almost as powerful as when he was around. Maybe more, because the memory of somebody dead is always of a nicer person, one you ought to obey. Life never answers anybody's questions, but it seems like death makes you an authority on plumb near everything.

"It's good that you're getting help, Sugar. Just trust in the Lord, He'll see you through. You come soon, though, 'cause I ain't long for this world, you know. Without your daddy it ain't the same."

"I'll call again when I get the time." Mama proceeded to describe the fates of every family member and neighbor she thought I would remember, except for Joe. She talked so long that Dwayne, who was waiting for the phone, had to take the phone out of my hand, say good-bye to her, and hang up because my phone time had expired. I protested, but not a whole lot.

The typical day at Resurrection didn't include much free time. It reminded me of the snack food conferences I had gone to in the past, except that here the seminars and group discussions were mandatory. Breakfast took place from 7:30 to 8:30. Then we'd go to our jobs. Once we got back, we had a family-style supper at 6:30. From 7:45 to 10 on Mondays and Thursdays, we took a class on the steps out of homosexuality. The class focused on a bunch of things: it helped us identify and work through the root causes of our unwanted attractions, to center on the Lord and healing, to bond with one another and give one another strength, and to build strong masculine identities. We followed the principles laid down by Charlie—Dr. Charles Soffione, the founder of Resurrection Ministries, who had written a well-known book called *Stand Up Straight*. In the book, Dr. Soffione explains that SSAs aren't caused just by gender confusion, but also by the failure to bond properly with our same-sex parents. From the kinds of things people said about their parents in our sessions, it didn't seem like you could argue with that theory.

After 10 p.m. was Open Activity or Quiet Time. That meant phone calls and writing letters home for people who had family and friends, and playing ping-pong or pool or board games for everybody else. Tuesdays we studied the Bible from 7:30 to 10 p.m. Fridays we had Group Share at that same time. Group Share was like a confessional time, when we checked in and told the group about our daily struggles against homosexual attractions, usually for people we worked with at our nine-to-five jobs, or people from our pasts. If somebody had an attraction problem with another guy in the group, he had to report it to leadership, not confess it in Group Share. I decided to wait and see if my feelings for Nicky would go away on their own. Fat chance.

On the far wall in the rec room, we had a big whiteboard where Bill had drawn a grid. We wrote our names in rectangles that ran down the left side, and up top we numbered the boxes with every upcoming day for about a month. During our first Group, Bill opened a puzzle box of the United States. We each chose a state and wrote our names on it above the real name of the state. I chose first, so I took South Carolina. Then we glued magnets to the backs of the puzzle pieces and put them into the rectangles. The hope was that we could race each other to rack up the most consecutive days without giving in to any homosexual thoughts or urges. Sometimes you could get an extra day for performing a good deed, or get put back for bad behavior.

"We're at day four," Bill said. "Is there anyone who hasn't let any same-sex thoughts or urges affect them in the last four days?"

Everybody stayed silent and peeked at each other with embarrassment. There was a little bit of nervous chuckling. "How about in the last three days? No? We've got our work cut out for us, huh?" he joked. "How about one? Can I see *one* day without SSAs?" Randolph shuffled up to the board and pushed Delaware one square forward. Everybody applauded.

After the first month, we were allowed to sleep in on Saturdays. Later in the day we could leave the dorms and go to approved locations like the mall or the movies, or on day trips to the mountains or downtown. But for the first seven months, we had to be in phase if we went anywhere. "In phase" meant that you kept two other people with you at all times so that you'd all stay accountable. And for the first month, Saturday meant we had short one-on-one meetings with leadership in the morning. In the afternoon we had Masculinity Repair, a monthlong workshop where we played football and learned how to build additions to houses and fix domestic cars.

On Sundays, we crossed the sloping lawn and filed into the cream-colored church on the hill to attend services until about 1 p.m. The rest of Sunday was Family Day. Not meaning our biological families—they had to wait three months before visiting. Family Day meant all the guys hung out together, played board games, and made supper. Nothing too complicated. Sometimes we molded our own burgers with ground beef and onion dip mix, or baked a mess of chicken wings. Keith made a stir-fry once, but he said he was worried that making fancy meals was a feminine thing to do. Jake shook him by the shoulders and said, "Don't be stupid, dude! Most chefs are guys!"

I loved life at Resurrection. The regimen probably seems tough to most people, but I found it comforting. I knew that I needed to be watched constantly or I would fall back into homosexual behavior. In my life, I had almost never had erotic thoughts about women, but I wanted to touch or kiss practically every man I saw, just to test him out. The tight schedule also brought back the good memories of my childhood. In fact, following it wasn't nearly as difficult as all the chores my father had set me and my brother to as kids. I liked waking up and knowing exactly what was expected of me every day, and when I would eat and play and sleep. It did away with the chaos of life and replaced it with a plan that would lead somewhere positive—to my being fixed.

Gay turned out to be my personal counselor. She was the first to notice that I was taking things in stride, and pretty fast, on the one-month anniversary of my stay.

"Wow, Gary," she said. "It's like you've been here for a year already." I had volunteered to lead a group in prayer the night before, and had joined the custodial and kitchen committees. She'd heard from Bill that I spoke up a lot during Group Share. Mostly I asked stupid questions, but participating mattered more than what you said. Gay praised my progress when I told her about any breakthroughs during my counseling sessions. The more praise I got from her, though, the harder it became to mention my problem with Nicky. If I caught myself admiring him powerful hard, I had a trick where I would replace his face with Christ's, so the Palmetto State stayed neck-in-neck with Delaware on the big chart. I avoided tense situations by staying out of our room most of the time, like I'd done with Russ. Soon I gained a reputation among my peers for helping others who had difficulty coping.

Bill also took notice. During Masculinity Repair, he realized that I had some knowledge about sports, so he encouraged me to show some of the other men how to hold the bat, how to catch with a glove, and how to throw a curveball.

My new brothers were so grateful that my belief in Dr. Soffione's theories rose up fast as a row of bean plants. For the first time ever, I spoke about an experience I had with molestation during a tear-filled Group Share, and Bill added it to my personal list of root causes.

Before I got there, I thought that touching men would be a no-no in the program. But Dr. Soffione's method didn't mean no physical affection between men. He believed that closeness with other men was exactly what we SSA-sufferers needed. But we had to regulate the contact and neutralize it. Lots of good masculine physical contact would test the sufferer's will power. Bill touched us affectionately and encouraged us to be playful with one another. But he warned us not to let Satan's lust spoil the experience. If we found ourselves attracted to another man in the program, we had to follow through and allow ourselves to experience the attraction, but turn it into something loving so that we'd stop far short of sin.

My first reaction to that policy was to get turned on in the secret part of my head about the possibility of touching Nicky. Any fool could tell you that making homosexual behavior more forbidden won't make it less attractive. I had *never* felt free to touch other men, not even when I went to gay bars. Now I could do it all I wanted. Of course, I wasn't fixing to disobey the rules, and I didn't intend to abuse the privilege of touching other men. I convinced myself not to admit my arousal, and thought that making male touch normal would help heal me, until one afternoon out on the lawn during Masculinity Repair.

We were playing softball. Before the game we had talked about our childhood experiences with sports, and especially how we'd failed to connect with our fathers through playing games. George said that the first time his father took him into the backyard to play catch and threw the ball at him, he let it fall to the ground. He stared at it and asked his dad, "Why did you do *that*?" His pop gave up then and there.

We divided up into two teams of six. Nicky ended up on my team. He struggled to hold the bat and swing properly. Dropping it several times, he giggled at himself and smoothed back his hair. He said he still wasn't used to the shorter haircut he'd had to get to enter the program. Everybody's attention always swung over to him—or maybe that was just my impression. His true vulnerable nature showed in his boyish looks and gestures. When he put his hand on his cheek or slapped his head with his palm it always made him more attractive to me. Of course nobody said anything, but I sensed that many of the other men in our group felt the same about him as I did. Nobody volunteered to help Nicky hold the bat. I looked into my brother strugglers' eyes and they all looked down or away.

Telling myself that it was in the interest of testing out Dr. Soffione's ideas, I took a breath, approached Nicky, and offered my help, reaching both arms around him to move his hands farther down on the bat. Raising his right elbow slightly, I instructed him to keep his eyes on the ball and hit as hard as he could. I smelled the faint odor of cologne or shaving cream around his neck. I caught myself breathing into his ear the way my father had done to me during my Little League games.

My lips got close enough to plant a kiss on his cheek. A hot, tingling sensation spread from my groin through my entire body. Holding my breath, I allowed it to flow through me. But instead of acting on it, I tried to enjoy the sensation for its own sake. I closed my eyes and held my tongue tight, like I was sucking on a butterscotch candy. The Lord, I reminded myself, was showing me the joy in fellowship, the nice side of desire. No need to take it further. Except that I couldn't control the stiffness in my crotch. I did my best to hide it and I think nobody noticed. That's one advantage of a fat stomach.

When Nicky's turn came at bat, I patted him on the shoulder to give him confidence. After a couple of strikes, he hit the ball pretty far. He was so pleased with himself that he bounced on his heels a few times before realizing that he had to run the bases. As he ran, the outfielders fumbled the ball, so we yelled at him to keep running. The ball didn't get to second base before he got to third, so everybody encouraged him to run home. Nicky got back safely and everybody shouted and rushed up to hug him.

Pride—and a rush of lust—pushed me toward him faster than some of the other players. Thinking of Dr. Soffione's words, though, I didn't worry. But when I embraced Nicky and we hopped up and down with the others in glee, I found that I couldn't let him go. It had been a while since I'd touched anybody. The warmth of his skin and his clean polo shirt increased my level of temptation. Even though he wasn't a good athlete and he hadn't worked out much, his arms and chest were naturally firm. Everybody swatted him on the butt like real baseball players. I looked around his shoulder and down his back. I meant to swat, but before I knew what I was doing, I squeezed him pretty hard.

Well, you bet I pulled my hand away like I'd gotten an electric shock. Resurrection had real strict guidelines against lustful touch, especially grabbing. But I couldn't take it back. I became extremely disappointed in myself. For the rest of the game, I could only focus on my failure to resist that urge. All three times I went to bat, I struck out.

As the last part of Masculinity Repair, when the game ended, everybody always shared his experiences. I knew somebody had seen the squeeze and would report me if I didn't confess. But I didn't want Nicky to know how I felt and be uncomfortable in our dorm. So without mentioning the act specifically, I admitted to the group that the home-run moment had aroused me in a way that didn't make me proud. I decided not to bring up the much more difficult moment of helping Nicky hit the ball.

Keith, the pitcher, spoke up. He was average height and slim, with a round head and meaty lips, and he stuttered slightly. I couldn't understand why the guys kept mixing us up. "That was a difficult moment for me, too, Gary. Just before it happened, I predicted that the hugging was going to be problematic for me. Nicky is a very handsome young man, I'm sure we can all agree on that." We acknowledged everybody's positive traits in public to make them feel good. The other guys nodded enthusiastically. "He's got a great smile," George said. Nicky rolled his eyes, but he blushed and held back that smile, too.

"So I had to take a deep breath," Keith continued, "and think about what Christ would want for me in that situation. I also reminded myself of the big picture. Giving in to those gay impulses is a dead end. They lead you down a path that's away from God. That's how you can tell that Satan is the one who puts them in your mind." The others expressed their agreement and added their own observations about the hugging. "Didn't you think of your wife and child, Gary?"

"You're right, Keith," I said. "I lost focus. That's always what makes me real disappointed in myself. Even after almost a month here, I feel like I'm moving toward the heterosexual life that God wants for me, but sometimes I lose control and—" I couldn't finish the sentence because I was becoming emotional. The possibility that I would never make progress opened in front of me like a deep cave. I shut my eyes.

Bill clapped his palms on my shoulders and massaged them. Another tingle of erotic feeling went through me and landed in my crotch. To focus, I imagined Christ in pain, writhing in blood beneath His crown of thorns.

"Gary," Bill said, "you're being pretty hard on yourself. You want your progress chart to be a diagonal line going right up to 100 percent straight in no time flat. But anyone here can tell you that it isn't going to happen in a month, or even in a year, am I right? We all have good days and bad days. Days where we beat the demons back successfully, and other days when our cravings for physical intimacy with another man reach practically unbearable levels, am I right? But we're here to repair the things that need fixing, guys. That means what?" Bill counted Dr. Soffione's guidelines on his fingers. "Learning to express our feelings for other men in a productive, nonsexualized manner. Building bridges back to our father-son relationship, which will lead to what? A full expression of our true masculine nature, culminating in an increased desire for the female companionship God created us to enjoy. Yeah!" He pumped his fist in a masculine manner. "That's a lot of work, guys. But Rome wasn't built in a day, am I right?"

We applauded Bill's pep talk and started walking toward the house. "Tomorrow's forecast is for rain," Bill announced on the way, "so Keith's suggestion is that we watch the Cubs game on TV in the rec room."

Nicky lagged behind as we walked back to put the equipment away. A strong wind bent the trees and then slowly released them. I thought I owed him an apology, so I slowed down and let him catch up to me. "Nicky, I'm sorry. I shouldn't have done that."

His face tensed. "Done what? Oh, that was *you*, huh? I was hoping it was Bernard," he whispered. Bernard, the pastor, was the team's MVP, a stocky guy with a neat beard, a gut, and thick hair on his arms and the back of his neck. Though his voice was kind of high, he didn't act like he needed his masculinity repaired at all. He helped out a lot during those classes, too. "I guess I'm supposed to tell you that I feel violated and that your touch was inappropriate and whatnot? But when I was turning tricks for smack, a lotta them guys done much worse all the time." He rolled up his shirt and pointed out a raised scar snaking up his side. It reminded me of the railroad tracks in North Charleston.

"This ex-Marine dude did that with a broken bottle while I was high. I lost a lot of blood." He turned and lifted up more of his shirt in the back. A bruise bloomed out from the small of his back almost to his waist, yellow at the edges, darkening into a horrible reddish black in the center. "That's recent, from my ex. So I mean, don't do it again, but it wasn't that big a deal or nothing. Compared to." I had seen his scars and bruises before, when he took his shirt off at night, but I didn't want to let him know that I'd looked. Steady, I said to myself. Think on Christ.

My eyes widened, even though by that time I had already heard about Nicky's days in Chicago. Many of the men at Resurrection had medicated their homosexual longings, suffered at the hands of parents and strangers who didn't understand, become alcoholics, drug addicts, and sex work-ers, gone bankrupt, and had wound up on the streets, on the wrong side of the law, or any combination of all that bad luck. Like me, many had attempted suicide, most more than once. Some had contracted STDs and would have to take huge pills with mysterious long-term effects for the rest of their lives.

"For me it *is* a big deal. You're more here for the drug problems, I guess," I continued.

"Kinda. But I also hate being gay, so I thought while I'm here I should take care of that, too." He giggled. "Two birds with one stone."

"If you really wanted Bernard to touch you in an ungodly way, why didn't you speak up during the talk-back? You know you're going to be held accountable."

"Oh, I was just kidding. Please don't tell nobody. If you tell anybody I said that, I'ma tell 'em you grabbed my sweet little butt. I'm really trying to live for Christ, I swear on a stack of Bibles." Bernard reached the top of the steps on the patio and stretched in a way that was almost provocative. Both of us couldn't help turning to watch him. "But before I lived for Christ, I lived for trade like that."

Hearing the strain in his voice from trying to lower his tone, I almost laughed in despair. The men and women at Resurrection had such wide gaps between who we were and what God intended for us. It broke my heart to think what a long road Nicky had ahead of him, from a terrible past of abuse in the streets to a confident, strong family man. But as we climbed the steps and spilled into the hallway, jostling for the water fountain and dropping our baseball caps on the multicolored chairs in the hallway, our past-life difficulties crumbled away. It gave me a thrill to think that retracing the negative stuff in our boyhoods could undo the terrible things that had gone wrong in our lives and turn us normal. I really did feel like a kid again, or at least a young guy with a second chance.

Keith saw Nicky and me speaking in twos as we climbed the steps to the main building and scrambled over. "Hey," he warned, "you guys are out of phase. Mind if I join you?" Being in phase was mostly meant for trips outside the complex, but Keith wasn't completely joking. Nicky and I brought our conversation to a halt.

Unfortunately, my desire for Nicky shot way up after our talk. Just when I thought it had reached its highest level, it always went farther. After our heart-to-heart, I understood that by praising Bernard, he had rejected me. This was Russ Part II. How could I not have seen it coming? To control the spike in my sexual appetite, I took a deep breath and concentrated on my future goals. In Group the previous Thursday, we'd drawn an image for ourselves of what our lives would be like once we learned to manage our same-sex drives. With the set of colored pencils, I had made a picture of Annie, Cheryl, and myself holding hands, standing in front of a colorful house with smoke coming out of the chimney. Angels and Jesus flew above the smoke, watching over everything. Gay told me to think on that picture whenever I thought I might slip.

Nicky ran ahead of me down the hall to the water fountain, his feet thumping the floor and ringing out with a slapback sound. I couldn't imagine going through the kind of experiences he had, but even those terrible times hadn't erased his youthful spirit. I concentrated as hard as I could on the picture of my wife and daughter in my mind and bit down hard on my tongue.

"Oh, Gary," Annie said to me one night as we ended another half-silent conversation, "I hate to think about us not being together anymore." She was more tired than angry.

I stood up in the phone booth. "No! We're going to work this out." Jake knocked on the glass to say that my time had run out. I waved him away.

"You think so? You don't believe in divorce, but you believe in running off to join the circus of sin."

"Annie! Don't you still love me?"

"Of course I do—but you have really tried my patience, Gary. Any sane woman would have thrown up her hands and said aloha."

"I thought you'd be overjoyed when I came back a changed man."

Annie sighed. "You have no idea what I went through. Everyone thought your body had burned up in the fire. In the back of my mind I held out a tiny hope that something bizarre had happened, because at first they didn't find anything at all. That you had hit your head and gotten amnesia and walked away from the accident. But then they found your wallet and I began to grieve. I bought five pillows and wrapped them in a sheet and clung to them every night for a while. After a few months, your mother and I decided to hold a funeral, so that we could start coming to terms with what had happened. At the service, we buried the wallet. That was your mother's idea. She wanted it to be buried in South Carolina, but I knew you'd want to be near Disney World, so we did it down here.

"I couldn't hear the word *Disney World* without becoming emotional, you know? I thought about leaving Orlando, because I couldn't watch TV or read the newspaper or drive down the highway or leave the house without seeing Disney World signs, and they made me so sad. Every day on the way to work I would pass a billboard of Mickey in his costume from *The Sorcerer's Apprentice*, and I'd think, Mickey, please use your magic to bring back my husband! And I would weep a little, because I knew that if Jesus couldn't do it, Mickey certainly couldn't." Annie chuckled at herself and coughed before going on.

"I quit my job at the travel agency. Every time I went to church, I begged your forgiveness in my prayers and consoled myself with the fact that you were saved, and you were with Jesus. I got a loan, started the restaurant, and tried to move on. I even looked at a few other men here and there. But then Lisette's friend, the Chinese girl, found me and said you were alive, living a homosexual lifestyle.

"It hurt me that you hadn't wanted to share the problem with me. I wished we could've worked on it together as husband and wife. But I knew that it must have tormented you a great deal if you felt you had to keep it hidden for so long."

Jake started yanking on the phone booth door. I had jammed my fingers into the handle and positioned my foot at the bottom so that he couldn't move it. I gestured to him to leave me alone, but his face became redder and more insistent. "Everything takes time, Annie," I said. "And this is a terrific opportunity. We'll work it out. No divorce."

"I've been through a lot," Annie sighed, "but I'll stand by you for as long as I can."

"Till death do us part?"

"I don't think I can do that again," she said, with a little sad laughter in her voice. We sort of made up, or at least stopped talking angrily, and she agreed to send some of my possessions on, including my Jesuses. We said good-bye and I stepped out of the booth. I apologized to the line of four people waiting for the phone. I knew I would be penalized for going over my allotted half hour. I was late for Group Share, too, and would probably be docked from phone privileges the next day.

Annie was right, I thought as I hurried down the hall. I wanted too many different things that didn't work together. I fought just as hard to up my desire for women as I did to get rid of my longings for males, and I wound up nowhere, failing at both. I had pretended to be the person Annie needed me to be and messed up royally. I wanted to try again, but without the risk of repeating the same blunders.

THIRTEEN

Two months of learning to put language on my inner struggles and cope with my past improved my attitude a whole bunch. Resurrection Ministries taught me the right words to describe everything that had happened to me. The language was like a cage where I could put all the nameless fears that had roamed around inside me from my earliest memories. A few weeks into the program, Bill gave us an assignment to write down a ten-page autobiography. Up until then, I hadn't understood the logic of my life story. I'd never taken the opportunity to reflect on the choices that I had made over the years, and how one thing had led to another. How had I fallen so far from what Christ intended, and how could I get on the path to righteousness?

In school, I'd hated writing. Ten pages seemed like an awful lot. But once I started the autobiography project, I couldn't keep away from the computer in the communal area. Truth be told, there were a number of nights when I snuck downstairs after lights-out and continued writing. Bill told me he knew I did it against the chain of command, but the sight of me tapping away on the keyboard, lost in memories and lit by the bluish glow of the computer screen, renewed his belief in his mission so much that he decided not to stop me. The positive, encouraging responses I got from my peers in Group also inspired me to continue working. Several of them started to expand their testimonials, too.

Writing triggered my memory. In Group, we had talked a lot about the broken places in us where homosexuality could get in. A lot of the other men told stories about childhood sexual abuse, but I had only suffered physical abuse from my father. Still, something dawdled in my mind, a blurry piece of a memory that I had not thought on in some years. While sitting at the terminal and trying to coax it out of my head, I suddenly sat up and remembered about the Black Witch.

Magic Harbor on Myrtle Beach. Folks nicknamed it Haunted Harbor because a bunch of robberies and accidents had ruined its reputation as an amusement park. It started out as a Wild West theme park. The summer I turned twelve, the Stage Coach ride crashed and killed a man from Charlotte. The park changed management, but bandits held up the office the next summer—some said they did it with antique pistols. The next managers owned an amusement park in England, so they made the place all British. The barmaids at the restaurant called you "Luv" and said "Bloody this!" and "Bloody that!"

Of course, Mama and Daddy wouldn't let me go on some rides. Roller coasters were okay, but haunted houses came in high on the list of Christian no-nos, because they made Hell seem like fun, like eternal damnation would end in five minutes. Mama hated the Black Witch the most. They'd painted the head of a witch on the front, with black skin and yellow eyes. The grinning old crone didn't look like a black person, though; her skin seemed like it had gone black from dirt, falling down a chimney, or pure evil.

On the first fair day that spring, Joe and I were supposed to be looking for my daddy, who had gone out looking for Joe to beat him the night before and hadn't come back. He'd just found out about Joe's Gullah girl Desiree, but not her pregnancy. Daddy called Gullah people "countrified niggers" and told us to mind that our people were from upcountry, around Bishopville and Columbia. "Why the fuck would I want to find Daddy?" Joe said once we got far enough away from the house. "So he could beat the shit out of me?"

I covered my ears. "Joe, don't curse!"

Joe hooked his hands into my elbows and pulled my hands away from my head. "Don't you get sick of being a goody-goody all the time, Gary? Don't you want to *live?*"

"All I know is we've got to find Daddy."

"You can look for him if you want. I hope they find the motherfucker hanging from a fucking oak tree by his nut sack." Joe pulled a pack of cigarettes out of his sock and tugged a matchbook from behind the cellophane. When he blew smoke through his nose, his nostrils flared like a dragon's. "I know who I'ma find, and her name is *Desiree*," he breathed, saying the name like an enchanted city.

Blabbing about trivial things, I walked him to the bus stop and waved when the bus pulled off and covered me in a black cloud of exhaust. I watched the bus, thinking Joe had crossed a bridge into a world where I could never follow.

Even though it felt dumb, I looked into people's side yards, over their walls, and around the thick trunks of sycamores. I pressed my face against the windows of the shops on King Street, though I knew my father would sooner be caught in a cathouse. I zigzagged through the tight cobblestone streets downtown until it hurt to walk. My steps came to a crawl and I took deep, sweet breaths by a brick wall draped in honeysuckle.

When I got to the Battery, I climbed up the railing and watched sailboats leap over sharp waves in the harbor. I dropped some pebbles into the water. Stretching my arms, I closed my eyes and pretended to be a seagull soaring out to the Atlantic Ocean over Fort Sumpter and Sullivan's Island. Feeling the breeze on my cheeks, I said my usual prayer to Jesus to stop me from being evil.

But when I opened my eyes, I saw Eugene McCaffrey down the walkway. He stood with his back against the iron railing. I hadn't spoken to him in two months. I caught my breath because he didn't have a shirt on. Euge kept his elbows hooked over the top bar and turned his round face up into the sun. The gold in the tips of his messy hair glowed in the light, and that made me think of the Savior, who was also blond, on the cross. Eventually Euge saw me, waved, and galloped in my direction. I didn't move.

Euge and his sister Kinky were waiting for their aunt and uncle. Gizzy, their mom, wasn't recovering well from a third bout with lymphoma. Eugene Sr. had a drinking problem worse than my father's, so Lorna and Dave would take the kids off their hands sometimes. Euge bragged that he'd conned them into driving up to Haunted Harbor on opening day, which was that day. I couldn't have improved my luck if I'd had three wishes.

"Got plans?" Kinky asked me, biting candy dots off a strip of wax paper. For some reason I thought about Joe kissing Desiree right then.

Pretty soon Dave and Lorna caught up to Euge, Kinky, and me. They asked if I needed my parents' permission to go with them to Magic Harbor and I told them no. Eugene grinned at me and his eyes twinkled because he must have known I lied. Technically, Mama hadn't said I couldn't go there, and as long as I kept looking for Daddy, how could she complain? As we walked to the car Euge put his nose right up in my ear and whispered, "I'm glad you're my friend again." A big shiver went down my spine, so big that it made me sort of wiggle my butt.

I won the coin toss for the front seat and we piled into the Plymouth Duster. Being included in a white person's family felt strange but familiar, like stepping through a mirror. Euge's people talked more like Negroes than Daddy ever allowed Joe and me to do at home. They used a lot of slang, all sorts of bad grammar, and rude expressions—Dave cursed in front of us and let Euge call him by his first name.

Up front I had the best view, and a ringside seat to Dave. Dave had what you might call an eager smile. When he flared his soft gray eyes, you thought that he might lick your face next. He reminded me of a performer who came to Sanders-Clyde Elementary School once and made balloon animals for us, including a parrot that sat on its own balloon perch. I'd never seen such thick veins on anybody's arms.

Dave never stopped fidgeting. He could drive, smoke, listen, and talk all at the same time. When everybody else got quiet, he sang along with "Black Water" on the radio. I mean screamed: *And I ain't got no worries, 'cause I ain't in no hurry at all!* It sounded like a dog howling, so we all covered our ears. Dave drove fast, and when he talked, the cigarette in his mouth bobbed up and down in time with his voice, hypnotizing me. He tapped the long ash outside before it fell, and patted his stomach. "I got me a letter in wrestling 'fore I turned into a lardball," he said.

We laughed at everything he said. When Dave smiled, he showed off all his teeth, top and bottom, and he made me guess which one wasn't real. I chose the wrong one. He gave us a lot of advice about how to get divorced, what fishing poles to buy, and how to cheat Breathalyzers and polygraphs. "You stick a thumbtack in your sneaker, see, and ever' time they ask a tough question, like 'Didja kill him?' you step on that sucker. Remember that."

Clouds blew in from the west as we sped north, cooling the air and bringing down little pinpricks of rain. Euge pulled a T-shirt over his head. The weather sure could change fast in South Carolina. Windy and cool in the morning, warm and smelling like the ocean around midday, then sweaty like a hog in the afternoon, with delicious barbecue smells from every smokehouse in town hanging in the air.

Euge and I broke off from the other three when we hit the park. We stood under a British flag. "They call it the Union Jack," he said, almost proudly. "Don't that sound like a dude? Like, 'Hey, my name is Union Jack!'"

Everybody agreed to meet back under one of the metal umbrellas near the King Charles Pub in an hour or so if the rain got heavy. I started to feel guilty. What if God had sent the clouds because he disapproved of my running off to Magic Harbor? What if my father was lying facedown in a ditch somewhere? How would I feel then? Before he whipped me and Joe, Daddy would sometimes remind us that the commandment "Honor thy mother and father" ranked higher than "Thou shalt not kill."

We started with the Tilt-A-Whirl, braved the Scrambler, and made our way to the Trabant. To get to the Trabant you had to pass the Black Witch. I hadn't told anybody that I couldn't ride some rides. I took a deep breath as we passed the nasty mural, staying behind Euge so he couldn't tell I was nervous. A chilly breeze flew up my shirt—maybe it was her breath! I tried not to look, but I couldn't resist a peek over my shoulder. Looking away quickly, I warded her off by reciting the Twenty-third Psalm.

Aside from the Magic Mountain, where you paid a separate fee, the only ride with a line was the Bumper Cars. We got in line and Euge spotted Ye Merrie Sweet Shoppe across the walkway. He got an urge for almond toffee, so I held our place. When he came back, I was leaning against one of the guideposts, like Euge had done earlier. I was lost in a daydream about living at Gizzy's and going to Magic Harbor with Dave and Lorna every weekend.

Euge had a white paper bag full of chocolate-covered squares shoved into his armpit. I hadn't moved forward in line very much. With a sigh, Euge turned and rested his back against me. His shirt heated up my chest, the bag crinkled, and I felt his body up against mine, from his chunky legs to that silky mess of hair. When it brushed across my face, it smelled like soap, and that took me by surprise. Euge turned around and smiled, at the same time as he put one hand in the bag and offered me a toffee. For a split second I wanted to pull him closer. I thought about resting my nose against the sweet skin behind his ear, pulling his scent up into my lungs. But I suddenly thought of his naked, rubbery body trembling next to me, my hand pulling on his slimy pecker and getting all dirty. Suddenly I couldn't take the lovebird stuff and I pushed him off. "What do you think you're doing?" I burst out in a whisper.

Euge stumbled forward, caught himself, and turned around. Carefully, he showed me how to bite all the chocolate off a toffee until there was just the gold under it. Talking with his mouth full, he started prattling about Mr. Mullen, one of our English teachers, and how he had no ass. Euge loved to talk loud about stuff you shouldn't talk loud about.

On the Bumper Cars, he creamed me. Grinning like a demon, he called me a new curse every time he blindsided me. Sparks flew on the wire grid up above. We rode alongside one another and he bumped from the side. Then he reversed his car so he could collide with me head-on, even though you weren't supposed to do that. Once the cars slowed down, we stumbled to the exit, wild and dizzy.

Still flushed from the ride, we headed toward the King Charles English Pub. "Say you're sorry," Euge demanded. In the collision I had jammed my funny bone, so I was focused on massaging away the tingle and throb.

"For what?" He'd nearly given me a concussion and now he wanted an apology?

"You know what." I couldn't figure out what to save my life.

During the rest of that trip, Euge kept giving me one-word answers and acting bored when I talked. He put his nose up at everything I liked. Playing keep-away with the toffee, he sat as far away from me as he could at the pub. I tried to sneak a chip off him and he pulled them away.

"We're going to ride the paddleboats," Lorna announced after lunch. We meant her and Kinky. "Who else is going?" I said I didn't want to, thinking that would win Euge back. But he volunteered to go with them. Paddleboats were suddenly the coolest thing in the park. I sulked, and I reckon it showed on my face.

"Union Jerk," I muttered.

"Hey, are Fric and Frac having a lovers' quarrel?" Kinky asked.

"Shut up, *Kimberly*," Euge spat back.

She kicked him in the shins under the table, and he howled. "Don't ever call me The Name!" she barked. He showered her with fries. Lorna broke up the quarrel by smacking them both in the arm. They told Lorna that she didn't have the right to hit them, and Dave hit them for complaining and sassing Lorna. When the hitting stopped, a tent of silence collapsed on us. We picked at the hard fish filets. I watched a piece of Kinky's hair wave in the wind like a feather above her shiny forehead.

"Hey, Gary," Dave said to me with his licking expression. "I'll bet you want to ride the Black Witch with me, don't you?"

Terror shot through me. I'd been so wrapped up in figuring out why Euge suddenly hated me that I'd forgotten about the Black Witch. It was like Dave reached into my mind and pulled out my worst fear, right when Euge betrayed me and I couldn't protest.

"I can't, sir," I said, hoping I wouldn't have to admit why.

"C'mon, don't be a wimp." Dave yanked me to my feet and started walking. I had to follow him just out of respect.

I still didn't know why Euge wanted me to apologize. When we got halfway to the ride, it fell on me like a sack of cornmeal. Without excusing myself, I ducked under the fence and ran toward the paddleboats. I'd swim across the moat and kiss Euge's paddling sneakers. If I could've swum. *I'm sorry*, I would tell him. *I'm real sorry*. But Dave came after me, grabbed me by the wrist, and dragged me back to the same place in line. People around us raised their eyebrows.

"You can't wimp out on me," he said. I failed to catch my breath. "If you see the Devil in there, we can turn around. But don't worry, he's an old buddy of mine," he giggled. I leaned my forehead against the rail, thinking it wasn't funny to pretend to be friends with the Devil. Slowly we edged toward the ticket-taker.

Dave kept talking. A book he'd read said that nobody needed a high school diploma to make a good living, and he agreed. Then he changed the subject, like something had just come to him. "You and Euge are real close, huh," Dave observed. I didn't agree but I nodded anyhow. "Do you think that's *natural*, Gary?" I couldn't answer. I couldn't tell if he thought two boys spending too much time together was unnatural, or if a black boy and a white boy spending time together was unnatural. "Don't you got other friends?"

"Yeah, plenty, sir," I lied. My nervousness increased with every step forward in line. Could he tell I was ashamed not to have other friends? Did he want to break me and Euge up? In my mind I started to recite the Twenty-third Psalm again. There were only five riders ahead of us. That meant three gondolas. I counted one, two, three. We were going to sit in *that* empty car bobbing toward us.

"You know what I think?" Dave said when we hit the front of the line. He never stopped smiling, did he?

"No, sir, what?" Dave kept me guessing; he didn't say anything else until we'd slipped into the gondola and the attendant locked the iron bar across our laps. The cars on the Black Witch were the hooded bell kind, more like little private places than roller-coaster cars. Dave leaned down, put his hand on my opposite shoulder, and let it rest there.

Poking me in the center of my rib cage, he said, "I think you're a fudgepacker."

I didn't know what that meant, and I couldn't tell if it was good or bad. He didn't explain. Did it have to do with the toffee? We entered the darkness, bumping through a pair of scary doors. The gondola took a twisty path, tripping lights on terrifying scenes splattered with brightly colored paint. You'd go toward one like you were about to crash into it and the monster inside would get you, then it turned at the last second. First we saw a coffin draped in cobwebs. When we bumped into it, a skeleton sat up from the casket and went *Ha ha ha ha ha!*

I tried not to scream like a girl, but I did. Boy, I covered my face lickety-split when that skeleton popped up. Dave put his arm all the way around me. His beer gut was right up beside me. That should have made me feel better but it didn't. Dave held on to my shoulder blade and stroked it, gently at first. Then he took to pushing on it so I would lean into his lap. "Don't be afraid, Gary," he soothed. He pushed me harder.

I peeked through my fingers and saw Frankenstein tipping his hat. That big old ugly head was still attached to the hat! Terrified, I let Dave push me down. "Don't be afraid, Gary," he whispered. "Be a man." Dave had pulled down his sweatpants. It smelled like an armpit down there. He held the back of my neck in place, pushed my hands apart and gripped my shaved head like a basketball. "Open your mouth," he said. "Open your fucking *mouth*." His movements got real strong and sharp. He twisted one of my ears and wouldn't let me sit up. I couldn't see anything, but I could still hear all the monsters whooping and cackling.

After the ride, I didn't stop crying for a while. A woman came by and asked why—did I lose my mama? Dave said, "He's with me. He got scared by the ride," and pointed to the Black Witch with his chin. Dave patted my hair. He blotted my tears with his T-shirt and threatened to tell everybody I'd cried if I didn't stop. He bought me a cotton candy and said that oughta shut me up. "Don't say I never did nothing for you," he joked. Except for inside the Black Witch, he never stopped smiling and acting friendly.

We sat on a bench where we could hear cartoon noises from the shooting gallery. After I bit all the sweet pink fluff off the cardboard stick, I pulled my arms inside my shirt to keep warm. A long, quiet mood came over me, like a movie that ends on a beach. It had gotten colder and darker outside, but that didn't bother Dave. He flicked his lighter again and again but couldn't get fire. He kept asking me how we were going to explain what happened. "What should we tell them, Gary?" he asked, "Huh?" the cigarette wagging in his mouth like a blaming finger. "Better not tell them you cried like a sissy."

I was teary-eyed when I got done typing all this up. I remembered most of what I thought had happened. But even through my tears, I couldn't remember for sure if the sexual abuse part happened for real or not. I tried pretty hard to be sure, but see, a little bit after that, I took a job at Dave's gardening center. Would I have done that after him sexually abusing me? I still am not quite sure. So when I told it to my brothers in Group, I made sure to say that I didn't know if the sex part really happened. But my brothers said it didn't matter, that the story felt true enough. George even said, "*I* think it happened." If a story can heal folks, then I suppose the truth of it doesn't matter so much.

The Black Witch was dismantled a few years after Dave and I rode it. A lady stood up in one of the gondolas and got her head chopped clean off.

* * *

With all the different types of silence, my calls with Annie got very heated over the next few months. Annie liked to remind me how much the program cost her. She felt like I had been away so long that she had forgotten what it was like to have a husband. She'd mention divorce and I would panic and weep.

Cheryl kept refusing to speak to me. Annie thought it had a lot to do with the promise I had made. She reminded me of the many betrayals I had subjected her and Cheryl to. Sometimes she threatened to divorce me and not to help pay for the program and never let me see Cheryl again. Once she even got Cheryl to agree. I cried a lot, and said that my SSA problem made me do terrible things that I couldn't even describe. I even confessed my belief that God had planned everything. She laughed at me and blamed me for not taking responsibility for anything, which hurt a whole lot. "No matter if Jesus told you to do it," she said. "He might have told you to do the wrong thing just to test your judgment."

"That's blasphemous, Annie!" I shouted.

"Jesus is a tricky guy," Annie replied. "He talks in riddles and teaches people by letting them make mistakes. He doesn't want you to take Him at face value, because you won't have your own epiphany about what He means. When He talks about mustard seeds, he doesn't mean mustard seeds!"

"Sure He does," I said. "What is that supposed to mean?"

"Think about it, Gary!"

Underneath all our yelling, I thought I noticed that we got back little sparks of what we had when we first met. Either that or I hoped for the sparks more than they existed. She opened up and told me more about how her life had changed. She and a friend had started the restaurant and named it Pago Pago. He cooked the food and she managed the place. They had done real well for themselves. Eventually she found a way of paying for my time at Resurrection using her health insurance plan.

A whole bunch of telephone dustups later, Annie found a special promotion on a plane ticket and she and Cheryl came to visit for a weekend after the waiting period ended. We toured the grounds together, I introduced her to Bill and Gay and the guys and took her to my job. Cheryl wanted to play putt-putt golf at the Big River Amusement Center next door to the hotel, so we spent part of Saturday afternoon there. Annie and I held hands and made nice like loving parents, partly to show our child how together we were and also to prove it to ourselves. Cheryl did better than we did at putt-putt and scooted to the giant willow tree while we got stuck at the hole with the riverboat on top. "It's hard to believe she was a mistake," Annie sighed, watching Cheryl run ahead, her young limbs whipping out in all directions.

"Do you really think of her as a mistake?"

"No, not anymore."

"Nothing is a mistake," I said. "The Lord—"

"Oh, plenty of things are mistakes," Annie interrupted, lowering her chin at me, "but some mistakes are like seeds, I guess, and they grow into—what's the opposite of a mistake?"

"A thing on purpose?"

"Yeah, purposes."

Many of Dr. Soffione's treatments focused on repairing our relationships with our fathers. So on the Friday before Easter, Bill told each of us to talk to our fathers. During the conversations, we would confront them about one of the issues that contributed to our same-sex attractions. Fortunately the guys didn't have to tell their dads about their SSAs if they didn't know about them. We were to write down everything we said, and all of their responses, too. My blood ran cold, knowing my father had passed and I couldn't do that. Across the room I saw a raincloud of worry cross Nicky's face. He hadn't spoken to his father since he left home, and didn't know how to contact him.

I raised my hand. "What if your father has passed, or you don't have his contact information?" A couple of other guys said they had wanted to ask the same question.

"Good point, Gary. Why don't those of you who can't speak directly to your dads write down a page or two of how you think the confrontation part of the conversation would go?"

None of us liked the idea for the assignment, but the more we complained about it to Bill, the better an idea he thought it was. In the end, he demanded that we do it. By the end of the long discussion, I was glad that I would get to create the conversation all by myself, even though it meant going back into difficult emotional territory. I still had fresh wounds having to do with my father's death, which I didn't want to admit had hurt me.

That night I took a break from working on the autobiography and opened a new WordPerfect document and wrote:

Hi, Daddy.

Address me with respect.

Hello, Sir.

That's more like it. Now what do you think you have to say to me?

Well, it's going to be Father's Day soon, and I thought I'd wish you a happy one.

Every day is *this* father's day. Do you think you don't have to talk to me on other days?

No, of course not. I've talked to you on other days. This is just a special day.

Well, I don't believe in anybody else's special days.

Happy Father's Day, Daddy.

I don't care about Father's Day.

So are you and Mama doing something special?

No. Are you deaf or just stupid?

I'm not stupid or deaf, Daddy. You know, there's something I've been meaning to bring up with you for a long time, but I haven't had the courage.

Have you gone fool? What's this mumbo jumbo you yapping about, boy?

It has to do with how severely you disciplined me as a child. I don't think it was appropriate.

What was appropriate was that you needed to get your ass beat because you were a punk. You got some nerve, going to tell me how to raise you. Too late now anywise.

But your punishments came between us and made me feel like I could never be close to you. They caused me to detach from you in a way that has turned out to be unhealthy and threatens to ruin my life.

Somebody brainwashed you, son. Your life is your own damn responsibility. You just blame your mama and me because you're weak. Always have been. Fat little weakling. Blame somebody else, that's Gary. Gary can't do nothing wrong, must have been his daddy screwed him up. Much as I hate the other one for what he did, and may he burn in Hell for it, I can't say he didn't have balls.

Joe nearly killed you, Daddy. How can you—

See, that's what you don't understand about being a man. That's a sissy mentality. Sissy doesn't know that every man got to kill his daddy someway. That one damn near done it for sure. But you were always too afraid of me to do anything near like what the other one did.

Daddy, stop! Don't say that!

'Cause as bad an apple as he turned into, he did something about it. He knew I'd have to give him respect for turning the tables. You don't beg anybody for respect, Gary. That's a contradiction in terms. You go out and you stick respect in the gut like a hog and drag it home still wriggling and bleeding and fighting you off with its guts spilling out. I do respect that other one. I do.

I hate you. I hate hate hate hate you.

You two weren't no different one from the other. You were raised in the same house. But see, I bet the other one don't have the same psychology brain problem you're talking about here, do he? He never had a problem being a real man.

Weeping, I stopped there and rewrote the entire dialogue to make my father more accepting before I presented it to Bill and the others in Masculinity Repair. I printed out a copy of the first one and hid it in the rapidly rising stack of pages of my autobiography. Re-reading it later, it had the eerie feeling of a séance, like I'd really contacted my father beyond the grave and taken down every word he said.

As I untangled my own history, I found that helping other men through their difficulties with same-sex desires came naturally to me. I enjoyed it a great deal, probably because it kept me from focusing on my own flaws. Keith had impressed me with his positive attitude, so I asked him to be my prayer partner. If he had a tough day fighting back the demons, he would come by my room that night. I'd buy us Cherry Cokes from the vending machine in the basement and we'd read from the Bible. Sometimes others joined us and it became a regular pajama party, though I would never have called it that then. Meanwhile, Bill leaned so heavily on my assistance during Masculinity Repair and other sessions that some visitors once mistook me for a staff member.

I'd begun to know myself in a new way. Every day the guys told me they loved me and appreciated everything I did for Resurrection. But I still didn't give myself credit for the positive impression I had made on everybody. That is, until Bill and Gay took me aside at the end of the ninth month.

We met in Bill's office, behind the front office. It was like a different universe in there. The cherrywood walls and gray carpet gave everything that happened in there a serious tone, like a hearing in Congress or a lawsuit. Even the garbage cans were made of polished brass. But when Gay sat down in the chair next to Bill's, facing me, her smile practically burst out of her face. I saw it and couldn't help smiling, too. Why was she smiling so much?

Bill leaned back in his chair and twirled a ballpoint pen over his thumb. In the past few weeks, I'd seen how much work he did, and my sympathy for him had grown a whole lot. Now when I looked at his connected eyebrows, I didn't see a frown. Instead I saw a fan, spreading out across his face with all the love he had for his job and the clients at Resurrection underneath his businesslike attitude.

"So, Gary, how are you feeling about your stay here? You know that you've made a lot of progress, am I right?" The terrific thing about Dr. Soffione's method was that it allowed you to evaluate your healing process with a special diary and a chart, in addition to the United States one on the wall. Everybody kept their charts in their notebooks and the notebooks always nearby, under their arms during the day and under their pillows at night. "Are you done with your autobiography?" he kidded.

"I've got quite a way to go, sir," I told him.

"But your enthusiasm is abundant. And terrific. Gay and I have been discussing you. We were wondering if once your year is up, you'd consider staying on."

"I thought y'all said I've made great progress."

Gay threw her head back and belly-laughed. "Gary, you are such a goofball! Bill meant to ask if you'd like to help the clinic with a certain project."

"Like a job?"

Resurrection's most famous graduate was Alec Braverman, who had written a popular book called *Jesus Loves Homosexuals*. It provided a hip, youthful guide to the dangers of the gay lifestyle, and a new approach to loving the sinner but hating the sin. Everybody there spoke of Alec with admiration, and many dog-eared copies of his book sat on tables in the library. He was very handsome, too, so he had a busy schedule of appearances on TV and at conservative and religious fund-raisers, but he still took the time to visit the center. Once, he gave us a pep talk using the book of Job as his starting point. Visions of myself as Alec, spreading the gospel of ex-gayness on TV, popped up in my head. I couldn't be like him, I thought. Could I?

Gay nodded and Bill put down his pencil. He sat up in his chair to emphasize the seriousness of the offer. "But the larger picture is, Gary, we're looking to start a new chapter in Atlanta. If you enjoy working here, perhaps you'd like to help us with that, since you're based there."

The air left my lungs. I supposed they didn't remember that I'd run away to Atlanta, and I'd have a lot of triggers to face there. Plus, Annie and I had assumed that I'd head back to Orlando after the program, even though we hadn't made definite plans. But maybe this Atlanta chapter could serve as a transition between the program and real life. Maybe Annie would agree to move there with me once I had overcome my past. Almost without thinking, I accepted Bill and Gay's offer. I knew that I had to accept it now and iron out the details later. I didn't want them to offer it to anybody else.

Naturally, they were delighted. "I'm so glad you're interested, Gary!" Gay shouted. "This is going to be terrific!"

Bill turned to Gay. "If he's really serious about coming on board, he should meet Charlie, shouldn't he?"

"You haven't met Charlie yet, have you? Ohmigosh. You should definitely meet Charlie."

Dr. Soffione had been out of town a lot. For most of my year there, in fact. Among his recent triumphs, he'd appeared on *The 700 Club* and provided a couple of quotes for a *Time* magazine article, speaking out against gay adoptions and gay teachers. I had seen him just once, from pretty far off, in the larger office behind Bill's, when I'd come to ask for a paper clip. His head, full of straight white hair, was focused tightly on something he was writing, so he didn't look up.

Dr. Soffione's name got mentioned a lot around the center in admiring, hushed tones, mostly by Bill and Gay. They didn't really want us to read his book during our treatment because it could interfere with our recovery. We couldn't have found it easily, because it had been put out by a small press that specialized in therapeutic types of books. Also, we all saw the principles of *Stand Up Straight* in practice every day, so nobody really felt the need to read the book.

Of course, Bill and Gay had timed their proposal so that Dr. Soffione would be sitting in the large office behind the smaller one where Bill and Gay and a couple of helpers did all of the center's paperwork and mailings. During our whole meeting I had heard somebody back there, pecking at an electric typewriter. I could've figured it was Dr. Soffione, but I didn't want to scare myself by knowing that. Bill stood up and lightly knocked on his door, although it was already partially open. "Charlie? Do you have a minute?"

The typing stopped, and in a moment, a short, white-haired gentleman came to the door. Dr. Soffione made smacking noises on a lozenge. The small amount I'd seen of him—a picture from the dust jacket of *Stand Up Straight* lying on Gay's desk—made me expect a strong, solid man. Instead, he came off as wispy and scattered, like somebody thinking about a whole mess of things and trying to make them into a conspiracy. Bill introduced me to him as the guy who would be opening the Atlanta chapter, and I shook his hand.

"Thank you for your wonderful program!" I blurted out. I wrapped my other hand around his and, happily, found the tendons hard and masculine.

"I'm glad it's been a help to you." He smiled and nodded, almost like a king bowing. We said a few more words, then he excused himself and closed the door. From behind the door, the *tap-tap-tap* of the typewriter started again.

"He's working on a new book," Bill said reverently. "*Straight Ahead*. It's a guide that counsels ex-gay men and women in ways to maintain and optimize the practices he outlined in the first book. A little lighter, a little more anecdotal, more of a self-help book than the psychiatric focus of the first one."

"It's going to be terrific," Gay chimed in. "It *is* terrific. I can hear it in there every day, already being terrific."

I wanted to admire Dr. Soffione even more after having met him. It occurred to me that he might have his own story. "Did he used to be gay?" I asked.

"What does that have to do with anything?" Bill asked.

"Or… or somebody in his family maybe?"

Gay touched Bill's wrist. "What Bill's trying to say, I think, is that it isn't necessary for someone to have been a homosexual in order to establish his credibility as an expert in psychology. Dr. Soffione has a master's and a PhD, and he's published countless articles and done tons of studies."

"Oh, I wasn't doubting him. I just thought it would be nice if he had struggled with it himself and could sort of be on our side about it a little."

"He *is* on our side," Bill replied. "You don't know the man, so I can see why you might not understand that yet. But no one in the world is *more* on our side than Dr. Charles Soffione."

"Dr. Soffione is completely on our side," Gay reassured me. "When you get to know him, you'll understand." Her tone reminded me of the way Erica talked about Rex. Dr. Soffione's tapping became furious for a moment and then slowed down. "So, let's talk about your responsibilities." I sat up in my chair. Bill handed me a legal pad and a pen.

The news about my staying on and helping at Resurrection didn't make Annie happy. She wanted her child to have a father and to have her husband back sooner rather than later, she said. Plus, she didn't feel she could move to Atlanta. She brought up the d-word again, and I begged her not to leave me, so that I could prove to her how much I had changed. Eventually she agreed, and even got excited about moving the restaurant or opening a new branch.

That night, I lay down on my bed and spent some time searching the Bible for guidance. Keith knocked on the open door pretty soon after that. Keith had had a difficult day struggling with his attraction to a coworker. I had told everybody about Hank, so I gave him some tips I used to use for that situation. As I talked, I found myself reliving my lust for Hank in a way that made me uncomfortable. I saw my enthusiasm reflected in Keith's eyes. It was like he had come in and dumped his sins on me like a scapegoat. But that wasn't his fault.

When Keith got up to go, he thanked me and I gave him a hug. Keith let the hug extend past the acceptable limit. "Special hug," he said as the embrace went into overtime. After about fifteen seconds, I shifted my body to let him know I wanted to stop, but he didn't stop. He lay his head against my chest, maybe listening to my heartbeat, and hugged harder. I told myself the back-slapping made it a masculine hug. But then he stopped slapping. He closed his eyes and made a low, sad humming noise.

Keith dropped his arms and took a step back. He tucked his plaid shirt into his khakis and stared at me intensely above his glasses, like he would cry next. "It was just a hug," he muttered.

I lay awake that night thinking about the hug. Keith and I would have to talk about it the next day in Group. The hug hadn't been a sexual hug. Did that mean we hadn't broken the rules? At what moment did it become inappropriate? I could have pushed him away, but I didn't. I hadn't noticed a strong attraction to Keith before, but the possibility had now opened up in my mind and I couldn't help drawing it out.

Dr. Soffione's treatment didn't offer a 100 percent cure. From the way Bill and Gay spoke about it, nobody could. Did Christ really want that for us? Would we have to spend the rest of our lives counting the seconds to make sure our hugs didn't go into overtime?

My nightly conversations with Annie changed. She agreed with me that if I went to Atlanta, we could transition more smoothly into being together again. She would visit and I would go to Orlando some weekends. By that time I had almost spent more time trying to rebuild our relationship than I had living with my wife and child. To outsiders it probably sounded like betting our life savings on a dead greyhound. Annie confided in me that many of her friends couldn't believe she'd stayed strong for such a long time, or that I would return to her and Cheryl as a heterosexual family man.

"I have changed," I told her. "A whole lot. I know the rules of football now."

"Cheryl will be so happy. Gary, are you sure this is working?"

"I thought you believed that Jesus could make it happen," I countered.

"Of course I do… but…"

"But nothing. You're not going to be able to keep me off you when I get back."

Annie chuckled. "I've waited so long for that to happen."

"I promise I won't disappoint you," I said. "End zone. Completion. Touchdown."

FOURTEEN

When I envisioned our struggle then, I thought of it as a battle between twelve men—like the disciples—and a hoard of evil impulses, numerous as Philistines. As a leader in the Men's Group and in Masculinity Repair, I helped reinforce the idea that the war against homosexual desire was never-ending among my peers every day. We told each other that there would be times when we slipped, and we had to learn to forgive ourselves, repent, and move on in the knowledge that God loved us and was rooting for us to triumph over our problem. In shame we confessed our lustful feelings, then joined hands and embraced each other to combat them.

But when I think about Resurrection now, I remember that at the same time I was having a weird experience with the dandruff shampoo Head & Shoulders. During my first two months at the center, I started to grow my hair out because of the house rules against too-short hair. My scalp got itchier than a rattlesnake in a dryer. I used that shampoo because its famous advertisements say that it is the best at stopping dandruff. As I used the product, I didn't see a decrease in the amount of dandruff. I saw an increase. Tiny white specks appeared all over my clothes. People brushed them off for me, and that made me more ashamed. I poked into my hair while looking in the mirror and saw the flaky skin all over my scalp.

Thinking that I hadn't used enough shampoo, I lathered extra amounts of the creamy blue goop into my hair during showers, but nothing changed. By the end of the month, I was filling my entire palm with Head & Shoulders and working it around furiously during each shampooing. I lathered, rinsed, and repeated several times during every shower. But still my head itched all day and I couldn't concentrate when I spoke to anybody, because I thought they were just gawking at the snowstorm on my head.

I finished two bottles of the product and was about to request a third, but as I filled out the slip and gave it to Gay, I mentioned that it didn't seem like the shampoo was doing its job right.

"It creates a seal over the scalp," Gay said matter-of-factly.

"And the seal is what flakes off as dandruff?"

"Uh-huh."

In Gay's view, the makers of the product understood that the people who used it would be the same folks who worried most about dandruff. The advertisements targeted those people. The product made the problem seem worse, so that the worried people would worry more and buy more.

"Really? That's awful sneaky of the Head & Shoulders people," I remarked.

"We've all got to eat," she said, leaning over the request form with her pen held up.

Even though I didn't like it when the shampoo company did it, I wonder now if everybody at Resurrection Ministries lived under the philosophy of We've All Got to Eat. Many of the men I counseled became involved in a cycle of sin and forgiveness after sin and forgiveness that kept them emotionally dependent on the center. But as long as they confessed their thoughts and deeds, pledged their commitment to getting better, and didn't fall too hard, nobody could doubt the goodness of the program.

But it seems like we were only fooling ourselves when I look back. I truly enjoyed my job as assistant counselor to the men and women at Resurrection. I believed Bill when he said that the journey to heterosexuality was "a twisted path that never ends and never becomes totally straight." But even as I became more involved in the administration of the program, and a role model to my peers, my resistance to my own homosexual desires started to ebb. Nicky's attitude kept affecting me as I tried to counsel my brothers—the enormity of our burden weakened my will, though I loved every one of my fellow strugglers, and it hurt to think that even one wouldn't make it. But back in November, Tom, the smaller version of me with the double chin, had slipped badly.

Gay was on her way home at night during quiet time and saw him coming out of a local park where everybody knew men had sex at night. Tom denied it at first, saying he'd just gone in to relieve himself, but then he broke down. The moment Gay realized he was out of phase, she burst into tears. She cried the next day, too, when she told us that she had to separate him from the program. We all did. We tried to bargain with Gay because everybody wanted Tom to make it, but he'd gone too far. We got to see him one last time, and gave him presents of Bibles and books and neckties. I still get choked up when I think of that night. Tom wept through the whole thing and we did, too, because we couldn't help him anymore. Even though I grieved, I saw his banishment as a warning.

The one thing that could tumble my whole house of cards was if I had any trouble with Nicky. Nicky stayed committed to the idea of healing his sexuality, sex addiction, and chemical dependency. But he was very willful, as we said in Group. He listened to the lessons of the program and could recite the rules by heart, but he could never put them to work in his life, no matter how hard he tried. He violated the rules without meaning to. Bernard warned Bill that Nicky had sort of propositioned him, and Bill threatened to kick my roomie out. The threats became routine. Then, right after Tom got kicked out, Dwayne caught Nicky masturbating into a toilet and Bill put him on probation. And even after that, I discovered a ragged copy of *Exercise for Men Only* under his bed and he pretended that he hadn't touched himself while looking at the images.

"It's a workout magazine," he whined.

"You don't work out."

"Sure I do, when I'm on the outside. At least once a month. That's more than you."

I was hurt, so I ended the conversation.

Ever since the day when I helped him improve his batting stance, Nicky had started seeking me out. Because I had violated his personal space that day and he had kept it secret, I felt an extra duty to help him in his struggle. But I couldn't be anywhere near him, because I wanted him so bad and I knew he couldn't control himself. Nicky was like a cream pie set on a plate in front of me during a strict diet.

Keith and I often held informal group prayer or Bible study sessions in my room after the evening meeting. That was one strategy for staying accountable with Nicky in the room. Nicky usually hung around, but he didn't always join in, and even when he did, he seemed distracted. Keeping Dr. Soffione's ideas in mind, I let myself experience my attraction to him—up to a point. But every night when I was alone with Nicky, I took deeper breaths, thought of unappealing things, and tried to keep a comfortable distance. My desire for him didn't decrease one bit. I might as well have tried to catch a hurricane in a toy bucket.

One night, Nicky, Keith, George, and I sat on my bed discussing Sodom and Gomorrah. We nibbled on sugar cookies and sipped lemonade. I deliberately sat across the circle from Nicky and didn't address him unless it was necessary. His presence always threw me off, no matter how much I thought of Christ. I swear, sometimes I could feel that boy's body heat clear across the room.

We all had to wear clothing that didn't invite temptation or promote false images, but Nicky would leave the top button of his polo shirt undone. That would expose the top of his chest, a little hair, and his beautifully shaped collarbone. Khaki pants didn't look sexy on most people, but Nicky's fit against the backs of his thighs and curved out around the pockets to suggest the firm backside I had followed into temptation before.

That night he had on a royal blue shirt that accented his chest muscles just a little; he could get away with wearing it. Though it was the right length, it kept creeping up his torso. "Darned thing shrunk in the wash," he explained, tugging it down to calm our disapproval. Between tugs, he exposed the patch of hair that led from his stomach into his pants. When he bent down to tie his shoes, his boxer shorts puffed out of his pants and he showed off the bony knobs running down his back.

Nicky seemed to enjoy knowing that others lusted after him, especially me. Could be he thought of me as a safe person to flirt with because my size and color made me seem not sexual, like a big Aunt Jemima. Since he knew that I liked him, it probably confused him that I refused to pay attention to him anymore, and that made him want to provoke me more.

Or perhaps he really wanted fellowship, and he only knew how to befriend other men by seducing them. Many of us who had spent time in the gay lifestyle had that problem. Nicky had admitted as much in Group Share. Worst of all, I didn't know if any of these theories worked or if I was just perverting his intentions in my own mind.

We had just read Genesis 19:5, where the Sodomites keep asking about Lot's houseguests, and the translation of the verb *to know* had come up. Keith twisted his pink mouth to one side of his milk-chocolate face. "It means 'have relations with,' right? So this is a passage about the abomi-nations of Sodom, isn't it? They want the men to come out so they can you-know-what them in the you-know-where." He chuckled nervously at having to describe the act. "So this is against homosexuality."

"That's right, Keith," said George. Keith spoke up more and often tried to be funny when George was around. I still didn't know what to make of our extended hug, so I tried to ignore it or excuse it as the healthy kind of male affection. We had to avoid all types of emotional dependency.

Nicky raised his hand. "But are they gay?"

"What do you mean, are they gay? They're blasting each other in the seat!" Keith fired back. He and George belly-laughed.

"Pipe down, pipe down," I said.

"Um, when I was a hustler in Chicago—" he began. Keith shot me a look to say, "Oh brother." He often teased Nicky behind his back because many of his shared comments began with those words. Also, Keith had race issues that were much stronger than any I'd ever had. "A lot of them guys didn't think it made you gay to be on top, giving it, y'know." The three of us turned to him in shock. George pulled in his chubby cheeks and it made him look like a squirrel who'd just sucked a lemon. "I'm just saying! Can't I say that? Maybe this part ain't about gays being bad people. I mean, there are plenty of other things that do say that, but maybe this ain't one of 'em."

George closed his Bible with his finger to keep his place and cocked his head. A good education and coming from money had taught him ways of cutting people down using only the accuracy of the facts. His dislike for Nicky came from thinking the kid was ignorant and poor, and that maybe one had caused the other.

"Well..." he said. Keith and I knew a zinger was coming. "God doesn't make a distinction between homosexual acts and so-called homosexual identity. For Him, homosexuals don't exist, just homosexual *acts*. Engaging in sodomy makes you a sodomite. That's all there is to it. The Bible doesn't say anything about lesbianism per se, but it doesn't have to—we can extrapolate the moral wrongness of lesbianism from what God thinks about male homosexuality."

Nicky wasn't satisfied. "But what if a guy falls in love with a guy, but nothing sinful happens between them, and he never says nothing 'bout it? Is that a homosexual act? Do falling in love make you a sodomite?"

Keith jumped in. "Impure thoughts are the root of the problem," he explained, in a rote voice that suggested he knew Nicky had heard this concept many times before. "You're both males, and even when you do succumb to those desires, it isn't real, functional love. Remember, homosexuality is something you *do*, not someone you *are*. Lusting in your heart is almost as bad as committing the sin, because it's a *gateway*. Satan is tempting you." We always repeated these founding principles of Resurrection during any group discussion. "That's what George basically said."

"I guess I'm still struggling. I mean, what about things that ain't homosexual? What if God didn't want ballplayers and I had the urge to play ball real bad? Like, I thought about it all the time and snuck out to learn the rules and play ball, and got so good at it that the major leagues picked me up and I went to the World Series. That's Satan telling me to be a ballplayer, and it ain't part of who I am? Even though I wanted to do it, like I agreed with Satan about doing it?

"Because Satan wants folks to do worse stuff than play ball, right? He wants us to kill each other and steal and lie and party all the time. But he don't go after people who can't play ball and try to tempt *them* into doing it, do he? He goes after people who already want to kill other people and says 'Kill! Kill!' Like, if Satan came to me and whispered, 'Hey, Nicky, take this here baseball bat, go out to the pitcher's mound, and knock it out of the park,' I'd be like, 'You're crazy!' I wouldn't do it in a million years! So Satan goes with your weakness, but where do that weakness come from? Who put it there?"

"You mean go out to home plate," George said, tired of Nicky's rambling speech.

"Yeah, whatever, which proves my point!" Nicky giggled at himself again, and Satan tapped *me* on the shoulder, telling me to notice his vulnerable smile. He really wanted to know these things because they confused him, not because he wanted to undermine Resurrection's mission.

Keith stopped short of rolling his eyes. He shifted in his chair slightly. I saw him adjust his attitude to a nicer one, almost like I could see inside his head. "First of all, Nicky, you can't put baseball and same-sex desires on the same level. Baseball isn't destructive to the soul. God *wants* people to play baseball. Well, men, anyway. Second, Satan plants the bad weaknesses in you and then he tries to reap what he has sown."

"Right, Keith," I chimed in. I would have said the same thing if I'd been on my toes as a group leader, but I'd relaxed a little, and Nicky talking so much meant I had to look at him, and that unglued me.

"How can he do that if God made me?"

Keith threw his hands out and made a gesture like somebody shaking a toddler by the shoulders. "That's exactly the point! You aren't what you desire. You could drink coffee every morning and then one day just decide you'd rather drink tea. You're a tea drinker. So when you stop doing homosexual things, you aren't gay anymore."

"Even if it's like, you just took a break?"

"Nicky, you're not being serious."

"But see, what's a homosexual thing? It ain't just sex, is it? 'Cause everybody says I talk like one, and I definitely walk like one, and I like all the things that everybody says are gay to like. I mean, if it's coffee and tea, why are we here? Why's it so hard to change? Even if I started acting like Arnold Schwarzenegger tomorrow, there's still so much stuff I done in the past and memories I have that it's like, who would I be trying to fool? The whole time I been here, I've tried walking with less swing in my hips, I've tried to deepen my voice, and I feel like a B-movie actress or a street mime. If I ain't who God intended me to be, how do acting like a freak bring me any closer to that? Did God make a big mistake? Maybe I ain't what I desire, but I am what I *done*, or what I *think*, ain't I?"

"My my, the hillbilly Descartes lectures us again," George muttered. He stroked Nicky's biceps to keep him from overheating, but Nicky drew back.

"Nicky," I said, "we all have to do that stuff. It's silly sometimes, but you've got to have faith that it's going to pull you through in the long run. Don't give up. You can't give up. Me, and Keith, and George, we all want you to succeed in the program, and you can't let Satan plant all these doubts in your head, or you'll be lost. You know what it's like to be lost."

"You've already made the choice not to be lost," Keith warned. "So stick to it, man. Hang in there. You're almost home free. Now is not the time for questioning and doubt."

George lowered his eyes and looked at Nicky over his reading glasses. "Surrender to Christ," he said solemnly. "That's all there is to it."

Underneath, we all feared that Nicky might have another meltdown, as he had done during a Group meeting a month before, when he described a real rough time he'd had with a trick. Bill had escorted him out of the room because he'd become hysterical, shaking and crying.

George gently flicked the golden edges of his Bible. "It says in 1 Corinthians 5:17 that those who become Christians become new persons. From talking about our histories in Group we all know that our brokenness and confusion come from our inability to bond properly with our same-sex parents. Keith, your father abandoned you. Gary, you suffered physical and mental abuse from your father. I had a violent past with my mother. And Nicky, we need hardly mention how your father's sexual abuse affected you. I think we're seeing the results of that right now. So to say that you're the person God intended you to be right now is frankly ludicrous."

Nicky lowered his chin, crossed his legs, and rubbed his knee uncomfortably. I could tell he wanted to continue asking questions, but he knew they weren't going to listen any further. George had put him in his place by bringing up Nicky's dad. He probably expected me to beat him up and keep him quiet with my words as well. But I couldn't think of anything to add, and I had sympathy for him, even though I thought he was out of line to cast doubt on our reading. I also knew what it meant to try to become a new person.

Turning to Nicky for only a second, I noticed the hole above his collarbone and accidentally dreamed about filling it with my tongue. Suddenly he raised his eyes. Nicky met my eyes shamelessly and I turned away. "Wandering thoughts are all on their way to Hell," I'd read in some of the literature. We continued the Bible study like nothing had happened. A few minutes later, when I pointed to a passage, Nicky sat next to me on my bed to look on. He leaned into my personal space and tried to slip back into the conversation. Over on the desk, my Jesuses looked the other way.

At 11:30 or so, George and Keith yawned and got up to leave. We said good-bye in the hall, but Nicky didn't get up from my bed. I shut the door and turned. One of Nicky's eyes was set slightly higher than the other, and both of them turned down at the sides. His brow hung heavy above his eyes and made his expressions look serious and maybe desperate. He cleared his throat and blinked.

"I just wanted to thank you for sticking up for me."

"I didn't, though." My hand caressed the doorknob.

"Then I guess thanks for not criticizing me like the other two." The pleading look in his eyes made me think of Miquel. The doorknob became slick with my sweat. I fidgeted with it more anxiously, and it rattled. Then I thought about how a doorknob was shaped like the head of a penis and took my hand away.

"They weren't criticizing you."

"Does everybody here just hate me?" Nicky asked. His lower lip glistened in the light of the lamp on my nightstand. "You hate me, don't you?"

"Of course not." It almost made me laugh to think how wrong he was. I wracked my brain trying to think of ways that people liked Nicky and came up short. He had a reputation for behaving the way he did that night: talking too much, too emotionally, and casting doubt into places where it wasn't welcome. Although other clients—that's what they called us—put it in the gentlest terms possible, many of us had difficulty with his questioning attitude and his nasal twang. People often asked Bill why he didn't kick Nicky out of the program, like he always threatened he would. Knowing that others didn't see the same things in Nicky that I did only increased my attraction to him.

A little clear liquid escaped from his left eye, the one I'd always thought of as the sadder one. "Then why do y'all always treat me so mean?" He ripped a Kleenex from the festive box on the nightstand next to my Jesuses and wiped his eyes and nose with it. "Keith and George, I don't care, but you're one of the supervisors and, and, and, you're my roomie, and you don't hardly even look at me when I talk to you." I took a breath and he pointed at me sharply, shouting, "Don't try to deny it, neither!"

"It's because—" I began, and then changed my mind. "I think you know why it's because. Listen, Keith and George are doing their best. You know they struggle with the same problems as you. You have other places you can bring this up, you didn't have to make a scene during Bible study."

"I suck," Nicky moped. "I suck big fat cock."

"No you don't!"

I didn't like to hear him say words like that. Nicky's questions had started my own beliefs shaking in sympathy. The image also stimulated me. Right then Satan whispered into my ear that all of Nicky's behavior that night had just been a complicated way of seducing me. Get back, Demon! I yelled in my head. But once the Beast had put the idea out there, it caught fire and burned with foolishness. Anybody with one eyeball could see that this young man was in a great deal of pain. I had failed as a counselor if I couldn't recognize that and treat him with the appropriate respect.

"Let's pray," I said, extending my fingertips to him. He blew a trumpet blast from behind a Kleenex and slowly stood up. Letting the tissue fall gently into the trash can, he turned his palms up so that I could put mine on top of them, and we bowed our heads. I had felt something like the contact between my flesh and his before—when those trains collided.

"Heavenly Father, we ask that you give us strength this evening that we might—" I moved my hands slightly, so that my fingertips rested on his wrists. Just beyond where the tendons branched out, shiny hairs scribbled down his forearms. "—do battle against—" Nicky sniffled and I noticed his breathing. It was unfair that something so basic to life had an erotic charge if you paid attention to it. "—the seeds of doubt that Satan has put in our minds, tempting us to live outside your will—" This was a standard prayer at Resurrection. Unfortunately I could now recite it while thinking of other things. I thought of Nicky's firm, round rear end under my hand back when I'd slipped. I thought of the closed door. An animalistic impulse took hold of me. I let my hand travel up one of his forearms and caress the hair there.

Nicky raised his head but I didn't meet his gaze. As I finished the prayer I pulled him to me and buried my face in his neck. "Jesus," I said. "Jesus, Jesus, Jesus. I love you, Nicky. I want you to finish the program and succeed. I really want that for you." I held him close, like a parent would hold a child. My lips brushed against the nub at the front of his ear. I let my lips do that. Nicky opened his arms and wrapped them around as much of my waist as he could. We stood that way for a while, rocking almost without moving, like an old couple in the ballroom of a cruise ship.

"You're real cuddly," he said, almost laughing at me. "Like a fat ol' teddy bear."

That wasn't what I wanted to hear about myself right then. But instead of asking him to be quiet, I tried to prove I wasn't cuddly and keep him from saying anything more by pressing my mouth down on top of his.

The kiss didn't take Nicky by surprise. He didn't resist, but he didn't respond, either. I held my lips there, kissing, and he let me, without moving. I kissed his swollen lips like I'd just crawled across Death Valley and they were the only moisture left anywhere. But as soon as I knew he didn't share my fantasy, the dream began to droop. Remembering his stories about Chicago, I supposed this was the way he acted while he turned a trick. Maybe he was having a fantasy about lying under a thatched umbrella on a tropical beach. Disgusted with myself, I took a step back, looked away, and apologized.

But I had crossed that line again. When I faced Nicky, he hadn't moved. Maybe he tilted his head back and parted his lips slightly, but he kept quiet. The silence made me uncomfortable because the Devil kept saying it meant I could kiss him again. In the program, thinking about kissing a man was as bad as kissing a man. But kissing a man twice wasn't hardly any worse than kissing a man once. I stepped forward and pressed my lips against his again. They tasted as sweet and wet as the first bite of a summer peach.

Nicky continued to stand still without responding as I worked my mouth on top of his. After I had slobbered all over his face, the guilt became too intense and I pulled away. "You don't want me to do this, do you?" I asked. "Why are you letting me do this?"

"I guess I'm just sick of people around here not being able to do what they want to do. Don't it feel good to do what you want to do?"

Blood rushed to my face. "For the here and now it feels good. But we can't live for the here and now. We have to think about our immortal souls, Nicky. The cost of one selfish moment like I just had could be an eternity of hellfire."

"Yeah, people say that a lot. We talk about homo stuff all day and night. Even when we talk about Jesus, we talk about how Jesus don't want us to be homos and how Jesus can help us stop thinking homo thoughts and doing homo things. How can George say that God thinks homosexuality don't exist? That's like saying God thinks dust don't exist and then spending your whole life vacuuming the rug. No wonder it's so hard to get over these urges. How do you get rid of an urge if you're blabbing about it all day? Not being able to shut up about homosexuality is a homosexual act, too, ain't it? But ain't nobody asking forgiveness for *that* around here."

I folded my arms and bobbed my head thoughtfully. Bill always did that whenever somebody criticized the basics of the program. Then I sat down, knowing Nicky would have to sit, too. He did. My passion for him temporarily retreated into goodwill. "It's good that you're getting all this out. Having these moments of questioning is a healthy way of getting back on track."

"I'm not sure if I'm gonna get back on track."

Even as a counselor, I rarely heard words like these. My surprise at hearing them was amplified by a panic at the idea that once he left, they'd never allow me to see him again. "So you're too weak to do God's will is what you're saying. You'd rather go back to a life of sin, addiction, disease, and death."

"No, I ain't weak. I didn't kiss *you*. I guess I believe in God, but my heart's not in the whole religion thing no more, you know? You gotta believe in too much other stuff. Like angels and devils and Hell and Heaven and miracles and burning bushes and the virgin birth and on and on. See, if it was just *one* of them things, maybe it would be easier, you know? But it's all of that. It's like magic tricks or Disney World or something."

I let out a weak laugh. Disney World was the only thing I believed in as much as God.

"And it's like, if you commit sins and do self-destructive things on Earth, you go to Hell, and your flesh burns eternally. If you follow everything that God says, you go to Heaven, and that's what? Like, an eternal picnic. Fire, okay, picnic, okay. It's the *eternal* I can't handle. Ain't nothing eternal. Seems to me God didn't make nothing to be eternal. Not even the sun. And another thing, I'll bet that you could get used to your flesh burning eternally and it would get boring. Maybe that's the part that's Hell, the boringness. Plus, if only pious Christian people go to Heaven, it just don't sound like no *fun* to me. Heaven without good music and sex ain't none of my Heaven."

"Heaven is being with God, Nicky. When we cast off the flesh, we are only spirit. Spirit is free of the base cravings of the flesh."

"See! That's what I mean. Christians can't stand earthly pleasures. We think that Heaven means freedom from enjoying yourself. I heard that when a Muslim volunteers to be a martyr, they tell him he's going to get him a harem! A Christian martyr would get a deluxe edition of Scrabble and a Pat Boone record!"

Nicky's tone had escalated to blasphemy, so I thought it was time to end the conversation. "It sounds like you've thought this through pretty thoroughly, Nicky," I said. "But I want to remind you that Jesus loves you and will always love you, no matter how far you stray from His truth, and that I will pray for you, and everybody here will pray for you. I don't want your soul to die, because there's a chance for you. You already know that Jesus can bring eternal life, and once you know that, you're halfway to salvation. So maybe you'll go back to the decadent lifestyle of the homosexual prostitute and the drug addict, because you just haven't fallen far enough to understand why we all need the helping hand of the Lord. At our greatest times of doubt, Christ is more with us than ever. Nicky, I feel an obligation to make sure that you make it through to the promised land of faith and freedom from all the suffering that homosexuality has brought you. I feel a special bond of brotherhood with you."

"Is that why you kissed me?" An urgent knock came at the door. I didn't go get it.

"Shush. I apologized for what I did. I hope you'll find mercy in your heart for me. Now, if there's any way I can help—special counseling sessions, extra Bible study—I'll do everything in my power." I was almost crying, because I didn't want him to leave the program, or me.

"Look how late it is," he announced, staring at my clock radio. It said 12:39. Without responding to my offer of help, Nicky gathered himself and went to the door. "I'm just gonna go take a walk down the hall and clear my head." He shook my hand tenderly. "You tried, Gary. That's more than I can say for a lot of people." The knocking got louder, so I joined

Nicky by the doorjamb. Keith and George stood there with lines of concern crisscrossing their faces.

"Did George leave his Bible in here? He can't find it," Keith said.

Nicky stepped around them without speaking and shuffled down the hallway. George, Keith, and I ended up on our hands and knees looking for the Bible underneath the beds. It wasn't anywhere.

FIFTEEN

About a week after the night we lost George's Bible, I didn't see Nicky for a whole day. Not only didn't I have to wake him up like usual, but he had even stripped his bed. Or somebody had. Bill counted heads at breakfast but he acted like he didn't notice that Nicky wasn't present. Everybody must have known. But nobody else brought it up, either. Leaving our world meant spiritual death, and you didn't want to hear the details, because morale was fragile and next time it could be you. Everybody must have known. All day an uneasy hunch wandered down a path in my head, but since the bad suspicions didn't have any facts to go with them, I made up excuses. Surely I'd see him that night in our room. I didn't see him for another week and a half, but nobody knew anything. I didn't know if he'd run away or gotten kicked out. Bill and Gay wouldn't discuss it. At night I ran my hands down the blue and white stripes on his naked mattress, praying that he was safe somewhere and not dead.

Then one night at supper I was sitting with Keith and Jake, poking the meatloaf with our plastic forks and chatting. Keith zipped open his package of chocolate pudding and stuck a spoon in, and I started my second one.

"Did you hear about Nicky?" Keith asked, without looking up from scraping the container. An expression danced across his face that I could've sworn was satisfaction.

"No," Jake said. "What'd he do?" Jake loved gossip because it was forbidden at Resurrection but not specifically gay.

"Nicky stole Bill's wallet and went AWOL."

I forgot to breathe. I knew I would rush upstairs to check the room as soon as supper got done. Later I found that somebody had cleared out all of Nicky's things while I was at work. I searched the room for something of his. I found some paper clips and pennies, but those wouldn't do as mementos. Later I picked up some hairs from around the baseboards and put them in an envelope.

"Is that true?"

Jake stuck his chin out and said "Yeah," because anybody who broke the rules secretly impressed him. Jake had a tattoo of a dagger on one side of his neck that the chain of command made him keep covered up with a Band-Aid, but he'd show it to anybody who asked, and plenty who didn't, whenever he got the chance. "Holy holy. Where do you think he went?"

"Back to Chicago to turn tricks for smack, I bet," Keith said, dropping his pudding container onto his plate, where it made a woodblock sound.

"That's not such a brotherly thought," Jake said.

"We should go get him," I said.

"In Chicago?"

"He's probably not there yet."

"Right, Bill probably doesn't carry a mess of greenbacks," Keith reasoned. "He had to have gone downtown. Should we really go get him? Can we do that?"

"You don't sound like you really want to," I told Keith. His uncaring response shocked me. One of our brothers was missing, maybe lost. I felt like we had no choice but to risk it, but I didn't want to appear different from the group, so I kept that part of my opinion to myself. "I talked to him last week. He knows that some of us are not extending our fellowship to him, and that's part of why he acts out." I thought about what Keith had said for a moment and became slightly annoyed. "For people who are all struggling with the same problem, you'd think we could show some compassion."

"But he's a troublemaker and a thief."

"We all know the way SSAs can affect other parts of your life and the behavior patterns. We need to let Nicky know that he's forgiven as long as he repents."

"Maybe it's just about him needing to hit rock bottom," Jake drawled sadly, sticking his finger into his dessert cup, wiping the sweet stuff up and then sucking it in a way that would have gotten him disciplined if Bill had been watching.

"He's one of the fallen," Keith added. "Some people have the discipline to deal with this problem and, obviously, others don't. He's probably better off shooting up with his tricks."

"Guys!" I shouted. "You know what can happen!"

"The world can probably go on without another sad, screwed-up homosexual," Keith said, bitterness dripping off his tongue. Jake stretched his arms up and yawned a long red yawn—like the Devil's cave, I thought.

Now Keith's and Jake's lack of caring got me seriously angry. I wondered if they were saying what they said just to get my goat. If so, they had succeeded. "I'm going to go look for him. If you guys come with me then we can stay in phase. If not, I'll just find somebody else to go with me."

"Are you nuts, Gary? Bill won't authorize that trip."

"I don't care. Nicky needs us."

"You'll be violating chain of command," Jake warned.

Keith leaned forward and guffawed, slapping his fingers on the dining table. His round eyes bulged out even further and his skinny arms bent outward. The combination of looks and movements made him seem to me like an African American frog. "When did you start caring about chain of command, Jake?"

Silently, the three of us dared each other to overcome our fear of going off campus unauthorized. I cast a nervous look at Jake, hoping I had his support. Keith glanced back and forth between the two of us, because he probably thought I might not have the courage to go ahead. I shot an angry squint back, downright insulted that they couldn't see the necessity of rescuing Nicky, and also to make sure neither of them had figured out that I wanted to find him partially because I was in love.

"It's Friday," Jake reminded us. Group Share started right after supper and usually lasted a little over an hour. On Fridays we had quiet time after Group Share, but we weren't really supposed to go off campus. We could go to approved movies or other events in phase, but technically we needed to let chain of command know.

"I'm not sure," Keith grumbled. "It's dangerous, and even if we succeed, we'll only get Nicky back."

I lost my cool. "Keith! How can you call yourself a Christian if you don't believe we should care most for the least of our group members? Isn't that how we are to be judged? What is wrong with you? Nicky's weak, but he's as human as any of us. Why can't anybody else seem to understand that around here?" My voice took on a deep, urgent tone and I wagged my finger at them.

"Dag, Reverend Gray. You don't have to get all black on me." I was flattered that anyone would think of my behavior that way. Nobody had ever accused me of getting black before, or being a reverend, like I had once wanted to.

"Besides, we need a third for accountability," Jake chimed in, though we all knew.

"Is there a game in Memphis tonight?" Keith asked. None of us knew for sure.

"If not, we'll say we went to the movies," Jake said.

None of us had access to a car. I probably could have borrowed Gay's, but our mission had a hushed-up quality that I didn't want to mess with. Gay would probably not have minded, but I didn't want Bill to hear about what we were planning. During Group Share we passed nervous glances around and tried to hurry the proceedings without giving ourselves away.

Shortly after Group Share, we signed out and left the Resurrection grounds, careful not to walk too fast. As we walked, the sun dipped down behind the sycamore trees and hid in the Mississippi River for the night. By the time we reached the bus stop we had broken into a full run, and Keith raced Jake to the end. I fell behind, of course, and huffed my way up to them a few minutes later.

At the nearest main road, we waited forty minutes for a bus at a stop with no sitting place. Jake flopped down on the grass and Keith rested his hands on his knees. All three of us were exhausted and panting. For a split second, the noise of our breathing together put me in mind of what a three-way sexual encounter might sound like. So I started to sing "Your Sins Will Find You Out" from an album by Brother Joe May that

Aunt Vietta had played over and over one weekend when I visited her. My out-of-breath singing sounded terrible to Keith and especially Jake, who put his hands over his ears and howled like a coyote near a fire engine. I laughed and the bus finally came.

Jake and Keith shared the seat in front of me. Keith asked where he thought we should look for Nicky. Jake turned sideways in his seat, running his arm along the metal bar to face us both.

"Well, it's still early, so I think we ought to check Overton Park first. The sun's almost down, so there won't be much action, but if he's not there he'll probably hit the Paris Theater looking for the after-work crowd."

Keith and I agreed, and Jake swung his arm back over the seat again. Outside, the traffic signals and lighted signs for fast-food restaurants gradually took over from the daylight. Keith, Jake, and I became fascinated by the street scenes in the bus window. They passed by each other carelessly like strangers, one reflection blurring the other. It hit me for the first time that we would now have to enter the gay underworld, a place I'd hoped I had left behind forever. Watching my two friends leaning sideways to see outside in the starched white shirts and gray slacks Resurrection provided for us, I wondered if we hadn't made a huge mistake.

We didn't find Nicky hanging out by the concrete pillar at the entrance to Overton Park, and he wasn't behind the band shell either. Jake insisted that we try to get closer to the wooded area by the lake—he consiered that our best bet. We reached a grassy clearing nearby and Keith and I stopped walking, like we'd arrived at an invisible wall. Jake walked forward until he saw we'd stopped. He turned to us, unbuttoned the first two buttons of his shirt, and rolled up the sleeves to the middle of his forearm.

"Getting serious, eh?" Keith mocked. I couldn't figure out whether I didn't trust my friends' motives, or if my own fear was keeping me from moving forward. Probably all three of us dreaded the same thing— ourselves, and whether we could withstand the intense feelings of repulsion and attraction racing through us at the thought of maybe seeing a penis in a man's mouth, or, God forbid, thrusting into a male anus. Jake and I both had histories of public-sex addiction. Even the possibility of catching a sidelong glimpse of gay sex in the dark woods frightened me. If I saw Nicky soliciting in there, I'd be a goner.

"Do you want to find Nicky or not?" Jake challenged. I took a couple of steps forward and joined him beside a crooked oak.

"If you stay behind, Keith, we'll be out of phase," I said. Jake put his hands on his hips.

Keith stood his ground and made a series of pained faces as he kicked a small hole into the grass. "Maybe we shouldn't look *there*," he whined. "I mean, do we have to? If anyone finds out... Can we just *run* through?"

Without answering, Jake turned and hopped onto the dirt trail that led into the wooded area. I waited a moment until I became concerned that Jake would outrun me, and with a deep breath, I leapt after him. "Keith," I yelled back, "c'mon! We've got to stay accountable!"

Breathlessly I skidded through the woods, trying not to look to either side. I called out for Nicky, hoping I wouldn't have to see any perversions taking place. Or hoping that I would, depending on which second it was. With jackrabbit leaps, Jake bounded far ahead of me until I couldn't see him anymore. Behind me I could hear Keith's footsteps crunching through the dead leaves.

By this time the sun had gone completely, and the only light entering the grove of trees came from lamps along the edges of distant walkways, and an orange sliver of moon I could sometimes glimpse through the tree branches. As I turned around to see if I could figure out where Keith was, somebody in a suit stepped out from behind a tree, like darkness dripping out of the air. Shot through with fear, I planted my feet to keep from stumbling into the person's chest. Keith's footsteps grew louder.

The guy turned out to be short and stocky. The closer I got, the more his forehead shone in the moonlight, until I understood that his whole wrinkled head was a forehead. From what I could see of the crags across his face and blobby nose, I guessed that he was in his sixties. He had a dark red silk scarf tied around his neck. He looked like Alfred Hitchcock coming from a fancy Hollywood to-do.

"Hi," he said, in a short tone almost like a blast from a party horn. "Looking for trouble?"

Careful not to make eye contact, I started to step around Alfred to let him know I wasn't interested. This usually worked in public-sex situations without too much fuss. The fellow got part of the message and moved to the other side of the dirt path. Right then, Keith caught up to me.

"Ugh," the man sighed to Keith, in a voice whose femininity instantly embarrassed me, "is there no action anywhere in this damned town? Wait. Are y'all Witnesses? *Hot.* What about it?" Alfred unbuttoned his jacket, then started unbuttoning a vest with about twelve more buttons.

"Don't touch me, faggot!" Keith yelled. Shocked by his language, I turned to see his elbow connect with the man's jaw. Alfred hadn't even looked up from his unbuttoning yet. He staggered backward, falling against a sapling. The tiny tree couldn't support his weight, and in a matter of seconds he crumpled down. I tried to rush forward and help him up, but Keith stayed me with the same elbow that had done the violence. Using me to support his weight as he moved forward, he approached the man, swung his shoe backward, and dealt him a hard blow in the privates. I reached out too late to stop him and yelled out his name. This couldn't be happening. Sure, we didn't agree with the pro-gay people, but we had less reason to beat them up than anybody. If they came over to the Jesus side, they could sign up tomorrow and they'd be us. I wailed at Keith to leave the guy alone.

The man let out a high-pitched yell, hollering "Help! Assault!" His girlish voice echoed through the trees, and before I knew what had happened, Keith pushed me forward and we ran, faster than we had all day, to the other side of the wooded area. I ran so fast I felt like I might leave my fat behind me. How could a fellow that weak send us rushing away in terror?

We found Jake waiting outside by a park bench across a meadow next to the path. He was sharing a cigarette with a slim, heavily tattooed guy in a tank top. Keith saw him and stumbled desperately across the grass. Yelling, he shoved Jake's shoulder the way he had done to me, and then continued running. I tried to explain what had happened to Jake but I was too out of breath, so instead I gestured for him to follow. He said a quick, confused good-bye to his friend and took off after Keith. Behind them, I thought I could still hear the faint wail of a scared, womanly voice.

The second I got to the stone wall by the main road, Jake shoved me back a few feet away from Keith, squeezed my upper arms, and looked directly into my eyes, hungry for truth. "What happened in there, Gary?"

He and Keith had already had some kind of discussion—I didn't know what about. In the corner of my eye, I could see Keith's face, lit by a white streetlight. I had never seen so angry a scowl cross it before. I couldn't turn away from the rage I saw there, naked for the first time. I shared his rage, and I suddenly resented Jake for trying to get me to rat on another black man. This probably wouldn't have occurred to me if Keith hadn't called me a reverend earlier and told me not to get black on him. Even so, it made me feel like I would rather let Jake rip out my liver before I betrayed Keith, the same way I had carried my brother's rage against my parents for so many years. The effeminate man wouldn't die or anything. He'd be okay in a few hours.

"Some guy tried to touch Keith. We ran."

"Is that all?"

I hoped he hadn't heard the wailing. "Pretty much. It was disgusting."

"You're sure?"

"Yeah."

Jake raised his eyebrow, but calmed down. Keith's face also relaxed for a second, first into surprise, then into its normal, slightly befuddled expression. Jake let go of my shoulders and allowed me to rejoin him over where Keith stood by the streetlamp.

"You were smoking, huh?" I joked.

He waved his hand in the air. "Yeah, okay, sure. That guy back there was a junkie I knew from way back. He told me he'd seen Nicky."

I tried not to let my excitement show, but I let out a sigh of relief.

"He said it was a 99 percent sure bet that Nicky would be at this dive bar off Beale Street, Thorny's. That's where his guy hangs out."

"What? He has a boyfriend already?"

"No, his connection, his dealer. There's a problem though. The dude usually doesn't get there until two in the morning."

"Oh," Keith said warily. "I guess that's it for me."

"Sometimes he gets there earlier."

"Maybe tonight will be one of those nights," I said. "It's only 9:30. If we go there now, maybe we can talk him into coming back before curfew ends."

It took us a little while to regroup and make our way downtown. Once we figured out where Thorny's was, we realized that the best route was to take the trolley through the historic district. The beautifully preserved old-time car, with its wooden seats and yellow lighting, provided a strange contrast to the unpleasant business of earlier that night. For a moment during the shaky ride, we had traveled back in time, and we were three innocents enjoying a rollicking Friday night in Memphis—soldiers on leave, maybe.

Two arguments and a wrong turn later, we found the place, smashed into a nameless, grimy side street. The entrance was up a brightly lit flight of stairs. Some strains of rock music, but not a scary kind, drifted down to us along with the hum of conversation. My heart leaping like a crazy toad, I led the way up only to find that the corridor suddenly became sooty and dark as soon as we turned the corner on the first landing. The music blared out of a slate-gray door held slightly open by a triangle of wood jammed into the hinge. I touched the doorknob—a metal handle screwed into the gray rectangle—but I was afraid to push it. A deep red glow lay waiting behind it. I could see a sliver of the interior, and I asked Jesus to make sure our mission didn't take long.

"All the FedEx guys come here after work, that guy Tommy was telling me," Jake announced. "Do you think they're still wearing their jumpsuits?" He took over from me, confidently pushing the door open. The music swelled and Keith and I followed him in.

Thorny's was about half-full, and the patrons all stood at the far end of the room by the bar. It had that bar smell, the bittersweet stench of cigarettes and stale beer. We passed a pool table lit by a fluorescent light. Behind it sat a pinball machine that said MONTE CARLO, with a drawing of a woman in a skintight dress, a man with a gun, and big dice behind them. Most of the patrons were thirtyish men, thickset but not fat. Only one of them had on a FedEx polo shirt, but most of them could have been FedEx guys, as far as I could tell. I saw Nicky everywhere in strangers who shared one or two of his features, but the real Nicky wasn't there.

We knew we shouldn't drink—especially Jake. In addition to the reparative therapy, his strict drug rehab didn't permit him to have even one sip. He couldn't even take communion. Keith and I stood with our hands in our pockets while Jake bummed another cigarette from one of the tubby men at the bar. Cigarettes weren't allowed at Resurrection either, but they were less not allowed than alcohol or men. Jake got quarters from the bartender and we practically ran to the pool table, a safe space where we could keep our vices at bay during the stakeout.

We played sudden-death pool until we ran out of money, and still no

Nicky. Idle and nervous, the three of us sat on a banquette by the restrooms and Keith tried to tell a joke about a coyote walking into a bar, but we couldn't hear him very well. I laughed at the punch line out of courtesy. Jake shoved his hands under his thighs to prevent himself from getting up to buy a drink or smoke another cigarette. He looked at each of us in turn and said, "Accountability, right?" We shook hands on it. Soon it got near midnight—long past curfew. Keith said again that he didn't really care what happened to Nicky, and we should get back as fast as possible.

"I'm gonna have one more cigarette and then we'll go, okay?" Jake pleaded. Even though I wanted to, I didn't think it would make sense to stop him. Keith shrugged and said something about Christ.

It was a good thing that Jake had that cigarette, because just as he gave up on it and stubbed it out in an ashtray that looked like a black crown, Nicky shuffled in. My heart bloomed like a time-lapse movie of a rose.

The other two didn't notice, but I had not stopped watching the front door during the off moments of our pool games. Nicky had started letting his facial hair grow. Already his stubble exceeded Resurrection's guidelines. He took short steps, like he'd injured his feet, and I thought shamelessly of massaging them. Automatically I got up from the banquette and made my way toward him in such a hurry that I didn't explain to Keith or Jake. If I didn't capture this rare butterfly, I would lose him forever.

When I got closer, I noticed that he looked like he hadn't slept or changed clothes for a while. He'd fallen pretty far after only ten days on the lam. The front pockets of his jeans had holes in them where his boxers showed through. His T-shirt had sweat stains in the armpits. His cheeks were hollow and his eyes sunken, but the shabby look somehow increased his beauty. I gave him a bear hug and shouted his name, but he struggled, so I released him. A cloud of cheap bourbon smell blew out of his mouth. The odor triggered a childhood memory of my father, waking me up at 2:30 a.m. the night before a final exam to show me a corner of the yard I had not mowed to his satisfaction, swatting me in the face with a newspaper like you'd do to a dog.

"Gary, man. The hell you doin' here?"

"We came to get you, Nicky." I indicated Keith and Jake. "We wanted to bring you back into the fold."

Nicky stuck his hands into his pockets. "Now, I appreciate that, but it ain't necessary, besides which I don't think I want to. The fold don't want me. What did Bill say about it?" The doubts of the secular world had fallen on Nicky already, and they had sucked some of the color out of his cheeks.

"Did you go home at all? Where are you staying?"

Nicky thought and smiled and said, "Old habits die hard," which I didn't quite understand at the time. He scratched the back of his head. "You know, thanks, Gary. Thanks. You were the only one at that thing who ever stood up for me."

"I didn't always do the right thing."

"Right, right. But they're always talking about fellowship up there, and Christ, just give 'em the opportunity to stigmatize somebody else, you know, and crush them underfoot. I wasn't never trying to make trouble, Gary. You know that. I just wanted to figure stuff out. Reckon I should've known better than to ask."

"Will you at least consider coming back?"

"Yeah, yeah, sure. If Bill the Old Testament God will let me. You know what Bill said to me before I left? I told him I had some questions about the whole thing and he said, 'I'd rather you dropped dead right now than leave. If you go back to the homosexual lifestyle, your soul will die forever. If you die now, at least you'll have a chance at eternal life.'"

I sighed. "Bill's very committed to the program."

"Give me a second," Nicky said, holding up a finger as he stumbled backward. "I have to go to the bathroom. Remember what we was talking about, okay?"

"Okay." I watched him go, and it felt good to watch him. The spark of mischief hadn't left his green eyes. For all his pessimistic talk and his sudden decline, I had a lot of hope for his return. Jesus wouldn't let him down. I knew from personal experience.

I went back to the banquette, a little drunk from seeing him again, and told Keith and Jake that I'd found Nicky. Keith told me that they'd noticed, but they thought I'd bring him back near the pool table.

"Is he ready to come back?" Keith asked.

"He said he might."

"Where is he now?"

"In the bathroom."

"There's no window in there that he could jump out of, right?" Keith asked, half-seriously.

"I didn't see one when I was in there."

The earlier heavy mood lifted, and even though we'd be lucky to get back to Resurrection before sunup, we'd had a naughty taste of secular life without knuckling under, and we were real pleased with ourselves. Keith volunteered to go to an ATM and get cab fare as soon as Nicky got out of the bathroom and agreed to go with us. Jake bummed yet another cigarette, and by the time he finished, Keith wondered if something might be wrong.

"What's taking him so long?"

"He didn't say which thing he was going to do. And he said to remember what we were talking about."

Jake sat up straight and slid forward, about to stand. "You don't think he met the dealer outside, do you? In the stairwell or something? Holy holy." The three of us followed Jake to the men's room door and found it locked. I banged on the door and called out Nicky's name, but he didn't answer, so I pounded and yelled harder. Jake said the lock was a deadbolt as thick as an index finger.

Keith went to find the manager. He came back with the guy, in the middle of explaining what we thought had happened. The fellow he brought was a big Viking-type man with a wrinkled brow. He showed no sign of surprise or alarm. Keith told us that the manager was on vacation in Belize and that this guy, Mike, was the assistant manager.

"You guys work in corporate or something?" he asked. Jake said yeah, and Mike turned his attention back to the locked door. "The only thing I can think of is, there's a sledgehammer in the back, no idea why, maybe for stuff like this. I'd rather not, but if you think your friend is really gonna... Damn junkies." Mike banged on the door and shouted to see if he could get a response. He didn't. I swallowed hard.

"Get it," Jake spat.

"We might have to hold you liable for the damage, you know."

"Just get it!"

Mike returned after the longest three minutes of my life, slinging the heavy tool with some difficulty. We stood to the left and Mike planted his feet apart, parallel to the right side of the door. Raw manliness glowed in his tight biceps and craggy face as he heaved up the hammer and smashed it against the place where the deadbolt must have been on the other side. It made a terrific clang. A few guys from the bar gathered to watch and give advice. When I turned to the left and right, I saw both Keith and Jake staring in awe at Mike and at the dent he had made in the door.

It took several more swings to break the lock. Finally it gave, and the door slammed backward and then forward with a bang, settling in a half-open position. The scene was like something from a haunted house, but real. The bloom of my heart turned brown and crinkly and the petals fell. Nicky sat slumped backward on the toilet with his pants down, lit by the bathroom's faint bulb and a green neon glow coming from a high window. He'd thrown his head back and a needle dangled from his calf, wagging along with his weak pulse. His calves had small purplish dots all over them. I realized he had never let me see them before, and now I knew why.

Keith stayed at the door trying to prevent any of the gawkers from following us in. Jake grabbed some paper towels and pressed them down on the needle, slowly tugging it out. I pulled up Nicky's pants, hardly even thinking about it, just trying to put everything right. Jake examined our brother's eyes and squeezed his chin, trying to get him to respond. A rapturous grin opened up on Nicky's face, but it had nothing to do with anything Jake had done. I took his other hand, and Mike stood back admiringly.

"That guy's feeling no pain. Okay, let's get him out of here."

"I think we should call an ambulance," Jake said calmly to Mike.

"There's a pay phone downstairs," Mike told us, in a way that said we had to leave. Keith dashed out to make the call. Jake and I leaned Nicky forward. His limbs bobbed in all directions and he drooled on my shirt. Keeping the door closed, we stayed with him to wait.

"Did he overdose?" I asked.

Jake tried to frown a thought out of his head. "It might have been cut with something. A bad something. The alcohol couldn't have helped." He growled with pity and fear.

The ambulance arrived and the EMT workers, a man and a woman, carried Nicky through the bar on the stretcher, cutting a path through the crowd and downstairs like a movie star's bodyguards. Jake squatted into the ambulance with Nicky and the paramedics, while Keith and I got the hospital's name. A bystander told us the address, and we followed in a cab.

When we finally found him outside the emergency room, Jake said it didn't look good. He thought Nicky had done a combination of drugs that were all bad by themselves—meth, crack cocaine, and something else I hadn't heard of. I felt stupid for not having realized that during our conversation, and not stopping him when I had the chance. *Wait, don't go to the bathroom*, I repeated in my mind, wishing I had said it at the right time. I whispered it out loud to myself. After a couple of hours of failing to stop watching forbidden television shows in the waiting room, the doctor greeted us seriously and said that they'd stabilized our friend. We filed into the ICU, admiring all the technological gadgets that circled the bed and the tubes entering Nicky's nose and mouth, feeding his unconscious body. I couldn't contain myself and wept openly.

"Be strong," Keith told me, massaging and hitting my shoulder.

"What for?" Jake muttered.

I gave the doctors all the information I knew about Nicky, and at 3 a.m. we called a cab to take us back to Resurrection. The attending physician said somebody from the hospital would call if Nicky regained consciousness, or, as he put it, "otherwise." We had the driver stop far from the building so that nobody would hear us coming back. Sometimes the doors weren't locked or a window was open on a lower floor. We circled the building, trying everything, and finally yanked open a rusty transom that led into the basement near the clothing storage area. Keith was just small enough to make it through, and with Jake's keys in hand, he crept into Jake's room on the first floor to let us in. We managed not to disturb Dwayne's sleep. After saying goodnight and pledging our loyalty like the Three Musketeers, we went off to our bedrooms. None of us slept well. Nicky least of all—he never woke up.

SIXTEEN

I believe in ghosts, of course. But until Nicky died, I figured ghosts were dead folks' spirits come back looking like somebody under a bedsheet, who leaped out of your cellar and said *Woo-woo* to scare you. Now I know they're more like memories that get trapped in your mind and make you think them too much, even though you wouldn't if you had your druthers. Like the memory of mine where Nicky's breath inside his oxygen mask made a misty little greenhouse over his face. Or the image of him with his pants down at the only time I wished I hadn't seen that. Or thinking about how bad it broke me to watch a paramedic pull Nicky's eyelids open and see those green eyes gone blank.

I overspent my phone time talking with Annie about it. Or around it. Bill and Gay didn't scold me; they must have understood my sadness. With Annie, I shared the terrible story of running off and finding Nicky, blamed myself for his death, and explained my frustration that the rules of Resurrection wouldn't let me show my sympathy because of Nicky's fallen nature. I told her about the extra emptiness in my room now that I knew he'd never return. Annie listened patiently for the most part, but sometimes she probed.

"You loved him, didn't you?" she asked one night.

"As a—as a brother I did. Yes. I loved him."

"Okay." Annie didn't say anything for quite a while. Her silence had a disbelieving quality in it, but I didn't want to point out any extra issues between us if I could pretend that they didn't exist, so I let her silence keep suspecting. With him dead it didn't matter.

For graduation two months later, they filled the church with yellow roses and wreaths. People sneezed on account of the pollen. Fine old ladies wearing fresh corsages jammed the pews, and the brass railings across the altar shone crisp and clean in the tinted sunlight that spilled through the stained glass. Annie couldn't make it because it was Independence Day weekend and her restaurant had become very popular. Even surrounded by people who loved me, I felt alone. Alec Braverman came and gave an emotional speech, tossing his curly hair and gazing down at us with pride and sympathy. "The whole world is going to feel different now," he told us. Doesn't that always feel more true when a handsome man says it? Bill called each of us up and gave us a diploma and a bear hug.

Chain of command forbade paying tribute to the fallen, so we couldn't express our grief about Tom or Nicky in a public way. But during the reception, George patted my back and we talked about how sad and lonely it was to finish the program across from empty shelves and a bed instead of a brother. "We should have moved in together," he said. "Why didn't we think of that?"

As a private thing that day, George wore a cardigan he'd borrowed from Tom and now couldn't give back. I only had a few of Nicky's hairs in an envelope, a souvenir too strange even to admit I owned. I could hardly prove he'd existed, let alone that I'd known him. But if you could have hooked a TV camera to my head and broadcast my thoughts, you would have seen mostly Nicky on the screen, without commercial interruptions.

Though I was happy and proud as I left Memphis, Nicky's ghost remained in my mind. We never could've gotten permission to go to his funeral. "You can't even be fraternizing with them," Keith warned me about dead sinners. During every free moment in the office, I tried to find Nicky's contact information. I wanted to send a note to somebody; I needed to apologize for my part in his downfall. But Gay and Bill had erased Nicky from the files. Once, in a righteous moment, I snuck into Charlie's office and tried his desk, but he always kept it locked. Searching phone directories didn't get me any further. So many Johnsons lived in Baton Rouge that I couldn't narrow my search at all.

Unfortunately, instead of putting the fear of God in me, my memories of Nicky gave my doubts about Resurrection something to stick to. Even if the center could teach some men to manage their unwanted desires, I said to myself, was it worth even one of them dying because he couldn't change enough?

Nagging questions like that scratched up my confidence as I hauled my suitcase out of the empty dorm. For the time being, I had changed my behavior, and I believed that sticking to the program would mean freedom from homosexuality. Bill had always insisted on calling us "former homosexuals." But as I passed through the invisible doorway to real life, that didn't sit so well with me. Even your garden-variety alcoholic has more horse sense than to say he's cured. All of us would have to spend the rest of our natural born days in recovery.

Not long after Gay and I arrived in Atlanta, I dialed the phone number I had for Concerned Relatives' place in Cabbagetown, but it didn't work anymore, and the recording didn't say the new number. I had no idea what might happen if I visited.

It took some doing, but I convinced Gay that I could go back to my old place to say hello again, apologize, and get a few of my possessions back. She insisted on coming along, though, because she was worried that I couldn't handle it alone. As we rode the MARTA I stared out at the treetops, making mental notes about how Atlanta had changed. Every time I moved to a new place, I thought to myself, I had tried to become a different, normal person and failed.

This time would be different. In my wallet I had a stack of crisp business cards, stamped with the logo for Resurrection Ministries—a golden cross in the center of a valentine. The stack made a neat rectangle that stood out on the wallet. I traced the rectangle with my finger, for luck.

Something didn't seem right at the house. All the windows had been replaced with sand-colored boards. The grass in the front yard had grown waist-high and gone to seed. A couple of planks of wood covered one corner of the property, and I recognized a plastic bucket overturned in another. A striped mattress with brown water stains covered the steps like somebody had tried to ride it down months ago. When I moved the bucket, I revealed a pale yellow circle of grass with bugs hurrying up and down the blades. I couldn't help thinking that poetic justice had come down on me. The house had a history separate from me, one I felt I should have taken part in. When I went away, had I become like that house to Annie and Cheryl? An empty, musty old place with boarded-up windows, in need of renovation?

Our old neighbor from across the street, a white fellow with a big gut, told us the bad news. "See, that was a *cult*," he said, even after I tried to correct him. "'Bout five month ago, this *cult* done a performance with a fire dancer in the street here or something of that nature, and it got out of hand—this made the papers, y'all ain't seen? Anyways, they refused to stop the show, even after the police come and tried to subdue them, and one of them cops got his leg broke someway. So the landlord had to throw them out after that." He nodded with satisfaction, like he'd chased the "cult" away himself. Gay and I were so surprised and confused that we went to the library to check the man's facts. The broken leg was a fractured skull, but otherwise he'd told the truth. What a disaster! I resolved to find my old housemates as soon as I could get away from Gay.

At that very moment Annie and Cheryl were driving up the coast, picking my mother up in Savannah for our reunion that night. Every time I imagined the kind of conversation they might be having, I cringed. But otherwise, the day felt like a chance to correct some of the things that had gone wrong before. I could apologize in person for all my bad behavior and start anew in a positive way with everybody I had hurt. Cheryl especially. She had only spoken to me a handful of times over the last year. Her mommy and I always yelled, she told us, and she didn't want to have to yell, too.

Gay had worn a pink golf shirt and a blue denim skirt that day. She sat with her legs apart, a hand on each knee. That wasn't feminine behavior, but I didn't correct her. As I watched her across the train car, I remember thinking that aside from her large bosom, no matter how she dressed she would still look like a handsome teenage boy, and that thought made me pretty uneasy, because I was supposed to like women as women, not find them attractive for looking like boys. It also might mean that some women were naturally masculine and some men naturally feminine. Thoughts like this always disappeared quickly, however, and for a while I could ignore them.

We'd gone to the Coca-Cola Museum after leaving the Concerned Relatives' house. Exhausted by all the traveling, Gay and I could hardly move. We only wanted to sit down and drink cold drinks. Unfortunately, we didn't have enough time to go back to the bed-and-breakfast and shower. We had a ton of presents, and we were within walking distance of their hotel, so we didn't bother going back. I hoped that they'd be so overjoyed to see me for the first time in a long time that they'd overlook how dirty and tired I was.

Much of the country was experiencing a record-setting heat wave, so the air conditioning gave us a refreshing chill as we passed through the revolving door at the Marriott. A fountain stood in the middle of the lobby, decorated with rocks and plants that looked almost real. I checked under my arms for a bad odor and was pleased not to find one. A shudder went through my body as we rode the elevator, so strong that it knocked my Coca-Cola baseball cap down over my eyes. I belched out of nervousness.

The hallway was completely silent except for a noise that sounded like wind blowing through an air shaft. Our feet didn't make any sound against the thick maroon carpet. In an open doorway, a black maid with a sour face shoved a fitted sheet under the corner of a king-size bed. I thought maybe she made the face because I was with a white woman. It would have been funny to explain the whole truth to her.

"Are you ready, Gary?" Gay asked, squeezing my fingers together.

"No, ma'am. Not really."

"It'll be okay," she promised. I didn't believe her, but I didn't want to hear the truth either.

The door was ajar. Inside the room I could hear the voices of my mother, Annie, and Cheryl. The noise of a movie musical came from the television, almost drowning out their voices. I pushed on the door with one of my bags of gifts and shouted "Hey everybody!" as I opened it. Annie came over and swung the door the rest of the way, announcing to the others that I had arrived. My mother's voice screamed "Gary! Gary!" I couldn't see her yet. Cheryl sat in a chair by the window in a blue dress with frills at the ends of the sleeves, playing with a doll. She didn't look up when I entered.

In the small hallway that led to the bedroom, Annie wrapped her arms most of the way around my waist. I kissed the top of her head at the place where her hair parted. I bent down and kissed her on the lips. During the kiss I tried to feel aroused. A small spark of static electricity happened when our lips met, and we laughed, but that was it.

When the kiss finished, Annie peeked around my left side and saw Gay. "You must be Gay," she said, shaking hands with her.

"Yes, but it's just a name!" she said. I had heard that joke a bunch of times now, and it usually made me chuckle, but this time I didn't want to remind anybody of the thing that they couldn't mention. Nobody could say *gay*. It's the opposite of John 1:1—*In the beginning* wasn't *the word, and the word* wasn't *with God*. Mama didn't know the real reason for my problem, so I didn't want the conversation to even come close to the topic. I would tell her once I had my impulses under control. "I used to have this problem," I would say to my mother, and she would be proud that I had conquered it and thankful that I had never told her during the process, so that she hadn't had to worry. I turned to Gay and widened my eyes to say *Don't talk about that*. Annie either didn't hear Gay's comment about her name or ignored the joke, and plunged her hands excitedly into the Coca-Cola bags.

"We come bearing gifts!" I announced. Cheryl stood behind the desk across the room. She held the doll upside down and bent her limbs in all directions. We'd bought Coca-Cola presents for everybody: a snow globe, T-shirts in all sizes, Santa ornaments, calendars that were on clearance, bottle openers shaped like Coke bottles, pencils and pens in a metal Coke box, and a baby seal plush toy.

As Gay helped Annie remove all the goodies from the bag, I stepped around them and into the main part of the hotel room, where my mother was still calling out for me. She lay on the bed, even larger than my memory of her. Mama screamed and screamed when she saw me. "My baby! My baby!" I gave her a big smile and a bigger hug. Her hair was short, straightened and combed, but not really styled. It had turned grayer than I ever imagined my mother's hair could get. She had on a plus-size cotton dress covered with daisies. Tears streamed down her face, and her eyes were red. The dark pockets at the top of her cheeks made her look permanently sad. She held out her hands to me for another hug.

As my body sank into hers, I cried, too. While crying, I noticed a four-footed cane by the bed. For a while I couldn't understand anything she said through her tears, because my hug covered her mouth. I thought Cheryl would get excited, too, but she still hadn't come over. I hugged Mama and turned to see my daughter sitting at the desk, posing her little doll all kinds of ways. The doll had on a bikini bathing suit. I recognized the long limbs and blond hair of Barbie. Why had Annie let her have a secular doll?

Annie and Gay came into the room to watch us, smiling broadly. Slowly we separated, and Mama scooted over on the bed so that I could sit on the edge. She pulled a tissue from a box on the nightstand and wiped her eyes and nose. We had dinner at a cheap family restuarant on the same block as the dirty bookstore I'd visited when I first came to Atlanta. I prayed that we wouldn't run into anyone I had known as August Valentine.

The firecracker thrill of seeing everybody after so much had happened settled down a little, and Annie and Gay and I dodged my mother's questions about where I would end up and what I had done in my dead years and "at the rehabs," as Mama called it.

During dessert, Annie got up to go to the bathroom. Cheryl tapped me on the arm. "Daddy?" she requested sweetly. She hadn't said much to me during the meal, but she hadn't acted out either, and I didn't want to tip the balance by saying something to upset her again. I was happy that she had decided to speak to me, and eager to grant her wishes. I leaned down into her space to hear her question. She pushed a blob of strawberry ice cream into the center of her spoon.

"It's okay if you don't come home," she said, bobbing her head up and down and grinning. She said it quietly enough that nobody else at the table heard. "I don't want to move." Like anybody else, I assume that a child doesn't know what she's saying, but this crushed me. She put the entire round part of the spoon into her mouth and pulled it out. Pink ice cream covered her lips. Then she licked the tips of her fingers and giggled like she had been joking. I tried to laugh along, but I wished I had stayed dead.

I would visit home anyhow, I knew, once Gay and I had taken a couple of months to get the new chapter up and running. I'd ease back into married life—I would return to Orlando in a couple of weeks, then Annie would sell her business and move everybody up here. But I couldn't adjust to the idea that Cheryl didn't want me around. In our hotel room that night, after Cheryl and my mother conked out on the bed near the window, I told Annie what our daughter had said.

"She needs a daddy," Annie told me. It didn't explain a darn thing, but it sounded good because I wanted to hear it. I nodded and put my arms around Annie and kissed her open-mouthed. During the kiss I thought about the fact that "She needs a daddy" doesn't mean the same thing as "She needs *her* daddy," or "She needs *you* to be her daddy." I kept on contemplating that word choice until I fell asleep, and then the whole next day, too.

SEVENTEEN

Darby, the manager whose sex habits Miquel had told me too much about, stood behind the counter at Over the Rainbow. His bushy beard looked like somebody had attached a possum to his neck. He wore a dirty T-shirt and a leather vest, and he rubbed the display case with Windex. I'd tried to avoid my old life, but all the curiosity, regret, and unfinished business stuck in my craw and reeled me in.

"August!" he called out. I froze inside, because the fake identity I left behind had stayed here in Atlanta, growing and changing in other people's minds. I would have to play the part of that sophisticated phony again, with his olive baguettes and his Martha Graham. Darby tried to bear-hug me, but the countertop got in the way. I informed him that I'd left homosexuality, and told him a little about Resurrection. Not the whole truth, but he didn't need to know everything. He didn't react much, just said "Oh" softly. I asked after Miquel.

"Miquel..." Darby shook his head. "He don't work here anymore, you know. I had to let him go. He's been having a powerful bad time with the booze, bless his heart."

"Here's my business card," I said. I gave him a business card, but I'd forgotten that it had my real name and Resurrection Ministries' new

Atlanta number and address on it. I wrote August on the back, and my personal phone number. Mistake.

Every Tuesday at 6:30 p.m., Gay and I ran drop-in group sessions for people struggling with same-sex attractions. Attendance wasn't high at first. We would both run the talks, so that it seemed like we had more members and the ex-gay movement was going strong.

Our third meeting, Gay and I sat in the office with the door open, like always. Chloë, a bad-tempered young lady who had been there from the first, came in and sat down on the other side of the circle of chairs we had set up in the office. I suggested that she move closer, since there were ten chairs and only three people. Then a gangly boy we hadn't seen before came in and sat across the room. He took out a pen and a datebook and started scribbling things in his agenda. His hand shook and he deliberately didn't glance at us. The small refrigerator in the other room hummed, and nobody spoke.

It came up on 6:45, so Gay started, welcoming Chloë and the new guy. We then went around the circle and said our names and one of our best qualities. Chloë said she had a good sense of humor. The boy introduced himself as Smith, and said he had excellent vision. Gay described her terrific spatial skills, and I said I had the biggest heart. Because we had a new person in the group, Gay said a few words about the program, its history, and how it was expanding, helping people heal, and spreading God's love. During her description, the elevator bell went off and somebody's footsteps came down the hall. For latecomers, we always left the door ajar with a note on it that said COME IN! in friendly letters.

The face on the other side of the door made my heart leap with excitement and churn with fear. It was Miquel. I had expected to hear from him, if at all, on my personal line, asking for August. So I hoped against hope that he had come in on his own to solve his alcohol and SSA problems. He had a shorter haircut than before, and he had gained a little weight. His eyes went to me, smiling, and he waved with his fingers, then his glance darted to the other people in the room and he smiled and took a seat. What a miracle! Maybe.

When Gay got done with her description of the program, she introduced herself. Then she introduced me as Gary Gray. She slapped her hands against her thighs and said "Hello, Stranger!" to the new guy. She asked him his name and his best quality. I figured things would make themselves clear when he spoke. Already I was daydreaming about how much fun we'd have as prayer partners. When all our suffering ended, we'd have family cookouts together at a long picnic table full of potato salad, fried chicken buckets, and burgers. Our wives, babies, and cocker spaniels would frolic around the park with us.

"My name is Miquel," he said, "and I mix a mean margarita." He crossed his legs. Though true, it was a typical Miquel comment. I let out a small, nervous chuckle. Using that as a good quality let me know he wasn't committed to changing his lifestyle. But I couldn't throw him out.

"Great, Miquel!" Gay exclaimed, with her amazing ability to turn a negative into a positive. "So alcohol is an important part of your life? Do you feel that you want help changing that, or no? Maybe that's part of why you came to Resurrection?"

"Alcohol has gotten me through some tough times," Miquel said. "It's been a good friend."

"That's great to hear, because this program is going to help introduce you to an even better friend. I probably don't even have to tell you His name. You've probably met Him before. But alcohol probably told you not to pay Him any attention, right?" Jesus' face was on a poster behind her, and in several other places in the room. Gay's spiritual energy glowed throughout the space. "When I was engaging in lesbianism, alcohol was always right there with me, saying, 'Go for it!' I'll bet other people in the room have had similar experiences with alcohol, right?"

"I would always have to get drunk before I could—you know," Smith confessed. Chloë nodded thoughtfully.

"With a man," I volunteered.

"Uh-huh. Even *talking*." Smith smiled nervously. He stuck a finger under the band of his wristwatch and snapped it.

"How old are you, Smith?" Gay asked.

"I'll be eighteen in a couple months."

Gay shook her head. "So you're underage and homosexuality is already encouraging a dependence on alcohol. Do you see how it works? This isn't the Lord's plan for you, Smith, I want you to know that. God loves you."

"I know! It's so obvious that the Lord wants a man to be with a woman," Smith said. "That's why we're made the way we are." He made a ring with one hand and stuck his index finger into it with the other. "See, this is a man and a woman." Then he crossed his index fingers like swords, and banged two circled fists against one another. "Those other ways don't work. And you can't make a baby or nothing."

Miquel snorted softly, holding back a laugh. That's how I knew for sure that he hadn't come in to seek help changing his wicked desires. He had come to mock me and my struggle. I wouldn't have minded so much if it had only been me, but he was also making fun of other people who had nothing to do with his life. I got hopping mad.

He raised his fist and his thumb. "But see, Smith, Smitty—can I call you Smitty?—this is a man's anus, and this is another man's big fat wiener." Smith started at Miquel's frank language. Miquel made a gesture like Smith's. "See how tight that is? And there's something up there called the prostate gland that—" Smith raised his hand as soon as Miquel began his crude demonstration and then started to talk over him.

"Sure, sure, but you still can't make no baby!" he shouted. "You can't make no baby!"

"So men and women never get it on just for pleasure?" he asked. "It's always about babies? How downright dreary!"

I knew Smith was too inexperienced to field this typical question. "We're talking about using the gift of sex for its highest purpose here, Miquel," I informed him. "And that is procreation, yes."

"All I'm saying is if procreation is such a holy sacrament, why don't straight people who feel that way stop debasing it by having sex? You don't need to do the nasty anymore if you want a kid. You can just get a little petri dish, swirl everything around in there, and if your wife's too lily-white to squeeze the puppy out herself, then you can just implant it in the Mexican maid. Or better yet, cut out the middleman and screw the maid! That's even more efficient than adopting a disadvantaged kid—make one from scratch! Hell, that's what *my* daddy did!"

"Miquel!" I shouted, to stop his offensive outburst. "When you first came in, I hoped that you were seeking healing. But if you just came to make fun of me and these other young people who are struggling, why don't you leave? Don't interrupt other people's process with your negativity."

Miquel sighed, like I'd interrupted *his* meeting, and let his shoulders fall. "I needed to talk to you about something, and I was trying to come early but I got here late, so there you go. And I'm not being negative, I'm genuinely interested in what your organization believes. Because it's so *nutty*."

"You're right, it is nutty," Gay told him, folding her arms. Her happy attitude took on an edge. "I'm nuts about Jesus Christ, and I'm determined to get better and truly live for Him instead of doing whatever the Devil tells me to, or alcohol influences me to do. Now, if you're serious about listening, you're welcome to stay, Miquel, but otherwise I think you ought to take Gary's advice and wait for him outside. Please."

"I'm sorry... um, Gay. I'm just curious. I've always wanted to find out what people in places like this actually think. Do you really think that gays can become completely straight?" A miserable note in Miquel's voice made me wonder if maybe his mocking tone hid a deeper longing. Perhaps he did want help, but he couldn't tell us through the wall of sarcasm he kept between himself and others. Some of the good memories from our time together bubbled up into my heart and warmed me.

"Homosexuality is a choice," I told him in a soothing voice.

"Really? Well, I didn't pull that lever. How come I'm a big queer?" Everybody laughed at this joke, because we had no doubt asked ourselves that very question many times in our lives. It had gotten so tense in the room that we needed a laugh pretty bad. Patiently, I explained Dr. Soffione's beliefs about homosexual identity versus behavior to Miquel, and said that the choice you had was whether or not to *express* your longings for same-sex contact.

"So it's the demons that tell you to go out and sin."

"Hey," Gay said. "He's getting the hang of this!"

"Because God only wants you to have sex for the practical reason of children."

Smith stretched his arms out and cracked his knuckles. "Sounds right to me," he said.

"And sex without babies is purposeless—like, to you guys, it's in the same category with art, it's like synchronized swimming, or interpretive dance, right?"

"Art is not purposeless!" Chloë suddenly blurted. "Art serves the purpose of self-expression!" Her voice had a rough, husky sound. She would have to do a lot of vocal training to change it. I made a mental note to bring that up with her.

"We're not here to talk about art," Gay reminded the group. Holding our attention for a moment of silence, she let the mood become calmer and refocused the discussion. "I thought what we should do in tonight's session is talk about the reasons why homosexuality happens and why God might have given some of us the challenge of moving beyond it." She went to an easel we had set up before the session and uncapped one of the magic markers on the shelf underneath. With a *whip* sound, she tossed the top sheet over to reveal a fresh page and held the marker above the paper, eager to start jotting.

"Because cock tastes good," Miquel said, unable to control his laughter.

"No!" Gay snapped. "Please. You're going to have to leave. Get out now." Miquel didn't get up, so Gay turned to the rest of us. "I'm talking about psychological reasons. Places inside us that got broken, where the Devil might get in during early childhood development and put in the wrong desires."

"Oh. Because your *father's* cock tastes good." Miquel had an even more hysterical fit of laughter, but he was the only one laughing. I thought he was behaving in a disgusting and immature manner. I should have known he'd been drinking.

Gay growled in an almost masculine way. "Gary, will you escort Miquel out of the room please, unless he decides he'd like to participate in a meaningful way?" Gay stopped cold and fumbled with the magic marker. "Hold the phone! Is this the Miquel that—?"

"Yes," I said, as blood pumped into my face.

"I'm sorry about this," she apologized to Chloë and Smith as I stood and crossed the circle. "Sometimes people come in off the street and they bring the street with them. They just want to disrupt our mission and pretend that God doesn't matter." I grabbed Miquel by the arm and brought him to a standing position. I was surprised that I had the strength, but Miquel didn't resist.

"I'm not trying to say the same thing or nothing, but parental abuse?" Smith offered.

"Great!" Gay said, writing it down on the easel. "Have either of you experienced anything like that before? Physical abuse? Sexual abuse by your same-sex parent?"

"No," they said, almost in unison. "My folks have always been okay with it," Smith added. "They don't like that I'm coming here. They think it'll make them cool in the neighborhood to have a gay son. Ain't that sick?"

"Oh, I feel so sorry for people who think it's fashionable. Okay, we'll talk about that in depth later. Any other things?"

Miquel opened his mouth, about to say something else off-color. I'd had enough, and I didn't want him to offend me another time. Furious, I pulled him into the hallway, then around the corner to the elevator. I pressed the button, ready to throw him into it and kick him out of the building and my life.

"What do you want, Miquel? You said there was something you wanted to talk to me about. Make it quick, because I'm in the middle of a meeting—though you can't seem to respect that." His voice reverberated and rang in my ears.

"Oh, Augie Bear, I've never seen you so mad! I'd better not ask what I was going to ask. I'm just going to get on the elevator and you can go back to your nutty ex-lesbians named Gay and we'll just forget we ever saw one another again. This wasn't what I meant to happen at our little reunion."

Miquel's eyelids flared and his mouth turned down into the helpless look that had always attracted me. He had called me by my old pet name. Against my will and in spite of my anger, some of the strength of that old desire broke on through. It was like a ravine lined with slippery memories had opened below me and I was trying to keep myself from falling in. It struck me that Miquel was the person who had believed in August Valentine the most, and even though August didn't exist anymore, he was an even more powerful symbol of the man I wanted to be, because now he was a man I could never be. Miquel still thought of me as August. And he had loved August.

I reminded myself of the Lord's plans for my eternal soul and pushed the feeling aside. "What did you mean to happen?"

"Oh, I'm kind of strapped these days, Augie. I guess you haven't heard as much about me as I have about you. It's nothing really, I'm just going through a rough period." The elevator showed up and he held the door back with one hand.

"You came here to ask for money? And behaved like *that?*"

"You know I have trouble controlling myself in certain situations. I just thought it was funny. Y'all put so much effort into not being who you are. Wake up, honey! Those normal people you want to be aren't so normal either! And *you!* Apparently you've never known what it's like *not* to lead a double life!"

Now I got it—Miquel hadn't come only to ask for money. He was very upset with me. Maybe asking for money was only an excuse. He had heard that during our relationship I wasn't the person he thought I was, and he wanted to let me know that I hadn't made a fool of him. Right then I remembered what I'd done with the business card, too, and felt doubly stupid. I knew I owed him an apology, but I didn't like that he had barged in on the meeting and made inappropriate comments. I couldn't form the word *sorry* on my lips.

As usual, Miquel couldn't resist making a bad situation worse. "So once you're straight, are you going to go for broke and try to turn white?"

In the tense silence where I should have replied with anger, the elevator door tried to jerk closed and knocked Miquel off-balance. He pushed the rubber guard in the center and held the door open with his foot, then raised his chin and cut his eyes at me. "In a way, we've had it easier, haven't we? Being gay saves us from having to be colored, and being colored saves us from having to be white. It's really tough to be 100 percent anything, ain't it? Well, I'm 100 percent faggot and 100 percent drunk! To thine own self be true, I say. Even if it kills you. And it always does."

I fished in my pocket and opened my wallet. "I've got forty dollars," I said. "Take it."

"I don't need your stupid money," he spat. My patience for him had run out. I couldn't keep back a growl at his unstable behavior. This was what it was to deal with an alcoholic. Miquel needed the healing love of Jesus Christ more than nearly anybody I'd known, but I feared it would be impossible for him to open up to it with his willful attitude. He had confused his illness for his identity, as Dr. Soffione would have said.

I lowered my wallet, but he grabbed my wrist with one hand and tugged the bills out. "I mean, yes I do need your stupid money." In one swift motion he took the cash between two fingers and slipped it into his pocket. There was something whorish about the way he did it.

"Thanks," he muttered, letting go of the elevator door. "It'll go to a good cause."

"Good cause? You're going to buy alcohol with it."

"That's what I meant, *Gary Gray*." He spoke my real name like a curse. The elevator door started to close again. He said "Keep in touch" in a tone that meant *Go to Hell*. My head filled with a mixture of anger, sadness, and repulsion, like some hot, dangerous mental swamp. Had I contributed in some way to his downward slide? Once I returned to the meeting, I couldn't pay attention to anything. Mostly I was upset about the things Miquel had said about me. Try though I did, I couldn't dismiss them, or him.

I hadn't stopped thinking about Manny from time to time during my recovery. He was the one man with SSAs I could think of who seemed not to conform to Dr. Soffione's theories. I didn't know about his history with his father, but he didn't seem to have the sort of masculinity issues that *Stand Up Straight* said you had to have for the illness to take root. He had even gotten a job as a police officer. The fact of a gay man in a traditionally masculine profession made me awful curious. The words *gay police officer* sounded outside reality to me, like *female bodybuilder* or *black president*.

Dr. Soffione said that men with my condition longed to be considered real men. They identified with their mothers and other women. They sexualized men because they thought of men as different from themselves. Difference didn't just make procreation possible, like Smith had demonstrated in the meeting. Difference *caused* normal sexuality. But Manny didn't seem to have this problem. He behaved exactly like a masculine man except for the sleeping with men part.

On top of that, Manny wasn't a large, beefy guy who lined up with my image of a cop. I'd never seen him wearing his uniform, so I daydreamed about this short man in the blue outfit and the stiff hat. When I ran across policemen in the street, I hoped that they would be him, but all the ones I saw downtown had larger frames than Manny, even some of the police-women. Maybe they kept him at the precinct, answering phones. I had to find out.

I unfolded the piece of paper and smoothed it out on our coffee table. Manny had jotted down his number first and his name below it in blue felt-tip marker. I wondered what the block print said about his personality. Did it mean natural masculinity? Wondering about something so minor made me think that I might be in love with him, like when I loved Hank's coffee stirring. When I reached that forbidden point of fantasy, I would fold the piece of paper back up tightly, stick it into the secret compartment of the book bag, and push it underneath the sofa again, farther back every time. I reckon I did this as a substitute for masturbation.

Aside from the things that happened with Nicky, I had remained celibate and kept my male yearnings from getting the better of me for almost a year. I was real proud of myself. Even when Gay left town, I had controlled the urges. I had asked her to call me every two hours and make sure that I hadn't given in to the bad desires. In the area of self-control, Dr. Soffione's therapy appeared to be working for me. The second-best option for recovery as a man with SSAs was celibacy. I supposed I could adjust my goals and shoot for that.

But like he was making up for the physical discipline and submission to Christ that had served me so well, Satan flooded my mind with sexual thoughts about men. I had an erotic thought about nearly every man I encountered. But then stranger things happened. I started to imagine people naked in a way that wasn't sexual. Men, too. If I noticed hair coming up out of the collar of a man's T-shirt, the image of his wooly chest would come to me immediately. When a man standing in line at the post office in front of me had a flat behind, the skinny rear end in front of me became naked. I imagined children naked when I passed them in the street, but girls as well as boys. I wondered what Gay looked like when she got undressed in the next room or when she sat on the commode. I never told anybody about these thoughts, because they were even more unclear and puzzling to me than my erotic fantasies about men. Those hadn't disappeared either. I just pulled in more than before with the same large net as my curiosity with everybody's nakedness. Maybe talking about my struggles made me emotionally naked, and as a result I wanted to see everybody *really* naked.

The pressure cooker boiled over the day before I took my first trip back home. Gay had gone running. Instead of folding up the piece of paper and hiding it again that time, I flattened it out with my palm. Each of the little squares in the folds seemed to wink at me, so much that I got up to look for the cordless phone. I bet myself I could interact with the world of secular gays without returning to their ways. I dared myself to find the strength. My first task in this quest to prove that I didn't have to lead a double life at all times was to make contact with Manny. I could convert him pretty easily, I bet. He would have an easy path toward true masculinity, since he probably didn't see males as his opposite as much as the SSA men I met at Resurrection did. Maybe Dr. Soffione's theory didn't apply equally to every homosexual.

I located the phone under some of Gay's laundry and brought it to the coffee table. Kneeling in front of the paper, I dialed the number. It was just a friendly phone call, I told myself. Just to talk. I had some questions for a gay police officer. But my stomach jumped with each ring. I held my breath to keep from hanging up in fear before Manny answered. I rehearsed in my head what I would say to him. Nobody answered the phone, so I hung up and sat on my bed listening to an inspirational cassette tape. The woman's voice told me to stand in my power, so I got up, and somehow a little of the guilt and disappointment left me, like a mean pussycat had jumped out of my lap. Twenty minutes later, as soon as I had put the event behind me, the phone rang.

"Gary Gray," I said.

Somebody laughed. "Gary, it's Manny! Did you just call?" I fell backward onto the bed.

"Well, I'll be. I did call. I just had this number lying around and I couldn't remember whose it was so I thought I'd call. And lo and behold. Nice to hear from you."

I spent a tingly couple of moments thinking about all we'd done back then. He wanted to get together, and when I said I was leaving town tomorrow, he said, "Then I guess we'll have to see each other tonight." I almost asked if he had a lover, but I thought that might make him assume I wanted sex. Maybe I did want sex, but didn't want to realize that I wanted sex until all my defenses failed and it was too late—about four days after the fact probably would've been best.

"Great," I said. "Let's go grab a beer. And talk."

"I have beer at my place."

"Beer's always better free, I say." We laughed.

At his apartment, I searched for signs of a boyfriend. Photos, shoes that wouldn't have fit Manny, another name on the mail by the door. I saw nothing. I supposed he'd tell me on a need-to-know basis. I promised myself I'd only talk through my troubles, but then we brushed against each other in the hallway. I grabbed and hugged him. Then I held him. I stuck my nose in his ear and sniffed deeply. My large body towered above his small but strong frame, and when I leaned over to make him walk backward into the living room and onto the couch, he stepped on the arches of my feet so I did all the walking. Our motions turned frantic. Shirts flew off. I tugged his belt open and we removed the rest of our clothes. When we came back together, though, he slid his legs out from under me and walked on his hands to the other side of the bed where I couldn't reach.

"Listen. We can't," Manny said.

"What's the matter?"

"I have a husband. He's roughly your size, also in law enforcement, like me, and he may come home at a later point in the evening. You're really a nice, upstanding guy, but I don't want any drama."

I would have been angry, but the idea of two gay macho cops in love, living together—I couldn't wrap my mind around that. It almost made me snort through my nose. I tugged my shirt down as Manny circled the bed, straightening the comforter. I wondered if he'd had the husband the first time I met him.

"No hard feelings," I said at the door.

He reached into my pants and raised his eyebrow. "Well, I'm feeling *something* hard!" He laughed and punched me in the arm like a straight guy friend would. "Hey, next time we'll have an actual beer. As friends."

Like most folks, I don't much enjoy rejection. Even less do I enjoy getting joshed by a fellow who has just given me blue balls. I reacted with a powerful urge to walk the streets alone and get off, the way I had during my year of free checking. But first I needed to calm my aching crotch and learn to walk again so that I could go home without arousing Gay's suspicion. The bronco strength of my desire at that point, chained with a hot determination to satisfy myself, momentarily wiped out everything else. I passed a bar I recognized, a hustler joint called Trixx. I had some brochures from

Resurrection in my jacket pocket; if anybody recognized me, I would say I meant to save souls. I ordered a cranberry and seltzer because it looked like a real drink, and stood watching a fortyish dude in tight jeans play pool. So few guys walked in that I took out the brochures and re-read them. On the final fold, a picture of Alec Braverman caught my attention. His arm held up, pointing, he seemed to rise up out of a field of trees near what I recognized as the Rictus Bollard Church. I held the photo to a nearby light. The color saturation of the print might have had something to do with it, but damned if Alec didn't have the most intense blue eyes in creation, bright as glass cleaner and determined as an ambulance. He wore a flattering polo shirt and he seemed to walk forward in a way that showed off the curve of his thighs and butt. I wanted to touch him, be him, to bury my face in the hot flesh around his belly button.

In a gay bar, fantasizing about a struggling brother—What could be more forbidden? As soon as I'd had any kind of freedom, the door in my head banged open and lust rushed in. But after a while, lust and guilt curled up together. One increased the other, and both got mixed up into a third emotion that made my body tingle from my toes to my temples. Even begging the Lord's forgiveness gave me a sexual charge. When I asked for absolution, I surrendered my will and my body. Wasn't that just like sex?

A dramatic disco song on the jukebox sang, *When I look back upon my life, it's always with a sense of shame... Everything I've ever done, it's a sin.* The singer sang the letter *s* in a way that sounded gay. Horrified, I shoved the brochure into my jacket and jogged out. Comparing God and sex wasn't right. Everybody knew you could only have one. Soon I had to slow my pace, but I missed the last train and had to walk all the way back home.

Gay had waited up; she wanted to know how far I'd slipped. She sat at her desk in a nightgown decorated with strawberries, her toenails painted a feminine shade of rose. I watched her chunky thigh as it moved toward her privates. If she'd shifted in the chair, I could've seen more. There were stories in the movement about ex-gay men and women becoming man and wife, but I had never heard of an ex-gay man having an affair with an ex-lesbian who wasn't his wife. The thought was too strange, plus I didn't like Gay in that way.

I told her about the bar. Worrying had kept her awake. She feared that some toughs had cornered me in an alley and beaten me up, the way they'd done to Enrique in the middle of the program just for walking down the street. When we visited him in the hospital, Enrique had said the attack was a warning from the Lord. He said it through bloody, scabby, fat lips, with an eye swollen shut.

"I'm going to have to report this," Gay told me. "If you're going to represent the new chapter, we can't risk your being spotted publicly cruising in a gay bar."

"I wasn't cruising," I corrected.

"Well, just *in* one. We've had trouble like this before. The gay-positive people find out and use it to undermine our efforts. It looks bad."

"I had brochures." I slipped them out and waved them as proof.

"This wasn't an official mission. It could be very serious, Gary. I don't know what Bill and Charlie are going to say about your leadership ability after this. I'll tell them that you're praying for guidance. But maybe you should speed up the process of moving your family to Atlanta. That'll keep accountability high for when I'm gone, and it's a great method of improving the image of the program."

We kneeled on the rug with our hands touching and prayed. She had warm, chubby hands, and her nightgown barely contained her very full bosoms. Imagine my confusion when I thought of squeezing them during our prayer, and some blood began to swoosh into my agonized private area. No! I thought. Not now. Not here. Wrong.

As Gay and I talked to churches farther outside Atlanta, we found more people receptive to the Resurrection philosophy and mission. Gradually, folks started to trickle in. In general that was a plus, but it also meant added responsibility for me at a time when I felt insecure. That put worry on top of worry. When I talked to Annie on the phone, in the days before my visit, I'd had trouble concentrating. I forgot how to bring up new subjects. But if Annie noticed, she ignored my distracted attitude. She would ask about what happened in our meetings and whether lots of new people were signing up. Douglas, one of the waiters in her restaurant, turned out to be gay. Instead of shunning him, she'd decided to befriend him first and wait to encourage him to get treatment. But he didn't seem to want help, and they were having too much fun—going to theme parks and restaurants and babysitting Cheryl, who loved him. She kept putting off bringing up his damnation. I felt jealous and confused. My wife was replacing me with a gay man.

I boarded the plane to Orlando in a real weird mood, like somebody had tied my feelings to four different horses and fired a pistol. The night before, I had needed release so badly I'd doubled over with pain, sweating and hyperventilating. I felt I had no choice but onanism. I began thinking of female images, but they took so long to arouse me that I broke my skin and had to keep from touching a raw red patch as I continued. I gave in and peeked at Alec Braverman's brochure photo, then thought of Manny. In my mind, I returned to his apartment. His wiry naked body didn't slip out from under me this time. Our motions turned frantic. He disappeared under me, then our fingers and thumbs and tongues disappeared inside one another. I aimed into a tissue. When I came, I saw stars.

Gay had informed Bill about my bar episode—it felt piddling to me now. I hoped he would go easy on me, knowing that I hadn't taken it to the level of sexual relations. I feared what Dr. Soffione might say. I pictured him shaking his feathery white hair from behind his desk and sighing to himself, "Another weak homosexual," as he marked my employment papers with a big black x and tossed them into the trash. This scene played over and over in my head as I boarded the plane. I hoped Bill and Gay would give it their best. The job mixed my faith, my social ties, and my path to recovery with my means of support. How would I live without it?

Staring at the ground through a porthole streaked with rain, I hoped that the plane would crash so that I could die a hero.

But once we passed above Florida, I thought I might have actually gone to Heaven. We flew through a high-pressure system. Florida's whole landscape spread out below, the biggest golf course you've ever seen. The clouds all had flat undersides and huge puffy plumes like explosions of pure joy. When we flew in between them I could see down to the ground through steep white tunnels, and that made me dizzy. The green hills curved around every which way, and all those lakes shimmered like new coins. No wonder old people came here to die. Going to Heaven from Florida, you wouldn't notice the change. I spotted palm trees as the aircraft flew down, then I saw Disney World just before landing and thought, I am returning to paradise. Not even Adam and Eve got to do that.

Annie and Cheryl met me in the food court before baggage claim. Annie hugged me and I was so nervous and excited that I picked her up off the ground. She laughed and struggled in my arms and I put her back down and kissed her. One thing I liked about straightness was that you could kiss in crowds without getting other people upset. Everybody approved of men with women. Men kissing, even in the dark, got people like my mother angry and could start an argument or a fight. It seemed like everybody had the responsibility to prevent that sort of thing from ever showing its face.

Cheryl hugged and kissed me, too, but not as much as her mother. "You got here in time for my birthday," she told me. "I'm gonna be six." She had lost a baby tooth, and she showed me the gap and the tooth, too. She kept it in a box that used to have mints in it. The Tooth Fairy had given her a whole dollar. Miquel, I thought, would have made a joke about fairies and money. I searched her face for signs of still hating me. She stuck her tongue out at me, but playfully, giggling.

We appeared to be just another happy Florida family as we got into the car. Annie had a new sedan with power windows and velvety seats. It smelled like pine trees. Cheryl sat between us and pretended to help her mother drive, while Annie pointed out things that were new since the last time I had lived there and businesses that had failed or moved. The pace of life surprised me—it always went too fast. I wanted to tell everything to slow down because I was getting lost, falling behind. I thought that and then I touched my daughter's forearm, making a list of everything I had already missed in her life. Silently I vowed that if I got better, I'd stop missing all those events. Annie saw my face and asked if something was wrong. I said, "No, nothing," smiling at her through my tears.

Annie still lived at the Ponce de León—they had never raised the rent. She had also stayed there to keep the memory of me alive, and to wait for me to get back, she said. I had always liked the place and was happy to see it again, even though it had become shabbier. The fountain in the courtyard had broken and the fish in the center of the blue bowl didn't spit water anymore. On the far side of the courtyard was an apartment with a FOR RENT sign in the window hanging by one corner. But the rest of the place had the same cheery atmosphere as before. Palms and almond trees decorated the arch out front. Vines climbed the stucco walls, and iron furniture circled the pool.

We had another celebration supper, this time at a Mexican restaurant called Caramba's. I wanted to go to Annie's restaurant, Pago Pago, but she said we would go there some other time—she had taken time off and didn't even want to see the place.

Cheryl told me everything about her first days in first grade. Annie reached under the table for my hand and held it there, all sweaty. From time to time I remembered that something might have to happen in the bedroom that night. I knew Annie would understand if I couldn't be a real man with her, but that didn't take the pressure off.

Cheryl's bedtime had come when we arrived home, so I read her a story and tucked her into bed for the first time. The story was about a pig who leaves home and finds that the world is a scary place so he comes back to a warm trough of his mama's best slop. Cheryl giggled uncontrollably as I closed the storybook. "That's you, Daddy," she said. "You're like the pig!"

I laughed at how right she was, and how little she knew about that painful journey. I wanted to protect her from that same scary world, but I didn't know how. "Sleep tight," I said. I kissed her on the forehead and she kissed me on the cheek. Lord, I asked, how can I be a good father to her?

The moment of truth came after Annie and I watched some religious TV and drank some tea. I wasted time by carefully refolding some of my clothes as I unpacked. I traveled with my Jesuses and arranged them on the nightstand just so. I had stopped putting the one Russ gave me in front of the broken one to hide its imperfection, and stood them up side by side instead. We went to the bedroom and locked the door. Annie removed her clothes and slid under the covers. She didn't even wear a nightie. Peeking at me from under there across the room, she winked. I took a breath and tugged my boxers down. I stood in front of her naked, but not proud. The moment passed without anybody saying anything, so I got into bed with her. I held her breasts in my palms and rubbed her nipples with my thumbs. Annie wiggled and moaned. I kissed her and ran my hands up and down the folds and bulges of her body. As I kneaded her behind, my chin over her shoulder, I caught myself thinking about being a pastry chef and rolling dough all day.

I kept my front pressed tightly against Annie's thigh, knowing it kept her from reaching between our crotches and finding my spongy little penis. Dr. Soffione's book advised thinking manly thoughts in this situation, even vulgar comments about women and their bodies. That would keep the focus on your masculinity being different from and maybe superior to her. He also said you should keep focused on the sensations happening in your male member, and the good feelings of man-woman sexuality.

I thought a whole lot of very bad sayings that I can't bring myself to write down. Phrases about how I wanted to conquer my wife's body and exercise my natural dominance over her. Connecting with the macho part of me turned me on a little, but it still took a bunch of effort to get anywhere. Soon as we rolled over for a little rest, Annie shoved her hand between my legs and flopped my thing around like a rag doll. Without realizing, she tore the scab from my activity the night before.

"Nothing doing, eh?" she asked. As any man knows, the second-worst thing anybody can do when a fellow can't perform is to call attention to it. Number one is laughing.

"I guess not," I said.

She whacked at it, gently first, then almost violently, and I put up with the pain a mite longer than any man ought to.

"Ow," I said, softly but firmly.

"Oh no! Did I hurt you? I'm so sorry!"

"It's okay."

For the next half hour we tried a whole bunch of different things to raise the barn, so to speak. But it turns out that getting an erection is also like a sneeze. By and by, Annie got a cramp in her leg. She stood up, stretched her leg against the wall, and shook her hand out. Then, giving us a fright, Cheryl tried the door and asked for a glass of water. Annie put on her nightie and ushered her into the kitchen. "Why can't I sleep with you tonight?" I heard her moan in the hallway.

"Your father is here, honey."

"It's not fair! He gets to sleep in there and I don't?"

Annie didn't answer, but it took almost an hour for her to get Cheryl into her bed. By the time she locked the bedroom door, I had nearly fallen asleep.

In the second round, I had an even tougher time finding the spot and staying hard. My skin was so chafed, and after I rubbed lotion on it, it burned something fierce. I didn't want to use any of my old male fantasies, but the masculine phrases didn't help much either. In the end, neither of us came and we conked out, lying diagonally across the comforter like beached orca whales.

"I'm exhausted," she said.

"So am I. Let's try again in the morning."

"Maybe we should wait a couple of days," she sighed. "To give you a running start."

"Maybe," I replied. "Do you think that would help?"

Annie murmured something that wasn't yes or no and pulled the covers over her shoulder to go to sleep. I thought about my encounter with Manny, and finally my juices started flowing, so much that I had to get up and go to the bathroom and masturbate carefully.

The following morning, we loaded up the sedan and drove to Daytona. It was off-season and not a great beach day. Warm but mostly overcast. We set out anyway because we had faith that the weather would improve like they said it would on TV.

Cheryl and I built a huge sand castle using only her bright pink pail and green shovel. I tried to make the sculpture look as much like Cinderella's castle as I could, but nobody else thought it looked like that. I helped her swim for a while and then we got corn dogs on the boardwalk.

After lunch Annie and I sat back in our half chairs and talked. In sunglasses and a straw hat, she looked very cool.

"It's always going to be like that, isn't it?" she said with a sigh, like we had already started a talk. I guessed that she meant the poor-quality sex of the night before. It had been loitering at the back of my mind the whole day, too.

"I wish I could say it won't. It's a lifelong struggle."

Flat waves kept rushing up the sand like kids leaving school on the last day, but then the ocean would drag them right back down under the new ones. It had never seemed like such a sad story before. The story kept repeating as I watched, and as far as I knew, it would go on forever.

"Doug thinks that he was born gay."

"Doug can think all he wants." The shore fizzed up to our blanket.

"Gary, maybe you should just be gay."

"But it's against the Lord and the family, Annie. I can't."

"It is? But everything you've done to stop being gay has *ruined* our family. Everyone in the program wants to be in a family. That's why they're trying to change. Their families kick them out or treat them bad or don't understand. Doug's twin brother tried to strangle him but Doug still wants a relationship with him. It's like what happened to me with my family. I don't want that. Maybe if you stop struggling we can all get some peace. This is such a big problem."

I sat up. "Yeah, I know," I said. "But see, it's the *only* problem."

"Sometimes one problem's all you need, honey."

"The Bible says it's wrong."

Her voice struck a deeply weary note. "The Bible says a lot of things. It says you can have three hundred concubines. It says Elisha can get a she-bear to kill forty-two children and that's okay. We have to live our lives."

"No, Annie. No. That's wrong. Our lives aren't our lives."

Annie gave me a strange look over her sunglasses and then looked off at the waves. The conversation ended there, but the idea had already been growing in my mind. Before, I would have lost control and begged her not to reject me, but this time I heard the high-pitched music of true love in her tone, the tenderness that sings above the rules people enforce on each other by saying God made them up. Her sacrifice staggered me. So often I had heard about Christ's gift to humanity, but now that I'd experienced it through another person, it took on a whole new meaning. It began to dawn on me that I could maybe step into myself, into August, and into the Lord all at once.

The clouds never blew away that day. But it didn't rain, and parts of the weather cleared. The sun sank into a bright area on the horizon, and the rays played across the bottom of the clouds like the world had turned upside down. As Annie drove us back to Longwood, Cheryl plopped her head down on my stomach to take a nap. She said I was her pillow. For a little while, I was glad to be fat.

EIGHTEEN

Annie didn't have to work until the afternoon, so we drove Cheryl to school and had breakfast at a chain restaurant the next day. Annie kept at me about my thoughts on gayness. I told her I didn't know how to continue serving the Lord under those circumstances. Would I have to become a weakling who gave up on the hard work of changing myself and joined one of those illegitimate, gay-friendly congregations? I didn't think Annie had thought it through carefully enough.

"I couldn't have a relationship with a man while I was still married to you. That would be adulterous," I said.

"It didn't bother you when you were running around behind my back."

My heart sank into my feet. I had discussed this aspect of my personal life a great deal at Resurrection, but I didn't think Annie knew that it had started long before Atlanta. My eyes widened and my spine curved under me, like a dog putting his tail between his legs.

"How did you find out? Did Gay tell you?"

Annie was silent and took a drink of water. Water droplets had formed on the glass. She put it down and the shapes of her fingers remained on the sides. She salted her last few home fries and put them into her mouth. When she finished chewing, she said, "I was bluffing. But I suspected."

A garbage truck full of shame emptied its payload all over me. Worst of all, she didn't know how recently I'd slipped. I saw that I had torn my napkin to shreds and started on the placemat. "You want to divorce, don't you? You said so before."

"I don't know," she said.

"Well, what do you want?"

"The truth?"

In the picture window, a man in a chicken costume took off his enormous yellow head so he could get into his van. We watched without speaking until he drove off. Then she made me tell her what I'd done with men, but I had to sum up a lot, and I didn't mention the recent thing with Manny. Honest to God, the shame of telling her just about liquified me. I could hardly remember half of my encounters with other men, and only a couple of names here and there. Annie turned away from me with her hand over her mouth, and tears ran hot and fast down her face.

"You're going to divorce me, aren't you?" I said when I finished.

"It will probably have to happen. But I'm not in a hurry."

"Why not?"

"Because... I forgive you, I guess. Or I know I will eventually."

"Why?"

"I don't know. I'm trying to be Christ-like. It's too heartbreaking not to forgive you. I don't want to add to everything. I'd rather be the turning point. Maybe it's because you gave me Cheryl. It doesn't mean I'm not angry. It's an angry forgiveness."

We spent the rest of the afternoon shopping and running errands for Annie's restaurant. At one point, we had to drive near the strip mall where it was located, so she took me in just to have a look and meet some of the people.

The restaurant had a lot of similarities to the Polynesian Resort Area of Disney World, but it also had a miniature volcano at the far end of the room. The volcano could erupt with sparklers at the top. Pago Pago had a more intimate atmosphere and lower prices than the Disney place. Annie introduced me to her business partner, a chef they called John, even though that wasn't his Samoan name. I also met her gay waiter friend, Douglas, and a few of the other waiters as they set up for the lunch crowd.

Annie and I got Cheryl from school, then we drove back to the Ponce de León and she went back to work. Cheryl watched Droopy Dawg cartoons and I called home for my messages. One had come from Gay, saying she needed to talk to me and could I call back as soon as I got the message. She would be in the office until later because there was a meeting at 6:30. I didn't like the grave tone in her voice. It didn't fit my concept of Gay. The news was probably bad.

I took the phone into the bedroom, pulled the door almost all the way closed, and dialed the office. Gay answered the phone in a cheery voice and I told her it was me. Instantly, her manner of speaking became uneasy.

"Gary, how's it going?"

"Gay, I feel so blessed," I said. "It's so beautiful to come back to my wife and daughter. The Lord really does work miracles. My whole life feels like a miracle right now." I told her what she wanted to hear in the words everybody used like shorthand.

"That's terrific, Gary. Praise the Lord. So is it hot down there?"

"There's a high of about eighty-eight degrees today. How's Atlanta?"

"About the same."

The small talk was a way of avoiding talking about the thing we knew we had to talk about. But I couldn't stand to let it go so long. "What did Charlie and Bill say?"

She huffed. "It's actually weird. Charlie thinks you should go on some kind of probation. But Bill blew his stack. He told me some things you did that I didn't know about, which explains why he was nervous about you opening the Atlanta branch without me. Did you and Jake and Keith really lie about going to the movies and stay downtown until 3 a.m.? Did you kiss Nicky? Needless to say, Bill's talking about termination, and he's trying to get Charlie on his side about it. But I think just a reprimand would be enough."

At first it didn't make sense to me that the higher-up person would be more merciful. But Dr. Soffione was busy working on his book, so he had less at stake. Dr. Soffione had a quiet faith in the truth of his theories and their ability to work in the long term, while Bill had firsthand experience with the defective people who needed Dr. Soffione's wisdom. He probably thought I was trying to get back at him. And how had he found out everything that happened? Was everybody wagging their tongues now that we'd graduated?

"There's a call coming in on line two. Can you hold, Gary?"

I said "Sure," but I didn't mean it. She put me on hold. I expected music but I got religious talk radio, reminding me of my failed dreams. I bounced up and down on the bed nervously, playing with the strap of one of Annie's shoes with my toes. Outside, Cheryl laughed and all kinds of crazy sound effects came from the television. Gay took a very long time. Ministers on the line said that prayer should be in the schools. The moment became suspended in time as I waited for Gay to return, and gradually grew heavier and heavier. I begged the Lord not to give me the challenge of separation from Resurrection Ministries.

Once Gay returned to the line my nerves had reached their limit. She spoke slowly. "Gary, that was Charlie. He says that he and Bill have decided that it's probably best to terminate. Bill wanted me to make sure you knew that it wasn't personal. He says that the image of the program can't support the kind of behavior you've been involved in, even though he knows that you weren't intentionally trying to hurt us. He said best of luck in your journey and Christ be with you."

I went nuts. I always forget how I can do that. It frightened me to hear myself yell at Gay about the harsh justice of the program. "We're supposed to be about forgiveness!" I shouted. "If God can forgive me, why can't y'all?" I said that about ten times, but Gay didn't raise her voice. Instead she apologized and tried to calm me down.

"Gary, Gary, it's okay," she said, trying to cool my jets. I noticed that her voice always sounded a little congested. "I'll see if there's a possibility that they'll reconsider."

"Don't bother," I spat, and pressed the OFF button on the phone. It made a tiny beep. For a second I marveled at how big parts of a person's life can end with the little beep of a phone. Then I curled over forward and dropped the phone on the floor. I held my head and tried to weep, but my anger was still too high. Instead I hit myself in the shoulder again and again, making low growling noises so Cheryl wouldn't hear me over the television noise. I wanted to break the mirror, but I didn't. Then it dawned on me that Nicky must have ratted on me when Bill kicked him out, and that was why they decided to terminate me. My firing was his sneaky present from the grave. To think that he had really communicated with me from the other side made me laugh until tears streamed out of the sides of my eyes.

Once I pulled myself together, I left the bedroom and joined Cheryl in front of the television. It seemed like Annie let her do anything she wanted. She was watching a cartoon with two male animals. I couldn't tell what animals they were. They lived together and everything that happened was disgusting. I found the remote on the couch behind her and changed the channel. Cheryl howled like I had smacked her and tried to grab the remote out of my hand. Her screeching almost didn't sound human. I stood up to keep the remote out of her reach. I changed the channel to a less bad cartoon and put the remote on a high shelf. She sulked in front of the couch with her arms folded.

"Daddy, why can't I watch?"

"Your mother says it's okay for you to watch that?"

"Mrs. Lucas does." Mrs. Lucas, who was in her seventies, lived down the hall and usually came over in the afternoons to look after Cheryl until Annie got back from work.

"Well, I say you can't."

"I wish Mrs. Lucas were here and not you."

My anger and disappointment about Resurrection carried over into my reaction. "You shut up!" I bellowed at her, so hard I hurt my throat. I shook her and raised my hand to hit her across the face, but I caught myself. The only way I knew how to be a father was to be like *my* father. Stunned by my behavior, I froze. During the freeze, Cheryl fled into her room and locked the door. I sank down on the couch and watched the Family Channel for several hours, even though it was a marathon of westerns. Cheryl wouldn't come out of her room, not even when I heated up supper and sweet-talked her through the door.

Annie returned at 11 p.m. and we talked about everything until 2 a.m. We agreed that I should find a place nearby and slowly get the hang of being Cheryl's dad, rather than jumping right back in. Then I remembered the vacant apartment downstairs and volunteered to find out about it. That night I laid my second Jesus down in a dresser drawer, and prayed to the one with the hole in his heart. I didn't need a perfect Jesus anymore. Tired and drained, Annie and I kissed goodnight and I clicked off the lamp. Lying in the dark and trying to fall asleep with just my fingertips touching Annie's, I felt like after all the trouble we'd gone through together, and even though I'd never be her sexual partner, I had finally earned the right to call myself her husband.

NINETEEN

Breakfast smells came into the bedroom the next morning and woke me up. I trudged into the kitchen to find Annie at the stove and Cheryl sitting in front of the television, her hand in a box of sugary cereal. Annie slid a pair of sunny-side-up eggs onto a plate with two stiff strips of bacon on it. Cracking two more eggs, she dropped them into the pan and they sizzled loudly. She asked if I wanted any and I said I did. I was hungry, of course, but I also had a hunger to add myself to their day-to-day existence. I sat at the table and played with the silverware, flashing the blade of my knife in the kitchen light. Annie had brought the paper in, so I unfolded it to the funnies and read a few out loud to Cheryl.

Annie called Cheryl to the table and she came with the box still on her hand. I made like I was going to grab her and pull the box off, but she ran around the other side of the table to avoid me. Getting her trust back wouldn't be easy. She took the box off herself and sat down in front of her bacon and eggs.

"Your mother lets you do whatever you want, doesn't she?"

Annie turned to me with the spatula in her hand. I knew she wouldn't, but it looked for a moment like she was going to slap me with it if I said more of the wrong thing. "She kept getting sick is what it is. Chicken pox, and then a really bad flu, and then bronchitis. I think she was fine for about two weeks that whole time. I couldn't be strict. She had no daddy and she was ill. But we're paying the price now, aren't we, honey?" With her free hand she ruffled Cheryl's coarse curls. "Things are going to have to change."

I tried out my best Dad frown and nodded in agreement with Annie. Cheryl swung her head back and forth to say no, and her dimples deepened when she grinned. She picked up a piece of bacon with her fingers and crunched down on it disobediently.

"Use your fork and knife," I told her. I lay the paper flat and tried to get her interested in the funnies, but she didn't care anymore. She grabbed one of her eggs with two hands and bit open the yolk. It sagged and burst onto the plate and all over her fingers and she laughed. Without getting angry, Annie cleaned her off with a dishtowel and took the plate away from her.

"If you want to act like a wild animal, I'll take you to Samoa and leave you."

"Okay," she said. "Grrr!"

In a matter of minutes, Annie managed to clean Cheryl up and get her ready for school. She threw a modest skirt and blouse on and the two of them left. Annie had restaurant business to do during the day and early setup for lunch, so she wouldn't be back all afternoon.

When I finished with the paper, I went downstairs to the building office and spoke to Mr. Foy, a thin white man with brown spots all over his bald head. In contrast to the image of a landlord, he had always been nice to Annie and me. When I knocked on his office door and stepped in he looked up from his electric typewriter, suspicious for a moment. He squinted and pulled the curly arms of his gold-rimmed glasses behind his ears.

"Hey, haven't seen you around in a while," he commented.

"I've been away."

Mr. Foy didn't seem to know any of what had happened, or even to have a sense that three years or so had passed. I asked him about the downstairs apartment and he admitted he'd had a hard time filling it.

"You have a friend or something, interested in moving?"

"No, it's me, I'd be moving in."

His eyebrows went up and concern came into his voice. "Oh. Trouble at home? That's rough."

"No, no. Everything's okay. Better than it's ever been."

"Better than ever and you're moving out?"

I nodded. He nodded in a way that said he didn't believe me.

"I won't pry."

Mr. Foy handed me an application to fill out and turned back to his typing while I took care of it. As I finished, he came around behind me and read the application over my shoulder. "The place is yours if you want it, Gary," he said. I accepted and we shook hands. "Can I just make a photocopy of your driver's license and your social?"

I hadn't needed to replace my old August Valentine ID yet. The place in Atlanta was in Gay's name. I paid for things through a Resurrection account. I took the MARTA everywhere. Mama and Annie had given my real wallet a proper burial.

"Oh," I said. "I don't have it with me. I'll come back later." Thinking it better to leave before he could start figuring out what had happened, I got up hastily. Perhaps if he knew, or if I told him anything accidentally, he would think that I was still a fraud, even though being a fraud was what I was trying to overcome. Even nice landlords could make assumptions like that.

With little time to lose, I called a taxi and waited. I borrowed money from a jar Annie kept on top of the cabinets and searched the house for a trowel, or some other kind of shovel. The closest thing I found was Cheryl's beach shovel, the one we used to build sand castles that Sunday. Feeling downright silly, I hid it in a paper bag and wedged it under my arm as I went out to the parking lot to wait for the car.

It was about 10:30 a.m., so we—me and the taxi driver—had missed the rush hour. We got to the gates of Greenwood Cemetery in just under half an hour.

I couldn't see the caretaker's house, if there was one. The place looked like nobody watched over it, they just opened the gates and went off somewhere else to let the dead folks sort everything out. That was good. I didn't want anybody to see me. I wasn't sure that what I was fixing to do was legal.

I didn't know exactly where to look, so I started by looking everywhere, my head swiveling left and right. The Florida sun neared its highest position and the granite headstones sparkled one after the other in my eye as I passed. Some of them had last names that I recognized, or funny ones like Sleeper, Dunwith, Leakey, and Hello. Some were very light in color and blinding to look at. Many had small bouquets in little vases next to them. A few were new enough to be covered with a man-sized rectangle of dying flowers. I read some of the loving memoriams and hoped all the dead people were okay, whichever place they had gone to. My father, for example. Nicky for another.

One corner of Section H contained three rows of recently buried people. From my short walk, I had learned how to tell a recent grave by the amount of grass covering the plot. Then I would check the date of death. In this small area of Section H, most of the plots had thin lawns on top. The lawns were also very bright green, which meant young grass. Stepping sideways through the rows in Section H, I stopped and read every gravestone. Sooner than I expected, I stepped on the mound I was looking for—my own grave.

Boy, I stared at that stone like a fixed tomcat, my jaw wide. I only snapped it shut when a skeeter hawk flew past. Good God almighty, I said. This is what I look like dead.

Before they die, everybody should get the chance to visit their own grave. It felt like seeing into the future, and it turned all my worries small and stupid. Of course, I wasn't buried here, but my memory had been, and one day my body would come back for good. Everybody would die, and probably nothing mattered to the dead—certainly none of my SSA problems. I reckoned there wouldn't be discrimination against minority groups in Heaven. Or else it wouldn't be Heaven, right?

My family had bought a marker lower than any of the others. It had a cut-off peak, like somebody had sliced off the top of a regular tombstone, and my last name was etched into the slice: GRAY. The stone was also gray. The gravestone could have been a floor model used to demonstrate one of the available colors, except that they'd carved the GARY into the base, next to a pair of praying hands, and below that the words LOVING HUSBAND in fancy script. That phrase does not even begin to tell the story, I thought, shaking my head. But if I had never come back, nobody would have known any different.

Double-checking to make sure nobody was around, I saw only a car parked way in the distance and two people with their heads bowed by a monument. I took the shovel out of the bag and dug in the center, toward where my stomach would one day lie. I hoped that they hadn't buried my wallet at the same six-foot depth as a corpse. Luckily the sandy dirt gave way easily, without big rocks or roots holding it together. But the sun became extremely hot, and I had to stop several times to wipe off sweat, though I hadn't gotten very far. I only succeeded in wiping sandy dirt onto my face. Soon I dropped the shovel and used my hands, pulling the soil away from the mound.

After about half an hour, my hand hit something hard about three feet down. With the shovel, I loosened the dirt around it and found a strongbox made of cheap but hard tin. I pulled the box out of the dirt and lifted it up. Using a key and part of an umbrella I found in a trash bin as levers, I pried open the sides of the box and broke the lock.

A black wallet slid out, its edges burned, surrounded with dead roses and nestled in a royal blue lining. I picked it up and put everything that had fallen out of the box back in. I folded the cover down and placed the box at one side of the hole. Quickly, I filled the grave again. I had a thin crust of sand all over my arms and clothes, like a gigantic sugar-dusted donut.

I suppose nobody saw me. Plumb near everybody in this graveyard must be dead, I thought, and then had a chuckle at my own joke. Picking up the box and putting it in the paper bag with the plastic shovel, I rushed out of the cemetery, wanting to get away from the gravesite for a bunch of darned good reasons.

I walked by the side of the road until I came upon a fast-food restaurant. Hungry and thirsty, I went in and got a large orange Coke and two deluxe hamburgers. I sat down at a table near the window, ate one of the burgers, and sucked on my drink until my thirst left me. Then I ate burger number two. Wiping my hands on a napkin, I opened the box and moved the dried roses aside on the satin lining. I opened the wallet. My plastic student ID from Central had buckled and burned from the heat of the train fire, and so had a couple of credit cards. There were some of my business cards from Bradley Foods still in there with those of other marketing execs I had met only once, and a train ticket stub to Atlanta. My driver's license was burned. A lot of the picture had melted, but the words were almost all readable. Funniest of all, it hadn't expired yet.

From the restaurant I took another cab home, palmed my driver's license, and hid the box under the bed. I put Cheryl's shovel back in the bathroom in the net that held the rest of her brightly colored beach things.

When I knocked on the door, Mr. Foy was still sitting at his desk, typing. "I've got my license," I announced, holding it out. Moving around the desk, he took it from me with two fingers.

"Geez, who tried to cook this thing?" he asked, turning the card over in his fingers.

"It was an accident," I said.

"Don't let it happen again."

"Believe me, I won't."

As Mr. Foy placed the card under the photocopier, he muttered that he'd been worried I wouldn't come back. He hadn't asked for a deposit or anything, he said, because he knew Annie and me. We could handle all that later. He gave me the keys right then.

"Go take a look."

The new key was very shiny, but the same shape as Annie's. I figured I'd have to get another job lickety-split in order to pay for it, but I knew I had no other choice. Holding the key to the light, I stepped into the courtyard and found my way along the path to my new place. Inside, it had one less room than Annie's, checkered linoleum instead of white on the kitchen floor, and a couple of dirty handprints on the wall. Otherwise it was real similar. My footsteps rang out in the empty apartment as I took a look at all the rooms, thinking of good things that might happen in them—birthday parties, Sunday mornings, Christmases. Moving back in here made me feel a little foolish—I had gone next door by traveling around the world in the wrong direction. I walked over to the living room window, took down the FOR RENT sign, and paused to appreciate my new view. Across the courtyard, on the second floor, I could see my daughter's window through the shade trees. I could look up and see her there. She could look down and I'd be here. Nope, it didn't seem far at all.

James Hannaham would like to thank Jennifer Egan, Brendan Moroney, Clarinda Mac Low, Colleen Werthmann, Jim Lewis, Timothy Murphy, Andrew May, Helen Eisenbach, Troy Lambert, David Wright, Anne Stringfield, Katie Williams, David Rogers, Vendela Vida, Eli Horowitz, Jordan Bass, David Groff, Basil Tsiokos, Joe Cabaniss, Tom Cabaniss, Mary Giles and Armand Derfner, Colin Lingle, John Dicarlo, Dave Ramirez, Gary Gray, Anone Palolo, Cheryl Gray, Jamilynn Gray, Obadiah Jocephus (Joe) Gray, Mrs. Vietta Consequence, Trudy Schwartz and her husband, Mr. & Mrs. Larrymore Hope Walker and their lovely daughter, Ms. K.E. Walker, Gregg Goldston, Marcus Lira, Terry Witek, James Magnuson, Michael Adams, the Michener Center for Writers, the MacDowell Colony, Yaddo, and the Blue Mountain Center for their help, and, in many cases, love.